"Who are you?" she said to the man.
"What do you want?"

"You tell me," he replied. Obviously, he was enjoying this dangerous game of twenty questions.

"You're from Singleatheart," she said.

He smiled again—a chilling grimace that filled Ali's soul with dread. "I'm not just *from* Singleatheart," he told her deliberately. "I *am* Singleatheart."

Without warning he sprang from the couch and crossed the room, brandishing the gun like a club. Before she could raise her hands to defend herself, the blow fell.

RAVE REVIEWS FOR *CRUEL INTENT*

MORE PRAISE FOR
USA TODAY BESTSELLING AUTHOR
J.A. JANCE
AND HER "HEART-STOPPING"
(*PUBLISHERS WEEKLY*)
SUSPENSE NOVELS

"Jance delivers a devilish page-turner."

—*People*

"Engaging and entertaining."

—*Los Angeles Times*

"Jance deftly brings the desert, people, and towns of southeastern Arizona to life."

—*Publishers Weekly*

"[Jance is] an expert in the tricks of her trade."
—*The Tennessean* (Nashville)

"An intriguing plot, colorful characters."
—*San Diego Union-Tribune*

"Characters so real you want to reach out and hug—or strangle—them. Her dialogue always rings true."
—*Cleveland Plain Dealer*

"Addictive . . . You'll swear you are part of the book."
—*Statesman Journal* (Salem, OR)

ALSO BY J.A. JANCE

ALI REYNOLDS MYSTERIES

Edge of Evil
Web of Evil
Hand of Evil
Cruel Intent
Trial by Fire
Fatal Error
Left for Dead
Deadly Stakes
Moving Target
A Last Goodbye (A Novella)
Cold Betrayal
No Honor Among Thieves (A Novella)
Clawback
Random Acts (A Novella)
Man Overboard
Duel to the Death
The A List

JOANNA BRADY MYSTERIES

Desert Heat
Tombstone Courage
Shoot/Don't Shoot
Dead to Rights
Skeleton Canyon
Rattlesnake Crossing
Outlaw Mountain
Devil's Claw
Paradise Lost
Partner in Crime
Exit Wounds
Dead Wrong
Damage Control
Fire and Ice
Judgment Call
The Old Blue Line (A Novella)
Remains of Innocence
No Honor Among Thieves (A Novella)
Random Acts (A Novella)
Downfall
Field of Bones

J.P. BEAUMONT MYSTERIES

Until Proven Guilty
Injustice for All
Trial by Fury
Taking the Fifth
Improbable Cause
A More Perfect Union
Dismissed with Prejudice
Minor in Possession
Payment in Kind
Without Due Process
Failure to Appear
Lying in Wait
Name Withheld
Breach of Duty
Birds of Prey
Partner in Crime
Long Time Gone
Justice Denied
Fire and Ice
Betrayal of Trust
Ring in the Dead (A Novella)
Second Watch
Stand Down (A Novella)
Dance of the Bones
Proof of Life

WALKER FAMILY MYSTERIES

Hour of the Hunter
Kiss of the Bees
Day of the Dead
Queen of the Night
Dance of the Bones

POETRY

After the Fire

J. A. JANCE

CRUEL INTENT

AN ALI REYNOLDS MYSTERY

POCKET BOOKS

NEW YORK   LONDON   TORONTO   SYDNEY   NEW DELHI

Pocket Books
An Imprint of Simon & Schuster, Inc.
1230 Avenue of the Americas
New York, NY 10020

This Pocket Books paperback edition September 2019

POCKET and colophon are registered trademarks of Simon & Schuster, Inc.

For information about special discounts for bulk purchases, please contact Simon & Schuster Special Sales at 1-866-506-1949 or business@simonandschuster.com.

The Simon & Schuster Speakers Bureau can bring authors to your live event. For more information or to book an event, contact the Simon & Schuster Speakers Bureau at 1-866-248-3049 or visit our website at www.simonspeakers.com.

Manufactured in the United States of America

10 9 8 7 6 5 4 3 2 1

ISBN 978-1-9821-1027-7
ISBN 978-1-4165-6387-7 (ebook)

For TLG.

{ PROLOGUE }

Sipping a cup of freshly brewed Colombian blend, Peter Winter sat on the couch in his spacious family room, inserted the DVD into his computer, and then waited for the slide show to appear on his fifty-two-inch flat-screen TV. He kept the "before" photos in a group by themselves, and he flicked through those first. The befores showed five slender blondes, each smiling sweetly into the camera—into his camera. Rita Winter, Candace Miller, Melanie Tyler, Debra Long-worth, and Morgan Forester. The five of them looked enough alike that they could have been sisters. Their faces were remarkably similar, with wide-set blue eyes, delicate features, and flawless complexions. They all had straight white teeth and carbon-copy smiles—superior smiles, knowing smiles, cheating smiles.

In addition to their beauty-pageant good looks, that was another thing the five women had in common—they were all cheaters. Second, all of them were greedy, always wanting more—always requiring more—than they had been given. Finally, of course, there was the dead part. That showed up in the "afters"—in those, the women weren't alike at all, except that they were dead and looked it; well, four of them did anyway. The first photo was a grainy copy of a news photo with the body already covered by a tarp. Peter had missed the opportunity to take his own portrait, but since then he had corrected that oversight.

The photos showed Peter's handiwork in brutal detail. The women, all of them naked and bloodied, lay either where they had fallen or where he had placed them. Posed them, as the profilers liked to say. Most people would have been repulsed by the photos. He found them exciting. Invigorating. Especially when he had reached this point—the time when he was about to add one more to his collection.

He hadn't expected it would come to this with Morgan. He had figured he'd use her and lose her. That was the way he liked to operate, and it was a philosophy that had worked fairly well over the years, with a few notable exceptions. But some dumb blondes were smarter than they looked. It had come as a rude awakening when that pretty little piece of tail had turned on him and tried tracking him down at work. That had been the end of it. Or at least it had signaled the end of it. It had taken him some time—weeks, in fact—to get all the pieces in place, but today was the day. Let us rejoice and be glad in it.

Whistling that familiar Sunday-school tune, he switched off the DVD player and the TV set, removed the DVD, and stashed it in the safe in the back of his closet. At the same time, he removed his precious good-luck charm—the heart-shaped Tiffany key chain Carol had given him. It was loaded now with something far more powerful than keys, and on days like this—days when he was primed for action—he wanted the key ring with him. As long as he had that talisman in his pocket, he felt safe.

After pouring a second cup of coffee, Peter set about gathering and packing his equipment. He didn't need to carry much. He brought along a fully loaded syringe, a set of scrubs, a pair of surgical gloves, and a pair of paper surgical booties. Blood spatter on scrubs was easily explained and easily gotten rid of. Surgical booties left no traceable footprints at the crime scene, and when they went into the hospital incinerator, they left behind no traceable forensic evidence, either.

Gloves were another matter. More than one dumb killer had been taken down when damning fingerprints were found inside gloves worn while committing a crime. But working in a hospital made disposing of surgical gloves pretty much foolproof. As long as they and his used hypodermics went into the proper containers in the proper examination rooms, he could be relatively sure they'd never be seen again—and never examined for incriminating forensic evidence.

He added a pair of leather driving gloves. Those were a necessity. They were the only way to ensure that he didn't leave behind a damning fingerprint or two in the rental car. They also kept him from running the risk of being seen driving while wearing surgical gloves; that certainly would have raised eyebrows. With driving gloves, you had to be careful not to drop one at a crime scene. Watching O.J.'s long-ago murder trial had taught Peter all about that. When he needed to unload a pair that had reached the end of the road, he dropped them off in a Goodwill donation box.

The next thing he loaded into the briefcase was that day's weapon of choice. In this case, he planned to use an ordinary household hammer, and not one he'd picked up from his neighborhood Ace hardware. Those might very well have some distinguishing markings on them. No, he chose to use one he'd bought at a garage sale in North Phoenix. The woman, a relatively new widow, had been selling her husband's tools in preparation for moving into an assisted-living facility. Initially, Peter hadn't wanted the whole lot, but she'd offered the entire kit at such a bargain-basement price that he had taken all of it, rolling tool box included.

So far he'd used only one of the tools he'd purchased that Sunday afternoon—the hacksaw—on the nosy little bitch in Greeley, Colorado, who had asked way too many questions. Getting rid of her had been an especially gratifying experience, but it had also been very messy. Exceedingly messy, as the after photo clearly showed. He'd had a lot of trouble getting himself cleaned up afterward and had worried about leaving something behind that might be traced back to him.

He expected that using the hammer would be simpler. If he did it right, there'd be far less blood to deal with, and what there was would be easier to control. Having blood evidence lying around was actually quite helpful. It gave the cops something to focus on, and that was the whole secret to getting away with murder. You had to give the cops plenty of blood evidence and make sure they found it where they expected to find it. And if you could muddy the water enough by having two prime suspects rather than one, that was even better.

Last but not least, he picked up his digital camera. Before he put it into the briefcase, he replaced the batteries. These shots were important to him. He didn't want to miss a thing.

After closing his briefcase he snapped the locks. Stopping by the kitchen sink, he rinsed his coffee cup and put it in the dishwasher. At the front door, he paused long enough to look around. There was nothing out of place, nothing at all, and that was the way he liked it.

Squaring his shoulders and whistling "A-Hunting We Will Go," he set out to do just that.

Matthew Morrison left home that Monday morning a little past five-thirty. Knowing he'd be heading out early on Monday, he had checked a Taurus out of the motor pool late Friday afternoon. By a quarter to six, he was on the 101 and driving south, heading to Red Rock, heading to Susan.

The last thing he had done before he left the house was turn on Jenny's coffee. He hoped she wouldn't notice that the coffee would be a whole hour older than it usually was, but he doubted she'd pay any attention to the clock on the pot. As far as coffee was concerned, the important thing for Jenny was that she didn't have to make it herself when she finally scrambled out of bed around seven-thirty. When she deigned to appear in the kitchen, she wanted her coffee there and at the ready.

Matt's customary departure time of six-thirty meant that his drive to the state government campus in downtown Phoenix usually involved dealing with rush-hour traffic. This morning and this early, there was barely any traffic at all. Anxious and excited, Matt kept reminding himself to slow down. Today of all days, it wouldn't do for him to get a speeding ticket.

During the last week, ever since Susan had suggested they should meet at last, Matt had done his best to maintain an even keel. Last night, though, he had almost given the game away when Jenny caught him whistling as he loaded the dishwasher. "What the hell are you so happy about?" she had demanded.

Eighteen years ago, when they first married, Jenny had been a reasonably good-looking woman. That was no longer true. Her constant negativity had turned the corners of her mouth into a perpetual sneer. Frown lines marred her forehead, but her lack of beauty was much more than skin-deep.

Matt, who prided himself on keeping a positive mental attitude no matter what, had done what he could to change her. Predictably, that hadn't worked. Now, it turned out, he was changing himself and doing something for Matt for a change. He was going to get lucky. He had stopped at Walgreens on Sunday afternoon—not his neighborhood store, of course—and bought a package of Trojans. Just in case, he'd also brought along the sample of little blue pills that he'd ordered over the Internet.

Better to be prepared, he told himself. This might be his one chance, and he didn't want to mess it up.

As the after-school bus rattled toward the end of its route on the Verde Valley School Road, only three children remained—the Forester twins, Lindsey and Lacy, and little Tommy Breznik. Tommy, far in the back, was engrossed in a handheld video game and oblivious to everything around him. As she did every day, Lacy sat silent and apart, with her face pressed to the window while her sister, Lindsey, chattered away with Mr. Rojo, the bus driver.

"Miss Farber said we'll be taking a field trip down to Phoenix just before Christmas," Lindsey was saying. "Do you think you'll be our driver?"

Conrad Rojo liked kids, but he especially liked Lindsey, a bright child who talked a blue streak. Her sister, on the other hand, never said a word. It was strange to think that the two second-graders who looked so much alike could be so different.

"That depends," Conrad Rojo told her. "Somebody else sets up the scheduling."

"I hope it'll be you," Lindsey said. "Of all the bus drivers, I think you're the best."

Even though there was no traffic visible in either direction, Conrad turned on the flashers as he approached the turnoff to the Foresters' place. He was surprised not to see Mrs. Forester's white Hyundai Tucson parked at the end of the half-mile-long drive. For three years—as long as Lindsey and Lacy had attended Big Park Community School in the Village of Oak Creek—Morgan Forester had been waiting for her daughters at the end of the lane when the bus dropped them off. Conrad, who took the safety of his charges very seriously, was reluctant to leave the girls alone.

"Your mom's not here yet," he said.

"Maybe she's running late," Lindsey said brightly. "Maybe she got busy and forgot what time it was."

"Tell you what," Conrad said. "Why don't you stay on the bus until I drop Tommy off at Rainbow Lane. If your mother's running late, that'll give her a few minutes to catch up."

He glanced in the girls' direction. Lindsey clapped her hands in delight. "You mean we can ride all the way to the turnaround? And then we can be on the bus all by ourselves?"

"Yes," Conrad said. "Once Tommy gets off, it'll be just the two of you and nobody else."

Lindsey turned to her sister. "Won't that be fun?"

Lacy shook her head and said nothing.

Once again Conrad was struck by how different the two girls were. Last year, on another field trip, he had overheard two of the first-grade teachers talking about them. "Well, Lacy's certainly not retarded," Mrs. Dryer, Lacy's first-grade teacher, had said. "She can do all the work. She just won't participate in class."

Conrad had wondered at that. He didn't think teachers should be talking about kids being retarded. Weren't they supposed to use nicer words than that? Besides, the situation with Lindsey and Lacy reminded him of his two sons, Johnny and Miguel. Johnny was two years older, and he had been the one who had done all the talking. There wasn't any need for Miguel to find his own voice, as long as his older brother was close at hand. Miguel hadn't actually started speaking on his own until halfway through first grade, when he skipped the baby-talk stage completely and cut loose with fully formed sentences. *And he hasn't shut up since,* Conrad thought with a chuckle. It seemed possible that some of Miguel's teachers used to say the same thing about him. Now, though, his younger son was an honors communications major at the University of Arizona, so go figure.

Once Conrad had dropped Tommy off, made the turn, and come back to the Foresters' long driveway, there was still no sign of the Hyundai. Conrad pulled over, stopped the bus, and reached for his cell phone. He wasn't surprised to find that he didn't have a signal way out here in the boonies. Putting away the useless phone, he sat and wondered what to do. It was against the rules to take the bus onto a private road, especially since there was a good chance he might run into a spot where it would be impossible to turn around. If there was any kind of problem, he'd be late getting back to school to pick up his next load of kids.

"It's okay," Lindsey said. "You can let us out here. We can walk home. We know the way. It's not that far."

"No," Lacy said.

Conrad was surprised to hear Lacy state her opinion. In the three years the girls had been riding his bus, this was the first time she had uttered a single word in his hearing.

"Come on, Lace," Lindsey wheedled. "Walking won't kill us. If you want, I'll even help carry your stuff." Lacy Forester came to school every day with a backpack that seemed half as big as she was.

"Maybe I should take you back to school so the principal can call your mom," Conrad offered.

"No," Lindsey said. "I don't want to go back there. I'm hungry. I want to go home and have a snack. Come on, Lace. We can do it."

For a moment Lacy Forester resumed her stony silence. She seemed close to tears, but finally, faced with her sister's force-of-nature determination, she sighed, stood, and shouldered her backpack.

"You're sure you'll be all right?" Conrad asked as he opened the door.

"We'll be fine," Lindsey declared. "You'll see."

The two girls clambered out of the bus. Conrad watched them trudge side by side down the dusty red dirt track with the clear November sun at their backs until they disappeared from sight over a slight rise. Then he put the bus in gear and headed back to school. If he didn't get going right then, he would be late for the last bell.

"I shouldn't have done that," he told the other drivers over coffee later that week. "I never should have let them go home alone."

{ CHAPTER 1 }

For the hundredth time that day, Ali Reynolds asked herself why she'd ever let her agent, Jacky Jackson, talk her into being a part of MCMR, short for *Mid-Century-Modern Renovations,* a program aimed at the Home & Garden TV viewer, documenting restoration projects designed to bring back venerable old twentieth-century American houses that otherwise would have fallen victim to the wrecking ball.

Months earlier Ali had come into possession of one of those precious fixer-uppers when she had purchased Arabella Ashcroft's crumbling hilltop mansion at the top of Sedona's Manzanita Hills Road. She had been intrigued when Jacky contacted her about filming the entire project. According to Jacky, MCMR would be the next great thing. *Mid-Century-Modern Renovations* was due to air on Home & Garden TV sometime in the not too distant future, but there was always a chance it would follow the lead of some of the Food Network's cooking shows and make the jump over to one of the major networks.

Jacky had begged and pleaded until Ali finally agreed. At first her contractor had been thrilled at the prospect, and his crew had enjoyed mugging for the two cameramen, Raymond and Robert. Now, though, with construction seriously behind schedule, the workers were becoming surly at having the cameras forever in the way, and so was Ali. It was bad enough when things were going well. But then there were days like today, when Bryan Forester, her general contractor, had gone ballistic after Yvonne Kirkpatrick, the city of Sedona's queen-bee building inspector, had decreed that the placement of some of Bryan's electrical outlets in both the bathrooms and the kitchen were out of compliance.

The cameras had been there filming the entire epic battle as Bryan and the fiery-haired Yvonne had gone at it nose-to-nose over the issue. Later, they had been missing in action when Yvonne, who had returned to her office to check the rules and regs, had called back with the embarrassing admission that Bryan had been right and she had been wrong. From her days as a television newscaster, Ali Reynolds knew the drill. After all, confrontations make for great TV. Reconciliations don't. Compared to war, peace is B-O-R-I-N-G. And even though Yvonne had admitted her mistake, she had yet to come back and sign off on the permit. The drywall guys couldn't start hanging wallboard until she did.

Ali had hoped to have the place ready for a grand Thanksgiving dinner unveiling for friends and family. Right now her house had no running water or electricity, and the interior walls were nothing but bare studs. This latest delay made a turkey-day gathering in her remodeled home even more unlikely. Disheartened, she had retreated to the wisteria-lined flagstone patio where they had erected a canvas canopy over the worn redwood picnic table that served as a lunchroom for workers and film crew alike. Before Ali could summon a really serious funk, though, Leland Brooks appeared, bearing a silver tray set for tea.

"Tea?" he asked. "You look as though you could use a cuppa."

"Yes, please," Ali said gratefully, shivering in the late-afternoon chill. "That would be wonderful."

Ali had taken on restoring Arabella Ashcroft's dilapidated home as her personal rehabilitation project, and Brooks, Arabella's former butler, had made fixing Ali Reynolds his. Months earlier and already dealing with the end of both her newscasting career and her marriage, Ali had abandoned California and returned to her roots in Sedona, Arizona, looking for respite and a little peace and quiet. That hadn't worked very well. Instead of achieving idyllic serenity, she had been propelled into life-and-death struggles with not one but two murderous nutcases.

Afterward Ali had been drifting aimlessly into a sea of depression when Leland Brooks came to her rescue, determined to find a way to help her help herself. Refusing to take no for an answer, he had set before her the daunting challenge of buying and re-creating Arabella Ashcroft's mother's house. In the ensuing months, every time the resulting complications had threatened to overwhelm Ali, Leland had been at her side. He still referred to himself as her butler, but she saw him as her property manager and also as her trusted aide-de-camp. He had taken up residence in a fifth-wheel trailer set up in the driveway, where he could make sure tools and supplies stayed put when the workmen left the site.

Ali waited while Leland dosed her tea with two cubes of sugar and a wedge of lemon.

"I see that building inspector was here again," he said.

"Yes," Ali returned. "She rode in on her broom, out on same, and fouled up the wallboard guys for at least another day. I'm pretty sure Thanksgiving is a lost cause."

Leland handed over a cup and saucer. "Mr. Forester is a good man," he said thoughtfully. "Surely he'll be able to find a way to carry us over the finish line."

Ali took a sip of her tea. It was perfect. "Mr. Brooks," she said, "has anyone ever told you that you're an incurable optimist?"

Leland frowned. "I don't suppose that's a compliment, is it?" he returned.

Ali laughed aloud. No matter how bad things got, Leland always seemed to cheer her up. Just then a car came winding up the driveway, threading its way between lines of workers' vehicles. As it parked behind Ali's Porsche Cayenne SUV, she recognized Detective Dave Holman's sheriff's department sedan.

Dave, a fellow graduate of Cottonwood's Mingus Union High, was a longtime friend and recently a some-time beau. Several months earlier, he had been granted primary custody of his two daughters, nine-year-old Cassie and thirteen-year-old Crystal. Since then Dave had thrown himself wholeheartedly into his unexpected second chance at fatherhood. His newly assumed parenting responsibilities combined with a realization that both Dave and Ali were in full rebound mode had led to a mutual decision to back off for a while. As a result, he and Ali had been spending far less time together of late. On this occasion, though, Ali was delighted to see him—until she caught sight of the grim set of his jaw. Clearly, this was some other kind of visit.

At another time in her life, Ali Reynolds might not have thought the worst, but after months of dealing with one disaster after another, her heart went to her throat. Had the brakes failed in her father's doddering antique Bronco, or had her mother's Alero been T-boned making a left-hand turn across traffic into the Sugarloaf Café's parking lot? Or was it Christopher? Had something happened to her son? Holding her breath, she gestured Dave onto the patio.

"Hey, Dave," she croaked. It was a lame attempt at pretending she wasn't terrified. "Good to see you. Care for some tea?"

Dave shook his head. "No, thanks." He glanced toward the house. "I'm looking for Bryan Forester. Is he here?"

Relieved, Ali let out her breath. "In the far bathroom," she answered. "Would you go find him, please?" she said to Leland.

Leland nodded. "Certainly," he said and marched away.

"Is something wrong?" Ali asked.

"I'm afraid so," Dave answered. "Morgan Forester's been murdered. Their two girls came home from school a little while ago and found their mother dead in the front yard. Has Bryan been here all day?"

Even though all of Bryan's worker bees had shown up on time, Bryan himself hadn't appeared until later in the morning. Given that he had several different jobs going, his late arrival wasn't so unusual. Ali had noticed, however, that the generally even-tempered Bryan had seemed out of sorts. Even before his confrontation with the building inspector, Bryan had been barking at his people and growling at the guys wielding their cameras.

"He wasn't here all day," she said. "But he was here most of it. Why?"

Before Dave could ask anything more, Leland returned, bringing Bryan Forester with him. "What's up?" Bryan asked, looking questioningly from Ali to Dave.

Ali knew from personal experience what it meant to be given that kind of devastating news. Not wanting to witness Bryan Forester's heartbreak, Ali thought of taking Brooks and disappearing into the house. Before she could rise from the bench, however, Dave cut off that avenue of retreat by speaking immediately.

"It's about your wife," he said. "I'm afraid I have some very bad news."

"Bad news about Morgan?" Bryan asked. "What about her? What kind of bad news. Has she been in a wreck or something?"

"I'm sorry to have to tell you this. Your wife has been murdered," Dave said. "Your daughters found her this afternoon when they came home from school."

Ali felt a momentary flash of anger at Dave Holman. Couldn't he have found a gentler way of delivering such awful news? Couldn't he have couched it in less blunt terms?

Bryan's face contorted in grief and astonishment as the brutal blow landed. He staggered over to the picnic table and sank down onto the redwood bench across the table from Ali. "No," he said, shaking his head from side to side in absolute denial. "That can't be. It's impossible. Morgan was fine when I left for work. This is wrong. You must be mistaken."

"I'm afraid there's no mistake," Dave replied. "If you don't mind, Mr. Forester, I'll need you to come with me. Once the body has been transported, we'll need you to identify . . ."

At first Ali thought he had softened slightly, but then she noticed the odd shift from "Bryan" to "Mr. Forester." Ali was a year younger than Dave, and Bryan Forester was over ten years younger than Ali. Dave's turn to formality struck her as ominous.

Bryan, on the other hand, seemed oblivious. He surged to his feet. "No," he interrupted. "Where are Lindsey and Lacy? What have you done with my daughters? I've got to see them, be with them."

"The girls are fine," Dave said reassuringly. "I called in Deputy Meecham, the DARE officer from their school. She knows your kids, and they know her. I asked her to take them to the sheriff's office. The girls are probably already there."

"Let's go, then," Bryan said impatiently, changing his mind about going to the house. "Why are we standing around here jawing?" He took two long strides toward Dave's car, then stopped and turned back to Ali. "Tell the guys for me, please," he said. "They should probably plan on taking the rest of the week off. Until I—" He broke off, unable to continue.

"Of course," Ali said reassuringly. "I'm so sorry about this, Bryan. You do what you need to do. We'll be fine."

She watched as Dave took Bryan Forester by the arm and escorted him to the waiting patrol car. Dave opened the door—the door to the backseat, Ali noted, to let Bryan inside. Ali had to concede that was probably necessary, since there would likely be weapons and equipment in the front seat, but still, was it really necessary for Bryan to be locked in the back of the vehicle like a common criminal—like he was under arrest or something? But then Ali remembered that when her almost–ex husband, Paul Grayson, had been run over by a speeding freight in southern California, the investigating officers had driven her to Riverside in the back of a patrol car as well. Perhaps this was the same protocol and it meant nothing. Maybe Ali was simply reading too much into it.

"If you'd like me to, madam," Leland Brooks said quietly, "I'd be happy to track down the work crew and relay the bad news."

Ali knew that in the past, Leland had dealt with Arabella Ashcroft's periodic flights from sanity by retreating into that very proper butler mode. Dave's uncharacteristic detour into formality had disturbed her, but as Leland switched gears, Ali felt herself comforted.

"Thank you," Ali said. "That would be greatly appreciated."

Ali sat staring into the depths of her teacup and thought about two little girls coming home to the shock of finding their mother murdered. It appalled Ali to think about them being thrust into this awful turmoil and then being carted off to the sheriff's office by some stranger to await the arrival of their father.

Ali's cell phone rang. Glad to be jolted out of her grim contemplations, she hurried to answer, but it didn't do her much good.

"Have you heard about Morgan Forester?" Edie Larson asked. "It's positively dreadful! I still can't believe it."

Ali Reynolds had always marveled at her mother's uncanny ability to know everything that was going on in Sedona, Arizona, before almost anyone else did. Since Edie's sources were quick and nearly always accurate, Ali didn't bother questioning them now. Obviously, whoever had delivered the news knew what was going on.

"Just did," Ali admitted. "Dave was here a few minutes ago and told Bryan what had happened."

"Those poor sweet little girls," Edie went on. "Can you imagine coming home from school and finding something like that? The one is already such an odd little duck, I doubt she'll ever recover."

"Odd?" Ali asked.

"They're twins, you know," Edie said. "They've come to the Sugarloaf on occasion, usually with their daddy." The Sugarloaf Café was the family-owned diner Ali's parents had run for years.

"The two of them are the cutest little things. They look just alike, but the one—I don't know which is which—talks nonstop. She chatters on and on like a little magpie, while the other one never says a word. The one eats everything in sight and cleans her plate without the least bit of fuss. The other one has to have everything on a separate plate—one plate for the eggs, another for the hash browns, another for the bacon, and still another for her toast or sweet roll. God forbid if one crumb of food should touch another. It's always a problem when they come in, because there's not enough room on our four-tops for one person to use four separate plates." Edie paused and then added, "I guess you've never waited on them."

Periodically, Ali pitched in as a substitute waitress. She knew of several adult customers with similar phobias, but she didn't remember ever waiting on Bryan Forester's little girls. "I guess not," she agreed.

"I'm baking one of my tuna casseroles right now. Your dad will deliver it to their house a little later. I understand Bryan's folks moved down to Sun City a few years ago. His dad has arthritis, and the winters up here were too cold, but I'm sure they're on their way. I don't know about Morgan's folks. It seems to me they're not from around here."

Ali didn't know anything about Morgan Forester's family. Wherever her parents lived, once they learned the news, their hearts, too, would be broken, but Ali suspected that no one from either side of the family would be very interested in Edie Larson's excellent tuna casserole.

"If the house is a crime scene, it'll be empty," Ali said quietly. "No one will be allowed to be there."

"You're right, of course," Edie said after a pause. "Well, then, I'll talk to one of the neighbors and find out where your father should deliver the food once I have it ready. Now, what about Thanksgiving?"

Her seamless segue from tuna casserole to turkey and dressing left Ali momentarily confounded.

"I know you had your heart set on having everyone over to your new place," Edie continued. "But we have to be realistic. That just isn't going to happen. We need a new plan."

If Edie Larson had a sentimental bone in her body,

her daughter had never seen it. After spending her entire lifetime either working in or running a restaurant and being in the day-to-day business of food, Edie looked at life's ups and downs through a framework of what needed to be cooked, where, and when. Yes, Morgan Forester's murder was a terrible thing, but after taking care of that required tuna casserole, Edie was ready to move on to the next piece of critical culinary business—Thanksgiving dinner. Meanwhile, Ali had been so shocked by what had happened that she had yet to consider how the terrible disruptions in Bryan Forester's life might also impact her own situation.

"Don't worry about it, Mom," Ali said. "I'm sure we'll be fine."

Ali was hanging up when Leland emerged from the house and began gathering up the tea things. She passed him her cup, cold now but still half full.

"You told them?" she asked.

Leland nodded somberly. "I talked to Billy, Mr. Forester's second in command. He said that if it's all the same to you, they'd like to come on the job tomorrow anyway. If he can get the building inspector to come out and sign off on the permits, he said they'll be able to go ahead with the wallboarding with or without Mr. Forester. But only if you don't mind."

The fact that Bryan's crew was ready and willing to move forward without him seemed commendable. "It's fine with me," Ali said.

Leland nodded. "Very good, madam," he said. "I told them I'd let them know if you had any objections."

As if on cue, the workmen emerged from the building. Carrying tool belts, tool cases, and lunch boxes, they headed first to the Mini-Mobile, the metal storage unit where they stowed tools and supplies. Leland locked it each evening after the workmen left the job site and opened it every morning before they arrived. Minutes after the workmen left, the camera crew decamped as well, but they took their load of expensive equipment along with them. Leland picked up the tray, but before he could head back to his cozy fifth wheel, Ali stopped him.

"Detective Holman asked me if Mr. Forester had been here all day," she said casually.

Dave had come to notify Bryan Forester of his wife's death, but Ali had no doubt the man had been in Dave's sights as a possible perpetrator from the moment Morgan's homicide had been reported, and Dave had already started the process of tracing Bryan's movements.

Leland returned the heavy tray to the table. "I seem to recall he did arrive a little later than usual," he said thoughtfully. "Most of the time he's here early enough to park at the top of the driveway. Today I noticed that his truck was down near the bottom of the hill."

Ali nodded. "Did he seem upset to you?" she asked.

Leland frowned. "Now that you mention it," he said, "I believe Mr. Forester did appear to be slightly out of sorts. He spent a good part of the day talking on his phone."

"Did he happen to mention any kind of difficulty at home?" Ali asked.

Leland gave her a wry smile. "That's not the kind of thing one would mention to the hired help," he said quietly. "It's just not done. It's getting quite cool out here," he added. "Would you like me to light the heater?"

They had stationed a propane-fueled outdoor heater near the picnic table so the guys could have their morning coffee without freezing their butts off.

"That's all right," Ali said. "I think I'll head home."

"By the way," he reminded her, "it is Monday. Your evening to cook, I believe. Would you like me to come by and throw something together for you?"

Ali looked at this remarkably caring man.

"Thanks for keeping me on track," Ali said. "You've done more than enough for today. I'll handle dinner."

"Very well," Leland said. "Will we see you in the morning?"

"If the work crew is coming, I'm coming," Ali told him.

But as Ali pulled out of the driveway, she wasn't thinking about getting her job done. She was thinking about two little girls, Morgan Forester's daughters, who would have to grow up without their mother.

Poor babies, Ali said to herself. *Those poor babies.*

{ CHAPTER 2 }

Peter Winter left the car parked along the road half a mile away from the house and walked the rest of the way, knowing that his surgical booties would leave behind no discernible prints. Concealed behind Bryan Forester's workshop, he watched as Morgan loaded the girls into the car to take them to catch the bus. There was a chance that she might not come straight back, but he knew that Monday mornings were when she usually caught up on paperwork.

Walking up onto the porch, he settled into the swing to wait for Morgan to return. He didn't have to wait long. Ten minutes later, she was back. She caught sight of him sitting there as soon as she got out of the car and greeted him with a radiant smile.

"James!" she exclaimed. "What a wonderful surprise. I didn't expect to see you until Wednesday. Why didn't you tell me you were stopping by today?"

It astonished Peter to think that Morgan was actually glad to see him. Naturally, he hadn't said a word to her about what she'd done wrong—that she'd crossed some invisible line and signed her own death warrant in the process. She came toward him with a pathetically happy smile, seemingly without noticing his out-of-place scrubs. Or the fully loaded syringe he had slipped into his pocket. Smiling back, he stepped off the porch and went to meet her.

James O'Conner was the name Morgan Forester knew Peter Winter by, and that was the name she had asked for when she had called in to the "work" number she had managed to lift from his cell phone. Of course, no one in the ER knew anyone named James O'Conner. In actual fact, James O'Conner didn't exist. Had never existed.

"Somebody wanted to trade at the last minute," Peter told her. "So here I am."

She fell into his arms willingly, happily, and was still kissing him when he retrieved the syringe from his pocket and plunged the needle into the flesh at the base of her neck.

"What was that?" she demanded, struggling and trying to push away from him as the painful needle point pierced her skin. "What are you doing? What's going on?"

Once the syringe was empty, he dropped it. She was still trying to escape him, but he grabbed her with both arms and held her fast. "Don't worry," he said. "It's okay."

But it wasn't okay at all. The Versed did its work well. When she sagged helpless in his arms, he half carried and half dragged her limp body up onto the porch and settled it in the swing. Then he went back and retrieved his syringe. He couldn't afford to leave that behind. Syringes came with identifiable serial numbers that could all too easily lead back to him.

He didn't bother undressing Morgan, as he had

his other kills. He knew the cops would be examining every aspect of the crime scene. Mixing up the details would make it more difficult for investigating officers to match this incident with any of his others. From a practical standpoint, if he wanted the cops to focus on Morgan's husband, he needed to downplay any sexual connections. Anger had to be paramount.

Physics had never been Peter's strong suit. Using the hammer with Morgan already in the swing didn't work all that well—not as well as he'd wanted. Each blow to her head sent both the swing and his target flying away from him, blunting the killing power. As a consequence, it took longer than he had expected. Once it was over, he did three things. He carefully set the bloodied hammer aside; he wanted to preserve as much blood evidence as possible. He dropped a little blood onto his hanky and put that in a baggy to keep it moist. That was what he hoped would seal Bryan Forester's fate. Next he removed Morgan's showy wedding band and the accompanying engagement ring with its three-carat rock. He slipped the wedding set onto his key ring along with all the others. Finally, he took his photo montage.

Once the scene was set, he made his way back to the rental car. Still in the underbrush, he slipped off the booties and then walked up to the rental car, which was sitting undisturbed where he'd left it. He had planned to put the bloodied hammer on some newspapers he'd left in the trunk for that purpose. Hearing a rapidly approaching vehicle, however, he was forced to ditch the hammer in a hurry, putting it down on the passenger-side floorboard before dashing around to the driver's side. He managed to start the car and drive away before the approaching utility truck caught up with him.

After that, it took a while to track down Bryan Forester's pickup truck. Peter had the addresses of Forester's several construction sites, and he found the Dodge Ram pickup at the one on Manzanita Hills Road. The problem was there were several ongoing construction projects in the neighborhood, which resulted in far more street and foot traffic than Peter had anticipated. He made several futile trips past the truck. In the early afternoon, he got a clear shot at the bed of Bryan Forester's pickup. The hammer needed to be visible but not obvious. He put it in the corner beside the rider's door, a spot Bryan was unlikely to look at as he got in and out of his truck. And then, for good measure, he left a smear of blood from the hanky there as well.

Peter was hungry by then, but he didn't dare stop to eat. He didn't want to do anything that would call attention to his face in the wrong place at the wrong time. Instead, he headed back to Phoenix. To his dismay, he found that there had been a serious rollover semi accident on I-17 on one of the steep downgrades between Cordes Junction and Black Canyon City. DPS had been forced to shut down the highway completely for over an hour while they cleared the roadway of debris, which included several tons of rolled roofing and countless scattered bundles of shingles. By the time he managed to drop off the car and retrieve his own from the short-term lot, he was almost late for his shift at work. He would have been late if he hadn't called his friend Brad Whitman, who had been willing to punch in for him.

Peter had hoped to stop by the house long enough to upload the photos and clear his camera's memory stick, but he had to stay focused. He was well aware that groggy doctors make mistakes, so he swilled coffee and tried to keep his mind on the job. Tomorrow, after he'd gotten some sleep, he would have plenty of time to treat himself to a victory lap on another job well done. Morgan Forester was dead, and her asshole of a husband would go to prison for it. What could be better than that?

The blue Ford 500 pulled into Bobby Salazar's lane at the car return facility ten minutes before his shift was due to end. Bobby knew he needed to leave right on time—at four. Otherwise, depending on traffic, he might be late for his five P.M. biology class at Phoenix Community College. There was a big exam scheduled for that night. Chasing after an A in the class, he couldn't afford to be late.

With that in mind and hoping this rental return wouldn't be a problem, he approached the vehicle, handheld card scanner in hand.

"How's it going?" Bobby asked.

The driver was a middle-aged Anglo wearing mirrored sunglasses, a Diamondback baseball cap, running shoes, an ASU tracksuit, and a pair of leather driving gloves. Over time Bobby had come to have a very low opinion of people who wore driving gloves. They were usually arrogant and unpleasant, and this one fit that bill to a T. He didn't bother acknowledging Bobby's greeting. Wordlessly, he handed over his rental agreement and then got out and opened the back door, where he extracted a briefcase.

Used to being treated as a nonentity, Bobby leaned into the driver's seat to verify both the odometer reading and amount of gas left in the tank. By the time Bobby popped the trunk, the driver was already moving away, walking briskly toward the shuttle buses that would return him to the terminal.

"Don't you want a receipt?" Bobby called after him.

Shaking his head, the man didn't reply. He just kept on walking. The scanner printed out the unwanted receipt automatically, and Bobby stuffed it into his pocket.

"Have a nice day, Mr. Morrison," Bobby called. No matter how rude the customers might be, company training dictated that they should always be addressed by name. If Morrison heard him, there was no response.

"Screw you, too," Bobby muttered under his breath. He turned back to the car and checked the trunk, certain that Mr. Morrison had forgotten to collect his luggage. Except for an array of day-old newspapers, the trunk was completely empty. That struck Bobby as odd. Briefcase-only guys usually wore the other kind of suits. Most of the time guys in sweats or running suits came complete with mountains of luggage and mounds of golf clubs, to say nothing of short-tempered wives and screaming kids.

Shrugging, Bobby returned to open first the driver's door and then the passenger door, continuing the routine check to be sure nothing had been inadvertently left behind. He found sand and gravel on the driver's-side floorboard. On the passenger-side floorboard carpet, he found a small rust-colored stain, smudged in a fashion that made it look as though some attempt had been made to clean it up.

Of all the attendants on the lot that afternoon, Bobby Salazar was uniquely qualified to recognize the ill-concealed stain for what it was—blood. He had seen bloody carpet before, and he had tried to clean it up with a similar lack of success.

One of his ex-roommates, Kiki Rodriguez, had been

home alone when he had gotten bombed out of his gourd on Everclear. Nobody ever knew, because Kiki couldn't remember and couldn't tell them exactly how he had broken the glass that cut his hand so badly. What was clear was that he had wandered aimlessly around the apartment, bleeding like a stuck pig and leaving a trail of blood everywhere, before he finally passed out on the couch. Bobby had been the one who came home and found him there. He had called 911. The EMTs had taken Kiki off to the ER, leaving Bobby to deal with both the cops and the bloody carpet. He wasn't sure which had taken longer, answering the cops' questions or trying to get the damned blood out of the carpet. He had tried everything, including calling in a professional carpet cleaner, but when he had moved out of the apartment two months later, the stains had still been visible enough that Bobby had lost his security deposit.

Concerned, Bobby got out of the car and gave the rest of the front seat a thorough examination. There was no visible blood anywhere else—not on the seat or the steering wheel or the door handle. The stains were on the floorboard and nowhere else. The guy had obviously walked in it. *What if he hit something?* Bobby wondered. *A deer, maybe. Or a dog. Please, God, not a person!*

Bobby walked to the front of the vehicle and studied the bumper, looking for damage. He was relieved when he found nothing—no dents, no dings, no sign of a collision with anything, living or dead.

Two more renters had pulled into Bobby's lane. Their luggage was already unloaded, and they were waiting impatiently for him to come check them in as well. He knew if he mentioned the presence of blood in the vehicle to one of his supervisors, there would be hell to pay. Questions would be asked. Forms would need to be filled out and filed. More than likely, Bobby would be late for class. Not only that, if he took that long with one vehicle, the guys who tracked productivity would no doubt give Bobby a black mark for slowing down the return process. You were supposed to check in so many customers per hour—or else.

Waving to one of the drivers, Bobby sent the Ford off to be washed, then turned and approached the next waiting customer. "How's it going?" he said. "Hope you had a good trip."

Late in the afternoon, Ali drove back to the Andante Drive mobile home, which had been left to her by her mother's twin sister, Evie. Permanently set on a concrete footing that had been carved into the steep hillside, the place boasted a very un–mobile-homelike basement that included Christopher's studio and Ali's late second husband's extensive wine collection.

Ali had lived there for the better part of a year and a half, most of that time with her son as her roommate. She hoped that by the time she finished the remodel and moved on to Arabella's house, Chris would have married his steady girlfriend, Athena, and Ali would be able to pass the mobile home along to them. Both Chris and Athena were public high school teachers whose low salaries wouldn't stretch very far in Sedona's stratospheric real estate market. Not having to buy a home of their own would give them a big leg up in starting married life together. Ali liked the idea that Aunt Evie's legacy to her would stay in the family.

Ali had never been a particularly capable cook, and she knew that what she brought home from Basha's deli section wouldn't be nearly as delectable as whatever Leland Brooks might have "thrown together." She had suggested hosting the Thanksgiving festivities primarily because she knew she would have him there to backstop her. For this Monday-evening dinner, she had raided Basha's deli counter for some enchilada casserole and a selection of salads and veggies.

When Ali walked in the door, Sam, her impossibly ugly sixteen-pound, one-eared, one-eyed tabby cat, trotted to the door to greet her, complaining at the top of her lungs that she was starving. Since Chris's Prius was already parked outside, Ali knew the cat was lying. For a time, her adopted kitty's weight had mysteriously edged up. It was only when the vet complained about the weight gain that Ali discovered that Sam had routinely cadged two evening meals by pretending she hadn't been fed. Once Ali and Chris had realized they were being suckered, they hatched the plan that whoever came home first fed Sam, no matter what the cat said to the contrary.

"Liar, liar, pants on fire," Ali told the noisy animal. Knowing full well the kitchen counter wasn't Sam-proof, she stowed the casserole in the microwave and deposited the evening's salads in the fridge. Then she headed into her room to shower and change clothes.

When she came out half an hour later, she was surprised to see that Chris had set the table—for three rather than two. The table was decked out in his mother's good china, complete with crystal wineglasses. He had also heated the casserole and opened a bottle of Paul Grayson's high-end wine—a Corton-Charlemagne from Côte d'Beaune.

"What's the occasion?" Ali asked.

Chris shrugged. "I invited Athena to come to dinner," he said. "Hope you don't mind."

When Ali had first heard about Athena Carlson, she had been a little dismayed. Athena was several years older than Chris and divorced. She was also a double amputee, having lost part of her right arm and most of her right leg, compliments of an exploding IED during a Minnesota National Guard deployment to Iraq.

Ali had always hoped her son would find the "perfect" girl. Initially Athena hadn't quite squared with Ali's idea of perfection. Over the months, though, Ali had come to see Athena really was perfect. Her midwestern small-town roots and rock-solid values provided just the right counterpoint to Chris's artistic temperament and occasionally unrealistic enthusiasm. And Ali had nothing but respect for the way Athena focused on what she could do rather than on what she couldn't. One of the things that fell in the "could" column was her ability to play a mean game of one-handed basketball.

"You should have called me," Ali said. "If I had known we were having company, I would have picked up something a little nicer than enchilada casserole."

"That's all right," Chris said. "Athena's not picky."

Ali knew that to be true, and as far as she was concerned, it was another mark in Athena's favor.

The doorbell rang, and Chris hurried to answer it. Athena stepped into the house. Underneath a pair of slacks, her high-tech prosthetic leg was all but invisible. The complicated device on her right hand was more apparent. Smiling and laughing, she entered the room and kissed Chris hello. When the two of them turned to face Ali, Athena's face was awash in happiness. Without a word, she held up her left hand, showing off a respectably sized diamond ring.

"He gave it to me last night," Athena said as Ali stepped forward to admire it. "I didn't wear it to school today. We wanted you to be the first to know."

"Congratulations!" Ali exclaimed, giving first Athena and then her son a hug.

"You're sort of the first to know," Chris admitted. "It's actually Aunt Evie's diamond. Grandma gave it to me so I could have it reset. But Grandma and Grandpa haven't seen it this way yet, and they don't know I've given it to her. You really are the first."

Ali couldn't help feeling slightly provoked that her parents knew more about her son than she did. Some of the irritation must have shown on her face.

"You're not upset about that, are you, Ali?" Athena asked warily.

Ali pulled herself together and laughed it off. "Not at all," she managed. "My mother always seems to know exactly what's going to happen long before anyone else does. I'm thrilled for you both."

Chris and Athena exchanged relieved looks. Obviously, they had been concerned about how Ali might react.

Ali moved over to the table, picked up the wine bottle, and began to pour. "How about a toast to the newly engaged couple?" she said enthusiastically. "I think you both deserve it."

Dinner was a lighthearted, fun affair. Athena, more radiant than Ali had ever seen her, was full of plans for the future. No, they hadn't set a date yet. Most likely, they'd get married after school got out at the end of May, possibly early in June.

"A small wedding," Athena said. "Maybe outside, with red rocks in the background and just family and a few friends in attendance. I already had the whole full-meal-deal church wedding with a white dress, half a dozen attendants, and a reception that cost my dad a bundle. Unfortunately, we all know how that one turned out."

For the first time that evening, a shadow crossed Athena's smiling face. Her husband had ditched her while she was in Walter Reed, recovering from her injuries. And since he and his second wife were now living in what had once been Athena's hometown, Ali understood completely why Athena had no desire to go "back home" for a second wedding.

Ali thought about the gnarled wisteria that shaded the patio at the house on Manzanita Hills Road. In May the venerable old plant would most likely be dripping with clusters of lush lavender blossoms, something that would make a perfect backdrop for a wedding. But she had the good sense to keep her mouth shut. After all, this was Athena and Chris's wedding. As mother of the groom, Ali needed to keep her opinions to herself.

"Your folks won't mind coming out?" she asked.

"My grandmother had never been on an airplane until she flew to D.C. to stay with me at Walter Reed." Athena grinned. "If she could fly for that, she can certainly fly for this."

"What about your parents?" Ali asked.

"My grandmother's the only one I really care about," Athena said.

Ali decided she was better off not asking anything more.

"We're going to have a little get-together at the gym tomorrow night before the game, and we'd like you to come," Chris put in quickly, diverting them from what was evidently dodgy territory. "About seven-thirty. We plan to go public with our engagement then. I'll invite Grandpa and Grandma. Athena's roommates will be there, along with the people in our basketball league."

"I wouldn't miss it," Ali assured them.

"It won't be much of a party," Athena said. "No champagne in the high school gym. We'll be drinking Hawaiian Punch and eating storebought cookies."

"I still wouldn't miss it," Ali said.

After dinner, when Athena left, Chris went out with her, ostensibly to walk her to the car. Ali knew that was bogus, of course. The process was likely to involve far more necking than it did walking and would last an hour or more. In the meantime, Ali cleared the table, put away the leftovers, and then hand-washed the china and crystal.

Standing with her hands and forearms plunged deep in soapy water, Ali recalled how she had chosen the Royal Limoges Beleme pattern at Paul Grayson's behest right after the two of them had become engaged. She had loved the creamy color of the delicate bone china and the subtle, understated designs around the borders. Ali had imagined using those gorgeous dishes as she presided over a lifetime's worth of joyous meals, complete with family and friends.

But the reality had been far different, more hell than heaven. The meals she had hosted with Paul, the ones where the dishes had been used, hadn't turned out to be what Ali had hoped for or expected. Yes, Paul Grayson had loved entertaining and had done so lavishly, but there had been an element of one-upmanship in everything he did. Dinner guests were invited because of who they knew or what they had to offer in terms of deal making. Places at his table were generally assigned based on who could provide the best political advantage at work. For him love had counted far less than leverage.

On this occasion, an inexpensive and simple meal— reheated deli food—had been served to guests in a mobile home that had once belonged to Aunt Evie, someone Paul, in his arrogance, had summarily dismissed as mere "trailer trash." Ali found herself smiling at the irony. Paul Grayson's command-performance entertaining was far in the past, and tonight's low-key celebration had fulfilled Ali's long-ago dream of how those lovely but costly dishes would be used.

Ali was drying the last of the plates when she heard the front door open. She peeked around the intervening wall, expecting to see Chris returning. Instead, Dave Holman let himself into the room.

"Sorry," he apologized. "Chris was outside with Athena. He said I should go on in."

Dave and Ali's decision to put their romance on hold while maintaining their friendship had led to a certain amount of confusion on both sides. Glad to see him under any circumstances, Ali put down her dish towel on the counter and hurried over to kiss him hello. He kissed her back with a lot more enthusiasm than mere friendship warranted.

"Sit down," she said, ushering him over to the leather couch. "Don't be such a stranger. How are the girls?"

"Great," Dave said. "Cassie's the same as she always was—never a bit of trouble. As for Crystal? She's back to being her old self—going to school, getting good grades, playing goalie on her soccer team. It's like she's really turned a corner."

Months earlier, unhappy that her mother and step-father had moved away from Sedona, Crystal Holman had staged an adolescent insurrection by getting involved with an online predator. Her rash behavior had come close to being fatal for her and for Ali Reynolds. But Ali wasn't the least bit surprised to know that Crystal was now happy as a clam. The child was a master manipulator. Risky though it had been, everything she had done had been calculated to bring her back home to her father. *And it worked like a charm,* Ali thought a little ruefully.

"Glad to hear it," she said aloud. "So this is work?"

Dave nodded. When the girls had come back to Sedona, Dave had moved out of his bachelor-pad apartment and into a three-bedroom rental near the old downtown business district.

"So who's looking after them while you're off on a case?" Ali asked. That had been one of Crystal's complaints—that cases were more important to her father than family. Ali suspected that was still true.

"Crystal promised she'd see to it that Cassie gets to bed on time," Dave said. "Believe me, I'm keeping the computer under lock and key these days. The only time Crystal gets to use it is when I'm there to supervise."

Crystal was an experienced thirteen, and not in a good way. Ali wouldn't have left her in charge of a younger sibling on a bet, but Dave hadn't asked for her advice about child care any more than Athena and Chris had asked for wedding advice. With some difficulty, Ali managed to keep her mouth shut.

"Meanwhile, you're working the Forester homicide?" she asked.

Dave nodded. "That's why I'm here—to ask you

some questions. I really do need to track Bryan's movements today."

"Is he under arrest?"

Dave shook his head and pulled out a notebook and pen. "Nothing like that," he said. "This is all very preliminary. We're just trying to get the lay of the land. What can you tell me about today? I believe you told me Bryan was at your place most of the day."

"That's right," Ali said. "We had a problem with a building inspector, and Bryan waited around until she showed up."

"Is he usually at your place all day, every day?" Dave asked.

"No," Ali answered. "He has multiple jobs and multiple crews—three that I know about for sure."

"What time did he arrive today?"

Ali had to think about that. "It must have been close to ten. I really didn't pay much attention. He's my general contractor, Dave. He isn't required to punch a clock. He supervises workers, picks up supplies, and chases after permits. When it comes to work ethic, I'd have to say Bryan Forester is right up there at the top of the list. He puts in some very long days—not unlike a certain homicide detective who shall remain nameless."

Ali's gentle jibe produced not so much as a glimmer of a smile from Dave. "And how was he once he got there?" the detective persisted. "Did you notice anything unusual about his demeanor?"

Ali paused before she answered. She didn't want to point the finger of suspicion in Bryan Forester's direction, but she felt obliged to tell the truth. "I suppose he seemed out of sorts," she admitted. "I chalked it up to what was going on with the building inspector. She's not a very nice person."

"But Bryan didn't say anything to you about what might have been bothering him?"

"Not to me, and I doubt he said anything to Leland Brooks, either. If he talked to anyone at all, it would be his workers—his foreman, Billy, in particular. They've worked together for years."

Dave jotted something into his notebook. "Billy?"

"William Barnes."

"Oh, him," Dave said. "Can you give me the names of the rest of his crew?"

"Not first and last," Ali said. "Leland probably keeps track of all that. I know them on sight but mostly by first name only. Ryan and Gary are the ones I remember; they both said they're planning on being on the job tomorrow. If you want to stop by and talk to them then, you're more than welcome."

"They're coming to work tomorrow even after what happened today?" Dave asked. "Why would they do that?"

"Loyalty, maybe?" Ali returned. "Bryan strikes me as a nice guy. His workers seem to think the world of him. Maybe they're just trying to help out. Or maybe they need the money."

Dave's grunt of acknowledgment let Ali know that even though he may have heard what she said, he remained skeptical. "I'll come see the work crew tomorrow," he said. "Probably fairly early in the morning, unless something else comes up."

"How are Bryan's girls doing?" Ali asked. She couldn't keep from thinking about those two motherless seven-year-olds. And the fact that they were the ones who had discovered their mother's body on the front porch.

"As well as can be expected," Dave replied grimly. "They're with their father and their grandparents right now. Bryan's folks came up from Phoenix. From Sun City. They're all checked in to the Best Western. Bryan and Morgan's house has been declared a crime scene. So's their yard. No one's going back there for the foreseeable future."

That was what Ali had expected. So much for Edie's tuna casserole. But remembering what her mother had said about Bryan's twins, Ali found herself more worried about one of them. What about the quiet one who never allowed foods to mingle on her plate? How would a child like that deal with what must seem like the total annihilation of her carefully organized existence? "Are they going to be okay?" Ali asked.

"They were pretty distraught," Dave returned. "And understandably so. Deputy Meecham, the DARE officer, is great with kids. She did what she could to help them, but they've been severely traumatized. I'm hoping we'll be able to schedule CHAP interviews for both girls tomorrow."

"CHAP?" Ali asked, not recognizing the acronym.

"Childhelp Advocacy Professionals," Dave said. "It's an outfit out of Flagstaff made up of psychologists and social workers. They do forensic interviews of at-risk children, including children involved as witnesses in homicide investigations."

Ali's heart gave a lurch. "You're not saying the two Forester children may have actually seen what happened to their mother?"

"No," Dave assured her. "Not as in eyewitnesses, no.

The ME's preliminary report says Morgan Forester died shortly after she put the twins on their school bus this morning. But if there was something going on in the house—if Bryan and Morgan Forester were feuding in some fashion—I'm guessing those girls know all about it. That's one thing I learned from dealing with Crystal this past year. Kids know a lot more about what's going on with their parents than they're willing to let on."

The door opened, and Chris bounded into the room in a burst of cold air. "Hey, Dave," Chris said. "Did Mom tell you the good news—that Athena and I are engaged?"

Grinning, Dave gave Chris a high five. "That's great," he said. "Congrats!"

"We're having a little get-together at the high school gym tomorrow night before the game," Chris continued. "You're welcome to come."

"We'll see," Dave said. "I'm up to my eyeballs in a case right now."

"The Forester murder?" Chris asked.

Dave sent a questioning look in Ali's direction.

"It's not my fault," she said. "I didn't tell him, not one word."

"I just heard about it from Athena," Chris explained. "Mindy, Athena's roommate, called and told us about it while we were outside. She couldn't believe it had happened."

"Mindy?" Dave asked.

"Mindy Farber," Chris answered. "She teaches second grade at the school in the village. Both the Forester girls are in her class."

"And the teacher is Athena's roommate?" Dave asked.

Chris nodded.

"I'll need that phone number, then," Dave said, "so I can talk to her as well."

Chris recited the number, and Dave jotted it down. Watching him, Ali knew it was necessary, knew he was doing his job, but she hated the idea of someone going through those little girls' lives. Bryan Forester's daughters had already lost their mother. And if Dave was able to get the goods on their father, they could be destined to lose him as well.

Chris said good night and headed for his room. Dave turned back to Ali. "Can you think of anything else?" he asked.

Ali gave him an appraising look. "I like Bryan Forester," she said. "I've been working with him for months now. I've never heard him raise his voice on the job. I've never heard him swear. He works hard, and he does a good job. I don't think he's a killer."

Thoughtfully, Dave closed his notebook and dropped it into his pocket. "The problem is," he said, "most killers don't wear sandwich boards announcing the fact. And as you and I both know, just because a marriage looks solid to outside observers doesn't necessarily make it so."

"Do you know for sure that the Foresters' marriage was in trouble?" Ali asked.

Dave shook his head. "The two of us have been through a lot," he said, "but I'm sure you can understand that I can't reveal details of an ongoing investigation—not even to you. I will tell you, though, that some details have come up that give us grounds to be suspicious of Bryan Forester."

"Those poor little girls," Ali murmured.

"Poor little girls indeed," Dave agreed. "Their mother was murdered in an act of homicidal violence. This wasn't random, Ali, it was personal. Morgan Forester's killer was someone operating in a blind rage. And if Bryan Forester is the perpetrator here—if he's capable of that kind of violence—I'm honor-bound to see that his daughters don't fall victim to it as well."

Reluctantly, Ali found herself nodding in agreement. Dave was right. If, behind his smooth facade, Bryan Forester was a cold-blooded killer, then someone had to stand up for his daughters. That someone was Detective Dave Holman.

"I'd best be going," Dave said.

Appalled by her own bad manners, Ali realized she hadn't offered him anything to drink. "What about a cup of coffee?" she asked belatedly. "It won't take long."

Dave shook his head. "No," he said. "Sorry. First forty-eight and all that."

Ali, like most American TV viewers, knew what he meant: If a homicide isn't solved in the first forty-eight hours after the crime, the likelihood that it will never be solved increases dramatically.

Dave started for the door.

"When you come to talk to Bryan's crew," Ali suggested, "you should probably plan on talking to the film crew as well."

"What film crew?" Dave asked.

"They've been taping the entire remodeling project for a possible series on Home and Garden TV."

"Oh," he said. "I see." He gave her a cursory kiss on the way out. Clearly, his mind was elsewhere. Like a bloodhound hot on a trail, he refused to be distracted.

Ali watched him as far as his car, then turned off the porch light and locked the door. She leaned her forehead against the door, and a sense of disappointment passed over her. Women always expected to juggle more than one thing at a time—family, work, relationships. Obviously, men did the same thing, but their priorities were entirely different. For Dave, duty came first. Being a good father had detracted from his ability to be a good lover. And now, with Morgan Forester's homicide case taking precedence, Ali worried that the fatherhood part might be losing ground as well.

Ali wondered if maybe the same thing was true for Bryan Forester. She could speak to the fact that the man was a conscientious worker, someone whose word was his bond. But what if being good at his job made him a bad husband or father? What then?

As for Bryan's two little girls? Ali was dismayed to realize that she didn't even know their names. Saddened by the reminder that real evil was alive and well in the world, Ali went into the bedroom.

After changing into her nightgown, she gently shifted Sam off her pillow and crawled into bed. Long after she turned out the light, though, Ali was still wide awake. At last, she turned on the light. While Sam stalked out of the bedroom in a huff, Ali took her computer out of the nightstand drawer and booted it up.

{ CHAPTER 3 }

In the aftermath of losing both her job and her marriage and encouraged by her son, Chris, Ali had started Cutlooseblog.com. Much to her surprise, what she had written about her own travails had resonated with plenty of other women. They had written in, sharing their own difficulties, their triumphs and tragedies. Some of those women, like the dauntless Velma T of Laguna Niguel, California, an eightysomething tough-as-nails cancer patient, Ali counted as friends.

But as her own life changed, Ali had found that Cutloose hadn't. Every few months a brand-new crop of women seemed to cycle through the website, dealing with the same kinds of issues Ali had already dealt with, drowning in their own pain, trying to put their lives back together. When Ali's direction changed, when she went from agonizing about her life and times to something else—like remodeling the house or choosing plumbing fixtures, for instance—many of the people who continued to visit Cutloose weren't interested. Her previous readers didn't want to learn about architectural drawings or getting permits or battling dry rot or sistering joists or any of the other countless new things the Manzanita Hills house was bringing to Ali's attention on a daily basis. It didn't take long for Ali to realize there was a looming disconnect between her own life and those of her readers. Once she did, she had done the only honorable thing—she cut Cutloose loose.

Months earlier a woman named Adele Richardson, aka Leda, had written in. Her history with a philandering husband paralleled Ali's in many ways. At a time when Ali's criminal defense attorneys were advising her to take a break from blogging, Adele had offered to step in and pinch-hit. Ali hadn't accepted the offer, but later on, when she realized she really did need to step away from the blog, she had contacted Adele once more. The transition had been seamless and relatively painless. Ali had written a farewell blog in which she announced she was handing the reins over to someone else, and Cutloose seemed to have gone on quite nicely without her, thank you very much. That was one thing the past few years had taught Ali Reynolds in spades. She was nothing if not expendable.

It had been true for her job and for her marriage and, apparently, for Dave Holman as well. Things happened. Circumstances changed. Life moved on. And as Ali logged on to Cutloose that night, it wasn't because she felt a need to revisit or wallow in her own misery. In fact, it was exactly the opposite. She had journeyed a long way from the awful pain she'd been in when she first started the blog. She went there now knowing that the stories she was likely to find would allow her to count her blessings.

For old time's sake, she scrolled through that day's postings. The stories were achingly familiar.

> *My husband ran off with my sister. I've got three kids, no job, no car, and no money. What am I going to do?*

Go to work, Ali thought. *Get a job. Pull yourself up by your bootstraps.*

As she scanned through the string of reader comments, she saw that was what the other writers were saying as well: Don't sit around blaming your husband; be responsible for yourself; get a life. Some of the correspondents couched their suggestions in less confrontational ways, but they were all pretty much of a piece—a course in tough love: self-love seasoned with ample amounts of good common sense. Obviously, Adele was keeping Cutlooseblog.com on track, staying true to Ali's original mission.

Ali was interested to see that Cutloose seemed to have attracted a fair number of male readers.

> *Thank you for showing me that I'm not the only man in the world who's a victim of domestic violence. It helps to know that there are others out there like me who are finding the courage to speak out. Maybe there's hope for me and my kids.*

The posts that followed that were a mixed bag. Two amazingly angry women declared in no uncertain terms that men were ALWAYS the perpetrators and NEVER the victims in domestic-violence situations. But one correspondent included a toll-free number where men could call to locate family-style shelters in their geographical area that would take male victims and their children right along with women.

> *While I was off on a business trip with my boss, I had too much to drink and ended up in his room. When we got back home, he fired me. What do I do now?*

Get another job, Ali thought. Again the accompanying posts echoed that sentiment, some of them with the added proviso of: *Quit drinking!!!*

Ali found it all interesting, but more as a trip down memory lane than anything else. She really had moved on, and she wondered how long her successor would be able to keep it up before she, too, would need to hand Cutloose off to someone else—to new blood, as it were.

Leaving Cutloose behind, Ali logged on to the virtual edition of Phoenix's daily newspaper, the *Arizona Reporter.* There, in the statewide news section, she found an article on Morgan Forester's homicide.

> *Morgan Forester, age twenty-seven, wife of prominent Sedona area contractor Bryan Forester, was found bludgeoned to death on the front porch of their rural home outside the Village of Oak Creek. Mrs. Forester had been dead for some time when the body was discovered by her two young children as they returned home from school.*
>
> *The Yavapai County Sheriff's Office is investigating.*

*"This is an extremely tragic situation,"
said Demetri Hartfield, Yavapai County media
relations officer. "We know she died of homicidal
violence. At this point, however, we have no
suspects and no persons of interest."*

That's not entirely true, Ali thought. Dave Holman
definitely has a person of interest in this case.

*Neighbors up and down the lonely length
of Verde Valley School Road reported seeing
nothing at all out of the ordinary. The house itself
is in a secluded area half a mile from its nearest
neighbor and screened from the road by a rise that
would have concealed events at the house from
passersby.*

*"Morgan was a wonderful woman and the best
friend anyone could ever want," said neighbor
Sally Upchurch. "She was a full-time mom who
loved being at home and who absolutely doted on
her two little daughters. She adored her husband
as well. They're just the nicest family, all of them.
I can't imagine how such a terrible thing could
happen."*

*Bryan Forester and his two daughters are
reportedly in seclusion somewhere in the Sedona
area. Through a family spokesman, he asked that
they be left to grieve in peace during this difficult
time. Services for Mrs. Forester are pending and
will be announced at a later date.*

The problem is, Dave Holman can imagine such evil
very easily, Ali thought, and now so can I.

Bad things really did happen to good people. Ali Reynolds herself was a case in point. Her husband had abandoned her to father out-of-wedlock children with not one but two other women. As a result, when he had been trussed in the trunk of a car and left on a railroad track to be run down by a speeding freight train, she had immediately been viewed as a prime suspect.

But all that worked itself out eventually, Ali told herself. *Dave Holman may be a less than perfect father and lover, but he's a good detective. If Bryan Forester is innocent of murdering his wife, then Dave is the one who'll sort it out. It's none of my affair.*

Ali looked at the clock and was astonished to see that while she had been staring at her computer screen, several hours had zipped by unnoticed. She logged off, shut down her computer, closed it, and put it away.

As soon as she turned out the light, Sam relented. The cat returned to the bedroom and to her spot on the side of Ali's bed, landing on it with a soft thud. As Sam curled up and settled down, Ali reached out and put one hand on the purring cat.

"Not our business," Ali said aloud as she drifted off to sleep. But Sam wasn't listening. Unfortunately, neither was anyone else.

Sleepless, Matt Morrison lay in bed and tried to figure out what had happened. For the thousandth time that day, he asked himself the same question. Why had Susan stood him up? After all, she was the one who had come up with the idea of meeting in the first place. Susan Callison—Suzie Q in her profile—was thirty-seven years old, married, had no children, and sold real estate. She had told him in their many online encounters that her fantasy was to meet up with a guy and "do it" somewhere they weren't supposed to be—preferably in somebody's model home. By seven A.M. that morning, an eager Matt had been at the appointed place sixty miles south of Phoenix, parked in the driveway of one of the model homes in a new planned-living development called Red Rock Ridge.

For someone like Matt, who had always followed the rules and kept his nose to the grindstone, Susan's explicit online chats had made the whole idea sound amazingly daring and out there. Making love with a stranger in a strange bed or elsewhere was something totally out of character for him, which was why he had jumped at the chance. It was why he had gone. He had driven down I-10 anticipating the idea that for once in his incredibly boring life, he was about to have the kind of sex he'd read about in books and seen in movies—something that would literally knock his socks off.

He had shown up early, a good twenty minutes before he was expected, but beautiful blond Suzie Q hadn't showed. Anxious minutes had ticked off one by one while he waited and waited. Worried that she might have been in an accident somewhere along the way, he would have loved to call her, but she had never given him her number. "Better not," she had counseled in an instant message. "Too dangerous." So he hadn't been able to call, and without his computer, he couldn't e-mail or instant-message her. Instead, he had waited for the better part of two hours. When construction workers at some of the other houses on the street had started giving him funny looks, he had driven away.

At first he'd had a hard time deciding where to go. Having left word at the office that he was on his way to Tucson, he couldn't very well show back up without some kind of explanation. He couldn't go home, either. Eventually, he'd made his way back to a truck stop in Eloy. There he'd sat at the counter and swilled several cups of coffee and thought about the call of the open road. What would life be like if he had become a trucker instead of an auditor? He tried to see himself at the wheel of an eighteen-wheeler with nothing ahead of him but mile after mile of blacktop. What if he didn't have to come home each night to a woman who barely tolerated his presence?

Unable to stand the suspense any longer, Matt had driven back to the office and told his supervisor that his appointment had been canceled at the last minute. In the privacy of his cubicle, he logged on to his personal e-mail account. His department maintained a zero-tolerance policy on personal e-mail, so he didn't send or open any, but he did scroll through his new mail, looking for a message from Susan. Nothing.

After work, he had hurried home, gone into his study, and fired up his home computer, where he had been disappointed to find there was still no e-mail from Susan, and she wasn't listed on his buddy list.

He had immediately dashed off a quick note:

Where are you? What happened? Did I go to the wrong place? Are you all right?

That one seemed too brusque. Unable to unsend it, he had written another:

I can understand it if you changed your mind. There's no harm in that. I just want to know that you're okay. I was afraid something bad had happened to you—that you'd been in a car accident and that you were hurt or in a hospital. Please let me know.

And then a third:

Please, please, please get back to me. The silence is killing me.

Matt had sat at his desk for a long time, staring at his computer screen and hoping in vain to hear the sound of an arriving message. Finally, startled by how much time had passed, he had hurried out to the kitchen to start dinner. He had just put the chicken pot pies in the oven and was starting to fix the salad when Jenny arrived.

"Dinner's still not ready?" she asked. "Did you forget that I have book club tonight?"

Matt had forgotten all about her meeting, but he had been thrilled to hear about it. If she was going out, that would give him a little peace and quiet for the evening, and maybe, with any kind of luck, a chance to hear back from Susan Callison. Just a single kind word from her, that was all he wanted.

Now, though, it was one o'clock in the morning. Jenny was back home, asleep in the bedroom, and snoring like a steam engine. Matthew Morrison was wide awake. Susan still hadn't replied.

Monday-night shifts were usually fairly quiet in the ER. Sometimes Peter could even duck into the lounge and grab a nap. But not that night. The place was a zoo all night long, from the beginning of his shift to the end. It took some doing for him to manage to dispose of the damning needle as well as the bloodstained scrubs, booties, and hanky. Once that was done without anyone in the ER being the wiser, he felt a rush of euphoria. Soon, however, it seemed as though the nervous energy that had sustained him through the day abandoned him completely. Fatigued beyond bearing, he could barely stay focused on what needed to be done. When his shift ended two hours late, Peter scared himself by almost nodding off a couple of times on his way home from the hospital. When he got there, he did the only thing he could do: He stripped off his clothes, fell into bed, and fell sound asleep.

By that time, a bedraggled Matt Morrison was already in his cubicle. He had never been much of a drinker, but this morning, lack of sleep had left him feeling like he'd overdosed on Captain Morgan rum and Coke. Matt felt sick to his stomach. His head ached. His ears rang. All because Susan hadn't gotten back to him.

By now he had sent her a dozen different messages. As each interminable moment of Matt's workday ticked by, he knew with heartbreaking certainty what he had already known in the driveway of that model home in Red Rock—he would never again hear from Suzie Q. Susan Callison was the one good thing that had ever happened to Matt Morrison, and now she was over—completely over. For Matt, the saddest part about his erstwhile affair was that it had ended before it even started.

Making love would have been nice. Matt would

have liked the sex part, but that wasn't the point. What he had really wanted was a connection—an honest, loving, human connection—to someone who, unlike Jenny, might somehow learn to care for him the same way he cared for her.

For a brief time, Suzie Q had held out that tantalizing possibility. It hurt him to think that what had almost been within his grasp had disappeared from his life. Without ever actually touching him, Susan Callison had wounded him deeply and had left a permanent hole in Matt's heart.

Staring blankly at the wall of his cubicle, Matt wondered if he'd ever get over it. *Maybe,* he thought. *Then again, maybe not.*

On Tuesday morning, Ali didn't bother making coffee at home. Instead, she drove straight to the Sugarloaf Café and took a seat at the counter, where her mother, coffeepot in hand, was holding forth on the previous week's local school board election, where her slate of candidates had won walking away.

Edie Larson glanced in her daughter's direction. "Ali's here," she called to her husband, who waved from his workstation in the kitchen. Edie hurried down the counter and filled Ali's mug. "From the look on your face, I take it I'm in trouble again," Edie said.

Ali suspected that it wasn't just the expression on her face that had alerted her mother. It was more likely Chris had stopped by the restaurant on his way to school to give his grandmother a heads-up on the engagement-ring situation. Ali tackled her mother straight on. She was glad Chris was close to her parents, but she worried that sometimes being close went too far.

"Why would that be?" Ali demanded. "Could it have anything to do with the fact that you and Dad knew all about the engagement situation, including the ring, and never said a word to me?"

"Chris asked us not to," Edie said. "He and Athena wanted to surprise you."

"I was surprised, all right," Ali said.

"Chris came to your father asking for advice about a ring," Edie explained. "Naturally, your father mentioned it to me. Evie's diamond wasn't doing anybody any good just lying around in my jewelry box, so I suggested he use that. End of story."

Ali realized that her parents had always regarded Christopher as the greatest thing since sliced bread. Things could be a lot worse. At least her parents cared, which was a lot more than could be said for Chris's other grandparents.

"What would you like?" Edie asked, changing the subject and writing on her order pad as she spoke. "Eggs over easy, bacon, no hash browns, biscuits?"

Because Ali was still a little provoked with her mother, she was tempted to order French toast out of spite—just to prove her mother wrong for a change—but for today eggs, bacon, and biscuits were what she actually wanted. She loved her parents dearly, but there were times when she could have used more distance.

Edie tore Ali's order off her pad and slapped it on the wheel in the kitchen pass-through. After delivering someone else's breakfast, she returned to Ali. "Have you talked to Bryan yet?" she asked.

Ali shook her head. "No," she said. "Under the circumstances, I don't really expect to. I'm sure he has plenty of other things to deal with."

"Dave's on the case?"

Ali nodded. In the old days, when Dave Holman had been an almost daily visitor at the Sugarloaf, Edie wouldn't have needed to ask that question. She would have had the answer straight from the horse's mouth. Now that Dave had his girls with him, he was evidently eating most of his breakfasts at home.

"People are really up in arms about what happened," Edie said. "The idea that someone could be murdered like that in broad daylight in her own front yard is appalling. And having those poor little girls be the ones who discovered their mother's body . . ." Edie clicked her tongue and shook her head. "Sedona is supposed to be a nice place. Things like that don't happen here."

Yes, they do, Ali thought. *Things like that happen in all sorts of places.*

"They're all saying Bryan did it," Edie Larson continued. "Although how a man could do something like that to the mother of his children is beyond me!"

"Mom," Ali objected. "Wait a minute. What makes you think Bryan is responsible for what happened?"

"I didn't say I thought it, but it's what people are saying. The husband is usually the responsible party."

Ali was taken aback. The article she had read online a few hours earlier had stated that investigators had yet to establish a person of interest in Morgan Forester's death. In the meantime, the good citizens of Sedona were already declaring Bryan Forester guilty before even being charged.

"What people?" Ali asked.

"Cindy Martin, for one," Edie said. "She works at the Village of Oak Creek salon. She's the one who always did Morgan's nails."

Ali sometimes forgot that her mother's unfailing ability to see all and know all was based in large measure on the fact that Edie Larson was tuned in to an intricate network of small-town gossip.

"According to Cindy, Morgan was tired of doing all the behind-the-scenes paperwork for her husband's construction company and was ready to do something else. I can certainly understand that," Edie added. "Not everyone can handle working in a family-owned business. When you spend every minute of every day with someone, it can turn into way too much togetherness. It's not easy, you know. There are times when I think I need to have my head examined for spending my whole life putting up with your father's foolishness on a day-to-day basis."

The Sugarloaf had been started by Ali's grandmother, who had eventually handed it over to her two daughters, Edie and her twin sister, Evelyn. Up until Aunt Evie's death, the two sisters had waited tables and managed the front of the house while Ali's father had done most of the cooking. Edie's current complaints notwithstanding, Ali knew that neither one of her parents would have wanted it any other way.

"And then there's the boob job," Edie went on, lowering her voice.

"What boob job?" Ali asked.

"Morgan had one a couple of months ago," Edie said. "When a woman signs up for a surgical enhancement, you can usually bet that she isn't doing it for the poor dope who happens to be her current husband."

In southern California, where Ali had lived previously, that hadn't been her experience. From Ali's point of view, lots of women had breast augmenta-

tion, many of them with their husband's encourage-
ment and approval. That Morgan had joined ranks
with other consumers of enhancement surgical
procedures didn't necessarily mean the Foresters'
marriage was in trouble. And it certainly didn't seem
like an adequate reason for anyone to declare Bryan a
person of interest in his wife's homicide.

Bob Larson pounded twice on a bell in the pass-
through, announcing that one of Edie's orders was
ready to be picked up. Edie shot off to deliver plates of
food, leaving Ali to mull over what had been said. Yes,
Ali knew Morgan Forester handled the bookkeeping
part of her husband's company, Build It Construction;
she sent out the invoices, paid the bills. The neighbor
had said she was a stay-at-home mom, although Ali
thought she had been more of a work-at-home mom.

Edie returned and refilled Ali's cup. "Cindy also said
that Morgan was always complaining that her husband
was a workaholic—that he lived and breathed for his
business. That's not good for a marriage, either."

The idea that Edie Larson was disparaging someone
else for being a workaholic would have been downright
laughable if Ali could have found anything in this dreadful situation even remotely funny. Bryan Forester had
lived in the community all his life. Ali didn't like the
idea that people were already turning against him based
on nothing more than flimsy hearsay from his wife's
manicurist. Ali felt obliged to defend him.

"One person saying it doesn't make it so," Ali
declared. "Yes, Bryan Forester is a very hard worker,
but that doesn't mean he's a workaholic. And it doesn't
make him a killer. Besides, most workaholics don't
have time for affairs."

Edie seemed taken aback by Ali's remark. "I see," she said, although Ali wasn't at all sure that her mother did see. It seemed instead that this was a subject on which they would simply agree to disagree.

Bob sounded the bell once again. This time Edie brought Ali's breakfast. While Ali ate, a seemingly abashed Edie hustled up and down the counter, busying herself with other customers. When she returned, she had evidently decided it was time to change the subject.

"About Thanksgiving," she began. "If the new house isn't going to be ready—"

"Bryan's crew is coming to work today," Ali interrupted. "Let's see how much they get done in the next few days. For right now I don't want to cancel."

"All right," Edie said. "Suit yourself. I hope it all comes together."

So did Ali. After breakfast, she drove from the restaurant to the house on Manzanita Hills Road. When she had left the night before, Bryan Forester's Dodge Ram pickup had still been parked at the bottom of the hill. Now the pickup was gone, but vehicles belonging to other workers lined both sides of her driveway. True to their word, Bryan's crew had turned up for work even if their boss hadn't. The same thing went for the videographers. Their van was there, too.

When Ali pulled into the yard, she was surprised that she had to move aside in order to make way for the departing building inspector. Yvonne Kirkpatrick had obviously stopped by first thing to sign off on that permit.

Thank you, Billy, Ali thought. *You're getting things done after all.*

The front door of the house stood open, with work-men coming and going. Ali followed one of them inside, where she was thrilled to see that after months of seemingly no progress but the framed skeleton of a building, studs were now disappearing behind sheets of expertly installed wallboard. She found Billy Barnes in the bathroom of what would be a master suite. He was deep in conversation with one of his crew of wall-boarders, walking the worker through some thorny issue.

"Looks like you're making good progress," she said when he looked up and noticed her. "And I saw that the permit got signed off on after all."

Billy Barnes nodded. "That one took some doing," he said.

"What about Bryan?" Ali asked. "Have you heard anything from him—how he's doing?"

"About how you'd expect," Billy answered. "I didn't talk to him directly, but I talked to his parents."

"So at least he wasn't alone," Ali said.

Billy nodded. "His dad said Bryan was in pretty bad shape—still in shock, couldn't believe what had happened, and all that. I don't blame him. I can't believe it myself."

"It was great that you and your guys came to work this morning. I really appreciate it."

"We're not the only ones," Billy said, waving aside her praise. "Bryan's other crews are doing the same thing. We're moving forward as well as we can without him. He can't afford for us to shut the jobs down. If he does, he'll go broke, and so will we. If any of us could afford to work for free, we wouldn't be here every day busting our butts, Bryan included."

That answered one of Dave Holman's questions: The employees being on the job had very little to do with loyalty to their boss or with sympathy for him, either. Their showing up had far more to do with enlightened self-interest. They were working because they needed the money. Bryan's regular paychecks fed their families and covered their bills.

"If you have a chance to talk to him directly," Ali said, "let him know I'm thinking of him, and if there's anything I can do to help—"

"Knock, knock," someone called behind her.

Ali turned to find that Dave Holman had followed her down the hallway. One hand held his notebook. In the other, he clutched a half-eaten doughnut. Dave glanced at Ali and then back at the doughnut. "At least I'm eating breakfast," he said, then he turned to Billy. "Mind if I ask you a few questions?"

Obviously, no introductions were required. From the guarded way the two men looked at each other, Ali was reasonably sure they were already acquainted—and that there was no particular love lost between them.

Billy had been cordial enough with Ali. Now he glanced pointedly at his watch, as if to say that he did mind—a lot. "I suppose," he allowed gruffly. "As long as it doesn't take too much time."

Dave polished off the last of his doughnut. "So tell me about yesterday," he said. "We're trying to get a time line on Mr. Forester's activities. He claims he was here on the job all day long. Do you happen to recall what time he showed up?"

Ali knew better than to hang around listening to the interview. Leaving the two men alone, she went back outside and made her way over to the canopy-covered patio. Leland had started the propane heater, and the outdoor space was warmer than it was inside the house. The butler had covered the redwood table with a clean white cloth and had stocked it with several thermal carafes of freshly brewed coffee and stacks of Styrofoam cups. The spread included a selection of baked goods—a platter of blueberry muffins and a box of mixed doughnuts with one (Dave's, presumably) conspicuous in its absence.

Ali was pouring herself a cup of coffee as Leland emerged from the fifth wheel with sugar, cream, and a fistful of spoons. "A good morning to you, madam," he observed. "A bit nippy, but lovely."

Ali looked out at the bright, cloudless sky arching overhead. "Yes," she agreed. "It is lovely."

"I see that Detective Holman is hot on the trail, as it were," Leland continued. "He's asking some of the same things he asked yesterday and checking our recollections for any inconsistencies."

"What did you tell him?"

"The truth. I told him that Mr. Forester is usually soft-spoken and remarkably even-tempered, but that he seemed a bit out of sorts yesterday—impatient and irritable."

That was how Bryan had seemed to Ali as well. They fell silent as Brooks laid out the spoons, lining them up with military precision.

"From the way Detective Holman asked his questions, I'm quite sure he believes Mr. Forester is responsible for what happened to his wife," Leland continued thoughtfully.

Ali nodded. "He's not the only one. According to my

mother, everyone in town has already decided he's the guilty party."

Leland shook his head. "I'd hate to think he would be capable of that kind of thing. Then again, I know for a fact that you can't always tell what someone is capable of, even if you think you know them."

Ali knew he was thinking about Arabella Ashcroft. Her seemingly normal appearance had belied the fact that she was a remorseless serial killer.

Before Ali could reply, tires sounded on the driveway. She looked up to see Bryan Forester's pickup truck come to a stop near the garage. As Bryan strode toward her, Ali hurried to meet him. Not surprisingly, the look on the man's face was grim.

"That's Dave Holman's car, isn't it?" he asked. "What's he doing here?"

"Asking questions about whether or not you were here yesterday, which you were," Ali said.

"Great," Bryan said. "Just what I needed, having him going around to all my jobs asking questions."

"But what are you doing here?" Ali asked. "Your guys are doing a great job on their own. After what happened yesterday, I would have thought—"

"We need to talk," Bryan interrupted. "In private."

{ CHAPTER 4 }

With a discreet but understanding nod in their direction, Leland disappeared into his fifth wheel. Ali led Bryan over to the canopy-covered table. "What about?" she asked.

Bryan sighed and ran one hand over his eyes as though he couldn't imagine where to begin. "It's about your cabinets," he said.

"The kitchen cabinets?" Ali asked. "What about them?"

"Since it seems likely that I'm going to have to be off track for a while, I was trying to line up materials so the guys could keep on working and we can finish up the jobs that are already in process," Bryan said. "I'm self-employed. If the jobs don't get finished, I don't get paid, which means I'll probably end up firing my crews and declaring bankruptcy. With the drywall going up, I knew it was only a matter of days before we'd be ready to install your cabinets. I noticed yesterday that they hadn't been delivered yet, so I called to check. The person I talked to said she'd look into it. Today she called me back to say that they were never ordered."

"Not ordered?" Ali asked. "How can that be? I distinctly remember giving you a check. You said I needed to pay half at the time we ordered and the remainder when they were delivered and installed."

"That's right," Bryan said. "I remember that, too. You did give me a check. So did the people on the other two jobs. All three checks were deposited in the company account, but as far as I can tell, Morgan never faxed the order to the cabinet company. They have no record of it. The good news is that I have a copy of the three files on the laptop in my truck, so at least we don't have to start over from scratch. I've already e-mailed the specs for each of the three jobs to High Design Cabinets. The problem is, they don't have any record of the payments, even though the money for those three deposits is no longer in my business account."

"It's not there?" Ali asked.

Bryan shook his head morosely. "None of it."

"But that was a lot of money," Ali objected. "I seem to remember the check I wrote for the cabinet deposit was well over thirty thousand dollars."

"Thirty-three nine, to be exact," Bryan answered. "And the other two orders came to nearly the same amount. One was a little more and the other a little less. Altogether, it comes to right around a hundred thousand."

"So where did the money go?" Ali asked. "Maybe your wife simply made a mistake."

"I believe I've found the money, and it's no mistake," Bryan said grimly. "A couple of years ago, when Morgan's grandmother passed away, she left her granddaughter a tidy little sum of money. Morgan had always been self-conscious about her figure. We agreed that she'd set that money aside in a separate account so she could use it if she ever decided to go ahead with breast enhancement surgery. Which she did. Once the surgery was over, I thought the account would be empty, but it's not. It has well over a hundred thousand dollars in it—almost the exact amount that's missing from the three cabinet deposits."

"You think Morgan was embezzling funds?" Ali asked.

Bryan nodded. "That's how it's starting to look. I think she was hiding money away and getting ready to take off. It's also what I need to talk to you about today. The money is in an account that's in Morgan's name only. With everything that's happened, the bank says I won't be able to touch a dime of it until after probate and this is all straightened out. High Design says they're willing to start building the cabinets on a rush-order basis, but to do that, I need to send them money—money I don't happen to have at the moment. I mean, I do have some money, but if I use that to pay the cabinet bill, I won't be able to meet payroll. One way or the other, I'll be out of business."

"So what do you need?" Ali asked.

"I was hoping you'd go ahead and pay the second half of the cabinet bill. That would be enough to get them started building them. Hopefully, by the time the cabinets are ready to ship, I'll be able to get the amount you've already paid freed up from Morgan's account."

"You're asking me to give you another check?"

Bryan shook his head. "The way things stand, that's probably a bad idea. I'd rather you have your bank wire the funds directly to High Design. That way, if something else happens . . ."

"What something else?" Ali asked. "What more could go wrong?"

Bryan let out a long breath. "Do you remember a couple of years ago, when we were afraid that fire was going to come down this side of the mountain and wipe out all of Sedona?"

Ali hadn't been living in Sedona at the time, but her parents had kept her posted with almost hourly reports. She nodded. "I remember the fire," she said. "What about it?"

"Our place was like a sitting duck out there in the middle of nowhere. Morgan did everything on the computer. I worried that if the house burned and took our computers with it, we'd be out of business. So I signed up with a Web-based off-site backup system. Every night at midnight, our computers log on to the Internet and back up all the files on our hard drives. I hadn't ever had any reason to look at Morgan's backup file. To begin with, I was just trying to figure out what happened to the missing money, so I didn't look at all of them by any means, but I learned enough to know that she's been playing me for a fool."

"More than just the money?"

Bryan nodded grimly. "Way more," he said.

"She's been cheating on you?"

"In spades," Bryan said. "I won't know the whole story until I have a chance to look into the files. And I have a feeling that once I dig deeper, I'm going to find out there was a whole lot more going on that I still don't know about."

Ali heard the hurt in Bryan's voice. Betrayals that are uncovered while someone is still alive are bad enough, but at least you can deal with them. You can talk them over, or not, and then move on. When something like that surfaced after someone was dead, the survivor was left to deal with the whole thing alone. Unfortunately, Ali knew all about that kind of pain—from the inside out—and she worried about Bryan and whether or not he'd be able to handle whatever else might be hidden in his dead wife's computer files.

"I'm so sorry," Ali said. "I'm not sure if you ever heard about it, but something very similar happened to me. There were things my former husband did behind my back that I never knew about until after he was dead."

"When it was too late and there wasn't a damned thing you could do about it," Bryan Forester added bitterly. There were tears in his eyes.

Ali pretended not to notice. "That's pretty much it," she agreed. Her heart went out to the man. How could it not? And even though she expected the rest of the world would deem her a fool, she decided right then that she would trust him on the cabinet deal. Besides, he wasn't asking for her money to go to him. He wanted Ali to pay the cabinet manufacturer directly.

"Where do you want me to wire the payment?" she asked.

Bryan let his breath out in a sigh of gratitude. "Thank you," he said. "You have no idea how much this means to me."

Before Ali could reply, her attention was drawn to the sound of raised voices coming from the open door of the house. The words, indistinct at first, became clearer as the speaker moved closer.

"You've got a job to do, and so do I," Billy insisted, his voice raised to a near shout. "I've wasted enough time answering questions. Now get the hell out of here."

Dave Holman emerged from the house a few minutes later, trailed by the two cameramen, one of whom had his camera shoulder-high and running. Obviously, it had occurred to at least one of them that, with a homicide investigation under way, their mundane Mid-Century Revival filming project may have morphed into something that might be more profitable.

The videographers may have been filming for some time, but this was the first Dave seemed to notice. "Hey, you two," he said. "What the hell are you doing? This is a homicide investigation. Turn that thing off."

The two cameramen, Raymond and Robert, were virtually interchangeable. At that moment, Ali still couldn't tell them apart, but on this score, she was in full agreement with Dave Holman.

"That's right," she told them. "This falls outside our filming guidelines. Do what he said. Turn it off."

Dave glanced toward Ali. When he caught sight of Bryan Forester, he stiffened. "What's he doing here?" the detective asked.

"Talking to my client," Bryan answered in Ali's place. "In case you haven't noticed, we have a job to finish here."

Without another word, Bryan rose from the table. He stalked off across the driveway and strode past both the detective and the cameramen. Billy Barnes and Bryan walked into the house together. Dave, meanwhile, came over to the table where Ali was sitting. "What's he doing here?" he asked again. "What did he want?"

"He already told you what he was doing here," Ali corrected. "We were conferring about the best way to get my project finished."

Dave made no attempt to conceal his disbelief. "The day after his wife was murdered? Sure he was. It's a lot more likely he's making the rounds, trying to make sure his people have their stories straight about where he was and what he did yesterday."

"Dave—" Ali began.

"Have you ever seen someone who's been beaten to death?" Dave demanded, cutting her off. "Morgan Forester died a horrible death on the front porch of her own home. She was beaten to death—so savagely that her face is barely recognizable. I can't believe those poor little girls came home and found their mother like that. Do I think this was a crime of opportunity—that some stranger just happened to stop by their place, found her home alone, and slaughtered her because he could? No way, Ali. Like I told you last night, when homicide cops see this kind of mindless fury, this kind of rage, we usually don't have to go looking for some kind of stranger/danger perpetrator. Killers like this are mostly found a whole lot closer to home."

"Bryan didn't kill his wife," Ali asserted quietly.

"Oh, really?" Dave returned. "How can you be so sure of that? Because he told you so?"

"Because I know the man," Ali insisted. "He's a nice guy who's worked for me for months. He just wouldn't, that's all."

"Right," Dave said. "Billy Barnes has known Bryan since high school, and he says the same thing—he just wouldn't. Don't be naive, Ali. When a man's world gets turned upside down, not even his mother knows what he might be capable of."

When Ali didn't reply to that, Dave pulled his car keys out of his pocket and walked away. Since he had arrived first, his car was parked on the far side of Bryan Forester's truck. Instead of going straight to his sedan, Dave made a slow circuit of Bryan's Dodge Ram, peering into the bed of the pickup. Halfway around the truck, even with the far back tire, he stopped cold, leaned over, and stared. Then, pulling a pair of latex gloves out of his back pocket, he reached into the pickup, removed something, and took it with him when he drove away.

For a moment Ali stood there in shocked silence. *What was that?* she wondered. But she knew what it had looked like—a hammer. *And why did Dave take it?* But she knew the answer to that, too. Dave had taken whatever it was because he thought it was evidence in his case—evidence that hadn't required a search warrant because it had been lying in plain sight.

"Are you all right?" Leland Brooks had appeared soundlessly behind Ali and was examining her face with some concern.

"Yes," she said, a little too quickly. "I'm fine."

"You don't look fine," he returned. With a firm hold on her upper arm, he led her back to the table. "Come sit down, then," he said. "Let me get you something—coffee, tea, or even something a bit stronger? Perhaps a hot toddy is in order."

Shaking her head, Ali managed to laugh off his suggestion. She reached for her now-cold coffee. "No, thanks," she said. "That's not necessary. I'll just sit here for a few minutes."

"Well, at least let me call and cancel your afternoon appointment," Leland suggested. "There's no point in going through with it if you're not feeling up to snuff."

At first Ali didn't remember what appointment he

meant, but then she did. As a high school senior, Ali had been the surprised recipient of the very first Amelia Dougherty Askins Scholarship, an award that had made it possible for her to go on to college. Now, over twenty years later and through a series of fluke circumstances, Ali found herself in charge of administering the scholarship program that had once benefitted her.

Rather than being part of the regular financial aid programs, the Askins Scholarship had a somewhat unorthodox selection process. There was no formal application. Early in September, Leland Brooks, after months of investigation, had presented Ali with a list of ten possible candidates. The deserving students were drawn from the Verde Valley's various secondary schools. Once Ali and Leland had winnowed that list down to three finalists, Leland had gone about collecting as much information as possible on all three. Ali had decided that before making her final decision, she wanted to interview each of the candidates. The first of those interviews was scheduled for later that day.

"So you don't want me to cancel your meeting with Miss Marsh?" Leland confirmed. Haley Marsh, a seventeen-year-old single mother, was a senior at Cottonwood's Mingus Mountain Union High School.

"No," Ali said. "Considering what's going on around here today, a drive over to Cottonwood would probably be good for what ails me. It's not until afternoon, though. In the meantime it might be a good idea if I spent an hour or so going over the files on all the finalists."

Leland nodded. "Very well," he said.

Just then Bryan emerged from the house. Ali was relieved when he merely nodded in her direction and walked to his pickup without bothering to engage her in conversation. He clambered into the vehicle, wheeled it around, and drove out of the driveway.

What if Dave is right about Bryan Forester? Ali wondered. *And what should I do about the cabinet order?* She had told Bryan she'd wire the money to get the rush job started, but should she? Wouldn't that be sending good money after bad?

Ali sat there for some time thinking about it, but then the whining sound of someone installing wallboard screws came to her attention. It was a wake-up call. Regardless of what was going on with Bryan, the job was moving forward. If her remodeling project was ever going to be completed, and no matter who was doing the actual work, Ali would need those cabinets on hand sooner rather than later. She spent the next little while making sure her rush order of cabinets was under way.

She was still at the table and finishing up on the cabinet call when the two cameramen came over to the table and helped themselves to coffee and doughnuts. They seemed surprised to see her.

"I want this morning's tape," she said.

"Excuse me?"

Which one is he? Ali wondered. *Robert or Raymond?*

"The tape," she said. "The one you were doing this morning when Detective Holman was here. You were hired to film a home remodel. You weren't hired to film a homicide investigation."

"But it's all part of the same—"

"Detective Holman's visit doesn't fall under the heading of home remodel," Ali insisted. "I want whatever film you may have taken of that. I clearly remember stipulating in the contract that I had the right to say what film would be released to the public and what wouldn't. That means I want a copy of the whole tape. That way, if all or part of it is released to any venue without my express approval, I'll know where the material came from."

"But what about the wallboard installation?" Robert/Raymond objected. "That's on the same set of footage."

"In case you haven't noticed, the crew is still hanging wallboard," she said. "You'll have plenty of usable footage on that, but the cop stuff is off limits—all of it."

"Well," Robert/Raymond said, "I can't just give it to you. It's not that simple. This equipment doesn't create an actual tape, as such. I can send you the file by e-mail, if you like."

"E-mail is fine," Ali said. "But I want it today, no later than five. And if I were you, I'd make damned sure that I didn't accidentally e-mail it to anyone else, either. I'm the one who determines who gets the material and who doesn't. If you try passing my film along to someone who isn't authorized to have it, be advised: I have plenty of trial attorneys at the ready who'll be only too glad to take you to court and hold you accountable."

The two cameramen walked away, grumbling to themselves, as Leland Brooks appeared with three file folders in hand. "Good," he said. "The two of them are forever throwing their weight around. It's about time someone put them in their places." With a ceremonial flourish, he set the folders on the table in front of Ali. "Here you are," he added. "The official dossiers, as it were. When I put these together, I always feel a bit like M from the old James Bond movies."

"Don't you mean Q?" Ali asked. "He's the one with the gadgets. Isn't M a woman?"

"I know," Leland replied with an impish grin. "I definitely mean M."

Ali remembered the night Arabella Ashcroft had realized that her long-term butler was gay. She had hit the roof about it. Ali liked the fact that Leland felt free to tease with her about the situation.

Ali spread the folders out in front of her and glanced at the three names. Two of the candidates were female—Haley Marsh, from Cottonwood, and Marissa Dvorak, from Sedona. The male was Ricky Farraday, also from Sedona High School.

Leland reached down and tapped Ricky's file. "As far as I'm concerned, he's out."

In the spring of his junior year, Ricky Farraday had gained some national exposure as the victim of Sedona High School's first ever documented hate crime when he'd been publicly outed by having his locker filled with swarms of fruit flies. The ACLU had come to his rescue and had obtained an undisclosed monetary settlement. He had also been thrown out of the house by his hard-nosed, homophobic father. Ali knew from things Chris had mentioned that Ricky was now living in an apartment on his own—at his parents' expense—as a supposedly emancipated adult.

Even though Askins Scholarship winners were traditionally female, Ali hadn't objected when Leland Brooks had put Ricky's name on the list. Ricky's grades up through his junior year had certainly merited that. Then there was the similarity between Ricky Farraday's background and Leland Brooks's own family history. After serving with the Royal Marines during the Korean War, Leland had been cast aside by his nearest and dearest because they hadn't wanted "his sort hanging about." Being rejected by his blood relations was the real reason Leland had emigrated from the UK to the States. Bearing all that in mind, Ali was somewhat startled to hear that Leland was prepared to kick Ricky Farraday off Scholarship Island.

"How come?" she asked. She more than half expected to hear that since he was living on his own, his senior-year GPA wasn't good enough. That was what often happened when kids went off to live without parental supervision for the first time.

"Because he's a fraud," Leland declared forcefully. "A lying, cheating fraud."

Ali was stunned. "You mean he's not gay?"

"He *may* be gay," Leland allowed. "Although I'm not sure I'm entirely convinced of that, either. My main problem with Ricky is that I've gotten to the bottom of the fruit-fly escapade. He's a victim of a self-inflicted hate crime."

"You mean he put those fruit flies in his own locker?" Ali asked.

"A friend of Ricky's put them there at his insistence. He was at war with his father and was looking for a way to get thrown out of the house, and he certainly succeeded in that. Yes, he's living on his own, but with that undeserved windfall from his court case, he doesn't really need any scholarship help. That's just my opinion, however. Go ahead and read all three dossiers. The final decision is yours, but I think either one of the two girls would make a better choice."

Ali didn't ask how Leland had uncovered all these details, but she was prepared to accept his considered opinion on the subject. Setting aside Ricky Farraday's file, she spent the rest of the morning in the canopy-covered break room, working her way through the two remaining dossiers. Although both Marissa Dvorak and Haley Marsh were capable students, neither was performing at the valedictorian or salutatorian level, where scholarship help would have been much more plentiful. The two girls were solidly second-tier students.

Marissa Dvorak had been adopted as a ten-year-old from an orphanage in Ukraine. Juvenile arthritis had left her confined to a wheelchair prior to her freshman year in high school. Lengthy hospital stays and prolonged absences had limited her academic achievement and had also contributed to a lower GPA than she would have had otherwise. Nonetheless, she was a serious student who gravitated toward classes in science and math. Her single extracurricular activity was the chess club, where she had easily walked away with the state championship.

According to what Leland had been able to learn from interviewing friends and teachers, Marissa hoped to attend the University of Arizona as a premed student with the eventual goal of doing medical research. For right now, her hopes and dreams were stymied by the fact that her parents, who ran a chain of dry-cleaning establishments, made too much money for her to qualify for most forms of financial aid other than student loans. Both she and her parents were reluctant to sign up for those—a situation Ali Reynolds understood very well.

Haley Marsh, along with her maternal grandmother, Nelda Harris, had moved to Cottonwood a little over two years earlier from Tuttle, Oklahoma.

Haley had enrolled in Mingus Mountain as a very pregnant fifteen-year-old sophomore. Despite being an unmarried teenage mother, Haley had managed to maintain a solid 3.2 GPA for as long as she'd attended Mingus Mountain. Nelda, who worked as a school janitor in the afternoons and evenings, looked after the baby during the day while Haley was at school, and on weekends while Haley held a part-time job as a cashier at the local Target.

Faye Gerrard, Haley's homeroom teacher and her junior-year English teacher, was the one who had brought Haley to Leland Brooks's attention. "The girl is smarter than she knows," Faye had told Leland. "What she's lacking is self-confidence. I don't think anyone else in her family has ever gone on to college. She's somehow decided that since they didn't, she won't, either."

Haley's file left more questions than it offered answers. Where were Haley's parents? Why weren't they in the picture or even mentioned? And what about the baby's father? Where was he? Who was he?

Ali Reynolds found it easy to relate to both girls. Like them, she had been a second-tier student. For her, receiving the Askins Scholarship was the one thing that had made going on to school possible. She suspected the same would be true for either Marissa or Haley. One would have to overcome tough physical realities. As for Haley? Ali knew that being a single parent and going to school wasn't easy, but she also knew it could be done. Ali Reynolds herself was proof positive of that.

Marissa had a definite career goal in mind. The information on Haley gave no hint as to what her possible career choices might be, but Ali didn't find that particularly alarming. After all, how many high school seniors already knew exactly what they wanted to be when they grew up?

Ali abandoned her spot at the picnic table when the workers came wandering outside for lunch. Relieved to leave the construction behind, she grabbed some lunch on the way and then stopped by a Hallmark store and searched until she found just the right card for Chris and Athena. After ordering a bouquet of flowers to be delivered to the high school gym in time for their engagement celebration, she headed for Cottonwood.

It wasn't until she was alone in the car that she started thinking about Morgan Forester again—about Morgan and Bryan, about how the love two people once shared for each other could go horribly wrong. After all, when she had first met Paul Grayson, he had showered her with flowers, one arrangement after another, so many that her friends at work had teased her about being able to open her own flower shop. The onslaught of bouquets had started to dwindle shortly after their wedding, and the deliveries had ended completely long before Paul had ended up dead under that speeding freight train.

Ali was relieved when she arrived at Haley Marsh's place, a modest duplex on the far-east side of Cottonwood. When Ali knocked, she heard a toddler, crowing and babbling, come racing to answer it.

"Get out of the way," Ali heard a woman's voice order from inside the house. "Let me open it." Ali recognized the gentle drawl that betrayed the mother's Oklahoma origins.

The child must have stepped aside because eventually the door opened. Haley Marsh was a petite blue-eyed blonde. One arm was filled with an overflowing laundry basket, while a wide-eyed child with chocolate-brown skin and a cap of curly black hair peeked shyly out from behind his mother's leg. Looking at him, Ali estimated that he had to be right around two years old.

"Haley Marsh?" Ali asked. "My name is Ali Reynolds."

Haley nodded, but she didn't open the door to welcome Ali inside. "Mrs. Gerrard said you'd be dropping by today," Haley said guardedly. "She mentioned something about your wanting to talk to me about a scholarship, but I haven't applied for any scholarships."

"May I come in?" Ali asked.

Haley sighed and set down her laundry basket. "I guess," she said. "But the place is sort of a mess." She hefted the child onto her hip and motioned Ali into the room. The crammed living room wasn't really a mess so much as it was lived in. A playpen empty except for a collection of outgrown toys was jammed into one corner of the room along with a changing table. Baby gear and more toys were scattered everywhere. Half the dining room table was covered with stacks of folded laundry. An open schoolbook and a notebook of some kind lay on the other end of the table as though an afternoon study session had been interrupted by Ali's arrival. A high chair, littered with the remains of the toddler's afternoon snack, sat nearby.

Still holding the squirming child, Haley ushered Ali over to a sagging couch, then she took a seat on a nearby straight-backed chair. As soon as she was seated, the barefoot baby scrambled out of her lap and scooped up a tiny plastic truck from the floor. With a face-wide grin, he brought the toy to Ali and offered it to her. Ali accepted the proffered gift with a thank-you. The child clapped his hands in glee, said something that sounded very much like "truck," and then dashed off in search of another one.

"Good sharing," Haley told her son. To Ali, she added, "He likes having company."

"He's adorable," Ali said. "What's his name."

"Liam," Haley answered. "After my grandfather."

Not after his father, Ali thought. She couldn't help wondering how this clearly African-American child would go about explaining his very Irish first name as he grew up. And was the fact that Haley had been expecting a mixed-race child part of why she and her grandmother had pulled up stakes and moved to Arizona?

"I'm here on behalf of the Amelia Dougherty Askins Scholarship fund," Ali explained. "The first Askins Scholarship was given to me years ago, when I was a senior in high school, and it made all the difference. My parents own the Sugarloaf Café in Sedona. At that point they had a viable business but not much money. Without the scholarship, I wouldn't have been able to go on to college; with it, I could and did. They say what goes around comes around. Now I've been put in charge of distributing the scholarship that was so helpful to me.

"You've been brought to our attention as an especially deserving student. I wanted to have an opportunity to talk to you about it. I wanted to see if your receiving a scholarship from us would help you go on to college."

"With him here and getting into everything, it's hard enough just going to high school," Haley said. "How could I possibly go on to college?"

"But you'd like to?" Ali pressed.

"I suppose so," Haley admitted a little wistfully. "But I hadn't really thought about it."

"What were you planning to do instead?" Ali asked.

"Work," Haley answered. "My manager at Target promised me a full-time position once I graduate. All I want to do is earn enough so Liam and I can rent a place of our own. Give Grandma a little peace and quiet for a change. She already raised me. It's not fair that she's having to raise him, too."

"If you could do anything you wanted, what kind of work would you choose?" Ali asked.

"I suppose I'd be a nurse," Haley said without hesitation. "I'd also like to be Santa Claus or the Easter Bunny. The chances of that happening aren't very good, either. For now all I want is to graduate from high school and for Liam and me to be on our own."

"But if someone would help you," Ali began. "If someone offered to help pay your way—"

Liam came back over to his mother, scrambled up into her lap, and cuddled up against her breast. Ali knew that, as a general rule, it was a bad idea for babies to have babies, but clearly, Haley Marsh was a good mother—an exceptionally good mother.

"If you had a better education, there'd be more opportunities for Liam," Ali said. "And more opportunities for you, too."

Suddenly, Haley's bright blue eyes sparked in anger. "You don't know that," she declared hotly. "You don't know anything about us. You don't get to come in here with your fancy checkbook and think that gives you the right to judge us or tell us what we should do or shouldn't do."

"I didn't mean—"

"Yes, you did," Haley interrupted. "But this is my baby. I had him on my own, and I'm raising him on my own. Grandma's been wonderful to us. I don't know how we would have made it without her. But I'll be eighteen in May. It's not fair to ask her to do any more. It's time for us to move out and be on our own. I can't do that and go to school, too. So thanks for the scholarship offer, but no thanks."

It wasn't quite the response Ali had expected. She had thought Haley would be as thrilled as Ali herself had been to learn she was even under consideration for a possible scholarship. She never expected that her offer would be turned down cold.

"This is important. Before you decide, shouldn't you at least discuss it with your grandmother?" Ali asked. "Yes, if you go on to school, it may take a few years longer for you and Liam to be out on your own, but obviously, your grandmother loves you very much. Surely she wouldn't mind—"

"No," Haley insisted. "I don't want it. We'll be fine. Give it to someone else."

"But—"

"I'm not going to ask her," Haley said. "My grandmother looks after Liam while I'm at school, and then she works from four o'clock in the afternoon until midnight. She can't go on working that hard forever. It's bad enough that she's doing it while I'm in high school. I couldn't ask her to do the same thing so I can go to college. I can't and I won't. She's done enough for us already. Now go, please. I've got homework to do."

"Won't you please reconsider?" Ali asked.

Haley was having none of it. "Thank you but no thanks," she said. "I appreciate the offer."

Rebuffed, Ali stood up and held out the toy truck. Liam scrambled out of his mother's lap and dashed over to collect it. As Ali made her way to the door, she opened her purse and pulled out a business card, which she handed over to Haley. "Given the cost of tuition, books, and room and board, the scholarship could turn out to be a substantial amount of money over the next several years," she said. "If you happen to change your mind . . ."

Haley took the card and then dropped it on a nearby end table. "Right," she said. "I'll let you know."

Moments later, feeling as though she'd been given the bum's rush, Ali found herself in the yard outside.

What kind of a salesman does that make me? she wondered. *I can't even give money away.*

{ CHAPTER 5 }

With both Ricky Farraday and Haley Marsh officially out of the running, Marissa Dvorak was the only remaining candidate for that year's scholarship. Ali's appointment with Marissa was scheduled for tomorrow. In the meantime, awash in a sense of failure, she headed back to Sedona. She couldn't help but contrast the ecstatic, grateful way she had felt when Anna Lee Ashcroft had told Ali about her scholarship with the way Haley Marsh had received similar news.

Ali picked up the phone and dialed Leland's number. "How'd it go?" he asked.

"Not well," Ali told him. "Haley Marsh told me to take my scholarship and shove it, then she threw me out of the house."

"She wasn't interested?"

"You could say so. She was vehemently not interested. Not interested in going on to school and not interested in receiving a scholarship."

"That wasn't the impression I got from speaking with her grandmother," Leland replied. "It sounded as though she was interested in Haley continuing on to university."

"You talked to Nelda Harris about the scholarship?" Ali asked.

"Only in the most general terms," Leland replied. "I led her to believe Haley was being considered for some kind of academic award, but I didn't mention the scholarship per se."

"Then grandmother and granddaughter need to get on the same page," Ali told him. "At this rate, we'll be lucky if we award an Askins Scholarship this year."

"Don't be discouraged," Leland counseled. "There's always Marissa Dvorak."

"She'll probably throw me out, too," Ali said despairingly. "What's happening on your end?"

"Bryan Forester came by and dropped off another load of wallboard," Leland said. "Dropped it off and unloaded it, too. The crew had run out of materials and gone home."

"He unloaded it by himself?" Ali asked. "That stuff is heavy."

"By himself," Leland confirmed. "And I can understand where he's coming from. Mr. Forester strikes me as a man of action. Doing some hard physical labor probably did him a world of good. Maybe he'll be tired enough to sleep. I doubt he did last night."

Ali doubted that, too.

"Oh," Leland added, "he wanted me to let you know that he heard from the cabinet company, verifying that the funds had been received and that your order was in process. They told him they have enough material in stock to do your entire order, and they're getting started on it right away. They're hoping to ship in two weeks, but that may be pushing it."

"So much for Thanksgiving," Ali said.

"What do you mean?" Leland asked.

Now that she had opened her mouth, Ali regretted it. Considering the fact that Bryan's whole family was coming apart, it seemed incredibly selfish for her to have brought it up. Now that she had started, however, she charged on.

"I was hoping I'd be able to invite people over to the new place for Thanksgiving dinner," she said. "Even if everything wasn't quite finished, I figured we'd be able to make do."

"Does Mr. Forester know about your dinner plans?" Leland asked.

"Not really," Ali admitted. "I never mentioned it to him. I didn't want to add any more deadline pressure than there already was. Besides, it's not that big a deal. I can always invite everyone over to my old house in Skyview. It's the principle of the thing—and a matter of changing my mind. That's all."

"Finished or not, if you'd rather have your guests come here, we'll have them here," Leland Brooks declared. "In case you haven't noticed, I'm a very capable cook. If I could cook food for the officers' mess in Korea in the cold and the mud, I'm sure I can manage this. How many people are we talking about?"

"Not that many. My parents, Christopher and Athena, Dave and his three kids, one of my friends from California. Mom probably wouldn't mind doing the turkey. She usually does, but she and Dad cook every single day of their lives. I wanted to give them a break."

"Not to worry," Leland said. "We'll work it out. You

come up with the guest list, and I'll manage the rest. We'll make it a memorable occasion. And speaking of occasions, the florist called. They said they tried to deliver your flowers to the gym, but the place was locked up tight. I'm having them deliver them to me here instead. I'll drop them off a little later myself. That will give me an opportunity to give the lucky couple my own good wishes as well."

Ali tried to remember if she had mentioned the engagement news to Leland. With everything else that had been happening throughout the day, it didn't seem likely.

"So you know about that?" she asked.

"Oh, yes," Leland Brooks replied. "Mr. Reynolds came to me a couple of weeks ago with some concerns about where to take the ring to have it redesigned and resized. I sent him to see the man who used to handle all of Miss Arabella's work. I hope he was pleased with the results."

"I'm sure he was," Ali said. "And I'm sure Chris appreciated having the benefit of your advice."

Ali couldn't help feeling slightly left out. Yes, she knew that Chris and Athena had wanted to surprise her, but her folks had both known about Chris's engagement well in advance of last night's ring unveiling. Obviously, the same was true for Leland Brooks.

I always tried to raise him to be independent, Ali thought ruefully. *I may have succeeded too well.*

When Peter woke up, he needed to pee like a racehorse and was astonished to see that he had slept for the better part of ten hours. When he was younger, he had been able to manage on far less sleep than that. It was, he supposed, part of getting older rather than better. He fixed coffee and some toast. Then he uploaded the memory stick from his camera and, after deleting some of the less-well-thought-out shots, added the remainder to his DVD.

Scrolling through them, he congratulated himself on the fact that the crimes were all different. Morgan, still dressed, lay half in and out of the swing with her face battered and bloodied beyond recognition. He had arranged Candace so she lay on the ground with her various pieces put back together in all the wrong places—like a macabre human picture puzzle gone horribly wrong. He had heard that a novice FBI profiler had claimed this indicated a highly disorganized killer. Peter had laughed outright when he heard that; he was anything but disorganized. Melanie Tyler had been shot to death with her husband's .38, while Debra Longworth had been stabbed to death before being the victim of a vicious postmortem sexual assault. And that was another part of being smart. Never do it the same way twice.

The pictures were fine, but Peter was feeling vaguely displeased with himself as he stowed the DVD in his safe. He spent some time examining the diamond he had removed from Morgan's finger. It was large and showy, though Peter understood enough about diamonds to know that it wasn't as flawless as it should have been. But then Morgan hadn't been flawless, either. With a sigh, he returned the precious diamond-loaded key ring to its customary hiding place.

After one of his exploits, Peter usually spent the next day patting himself on the back. After all, who else was going to tell him "good job"? This time he couldn't quite manage it. Yes, by trying to track him down, Morgan Forester had posed a threat to him. As a result, she had gotten exactly what she deserved. But had it been worth it? Usually, he came back from a kill with a euphoric sense of accomplishment. Today he was left with a lingering sense of foreboding.

When Rita had fallen off the mountain, he had been right there with her. Naturally, he had been a person of interest in that case, but the cops had never charged him. With the others, he had managed to make sure his name had never surfaced in the resulting investigations, and all those cases had gone cold without ever being solved. This time he worried that he might have made a mistake. He couldn't get that asshole from Hertz out of his mind.

One of the things Peter counted on in life was that worker bees would function that way—as miserable drones who collected their paltry paychecks without caring that much about doing their job. Peter's big problem with the guy running the Hertz check-in line was that he hadn't just been doing his job. He had actually been paying attention. How carefully had he been watching, and if questions were raised, how much would he remember?

For the first time, Peter realized that he might have made a slight miscalculation. He had used Matthew Morrison's name for car-rental purposes because he could. Because Matthew Morrison was convenient. Because he was as good a fall guy as any.

People said that being a doctor let you play God. That was especially true in the ER. Patients came in. Peter sewed them up and patched them up. Some lived; others died; and after Peter was done with the ones who survived, he turned them over to other doctors who helped them go on with the messy business of living. But what he did and didn't do with his patients in the ER was nothing compared to the havoc he could wreak in people's lives when, as Internet puppet master, he could run them up and down a flagpole at will—as he had with Matthew Morrison.

Much as Peter despised cheating women, that was nothing compared to his overriding contempt for weak-willed, pussy-whipped men like Morrison. Peter had created Suzie Q—her name, her profile, her e-mails, her everything. He had penned every word of Susan's half of the e-mail correspondence, and it had amused him to see how smitten Matt had been, how he had fallen under the faux Susan's spell. In return, Matt had poured out the details of his miserable, boring life—his deadly dull job and his loveless marriage to the appalling Mrs. Morrison, the loathsome Jenny.

As far as Peter was concerned, Matthew was less than nothing. Peter had used the man's hijacked identity for the car rental without the smallest concern that anyone would notice. And even if someone did notice, Peter couldn't help wondering how Matthew would manage to talk his way out of that. The man was utterly petrified of losing his job. It didn't seem likely that he would have the balls to tell someone that he couldn't possibly have murdered Morgan in Sedona, since at the time she died, he was down in Red Rock waiting to get it on with some hot-to-trot sexy babe named Susan—who didn't, in actual fact, exist.

Peter had looked forward to watching Matt squirm, but because of the guy at Hertz, he'd have to deny himself that pleasure. He scanned through a couple of the thirteen plaintive, groveling, apologetic e-mails Matt had sent to Susan in the course of the last twenty-four hours. Too bad there was no time to reply. With a few clicks on his keyboard, Peter closed the e-mail account. Then he went to Singleatheart .com, found Suzie Q, and deleted her so thoroughly that no one but the most determined of hackers could have found the smallest cyber trace of her.

That done, Peter turned his attentions to Matt Morrison's hapless computer. Peter had kept his file-eating Trojan lurking undetected in the background of Morrison's HP for a very long time. Again, all it took was a few keystrokes to bring the worm to life. When Matt came home from work that afternoon and tried to log on as he usually did, the worm would destroy his hard drive. He wouldn't be able to boot up. The only thing left on his desktop would be the blue screen of death.

Taking out Matthew's computer meant that Peter would no longer have an unauthorized window into the man's pathetic life. Though Peter had enjoyed the game as long as it lasted, now it was over.

So long, Matt, Peter thought as he typed in the command. *It's been good to know ya.*

And then, having set the worm in motion on Matt's computer, Peter turned his attentions to those that belonged to the Foresters. Through spying on Morgan's files, Peter had managed to gain unlimited access to Bryan's computer. Peter hoped that by waiting this long he had given cops ample opportunity to find the bloodied hammer in Bryan's truck and that they would now be focusing their investigation in that direction. He was certain that the homicide detectives involved would take a very dim view of having their prime suspect's files suddenly disappear from the family's computers. Forester could shout to all the world that someone else had destroyed the data, but under the circumstances, who would believe such a story? The missing files would make him seem that much more guilty.

With a few masterful key strokes, Peter launched that destructive process as well, then he turned off his computer and headed for the gym. What he needed before work was a good workout and a nice lunch or dinner.

With Morgan gone, he was once again ready to go on the hunt for a new woman. He knew he was blessed with relatively good looks. When it came to attracting women, that always helped. So did good muscle tone and properly defined abs and biceps. This time, though, he hoped he'd find someone who didn't ask so many questions.

Peter remembered his mother telling him once that curiosity killed the cat. He had been a little boy at the time, only seven or eight. He had wondered about the statement, trying to figure out exactly how it worked. He no longer wondered about it because he knew it was true.

So did Morgan Forester.

Ali was back home by four-thirty. After showering, still wearing her robe, she turned on her computer and logged on to the Internet. She had been reassured by Leland Brooks. Now, regardless of whether or not her stalled home remodel would be finished in time for Thanksgiving, Ali was determined to start issuing holiday invitations. To that end, she was relieved to see

Velma Trimble's screen name, VelmaT, on her buddy list.

Velma T, an eighty-six-year-old widow from Laguna Niguel, had started out as a fan of Ali's blog. Over months of regular correspondence, a friendship had grown up between them. When Velma was diagnosed with cancer, both her son and her doctor had been more than willing to write her off. Ali had been the one who had stepped up and encouraged Velma to seek a second opinion. With that dire second opinion, Velma, too, had been willing to give up. She had gone off on what was to have been a final splurge, an all-first-class, round-the-world tour. Much to Ali's surprise, Velma had returned from the trip determined to undergo treatment.

"That's what Maddy Watkins told me," Velma had said, referring to the retired schoolteacher from Washington State who had been her traveling companion on the trip. "Anyone who's tough enough to go see Mount Kilimanjaro is tough enough to fight cancer."

Now that Velma was finishing her second round of chemo, Ali wanted her to come to Sedona for Thanksgiving dinner. She immediately sent an instant message to that effect and received an almost instantaneous reply:

Velma T: I couldn't possibly. I'm bald as a billiard. I look a fright. Ghastly.
Babe: I'm inviting you to come have dinner. It's not a beauty pageant.
Velma T: Who all would be there?
Babe: My parents. My son and future daughter-in-law. A few friends.

Velma T: But how would I get there? You know I don't have a car. Don't drive.

Babe: Just say you'll come. Let me worry about getting you here.

Velma T: It's so close. You probably wouldn't get a very good fare.

Babe: See reply above. I'll worry about that.

Velma T: I already told my daughter-in-law that I was booked. That was a lie. Now it could be true.

Babe: Is that a yes?

Velma T: Even if I'm bald?

Babe: Especially if you're bald.

Velma T: Fair enough, then. It's a yes.

Babe: Okay. Details to follow.

Ali's phone rang as she was signing off. Her parents' number showed on the caller ID screen, but since her father avoided using the telephone as much as possible, there wasn't much chance Bob Larson would be calling.

"Hello, Mom," Ali said. "What's up?"

"Nothing much," Edie said. "I was just worried about you, that's all."

"Why?"

"Because of all this business with Bryan Forester. What's going to happen to your house? What if he gets thrown into jail and your job doesn't get finished?"

This was probably not the right time to mention the cabinet order for which, if things fell apart, Ali would be paying 50 percent more for than the original agreed-upon price.

"It'll be finished," Ali declared with more confidence than she felt. "I've definitely decided to go ahead with Thanksgiving dinner. Please mark it on your calendar."

"And where do you plan to have it?" Edie wanted to know. "In the driveway? I heard they were just installing wallboard today. You've got a long way to go before the place is going to be ready for occupancy."

"Turkey dinner is at my house," Ali said. "If not that one, then this one, and that's final."

"What do you want us to bring?"

"Nothing," Ali said. "I'll handle it."

The long silence that followed meant that Edie wasn't entirely convinced. "All right, then," she said. "But have you ever cooked a turkey before?"

"Don't worry," Ali said. "I'll figure it out. I can read a recipe." *And so can Leland Brooks,* she thought.

"Is Dave coming to Chris and Athena's get-together at the gym tonight?" Edie asked, changing the subject. "He loves my pumpkin pies. I've made one especially for him."

When it came to Dave Holman, Edie and Bob Larson were absolutely transparent. Ali's parents really liked the guy and were lobbying to the best of their ability for Dave and Ali to land in some kind of permanent arrangement. Ali had attempted to explain the changed dynamics in the relationship, but it made no difference. Bob and Edie's minds were made up. They weren't listening.

"He may be coming," Ali said. "He was here at the house for a while last night. I know Chris invited him tonight, but I don't know if he'll be there."

"Well, then," Edie said determinedly. "I'll bring his pumpkin pie to the gym along with everything else, just in case."

"Everything else?" Ali echoed. "I thought Athena said Hawaiian Punch and storebought cookies."

"Christopher is my grandson!" Edie said indignantly. "You don't suppose I'd let him celebrate his engagement with a batch of storebought cookies, do you?"

"No," Ali agreed with a laugh. "I don't suppose you would."

Just then her e-mail announced the arrival of a new message. And there, moments before the five P.M. deadline she had given them, was a video-bearing e-mail from Raymond Armado. Once Ali got off the phone with her mother, it took her a while to download the attached file. When she finally opened it, she fast-forwarded through the parts that consisted of Billy Barnes and the other guys dutifully hanging wallboard. Boring. Steady. Absolutely unexciting. Toward the end of the film segment, however, Dave Holman, notebook in hand, appeared on the scene. That sequence began with Billy Barnes glancing at his watch and with Ali exiting the frame.

"What can you tell me about Bryan Forester's situation yesterday?" Dave asked on the video without preamble.

"He was here from around ten A.M. on," Billy answered. "We had a problem with a building inspector. Once he got here, he was here for the rest of the day."

"He didn't come and go?"

"Nope," Billy said impatiently. "I already told you. He was here all day long."

"Did he seem upset to you?"

Billy made a face and shrugged, but Ali knew the answer to that was yes. When she'd had dealings with Bryan herself on Monday, he had appeared to be distracted and off his game. She had assumed it had something to do with the building inspector or with the slow progress of construction or even the missing cabinets. Now it seemed possible that something else had been bothering him.

"Were you aware of any difficulties he and his wife might have been having?" Dave asked.

"What husband and wife doesn't have difficulties?" Billy returned. "Of course they were having difficulties."

"Do you know what kind?"

"I'd rather not say," Billy said.

"Look," Dave said. "This is a homicide investigation. I need you to answer."

"Bryan Forester is a nice guy—a regular straight arrow. You'd think a woman would appreciate having a guy like that around, someone who goes to work every day in all kinds of weather, brings home the bacon, and turns the money over to her so she can spend it however she likes, and spend it Morgan did. I never heard the woman say a kind thing about him. All she ever did was gripe, gripe, gripe. Nothing was ever good enough for her, but still, finding out that she'd signed up for an Internet dating site. That just about corked it."

Dave consulted his notebook. "This Internet dating site. I believe Bryan mentioned something about that. That would be Singleatheart.com, right?"

"I guess," Billy conceded with a shrug. "Something like that."

"And Bryan told you about it?"

"Yes."

"When?"

"Yesterday morning," Billy said. "We were out at the picnic table having a smoke. He was fit to be tied. It was his first cigarette in three years, at least."

"You're sure it was yesterday that he mentioned it to you? He talked about it on Tuesday, not Monday."

"I'm sure," Billy said.

"Did Bryan mention to you how he found out about it or when?"

"The kind of woman she was, I wouldn't be surprised if she came right out and told him about it herself. Probably wanted to rub his nose in it. Morgan was like that. He did say that they'd fought like cats and dogs all weekend."

"About?"

"He didn't say."

"So they fought like crazy all weekend, and Morgan ended up dead on Monday morning," Dave muttered, more to himself than to anyone else. "How very convenient."

"He didn't kill her," Billy insisted. "Even if she deserved it, he wouldn't."

"Did he say that—that she deserved to die?"

"Bryan never said any such thing," Billy replied. "I'm the one who said it. As far as I'm concerned, Morgan Forester was bad news. Her family used to be dirt poor, and all she ever wanted was a meal ticket. I don't think she even liked the guy."

"You seem to know quite a bit about it," Dave said.

"You think so?" Billy answered. "Bryan and me go way back. We've been friends since high school. Once Morgan turned up on the scene, you could see she thought she was really hot stuff—like she was something special—but she wasn't. You don't have to take my word for it. There are plenty of guys around who can tell you Morgan Forester was a good-for-nothing tramp and that Bryan was way too good for her."

"Sounds like you didn't care for her much."

Billy simply shrugged.

"So where were you yesterday morning?" Dave asked.

Billy bristled. "So now you're accusing me of having something to do with what happened? For your information, I was right here on the job. Had to go out for supplies for a while early in the morning. We were running short on wallboard screws. Other than that, I got here at seven-forty-five and left at four. You can ask anybody. Try Leland Brooks, for starters. He's usually right outside."

Someone spoke to Billy from off screen. He nodded, then turned back to Dave. "Look, they need me. I've got to get back to work. You've got a job to do, and so do I. I've wasted enough time answering your damned questions. Now get the hell out of here."

Dave studied his notebook for a moment before pocketing it and walking away. The camera continued to roll, following him through the house and out the front door. Moments later, he seemed to notice the trailing film crew for the first time and ordered them to stop filming. Seconds later, Ali's voice said the same thing. Only then did the film fade to black.

When the clip ended, Ali sat staring at the screen. Morgan's neighbors had thought of her as the perfect stay-at-home wife and mother. But her husband suspected her of embezzling funds, and now it turned out that she'd been prowling the Internet looking for greener pastures while her husband was hard at work.

What kind of perfect wife does that? Ali wondered. *And what kind of place is Singleatheart?* The name implied that it was a hookup tool for people who were married but who wanted to carry on as though they weren't. The way Bryan had told the story to Ali, he hadn't looked at Morgan's computer files and learned about Singleatheart until after his wife was already dead. But what if that wasn't true?

What if he learned about it earlier? Ali wondered. *What if that was what Bryan and Morgan fought about over the weekend?* If that were the case, it made sense that Dave Holman would have settled on Bryan as the prime suspect in his wife's murder. And maybe the item Ali had witnessed Dave removing from Bryan's pickup would further implicate Morgan's widower. From the way Dave had rushed away after finding it, Ali suspected that to be the case.

Still, there was something about the interview she'd just witnessed that gave Ali pause, something that bothered her. Why was it Billy Barnes happened to know so much about everything that was going on with Bryan and Morgan? Were Bryan and Billy really close enough friends that Bryan would have confided in Billy about Morgan's infidelity and her involvement in Singleatheart? That struck Ali as odd. Most betrayed husbands wouldn't have admitted such things to anyone, not even their best pals.

And what about Morgan? Ali recognized that she must have been dreadfully unhappy to have risked everything—including life itself—to go shopping for romance on a dating website.

Without really thinking about it, Ali typed "Singleatheart" into her computer's search engine. Just then Chris came trotting upstairs from his basement studio. "It's my night to cook. I thought I'd fix some grilled-cheese sandwiches before we go."

Guiltily, Ali closed her computer before Singleatheart's home page appeared on the screen. On the night they were due to celebrate her son's engagement, she didn't want to spoil his happiness with tales of other marriages that had foundered and come to grief.

"Don't bother," she replied. "I'm sure there's going to be plenty of food at the gym."

"What kind of food?" Chris asked. "I thought we were just doing cookies and punch."

Ali laughed. "Guess again," she told him. "You invited your grandmother, remember? Just plain cookies and punch won't cut it. They aren't in Edie Larson's vocabulary."

In terms of the abundance of food, Ali's prediction proved absolutely on the money. Out of deference for the hardwood floor, the engagement party wasn't in the gym proper but in the tiled lobby right outside. A cloth-covered table inside the door sagged under a load of goodies. The centerpiece was a decorated white sheet cake. Bright red frosting roses were stationed on each corner, while in the middle, resting on a red frosting heart, were a pair of entwined frosting wedding rings.

That eye-stopping cake was only part of Edie Larson's caloric overkill. There was a tall German chocolate layer cake and a seven-layer straight chocolate cake along with six homemade pies—two each of lemon meringue, pumpkin, and pecan—without a single "storebought" cookie in sight. Those showed up a few minutes later, when Athena arrived followed by a young woman Ali didn't know. The newcomers came into the room, carrying several brimming grocery bags.

Ali caught the look of momentary shock on Athena's face as she took stock of the overloaded table. After some quietly exchanged words, Athena and her friend removed plates, napkins, and plastic forks from the bags and then tactfully stowed everything else under the table.

Once the storebought foodstuffs had disappeared, Athena went over to Edie Larson and gave her a hug. "You shouldn't have," she said.

"I couldn't help it." Edie was beaming. "I wanted it to be a real party."

Athena turned questioningly to Ali. "Don't look at me," Ali said. "It's not my fault. I'm responsible for the flowers, and that's it."

As the festivities got under way, they soon turned into a real party, starting with a series of Hawaiian Punch toasts. After that, by mutual consent, community-league basketball was canceled for the evening while the erstwhile players swilled punch or coffee and filled up on Edie's scrumptious collection of sweets. Someone found folding chairs in a closet and set those around the room so people had somewhere to sit while they juggled plates and paper cups. Toward the end of the evening, Ali wandered into a conversation where the young woman who had helped Athena bring in the groceries was speaking with her and two other high school teachers, Lois Mead and Gail Nelson.

"The whole thing just breaks my heart," the young woman was saying. "Lindsey will be fine, but what about Lacy? She's already so . . . breakable. I can't imagine that she won't shatter into a million pieces."

"Lindsey and Lacy?" Ali asked. "You mean the Forester twins?"

The young woman nodded. She seemed close to tears.

"I'm sorry," Athena said. "Have you two met?"

Ali shook her head. "I don't believe so."

"This is my roommate, Mindy. Mindy Farber," Athena said. "She teaches second grade over in the village. The mother of two of her students was found murdered yesterday. And this is Ali Reynolds, my future mother-in-law."

Mindy mumbled a polite acknowledgment and then went on talking. Ali already knew more about the situation than she cared to admit, but she stayed on, listening to what Mindy Farber had to say.

"Lacy has issues," Mindy said. "She's afraid someone might touch her books, so she carries all of them back and forth with her every day. She never leaves anything in her desk. She doesn't talk, either, not at all. Maybe she talks at home, but not in school. Last year the principal separated the two girls for first grade. He thought that would force the issue, but it turned into a complete disaster. This year they put them both in my room. Most of the time it's not a problem. Lacy may not say anything, but Lindsey more than makes up for it. That girl never shuts up. But they're both smart. And as long as Lacy can write out the answers instead of responding orally, she's a straight-A student."

"I heard they're the ones who found their mother's body," Lois Mead commented.

Mindy nodded. "It's true. They found the body on the front porch after the bus driver dropped them off at the end of their drive. Lindsey was smart enough to call nine-one-one and report it."

"Do the cops know who's responsible?" Gail Nelson asked.

"If they do, I haven't heard," Mindy said.

"I'll bet it's the father," Gail said. "Isn't that usually how it turns out? The mother gets murdered, and the father or boyfriend ends up going to jail."

"If the father did do it, what will happen to the two little girls?"

Mindy shook her head. "I have no idea," she said. "They're so young to lose both their parents. Maybe there are other relatives who can step in and help out, but the whole thing makes me sick to my stomach."

Me, too, Ali thought. Excusing herself, she wandered back over to the table where her mother was sorting leftover cakes and pies into a collection of Styrofoam take-home containers she had brought along from the restaurant.

"Aren't they a lovely couple!" Edie exclaimed, beaming at Chris and Athena, who were across the room bidding departing partygoers good night.

Ali nodded.

"And I hope they'll be very happy."

"So do I."

"Have they said anything to you about setting a date?"

"Not to me," Ali replied.

"June is very nice," Edie observed. "I think we could have a very nice June wedding. If we wait until July or August, it'll be way too hot."

Ali knew that her mother had a weak spot for weddings, and it was sounding as though, after turning Chris and Athena's "intimate" engagement party into a major function, she was determined to do the same thing for their wedding.

"Shouldn't we leave that up to them?" Ali asked circumspectly.

"Absolutely not," Edie declared. "We have way more experience with these things than they do. By the way," she added, "here's Dave's pie. Make sure he gets the whole thing. I wouldn't put it past that son of yours to try stealing a piece."

{ CHAPTER 6 }

A few minutes later, pie in hand, Ali left the gym. Shaken by her mother's over-the-top interference, Ali was glad to have her assigned pie-delivery errand as an excuse to bug out early. When she pulled up in front of Dave's rented house, she saw that his battered Nissan Sentra was parked on one side of the driveway, but the county-owned sedan that was usually parked next to it was nowhere in sight. That meant Dave wasn't home, but since lights were on inside, Ali figured his daughters were.

She parked in the street and carried the pie to the front porch, where she rang the bell. Seconds later, Crystal, Dave's older daughter, pulled the door open but only as far as the length of the security chain.

"Ali," Crystal said, peering through the crack. "Dad's not here. He got called out on a case."

Ali didn't bother asking what case. She already knew. Well into the first forty-eight hours after Morgan Forester's homicide, there could be little doubt that the officers charged with solving her murder—Detective Dave Holman especially—would be working pretty much round-the-clock.

"I'm not here to see your father," Ali announced. "I come bearing gifts. My mother baked a pie for your dad and you. I'm here to drop it off."

"A pie?" Crystal asked, undoing the chain and opening the door the rest of the way. "From the Sugarloaf?"

"Absolutely."

"Can we eat it?" Crystal asked eagerly. "Or do we have to wait until Dad gets home?"

"I don't see your father's name on it," Ali said. "Just don't eat it all." She waved at Cassie, Dave's younger daughter, who had appeared beyond her older sister's shoulder and was hovering in the background.

"Do you want to come in for a while?" Crystal asked.

"No, thanks," Ali said. "I appreciate the invitation, but I need to get home, and you and Cassie should probably go to bed."

"I know, I know," Crystal grumbled. "It's a school night."

A few months earlier, Crystal had been in full-bloom adolescent rebellion. The idea that she was concerned about getting to bed at a decent hour on a school night struck Ali as remarkable progress.

"Right," Ali said. "A school night."

She was happy to leave it at that.

Back home on Andante Drive, Ali was sitting with Sam purring in her lap, and still thinking about her mother's performance, when Christopher arrived home. He looked unhappy.

"Nice party," Ali said.

Chris gave his mother a disparaging look. "Thanks," he said. "But Athena's all bent out of shape about it."

"She is? How come?"

"Because Grandma managed to turn it into a circus," Chris said.

She did, Ali thought. *And I was right to be worried.*

"It was supposed to be this casual, fun time with our friends," Chris continued. "By the time Grandma finished her baking spree, it turned into something else entirely. Athena didn't make a fuss about it at the time, but she's worried that Grandma will try to hijack our wedding into some kind of huge event. That's not us, Mom. It's not what Athena and I want."

"What do you want?" Ali asked.

"Something small," he said. "Something private and nice."

Ali had suspected as much. "Here's the deal," she explained. "Back when Mom and Dad got married, times were tough, and they couldn't afford much of a wedding. There were the two of them, Aunt Evie and her then boyfriend, and a justice of the peace. That was it—the five of them. I'm afraid Mom has been trying to make up for that deficit ever since. It's a total blind spot for her. I doubt she even realizes she's doing it. When your father and I got married, she tried to pull the same stunt with us. If I'd let her have her way, our wedding would have been an out-of-control extravaganza."

"But you stopped it?"

Ali nodded.

"How?"

"By putting my foot down and taking control," Ali told him. "You and Athena will have to do the same thing. Tell your grandmother no and mean it."

"But how can you stop something when you don't even see it coming?" Chris asked. "By the time we got to the gym tonight, the food was already there. Mountains of it."

Ali understood far better than Chris that food was the coin of her mother's realm. That was how Edie dealt with the vicissitudes of life, with both the good and the bad, the triumphs and the tragedies. Arriving babies or returning soldiers were greeted with cakes and cookies and immense bread puddings. Hospital stays called for soups or casseroles. Rounds of chemo meant plenty of mashed potatoes and bowls filled with red Jell-O. Deaths and funerals brought back the soup/casserole theme.

"Try turning it into a chess game," Ali advised her son. "You win at chess by anticipating what your opponent is going to do several moves in advance. You'll need to learn to anticipate what your grandmother is going to do as well, then you'll have to come up with suitable countermeasures."

"Easier said than done," Chris grumbled.

"Don't be so grumpy about it," Ali said. "After all, that's what you get for being the apple of your grandmother's eye. You and Athena will have to sit Mom and Dad down and have a serious talk with them, but in order to make it stick, you'll have to present a united front, diplomatic but absolutely firm. By the way, Athena was exceedingly diplomatic tonight," she added. "She came in with her bags of groceries, but as soon as she saw what Mom had brought, she deep-sixed the grocery bags. I never heard her say a cross word."

"There were plenty of cross words for me," Chris complained. "As far as Athena was concerned, the whole engagement-party extravaganza was my fault."

"Dealing with difficult relatives is one of the hazards of getting married," Ali said. "And your grandmother isn't the only one who'll pull that kind of stunt. It turns out I'm putting together a little extravaganza of my own."

Chris rolled his eyes. "What kind?"

"Thanksgiving."

"Don't tell me you're cooking."

"Be nice," she told him. "But don't worry. Leland will be supervising the cooking, if not doing most of it himself. So this is my official notice that you and Athena are invited, as long as you don't have any other plans."

"Okay," Chris said. "Sounds good. We'll be there."

"Wrong," Ali said with a laugh. "We're talking Rules of Engagement 101 here, Chris. Don't fall into the old trap of making unilateral holiday decisions. If you want to be happily engaged and end up happily married, you won't accept any invitations without first consulting your significant other."

"You mean I should ask Athena and then let you know?"

"Exactly," Ali said. "If you know what's good for you."

"If she's even speaking to me," Chris added gloomily. He went off to bed then, leaving Ali absently petting Sam and reflecting on the conversation.

Where do I get off dishing out marital advice to anyone? she wondered. *When it comes to being married, my own track record isn't much to write home about.* For instance, when she had told Chris he needed to put his foot down about his grandmother hijacking the wedding plans, it had been a case of "do as I say" rather than "do as I do." Or did. Back when she and Chris's father had been in a similar situation, Ali hadn't exactly confronted the problem head-on. Instead, once the wedding arrangements had threatened to career out of control, she and Dean had taken the path of least resistance and eloped to Vegas. No fuss; no muss. Edie had been furious, but despite the instant wedding, Ali and Dean had been a match made in heaven—right up until his death from cancer a few short years later.

Ali's much later wedding to Paul Grayson had been far more to Edie's liking. It had been a splashy Beverly Hills social event even in a milieu where outsize weddings were the order of the day. Edie and Bob Larson, a little out of their depth, had sat proudly in front-row seats when Paul, dressed in an impeccable tux, had stood in front of several hundred other invited guests and had solemnly vowed to love, honor, and obey.

In spite of all the lavish arrangements, Ali had learned, to her regret, that it had all been for show. Paul hadn't meant a word of what he'd said, and he'd made a mockery of his wedding vows. In the dark of the night, sitting there alone with her aging, scruffy cat, Ali couldn't help feeling a small chill tingle her spine as she realized Morgan Forester had done the same thing. She, too, had made marital promises that she had been unwilling or unable to keep. And now the young wife and mother was every bit as dead as Paul Grayson.

Ali went to bed a short time after that, but it took hours before she fell asleep. Awakening the next morning to the sound of Chris's car pulling out of the driveway, she wandered out to the kitchen and poured herself a cup of coffee.

While she had been lying awake, she'd kept going back to Morgan Forester's involvement with the Internet dating site Singleatheart.com. What had compelled a supposedly happily married woman to sign up for something like that? And what kind of people had she hoped to meet there?

Other cheaters, no doubt, Ali thought. *Other people whose word couldn't be trusted.* So why had Morgan thought one of them would have more to offer than her hardworking husband, Bryan?

Without necessarily making a conscious decision, Ali retrieved her computer and dragged it over to the dining room table. Within a matter of minutes, she had surfed over to the Singleatheart website. At least she had arrived at the welcome page. In order to see more than that, she would have to register. To simply surf through the site or post a profile would cost a hundred dollars. To make a connection with one of the profiled parties was an additional four hundred.

Ali hesitated. She had no interest in posting a profile, but she wanted to know more about the people who had. She waffled briefly, but before long, her natural curiosity won out. In order to register, she had to provide both her name and a screen name. Fortunately, Babe, her Cutloose handle, worked very nicely. Her names, along with a working credit-card number and billing address, allowed her to log on.

Her browser was set to limit pop-up ads, but once Ali was inside Singleatheart, her computer screen was immediately besieged by a cascade of competing images. Unremittingly explicit sexual scenes sprang to life on either side of her screen. As a news broadcaster, Ali had done two separate news stories related to commercial porn sites. She had expected a dating site to be somewhat less graphic, but it wasn't. There were ads for sex toys that came in more varieties, shapes, colors, and sizes than she ever could have imagined. The lingerie for sale was outrageous, and the ads promoting it were even more so. This was a long, long way from eHarmony!

The middle of the screen contained an old-fashioned Mercator projection of the world with an arrow and a guide that advised visitors to click on a particular location in order to narrow their search. By the time she landed on the map for Arizona, she was told that the section contained 2,364 profiles. *That many?* she thought. *Just in Arizona?*

Ali whistled aloud. At a hundred or five hundred bucks a pop? You didn't have to be a math whiz to realize that Singleatheart meant big business. Even if you disregarded the lower-priced subscribers who were website visitors only, the people who ran Singleatheart were raking in piles of Internet dough.

Ali poured herself another cup of coffee and prepared for what she thought would be a long search, but she found what she was looking for almost immediately among the list of Arizona-based female profiles: the screen name Morgan le Fay.

From Camelot, Ali thought, drawing on her knowledge of Aunt Evie's extensive collection of musical comedies. *Like the fairy princess who caused all the trouble by packing off Merlin.*

It took some time for her air card to download the profile, which consisted of several paragraphs of printed bio-style material along with a video clip. When that one finally opened, Ali saw a young woman sitting in a wooden swing, probably on the very porch where Morgan Forester had been murdered. She was a blond beauty with fine features, a winning smile, and an air of absolute innocence. Had Ali not heard what Billy Barnes had told Dave Holman about Morgan, Ali might have believed that look. Instead, she hit the play button, and the taped image of Morgan Forester began to speak:

"My grandmother loved records. Not CDs, but the old-fashioned black vinyl ones that played on phonographs. One of her favorites—one she listened to when she was washing dishes or doing the ironing—was done by a woman named Peggy Lee. I came into the house one time and found my grandmother sitting on the sofa crying with a record playing in the background. I asked her what was wrong, and she told me, 'Oh, honey, it's just so sad.' 'What's so sad?' I asked her. 'This lady and her song,' she said. 'She's singing about her life.'

"I loved my grandmother to pieces. It worried me that something could make her that upset, so I made it my business to find out which song it was that bothered her so much. 'Is That All There Is?' Eventually, my grandmother divorced my grandfather and came to live with us. She brought her records with her. I still have that one by Peggy Lee, and now I understand it. Too well. I'm living that same kind of life.

"If you asked any of my friends, they'd be surprised. They all think I have the perfect life, and maybe I do. I have a nice house, a nice car, good kids, and a nice husband, but it seems like nice is not enough. I keep asking myself the same question: Is this all there is?

"My husband and I started dating while we were still in high school. From the time I first knew him, he dreamed of having his own business. At first he worked construction for other

people. When he was able to go off on his own, we both thought his dream—our dream—had come true. Now that he's successful, it's more like a nightmare. That's all he thinks about all day long—his business. He lives, eats, and breathes his job. Yes, I'll admit he brings in good money, but what good is money if we never do anything together or if we never have any fun?

"As far as I can see, I'm nothing more to him than a live-in cook and babysitter. Don't get me wrong. I love my two girls. And I guess I even still love him a little. But I'm looking for something more. I want someone who will look at me and value me for the person I am. Someone who will see that I'm more than an attractive doormat in a very nice house. I don't want to go to my grave still asking Peggy Lee's old question, because I believe with all my heart that there is something more out there for me. Something better."

For a long time after the clip ended, Ali sat staring at Morgan Forester's features, slightly distorted but frozen in place on the computer screen. The whole thing left Ali feeling incredibly sad. The vital and attractive young woman who had filmed that clip was no more. The life she'd had—with her boring but hardworking husband and challenging seven-year-old daughters—really was all there was or ever would be, just like in the song. It sounded like Morgan had fallen out of love with her husband and was looking for more than a quick roll in the hay. *But then she could be lying about that, too,* Ali thought.

Whatever Morgan had wanted, or however much

she had cheated on her husband, it seemed clear that she had cheated herself even more. Her craving for temporary excitement had robbed her of a lifetime of joy—of watching her children grow up and become adults themselves; of watching them marry and have children of their own. The real tragedy of Morgan Forester's life was that she had missed it.

How could a few tawdry sexual encounters have been worth all that? Ali wondered, although Morgan couldn't have known that she was putting her entire existence at risk.

When Ali had watched the tape of Dave's interview with Billy Barnes, it had struck her as odd that Billy would have such intimate knowledge about Bryan and Morgan Forester's private lives. Some men might go around pounding each other on the back and bragging about their various sexual exploits, but Ali couldn't see Bryan admitting to anyone—especially one of his employees— that his marriage was going south and that his wife was screwing around on him. If Bryan hadn't admitted any of that to Billy, how did Billy know so much? And why was the man so outspoken in his antipathy toward his boss's dead wife? And why had he taken it all so personally?

Ali had been about to exit the website. Now, though, working on a hunch, she clicked back to the navigation page and pulled up the list of Arizona would-be bachelors, the men who were stalking the Internet in hopes of hooking up with like-minded women, sexual partners who were willing to play around with no strings attached.

This time the search took slightly longer, but as soon as she saw the screen name Billy Boy, she knew she was on the right track. After a few more clicks, there he was—Billy Barnes himself. His run-of-the-mill profile contained no film clip, just a still photo and a laudatory bio that made Billy sound like a well-to-do contractor in his own right rather than a guy working for someone else. Ali also remembered noticing that Billy wore a wedding ring, but that was hardly a surprise. After all, this site was a place for people who were single at heart as opposed to being single really.

Was it possible that Morgan and Billy had hooked up and had a fling? If so, it would have been a stunning double betrayal—an unfaithful wife deliberately carrying on an affair with a man who was both her husband's friend and his employee. If it had happened, and if Bryan had somehow caught wind of it, would that—along with the missing cabinet deposits—have been enough to push him over the edge and set off a murderous rage?

But did it really happen? Ali wondered. *Am I leaping to conclusions here?*

The fact that both Billy and Morgan were members of Singleatheart didn't necessarily mean that they'd been involved. But still, it was possible, and it meant that if nothing else, Billy knew about Morgan's posting.

I know, Ali told herself. *When I get to the other house, maybe I'll ask Billy Barnes about this outright and see what he has to say.*

Just then, though, her phone rang.

"Good morning, madam," Leland Brooks said. "I'm sorry to disturb you, but it seems you have an unexpected guest. Mr. Jackson is here."

"Mr. Jackson," Ali repeated. "As in Jacky Jackson, my agent?"

"I believe that is correct," Leland said. "He evidently came into Phoenix on an early flight from L.A. and drove straight here to see you."

"Without calling in advance?"

"So it would seem," Leland replied with a sigh.

Ali knew that Leland Brooks held an exceptionally low opinion of people who failed to observe the niceties of polite behavior. In his book, showing up uninvited and unannounced at someone's home was a serious faux pas. Social anathema was more like it.

"I'm not sure how he knew to come here," Leland went on, sounding aggrieved.

That was easy. Jacky was the one who had set up the Home & Garden TV gig. That meant he knew all about the house on Manzanita Hills Road. He probably also knew that Ali spent time there on a daily basis.

"What does he want?" Ali asked.

"Other than hinting it's a matter of some urgency, he didn't say," Leland answered. "I gave him a cup of coffee and stowed him at the table outside. I used the excuse of making him an omelette to come inside and call you. If you'd like me to tell him you're unavailable and send him on his way . . ."

"No," Ali said with a laugh. "I'll handle it. I'll be there in a few."

"Very well," Leland said. "I'll do my best to keep him occupied in the meantime."

Putting down the phone, Ali closed her computer and threw on some clothes. After pulling her hair into a ponytail and without bothering to apply any makeup, she headed for Manzanita Hills Road. All the time she was getting dressed, she was trying to figure out what Jacky was doing here. After all, Sedona was a long way out of his natural habitat in southern California.

Although Jacky had been Ali's agent for years, she was more than ready to be done with him. In the aftermath of her divorce from the network bigwig Paul Grayson, Jacky had distanced himself from her completely. Yes, he had come up with the home-remodel filming project, but Ali suspected he had done that more because it would be good for him than because it would be good for her. Ali really was interested in the process of bringing back and preserving architectural treasures that were in danger of being bulldozed. Jacky, on the other hand, was interested in Jacky.

Ali had considered leaving him on more than one occasion, especially now, when she had no intention of going back to work. But with only a few months left on her contract, she had decided to run out the clock rather than making a break. Letting their agreement simply disappear would be a lot less messy than going to the trouble of ending it prematurely. Had he somehow gotten wind of her possible defection? Had someone mentioned to him that Ali Reynolds was about to flee the Jacky Jackson coop?

That brought her back to her original question: What was Jacky doing here? Maybe he had ridden into town at the behest of Raymond and Robert, the camera guys. Was it possible the enterprising videographers had found someone willing to pay top dollar for the off-limits homicide-investigation portion of their film? Ali suspected it wouldn't be terribly difficult to find someone willing and able to outbid Home & Garden TV's lowball offer. If Raymond and Robert were hoping to transform their remodeling gig into something else, maybe Jacky had come to see her in hopes of convincing Ali to change her mind and let them run with it.

As usual, the lower part of Ali's driveway was lined with pickup trucks, which meant that even without Bryan Forester, his work crew was on the scene. After threading her way up the hill to the top of the drive, Ali found a rented Lincoln Town Car in her accustomed parking spot. *Count on Jacky to grab the prime spot,* she thought as she made her way over to the covered picnic table where Jacky was seated. Wearing a down vest and huddled next to the roaring propane heater, her uninvited guest was polishing off the last few bites of what appeared to be one of Leland Brooks's fluffy three-egg omelettes.

"My, my, my," Jacky cooed as Ali approached. "Wherever did you find such a marvelous cook way out here in the sticks? I don't think I've ever had a better omelette." He handed his empty plate over to Leland, who took it with a stiffly polite nod and walked away. Jacky's referring to Leland Brooks as a cook was a joke. He might as well have called a Kentucky Derby–winning thoroughbred a nag. Yes, Leland cooked on occasion, but he was far more than that. At a time when he might reasonably have put himself out to pasture, he had stayed on to help Ali with the complicated remodel and had morphed into a friend. She sometimes suspected that in helping her, Leland was also helping himself as he, too, tried to move beyond his own set of betrayals.

"If you ever want to unload him," Jacky continued tactlessly, "I'm sure I could come up with a list of ten people who would be happy to snap him up."

"Mr. Brooks is fully employed," Ali said. "He's not available."

"Too bad," Jacky said. Belatedly, he rose to greet her.

After a peremptory kiss on each cheek, he held her at arm's length and examined her. There was no disguising the dismay that registered on his face.

"My goodness, Ali!" he exclaimed. "Just because you're stuck here in lovely, charming, perfect Sedona is no excuse for letting yourself go. What are you thinking? No makeup, bag-lady clothes, hair in a ponytail? Bad for your image, darling, very bad. What would people think?"

"They might think I was having to deal with company that hadn't bothered calling in advance," she said. "And if you'll pardon my saying so, you don't look all that great yourself."

"Oh, that," Jacky said with a dismissive wave. "That comes from flying at such an ungodly hour. Had to be at the Burbank airport at oh-dark-thirty this morning. I'm missing several critical hours of beauty sleep. And can you believe it? Even at that ungodly hour, the plane was totally packed. Not a single empty seat to be had. Squalling babies everywhere."

"Yes," Ali agreed. "I see what you mean. It's always a shock to see how the other half lives." It annoyed her to realize that Jacky somehow brought out the worst in her. It was as though his perpetual bitchiness were a communicable disease.

Leland returned from his trailer, poured Ali a cup of coffee, and handed it over. "Will you require anything else, madam?" he asked formally, nodding imperceptibly in Jacky's direction.

Ali smiled at him. "We're fine for now, Mr. Brooks," she said.

As Leland headed back to his fifth wheel, Jacky watched him go with mouthwatering intensity. "Such a lovely man," he said admiringly.

"Knock it off, Jacky," Ali ordered. "I already told you Mr. Brooks is not available. He's fully employed. He's also taken."

"Spoilsport," Jacky said.

Ali was tired of small talk. "I'm pretty busy at the moment," she told him. "What is it you want?"

"Don't be so cross," Jacky purred. "I've got this wonderful, wonderful opportunity for you, something you'd be utterly perfect for. And you know me. I never discuss important negotiations over the phone. I'm a face-to-face, belly-to-belly kind of guy. So that's why I'm here: to offer you a golden opportunity to go back to work doing what you love—to get you back where you belong, in front of a television camera. Fortunately, the project is being put together by some very talented people who happen to have enough money at their disposal to do things right."

"Sounds intriguing," Ali said. "What project do you have in mind?"

"All right, so maybe it's a bit of a knockoff—a second-generation *America's Most Wanted,* if you will, but do you know how long that program has been on the air? Besides, as they say, imitation is the highest form of flattery. You've built up a bit of a crimefighting reputation since you've been off the air. It seems to me this would be a great fit."

"What are you asking me to do?" Ali asked. "Host it?"

"Oh, no," Jacky said too quickly. "Nothing like that. They've already lined up a man-type to do the actual hosting job. They want you to be one of their personalities—one of the team of on-air folks and producers who go around the country and pull together various independent segments. You'd have a lot of autonomy, Ali. You'd be able to call your own shots."

Unfortunately, Ali was able to read between the lines. She understood what Jacky wasn't saying as much as what he was. No doubt one of his other clients—a male big-name client—was being tapped for the host job. What Jacky was doing was pulling in people to fill out the rest of the package.

"I'm calling my own shots now," she said. "I'm not interested."

"But you're not working," Jacky insisted. "Come on. Let me at least show you the proposal and bring you into the picture as far as the dollars are concerned. This is a good deal, Ali, darling. A very good deal, and despite the fact that you've been out of the loop and really need to make a comeback, they're still willing to pay some real money."

"Who says I need to make a comeback?" Ali returned abruptly. "And I don't care that much about the money. I don't *need* more money."

In Jacky's world, everyone wanted more money. The idea that Ali didn't left him stunned. The lingering silence between them was broken by the ringing of Ali's cell phone. A glance at caller ID told Ali her mother was on the phone. Oddly enough for that time of day, Edie Larson was calling from home rather than the restaurant.

Ali felt a moment of panic. *Is Mom sick?* she wondered. *Or has something happened to Dad?*

"This is a good deal, Ali," Jacky went on as though he hadn't heard her. "Surely you wouldn't just turn your back on it."

But Ali's attention was focused on her phone. "You'll

have to excuse me," she said. "I've got to take this." She got up and walked far enough away to be out of earshot before she answered. "Hello, Mom," she said. "What's up? Are you all right?"

"I just had a call from Chris," Edie said. "And it's all so upsetting. He lit into me something terrible. He's never spoken to me like that before, Ali. Not ever. He made it sound like the baking I did yesterday was some kind of criminal offense. I was trying to help out. I wanted to make their engagement party a special occasion. How could it go so wrong?"

There was an odd sound. It took Ali a moment to realize that her mother was actually snuffling into the phone. From what she was saying, Chris had taken Ali at her word and tackled his grandmother on the subject of wedding planning. Ali remembered mentioning to Chris that he should try to be diplomatic. Evidently, that part of the message hadn't gotten through.

"Mom," Ali said, "are you crying?"

"Well, maybe a little," Edie admitted. "I'm so upset, though, that I can't help it. Your father sent me home. He said he didn't want me making a fool of myself in front of all the customers. He's right about that, of course. Fortunately, the restaurant isn't busy, and Jan is holding down the fort."

Jan Howard was the Sugarloaf Café's long-term waitress. She and Edie handled the front of the house while Bob Larson handled most of the kitchen chores.

"Hold on," Ali said to her mother. "I'll be there as soon as I can."

For someone wanting to dodge Jacky Jackson, Edie's call was heaven-sent. "Sorry," Ali said, turning back to Jacky. "Family emergency. I've got to go."

"But—" Jacky began.

Ali didn't give him a chance to finish. "It's my mother. I'll catch you later."

Before he could build up to full-whine mode, Ali walked briskly away. She got into the Cayenne and drove down the hill. She went straight to the Sugarloaf and parked next door to the little house at the rear of the building where her parents had lived for most of their married life. Ali found her mother in the living room, plopped in the recliner usually reserved for her husband. A trash basket full of sodden tissues sat on the floor next to her.

"Just tell me," Edie demanded tearfully as Ali entered the room. "What did I do that was so wrong?"

Honesty's the best policy, Ali told herself. "You did too much," she said.

"Too much," Edie echoed. "All I did was bake a few things . . ."

"You baked more than a few things," Ali corrected. "I've seen whole bakeries with fewer pies and cakes. Chris and Athena wanted a small party. You turned it into a big party. They wanted to keep it simple and do it themselves. From their point of view, you took over. You made their party your party."

"But Chris is my grandson," Edie objected. "Why wouldn't I want to make it special?"

"You have to remember that Chris is only half of this equation," Ali told her. "The other is Athena. She's been married once before, and it didn't turn out very well for her. I can understand why she might be feeling a little glitchy about doing this the second time around."

"And then there's her physical situation," Edie suggested. "That might be a factor."

"No," Ali corrected firmly. "I think you're wrong there, Mom. I don't believe Athena's missing arm and leg have anything to do with it. But if they do, so what? She's a grown-up. She went to war and served our country. She's paid a hell of a price for wanting to do things her way—not your way or Dad's way or my way, but her way. Athena's way. She and Chris get to conduct themselves the way *they* want to."

"But still—"

"No," Ali said. "No buts. I could have raised a fuss when I found out that Chris went to you and Dad about the engagement ring instead of coming to me. But I didn't. It was Chris's decision. This is the same thing, Mom. He and Athena are a couple. We've got to let them live their own lives."

"So I suppose you're going to light in to me, too?" Edie asked. "Is that why you're here?"

"No," Ali said. "I'm here because you were crying on the phone. As far as I can remember, that's never happened before. I'm here because you're upset, but I happen to know Chris and Athena are upset, too. They're at a delicate point in their relationship. They're trying to figure out how to pull away from us and be a family of their own. That means that even though we have the very best of intentions, you and I need to back off. Not only that, I'll make you a deal. If you'll tell me when you think I'm meddling, I'll do the same for you. Maybe we can spare ourselves and everyone else a lot of grief."

"It's just like when you and Dean eloped, isn't it?" Edie said as a new spurt of tears coursed down her cheeks.

"Pretty much," Ali admitted.

"I never meant for that to happen, you know," Edie

said, blowing her nose one last time. "I just wanted to be a part of it."

Ali leaned over and gave her mother a hug. "I know, Mom," she said. "And I'm sorry, too, so let's see if we can both do better this time around."

When Edie had recovered enough to go powder her nose, Ali left her alone. Realizing she had skipped breakfast, she walked across the parking lot and into the restaurant.

"How's she doing?" Jan asked after taking Ali's order for French toast. "That poor woman baked like crazy all afternoon yesterday, and for what?" she added. "So she could be bitched out about it today? I swear, there's no pleasing kids these days."

So that's it, Ali concluded. *A generational divide.*

As far as Jan and Edie and probably even Ali's father were concerned, Edie had been trying to "help." From the point of view of Chris and Athena, however, that help had come across as unwanted interference. Ali realized it would fall on her shoulders to negotiate a peace treaty, and it wouldn't be easy.

I'm stuck in the middle, Ali told herself. *I'll be ducking shots from both sides.*

{ CHAPTER 7 }

Working four ten-hour days gave Peter Winter a lot of time off—three whole days he could devote to other things and to his other life. He tried to get in at least two rounds of golf a week, not because he liked the game all that much but because it was expected. Besides, playing golf was good cover. The rest of his free time went to Singleatheart. Sometimes he went prowling on the site for the hell of it, checking to see if any of the newly arrived profiles suited his particular fancies. Now that he was in the market for a new playmate, his search had taken on greater urgency.

Peter's private system automatically captured all incoming profiles and credit-card info and sent him those bits of information. Each week he made it his business to go over all of it in detail. You never could tell when something might prove useful for creating yet another virtual man or woman, as he had with the lovely and now departed Susan Callison. As far as Peter Winter was concerned, having a never-ending supply of virtual identities at the ready was essential.

Most of the time he used a stolen identity only once

or twice before shedding it the same way a molting snake discards its skin. As long as he was careful to keep any resulting bills under five hundred dollars, no one paid much attention—not the cops and not the banks, either. The banks quietly wrote off any and all disputed bills, mostly because they didn't want to let on that their supposedly secure systems were being breached.

At Hertz, Peter had used a phony credit card belonging to Matt Morrison to rent the vehicle he had driven to Sedona. He had done so in hopes of adding another possible suspect to the investigative mix into Morgan's death. Now that the damage was done, he wouldn't use it again; he ran the card itself through his shredder.

So far the only major exception to Peter's use-it-and-lose-it identity philosophy was Manny Wilkins, Peter's first fully cyber offspring, a fictional creation who was proving to be exceptionally successful in the real world. Manny Wilkins had come into being through a complex trail of fake and official documents it had taken Peter two years to pull together. Known as a canny businessman with a Las Vegas address, Manny was listed as the founder and CEO of Wilkins LLC and also as the bottom-line owner of Singleatheart.com. It was Manny who received all the checks and paid all resulting expenses and taxes before moving any remaining monies to numbered accounts in a series of offshore banks. Other identities came and went. Manny remained because, to Peter's astonishment, Singleatheart had turned into an inadvertent gold mine, and as long as all resulting taxes were paid on time, no one looked too closely.

The irony of the situation wasn't lost on Peter. He owed much of his good fortune to Rita—poor, dear departed Rita, who had stupidly refused to give him a divorce—or at least the divorce he had wanted. She had told him once that the only way he would get rid of her was over her dead body, which was exactly how he had done it—by making sure Rita was dead.

Their hike up Camelback Mountain had been part of a carefully orchestrated reconciliation after a period of marital turbulence. There had been no witnesses when Rita fell several hundred feet to her death. She had been so surprised when Peter had turned on her with a drawn weapon in his hand that she'd leaped backward and fallen all on her own. He'd made sure there was no one around to say Rita hadn't tripped and fallen exactly the way her grieving husband claimed she had.

Had Peter carried a big insurance policy on Rita, things might have been different. That would have given him a motive. As it was, after a fairly cursory investigation, Rita's death was declared an accident. That was done over the objections of Rita's mother, who insisted Peter had killed her daughter. The mother-in-law couldn't prove it, however, and neither could anyone else.

Rita had been gone for ten years now. Peter's friends at work kept telling him that he needed to get over her and move on. They kept trying to fix him up with someone else, but Peter wasn't interested in another wife. In fact, he was hung up on something else entirely.

Peter had liked how he felt as he watched Rita go tumbling helplessly down the steep hillside, flopping like a limp rag doll as she flew from one boulder to the next. He had exulted in hearing her fading screams as they melted into the far distance, and he had known right then that he would kill again when the first opportunity presented itself—even if he didn't know exactly how or when.

In contemplating this new compulsion, and before taking any action, Peter had become a student of murders. He searched out as many cases as he could find and sorted out who got away with it, who didn't, and all the hows and whys in between. As he researched his newly chosen field, Peter was struck by one recurring theme: how many stupid killers, mostly men lacking in imagination, killed first one wife or girlfriend and then another in exactly the same way. Later, once the hapless killers were caught, they were always astonished that some detective or other happened to pick up on the obvious similarities between cases.

Peter Winter was a doctor. That meant he was smarter than the average bear to begin with. Determined not to make the same kinds of fatal errors, he realized there was no need to kill his own cheating wife when he could always murder someone else's.

Peter had earned his way through school by being a geek. Putting his well-honed technical skills to work, he set about creating Singleatheart. In doing so, he discovered that the world was full of women just like Rita, all of them admitted cheaters and all available for the taking. Their numbers alone had been an amazing wake-up call. It turned out they were everywhere. As Peter scanned through the various profiles each week, that was what he went looking for—geographically diverse women who looked like carbon copies of Rita and deserved what was about to happen to them. By murdering women who bore an amazing resemblance to Rita Winter, Peter was able to do away with his wife over and over without ever getting caught.

Peter had covered his tracks by working through websites based in Russia. When it became apparent that he'd need a U.S.-based server farm, he had chosen one in Deadwood, South Dakota, for three reasons. For starters, the name appealed to him. Deadwood had a certain ring to it, and that was how he liked to think of cheating women in general—as so much deadwood. He also liked the fact that Deadwood was a hell of a long way from his home and respectable lifestyle in Phoenix, or from Manny Wilkins's phony condo office just off the Strip in Vegas. As long as Peter was careful to avoid attracting the attention of the feds, crossing multiple jurisdictional lines made things far tougher on the cops and easier for him.

Third, the server's South Dakota location was attractive for economic, moneygrubbing reasons. With gold mining not exactly booming at the moment, local city and state officials had enacted a series of changes designed to attract and keep new businesses. The resulting tax savings meant that the IP server Manny had chosen was able to do the same job for a lot less money than vendors in other locations.

Securing Singleatheart's business had been carried out by one of Manny Wilkins's minions—Peter Winter in yet another cyber guise. Once the site was up and running, all Peter had to do was sit back and rake in the dough and the occasional victim.

On that particular Wednesday morning, Peter turned to his computer with no inkling that something was amiss, not until he went scrolling through the credit-card information from that week's server-farm

data dump. What jumped out at him from the very
first listing of the day wasn't the person's name, Alison
Reynolds, but part of her address—Sedona. The place
where Peter had driven on Monday morning. Where
he'd used a hammer to beat Morgan Forester's pretty
little face to a bloodied pulp. Where he'd managed to
leave the murder weapon in the back of the victim's
husband's pickup truck.

Was it merely a coincidence that someone else
from Sedona was venturing through the Singleatheart
website barely two days later?

No, Peter Winter told himself. *There are no coinci-
dences.*

But there was something about the name Alison
Reynolds that was spookily familiar. Just for argument's sake, Peter went ahead and Googled the name
to see what might come up. There was far more
material than he'd expected, and none of it was good
news for Peter Winter. A former TV anchor, Alison
Reynolds now claimed to be a different kind of jour-
nalist—a blogger with an extensive following of fans.
Over the course of the past two years, she had been
involved in several high-profile homicide cases in Arizona and California. She had a concealed-weapon
permit, and she was evidently well acquainted with a
Yavapai County homicide detective named Dave Holman. And she was remodeling a house with Build It
construction—the company owned by Bryan Forester.

The light came on in Peter's head. That was why
Ali Reynolds's name was familiar: He had seen it mentioned somewhere in Morgan Forester's computer files.

That's not good, either, Peter told himself. *Not good
at all.*

Was she nosing around because Morgan had confided in her, or was she doing her snooping on behalf of Morgan's husband? Either way, Alison Reynolds was a woman who would bear careful watching.

From past experience, Peter knew that often the best way to watch someone like that was through her computer. A less adept man might have unleashed the dogs of war. Peter Winter didn't need to. Ali Reynolds had unwittingly wandered into the world of Singleatheart, so she had also opened her computer files to the Trojan horse he kept hidden there. The next time Ali Reynolds opened her computer, he'd be there, too, able to follow her every keystroke.

Peter didn't have a doubt in the world that observing what she said and did there would tell him everything he needed to know. And though he was tracking her activities online, he knew that if he needed to, he'd be able to take her out the old-fashioned way—just like he had Morgan Forester.

After dealing with her mother's meltdown, Ali had no intention of going back to see Jacky Jackson. When she left the Sugarloaf, she headed for Andante Drive. She had just parked and walked inside when her phone rang. Glancing at caller ID, Ali saw a Cottonwood number in the window. "Hello?"

"Is this Alison Reynolds?" a strange woman's voice asked.

"Yes. Who's this?"

"Nelda Harris, Haley Marsh's grandmother. I found your business card on a table in the living room last night. I believe you must have stopped by to see her sometime yesterday afternoon."

Great, Ali thought. *Now I'll probably be caught in the cross fire on this as well.* "Yes," she admitted. "I did stop by."

"May I ask why?" Nelda asked.

"Haley didn't tell you?"

"No, she didn't, and that's why I'm calling—to find out. As her guardian, I need to know what's going on with her."

"I came to offer her the chance of a scholarship, Mrs. Harris. A scholarship she could have used to attend any college of her choice. She turned it down. She says she wants to go to work for Target."

"An Askins scholarship?" Nelda Harris asked.

"That's right. It would have paid her way to virtually any school in the country. I suggested she might want to talk this over with you. She seems to be under the impression that she's a burden to you somehow. She wants to make her own way in the world, and she's afraid that going to school will mean you'll be stuck with her and her little boy for that much longer."

"Whatever would give her that idea?" Nelda demanded. "I never said she was a burden to me, or little Liam, either. I wouldn't."

"And I'm sure you didn't," Ali agreed.

"Liam," Nelda said, "stop that. Come away from there." Speaking into the phone once more, she added, "Do you believe in good and evil?"

For a moment Ali thought the woman might be referring to her granddaughter's cute little toddler. "I'm not sure—" Ali began.

"Not just good and bad," Nelda interrupted. "I mean real good and evil."

Earlier in her life, Ali might have been able to

answer that question clearly in the negative—at least so far as evil was concerned. But now that she had met and unmasked Arabella Ashcroft, now that she had seen beyond the skin-deep physical beauty of April Gaddis, the young woman who had come within hours of marrying Ali's former husband, real evil did have a presence in her life, and often a very human face.

"Yes," Ali replied at last. "I suppose I do. Why?"

"Liam, please. Grandma's on the phone. Come here and be still for a moment." Nelda sounded exasperated, as though the toddler was taking advantage of her being on the phone to get into all kinds of mischief.

"Let me ask you another question, Ms. Reynolds . . ."

"Please call me Ali."

"All right, Ali. I know you said Haley turned down your offer, but if I could convince her to change her mind—if we could convince her—would the scholarship still be available?"

"She doesn't actually have the scholarship at the moment," Ali corrected. "When she said she wasn't interested, I took her at her word. It'll most likely be awarded to someone else."

"Please," Nelda said as though she hadn't heard. "I'd really like to discuss this with you, but not right now, when Liam's driving me crazy. I need to put him down for a nap, but once he wakes up, we could drive up to Sedona to see you."

Ali looked around her house. Aunt Evie's very breakable knickknacks were still scattered here and there, well within reach of a toddler. And then there was Sam. A temperamental cat who didn't do well with most adult strangers would probably have a complete meltdown if faced with a busy-bee little boy. And

if this house wasn't kid-proof, the construction site at
Manzanita Hills Road was even less so.

"I'll tell you what," Ali said. "Do you know where
the Sugarloaf Café is?"

"Of course," Nelda said.

"Great," Ali said. "Call me at this number when you
head out. I'll meet you there. We can have lunch. My
treat."

"You don't have to do that," Nelda said. "Liam and I
can eat before we leave home."

"Don't be silly," Ali told her. "You said we need to
talk. Eating lunch will give Liam something to do in
the meantime."

"You must know something about little boys."

Ali smiled into the phone. "I had one of those once
myself," she said, laughing. "It's like riding a bicycle.
Some things you never forget."

Ali had fixed her hair and makeup and was in the
process of changing into something more suitable for
lunch when her cell phone rang.

"Mr. Forester just called," Leland Brooks reported.
"He's on his way here and says he needs to speak with
you. He says it's urgent."

"All right," Ali said. "I'm on my way. Is Jacky still
there?"

"Mr. Jackson evidently had another engagement,"
Leland said.

"Good news," Ali said. Relieved, she headed back
to Manzanita Hills Road. She stepped out of her Cayenne and was delighted when she heard the familiar
whine of drills working inside the house. That meant
that no matter what else was going on, wallboard
installation was still moving forward.

Bryan Forester arrived bare seconds later. When he stepped out of his pickup, she was startled by his gray pallor. "Come on," he said grimly, gesturing toward the picnic table. "We need to talk."

He settled down at the table, pulled out a cigarette, and lit it. Sitting opposite him, Ali was surprised. She remembered that Billy had mentioned something about Bryan taking up smoking again, but in all the months they'd worked together, she had never seen him with a cigarette.

"They fired me," he said at last, blowing a cloud of smoke into the air.

"Who fired you?"

"The people at the other two remodel jobs I was doing," Bryan said. "They're using the missing cabinet order as cover. They're claiming I was trying to defraud them by charging for materials that were never ordered."

"What does that mean?" Ali asked.

"It means both those jobs are shut down. My workers have been ordered off the two properties. Immediately. That's just an excuse, though. The real reason is what happened to Morgan. As far as the people in this town are concerned, she's dead, and I'm the abusive murdering husband who did it."

He sounded so beaten and discouraged, Ali had no idea what to say. "I'm sorry," she began, but he plowed on.

"You know, I put up with Morgan's crap for years because I didn't have a choice," Bryan continued. "The world may have changed in a lot of ways, but not when it comes to divorce. If there are kids involved, fathers don't get custody, period, not unless the mother happens to be a drug-dealing crackhead, and sometimes not even then. So I put up with Morgan's stunts, with all her whoring around and game playing, because I wasn't willing to lose Lindsay and Lacy. I kept my mouth shut and lived with it. But now that she's dead, all of a sudden people have decided I'm the one who's at fault—I'm the one who must have killed her. That I, someone who's never killed anything—who's never even shot a bird with a BB gun—would murder the mother of my children."

"I'm sure they're shocked by what happened to Morgan," Ali interjected. "We all are. They're looking for someone to blame."

"They're blaming me!" Bryan insisted, his voice trembling with outrage. "People I've known all my life are saying awful things about me. They don't say them to my face, of course. No one has guts enough to do that, but I'm not stupid. I'm getting the message loud and clear."

"What do you mean?" Ali asked.

"I went to the bank just now, and the teller there treated me like crap. The same thing happened to me at the hardware store with a clerk I've done business with for years. It seemed to me that with my wife dead, people would be nice to me and might even offer a little sympathy. What a laugh. Instead, they treat me like a leper. Why? What happened to that bit about innocent until proven guilty? And what about the deputy who's been following me around all morning? I'd be willing to bet he's parked at the bottom of your driveway right this minute. What do they think I'm going to do, try to take off somewhere? Take my girls and go live in another country?"

Spent, Bryan subsided into a bleak silence. At that

point, the man seemed so far beyond any consolation mere words could offer that Ali wondered if she should even try. But she did anyway. "As I told you, the same thing happened to me when my second husband died."

Bryan looked at her blankly and shook his head. Bogged down in his own troubles, he clearly didn't remember their earlier conversation. So she told him again.

"My ex-husband was murdered just before our divorce was due to become final," she said. "People found it easy to blame me, too. So did the cops."

"Even though you hadn't done it?"

Ali nodded. "Even though."

"And what did you say to those people—to the people who thought you were guilty?"

"They were entitled to their own opinions," Ali said. "I wouldn't be surprised to learn that some of them still think I was somehow involved in Paul Grayson's murder. The point is, what they think of me is none of my business. It doesn't matter."

"Do you believe me?" Bryan asked suddenly. "Do you think I did it?"

"I saw Morgan's profile on the Singleatheart website," Ali said quietly. "I know she was cheating on you. Or at least I know she was trying to cheat on you."

"More than trying," Bryan corrected. "Did." He didn't bother asking how Ali knew about Singleatheart. Obviously, he had known about it, too.

"You told me yourself that you thought she had misappropriated the cabinet deposits," Ali said. "I can see how you'd have reason to be angry."

"Not angry enough to kill her," Bryan said.

"No," Ali agreed, "but in the eyes of the world, the

fact that you were angry, even justifiably angry, also makes you a suspect."

Bryan looked at Ali closely. "What about you? Do you think I did it?" he repeated.

It was an honest question that deserved an honest answer. Ali met Bryan's questioning gaze without wavering. "No," she said. "No, I don't. If I had thought you were guilty of murder, do you think I would have gone ahead and reordered the cabinets?"

"But you're the only one," Bryan said. "My other so-called clients sure as hell didn't reorder."

"Maybe I have more faith in the justice system than they do," Ali said. "Maybe I believe in what you called 'the innocent until proven guilty' bit."

"Does that mean you'll help me?" Bryan asked.

"Wait a minute," Ali countered. "As I said, I've already reordered the cabinets. Your guys are still working here. I haven't ordered them off the premises. Isn't that enough?"

"I need more than that," Bryan said, lowering his voice. "I'm convinced someone is trying to frame me—someone who wants me to go to prison for murdering my wife. Gary, one of the wallboard guys, told me he saw Dave Holman take something out of the back of my truck yesterday afternoon. Gary didn't know what it was, and neither do I. But whatever it was, I sure as hell didn't put it there.

"Then, last night, when I was loading a stack of wallboard, I saw something in the bed of my truck—a rust-colored stain that looks like blood. If that's what it is, I have no idea where it came from, but I'm guessing whatever Dave took away with him had blood on it, too. They're probably running forensics tests on it right this minute. That may be why I'm not already under arrest—they haven't finished running whatever tests they need to run. But once they do that, it's game over. That's why I'm here talking to you now. There's been a cop on my tail all morning long, following me everywhere I go. I doubt I have much more time."

With that, Bryan reached into the pocket of his plaid flannel shirt and withdrew several items—an envelope with Billy Barnes's name scrawled carelessly across it and what appeared to be two computer thumb drives. He carefully returned the envelope to his pocket, but after placing the two drives on the table, he pushed them in Ali's direction.

"I downloaded these from our Web-based backup site," he explained. "One contains all the files that were on Morgan's desktop computer as of midnight last night. The other contains all the files on my laptop. I'm sure Dave Holman is trying like crazy to get himself a search warrant for all my property. Once he does that, I have to assume both of those computers are going away. He'll probably be able to freeze the backup files as well. In the meantime, I want you to keep these for me."

"Why?" Ali said. "Surely you must know that Dave Holman is a friend of mine. I'm not going to go against him on something like this."

"I still want you to have them," Bryan insisted. "I'm not asking you to do anything with them. Just hold them for me, for safekeeping, until I decide what's to be done with them."

"Bryan," Ali said, "if you think what's on either one of those drives will help your case, you're far better off giving them to your attorney."

"What attorney?" Bryan asked. "You're forgetting I just

had to terminate two full crews of workers. It took every last penny in my checking account to pay them off. And I've maxed out my credit cards making a deposit with the funeral director who's handling Morgan's services. I don't have an attorney for the very good reason that I can't afford one. Period. I'm not going to have any representation at all until the court gets around to appointing someone, and that won't be until after I've been arrested. From the way things are going, help like that could be too late. I need to know that someone is looking at this mess from my side, Ali. Right now it feels like everyone in the world is working against me—everyone but you."

As Ali struggled to find a way to reply, she realized that the whining drills inside the house had fallen silent. She saw Bryan's expression darken. His crew emerged from the house. With lunch boxes in hand, the three men sauntered in the direction of the canopy-covered table. They were followed by the camera crew. This time the cameras weren't running.

"Speak of the devil," Bryan muttered. Rising to his feet, he went to meet them. A few steps from the table, he barred their way.

"Hey, Bryan," Billy Barnes said easily. "Good to see you. What's up?"

In answer, Bryan removed the envelope from his pocket and handed it over.

Billy looked puzzled. "What's this?" he asked.

"You're terminated," Bryan said. "Ryan, you and Gary are still on the job until the wallboarding is done. Understand?"

"Terminated," Billy repeated. "Wait a minute. What's the deal? You're keeping these yahoos and letting me go? What are you smoking?"

"Unfiltered Camels," Bryan returned. "That's what I'm smoking, but I've also been reading the e-mails on Morgan's computer. Turns out she kept them all—the ones she wrote to somebody named Billy Boy and the ones he wrote back to her several months ago. She didn't even bother erasing them. Can you imagine that? And here I thought the two of us were friends." Bryan's voice dripped with contempt.

Billy Barnes's customary bluster faded. "Look, Morgan and me were friends," he said. "And I can explain. What happened was an accident. I didn't mean for us to get involved like that, and neither did she. Things just got out of hand."

"Things got very out of hand," Bryan agreed. "Now get the hell out of here, Billy. Everyone in town seems to think I'm capable of murder. Looking at your slimeball face, I'm beginning to think maybe they're right. I could do the world a huge favor by wiping your ass off it." Bryan took a single threatening step in Billy's direction. Fearing blows were about to be exchanged, Ali held her breath, but before the confrontation had a chance to turn physical, Leland Brooks appeared silently out of nowhere and stepped between the two men.

"Enough," he said. "You should probably leave now, Mr. Barnes, while you still can."

Brandishing his lunch pail, Billy glared back at him. "Nobody tells me what to do, you worthless little fag," he shot back. "Get out of the way."

"Don't start with me," Leland advised quietly, holding up a warning hand of his own. "Looks can be quite deceiving. I just might surprise you. Now, I suggest you do as you were told and go."

After a moment of bristling silence, Billy backed

down. He turned to the other workers, who had melted into the background, putting some welcome distance between themselves and the growing altercation. "Are you two coming with me or not?" Billy asked.

Gary and Ryan exchanged wary glances, but neither of them made a move.

"Suit yourselves," Bryan told them. "It's up to you. Go or not. Billy's the one who got terminated, not you. As far as I'm concerned, you guys are still on this job."

"Hey, you two, don't be stupid," Billy urged. "You heard what the man said. He's broke. Busted. Tapped out. Once he goes to jail, who's going to write your checks?"

"I will," Ali asserted quietly, moving into the breach. "No matter what happens to Mr. Forester, if you're still working on my job, I'll see to it that you get paid. Understand?"

"You think she'll pay you directly?" Billy asked. "What BS!"

"It's not BS," Leland said. "If madam says she'll pay, she will. The woman's word is her bond. As for you? It's time for you to leave. Now."

Heeding the warning, Billy stalked off without a backward glance. Bryan returned to the table and sank down on one of the benches, while Leland turned back to the two remaining workmen.

"It might be best if you went somewhere else for your lunch break today," he said. "I believe Mr. Forester and Mrs. Reynolds require some privacy."

{ CHAPTER 8 }

Gary, Ryan, and the two ever present cameramen disappeared into the house without any further discussion.

"Thank you for backing me up, Leland," Bryan murmured. "If it hadn't been for you, I might have decked the guy. Then the cops could have me up on an assault charge along with everything else."

"You're most welcome," Leland replied. "Think nothing of it. That's one of my responsibilities around here—dealing with thorny construction issues." With that, he turned to Ali. "And now, if you don't mind, madam," he added, "I'd like to take the key to your other home and go have a look around."

"Why?"

"In case we have to change the venue for Thanksgiving dinner in a matter of days, I should probably reconnoiter the situation—see what you have available. That way I'll know what equipment, if any, I should get out of storage."

Ali knew at once that she had been outmaneuvered. Had Leland pressed her for the key to her house under any other circumstances, she might have been able to tell him no. Not wanting to add to Bryan's difficulties by making more of a fuss about the Thanksgiving issue, she simply handed over her key.

"And the alarm system is still out of order?" Leland asked.

The previous week, the alarm had gone nuts. A technician had stopped by long enough to say that a new motherboard was required. He had yet to return. Ali nodded in confirmation.

"Very well, then," the butler said. He started away, then turned back. "You're not forgetting your three o'clock, are you?"

"Which three o'clock?" Ali asked.

"With Marissa Dvorak."

The other possible scholarship winner. Leland was right: With everything else that was going on, she had forgotten.

"Of course not," Ali replied. "What makes you think I'd forget that?"

For a long time after Leland Brooks left them there, Ali and Bryan sat at the table in silence while Bryan lit another cigarette. "Thanks for agreeing to pay my guys," he said at last. "I don't know when or how, but I will pay you back."

"I'm sure you will," Ali said.

"I really appreciate it," Bryan added. "I understand that you probably don't want to believe me, either. Thanks for giving me the benefit of the doubt."

Ali glanced down at the two thumb drives, still lying on the table. Then she looked back at Bryan. "So Billy was involved with Morgan?"

Bryan nodded dejectedly. "Some friend, right?"

"Is it possible he had something to do with what happened to her?" she asked.

Bryan shook his head. "I doubt it. The e-mails I found that went back and forth between them were from several months ago. Whatever they had going, I think it was pretty much over, but I may have turned up another clue."

"What's that?"

He reached into the pocket of his jeans and removed his wallet. From that he took a small piece of paper that he handed over to Ali. On it was a list of numbers—872-GYG, along with a freestanding H that evidently wasn't part of the number.

"What's this?" Ali asked.

"You don't know my daughters," Bryan said softly. "Lindsey is bright as a new penny—fun and engaging. Lacy is different, smart but different. She likes order. She doesn't like it if things are out of place or if they're not what she's used to. She notices things and can remember details that other kids don't. Numbers especially."

Ali studied the paper. "Is that where these numbers came from?" she asked. "From Lacy?"

Bryan nodded. "She saw a car parked along the road that morning when the bus went past on its way to school. It had never been there, so as far as Lacy was concerned, it shouldn't have been there at all. That's why she remembered the license number."

"Is the H part of it, too?"

Bryan shook his head. "That was on the bumper, not the license. So it could have been a rental car—from Hertz, maybe."

Ali handed the piece of paper back to Bryan. She

remembered Dave mentioning that he intended to have the two girls interviewed by one of the children's forensics specialists from up in Flagstaff.

"Did this information come from an interview with one of the child advocates?" Ali asked.

Bryan shook his head again. "Lacy doesn't speak to strangers," he said. "She doesn't speak to anyone, really, not even me. The only person she actually communicates with is her sister. She told Lindsey about this last night, and Lindsey told me this morning. She said the license was green and white and that it had mountains on it."

"So the vehicle is registered in Colorado, then," Ali concluded. "Have you told Dave Holman? If there was an unidentified vehicle in the vicinity of a homicide, the investigating officers need to know about it."

"There's no way to know for sure if whoever was driving this vehicle had anything to do with what happened to Morgan," Bryan said. "It could be totally unrelated—something as harmless as a hiker leaving his car parked along the road while he went for a walk."

"It could also be a lot more than that," Ali pointed out. "Dave needs to know about it."

Several long seconds passed before Bryan replied. "Here's the problem," he said. "If Dave learns about it, he'll want to question Lacy, and I don't want him hounding her about anything. My girls have already been traumatized enough—Lacy in particular. Their mother's dead. Their whole world is in an uproar. How much worse could it be?"

"Unfortunately, it could be a lot worse," Ali told him. "What happens if you go to prison for Morgan's murder? How traumatized will your daughters be then? If there's even the smallest chance that this license number might lead to the killer, or even to someone who might have seen the killer and could help identify him, then you have an obligation to your daughters and to yourself to let the authorities in on it."

Without another word, she picked up her cell phone and scrolled through the phone book until she located Dave's number. Then she handed the phone over to Bryan.

"What's this?" he asked.

"That's Dave's number. Press send and then talk to him. You can't sit on this information, Bryan. It's too important. It could be vital."

Bryan stared at the phone in his hand but made no move to use it.

"Look," Ali insisted, "you asked me to help you. I'm willing to do that, but not if you're not willing to help yourself."

"All Dave Holman is looking for is an excuse to slap me in jail."

"Dave Holman doesn't screw around," Ali returned. "He's a straight shooter. And he's got kids who aren't perfect themselves. If you ask him to leave Lacy alone, he probably will. But you decide. Either call him and give him the information, or you're on your own."

For a moment her ultimatum hovered between them, then reluctantly, Bryan pressed send.

"Detective Holman?" he said when Dave answered. "It's Bryan Forester. I have some information for you. Yes, I know I'm calling on Ali Reynolds's phone. She insisted that I call."

There was a long pause before Bryan spoke again.

"It has to do with a vehicle that was spotted in the vicinity of our place the morning my wife died." After another long pause, Bryan swallowed hard before he replied to Dave's obvious question. "That would be my daughter Lacy. And no, I don't have a description, beyond the fact that the car was blue but I have what I believe to be the license number—from Colorado. Yes. I'll wait." He turned to Ali and mouthed, "He's getting a pencil."

Several minutes later, Bryan had relayed the information. He closed the phone and handed it back to Ali. "There," he said. "I hope you're happy."

Ali nodded. "It's a start," she said.

Bryan stood up.

"Where are you going?" Ali asked.

"I'll go into the house and check on progress, then I'll head back to the hotel. My mother doesn't do well with Lacy, especially when it comes to mealtimes. Mother thinks Lacy is spoiled. She's not. She's just Lacy."

He walked away, leaving Ali to wonder if Lacy's different way of viewing the world might provide the one telling detail that could end up proving her father's innocence.

Bryan was still in the house when Ali's phone rang. She wasn't surprised to see Dave Holman's phone number.

"You had Bryan Forester call me on your phone?" Dave demanded. "Why are you having anything to do with him, Ali? He's a possible murder suspect, a dangerous man."

"Yes," Ali agreed. "That's the word on the street. I'm hearing the same thing from all the local hairdressers."

"Ali, he's playing on your sympathies. And this license thing. Where did that come from? It certainly didn't show up in the CHAP interview."

"I'm not surprised," Ali said. "According to Bryan, Lacy doesn't talk to anyone but her sister, but are you going to check the lead or not?"

"Of course I'm going to check it out," Dave said, sounding exasperated. "But I'm also telling you that it's in Bryan's best interest to have us running around in circles and following up on useless leads. It's what guys like him do. That's how they think and how they work."

"Bryan Forester didn't kill his wife," Ali asserted.

"How do you know?" Dave asked.

"Because he told me."

"Right," Dave said with a mirthless chuckle. "He told you, and you believed him. How does that old George Strait song go? 'If you'll buy that, I've got some oceanfront property in Arizona.'"

"But I do believe him," Ali said.

Dave backed off. "Look, things were going badly for him. I'm hearing that Morgan wasn't exactly walking the straight and narrow and that she was fooling around—a lot. I think it's possible he and Morgan got into some kind of argument, and he lost it. I'm not saying that he didn't have some real provocation, and I'm not saying it was premeditated. But that doesn't mean he isn't dangerous and unpredictable. Do yourself a favor, Ali. Do us all a favor. Stay away from him. Don't get involved."

"Sorry, Dave," she said. "Remember, I was a murder suspect, too—and not all that long ago." Ali ended the call knowing it was too late for Dave's warning. She was already involved—very involved.

Bryan emerged from the house. "Ryan and Gary are close to finishing up with what little wallboard they have left. I told them that when they quit for the day, they should call me. I'll pay them for whatever hours they've worked so far. After today, though, they should plan on taking the rest of the week off. I told them either I'll give them a call or Mr. Brooks will when it's time for them to come back."

Ali nodded. "That's fine," she said.

"Thanks for all your help," he said. "The best I can possibly hope for now is that Dave Holman won't throw me in jail until after the funeral and until after I can make some kind of arrangement for the girls. That's not asking too much, is it?"

"I hope not," Ali said. "When is the funeral?"

"Day after tomorrow," Bryan answered. "Friday at ten A.M."

What if Dave does have evidence that links Bryan to Morgan's mrder? Ali wondered. Here was Bryan, hoping he'd be able to be with the twins for their mother's funeral. But what would happen to them after that, especially if he ended up being tried for murder and going to prison? The idea of those two little girls—the one, especially—having to live with a grandmother who didn't particularly like them made Ali's heart ache.

Bryan had barely driven away when Ali's phone rang. "Liam didn't take much of a nap," Nelda Harris told her. "We're on our way."

Switching gears, Ali left the house and went straight back to the Sugarloaf. It was long enough after the lunch rush that the place wasn't crowded. She corralled the corner booth—the one that offered the most privacy—and asked her mother for a high chair.

"Whose baby?" Edie Larson asked.

Ali wasn't eager to go into detail. "A friend's" was all she said.

Nelda arrived a few minutes later. She walked through the restaurant with Liam following behind. He carried a miniature truck in each hand and grinned happily when he saw Ali.

Nelda nixed the high chair in favor of a booster seat and then hefted Liam into that. "He gets in less trouble if he has a truck in each hand," she observed.

Ali's mother followed them to the table, bringing along the one-page children's menu and a pack of four Crayolas. When she returned a few minutes later, she beamed at Liam, who was busily coloring, and handed Nelda a package of oyster crackers. "What's Mr. Handsome here having today?" she asked. He looked back at her with his wide-eyed killer smile.

For lunch, Nelda asked to share a grilled cheese with the baby. Ali, still full from breakfast, ordered nothing but coffee. As Edie pocketed her order pad, she gave Liam an affectionate pat on the head. "This kid is cute as a button," she said. "I'll bet he takes after his daddy." As Edie walked away, she didn't glimpse the dismay that flashed across Nelda's face at the well-meaning remark. Ali did and knew that her mother had stepped in it. *So that's it,* she thought. *Something to do with the father. Some kid knocked Haley up and then declined to do the right thing.*

Since Edie had already broached the subject, Ali went ahead and followed up. "I suppose this is the same old story," she said. "The boy gets off scot-free, and the girl is left holding the bag and the B-A-B-Y." Ali didn't know exactly how old Liam was or how much he'd be able to understand. Spelling some of the critical words seemed like a good thing.

For a moment, rather than replying, Nelda busied herself with doling out a few of the oyster crackers to Liam. "It wasn't quite like that," she said at last. "It was actually a lot worse. Do you remember what I asked you about this morning?"

"You mean about good and evil?"

Nelda nodded. "I think most people believe that good comes from good and evil comes from evil, but that's not necessarily true. My husband, Liam, was one of the nicest people who ever lived. And I consider myself a good person, too, but our daughter, Patsy, was pure evil. Still is pure evil. And yet Haley is her daughter. And Liam here is her grandson."

Liam took that as a cue to toss a handful of crackers over his head. And when his grandmother—his great-grandmother, Ali realized—chided him about it, he gave her a grin punctuated by tiny white teeth. Shaking her head, Nelda gathered up the crackers and gave him the menu and the Crayolas.

Ali sensed that this was the reason Nelda Harris had driven here—to tell Haley's story, whatever it might be. Now, though, with Nelda seeming to have second thoughts, Ali realized that it must be worse than a teenage affair gone bad. *It must be a case of rape,* Ali theorized. She knew from her years in the news business how difficult it could be for rape victims and their families to discuss such things.

"What happened?" Ali asked gently.

Nelda bit her lip. "She was a problem from the day she was born," she said at last. "We tried to love her, but it wasn't easy. She was a colicky, cranky baby who never slept. And once she got to school, she was a biter and a fighter. By the time Patsy was a teenager, she was completely out of control."

When Nelda first started speaking, Ali had thought she was referring to Haley. It wasn't until that last sentence that Ali understood Nelda was talking about her own daughter rather than Haley, her granddaughter.

"Patsy dropped out of high school her sophomore year," Nelda continued. "Nothing we said made any difference. As far as she was concerned, she had learned everything there was to learn. Besides, she had taken up with an older guy—a married older guy, a long-haul truck driver named Wally Marsh. Patsy had two abortions before she was twenty. By then Wally had divorced his wife. He and Patsy got married, and the next thing we knew, Haley arrived on the scene."

There was a short pause in the narrative while Edie delivered Nelda's grilled cheese and poured more coffee. Nelda cut half the sandwich into pieces and then passed those to Liam, who stopped coloring long enough to mow through them.

"I knew before Patsy ever delivered that she'd be a terrible mother, and she was. She had this strange idea that as soon as she had the baby, Wally was going to straighten up and fly right. He didn't."

"Yes," Ali said. "As my father likes to say, once a cheat, always a cheat."

"And now Patsy was stuck at home with a baby while Wally was right back to doing his cheating with someone else. So Patsy came up with this harebrained idea of going to school and becoming a truck driver, too. I'm sure she figured that once she was out on the road with Wally, it would be that much easier to keep an eye on him. She came to me and asked me if I'd look after Haley so she could get her license.

"Liam and I talked it over. We knew what kind of a person she was—mean and vindictive. Liam said that if she ever got mad at us, she'd take Haley away and we'd never see her again. We told Patsy that the only way we'd look after Haley was if she made it official— if she and Wally signed over their parental rights to us. We told her they could have visitation privileges, but they needed to make us Haley's official guardians. And that's what happened. They both signed the paperwork, and then off they went while we set about raising Haley."

"From what I see, you did a good job of it," Ali said.

Nelda nodded. "We still had the farm then. Patsy always hated living there, but Haley loved it. She worshipped her grandpa—followed him everywhere, rode on the tractor with him. And when he got sick, she sat with him for hours on end. Just sat with him, telling him stories that she made up on the spot." A tear appeared in the corner of Nelda's eye. She brushed it away with the back of her hand.

Liam peered at her with a look of concern. "Owee?" he asked.

"No, honey," she said. "Grandma's fine. Just eat your sandwich." As he returned his attention to the food, Nelda returned to her story. "At first Patsy and Wally came to visit every month or so, but then their visits started getting farther and farther apart. By the fourth year, they came for Haley's birthday and for Christmas, and that was it. But it didn't matter, not really. By the time she was five, she barely knew them. Liam and I were her parents, the only ones who mattered.

"But we started hearing rumors about Patsy and Wally—that things were going haywire with them. Tuttle's a small town. Wally's first wife still lived there with his two sons. First we heard that Patsy and Wally were having marital difficulties of some kind. The next thing we knew, Wally was shot dead at a truck stop near Dallas. It turned out that they had been doing land-office business, hauling drugs along with their other cargo. Wally had been ready to settle down and buy a farm somewhere. He bought the farm all right. Patsy and her new boyfriend, Roger Sims, saw to it. All the ugly drug dealing came to light during the trial, and Patsy and Roger both got sent up twenty-years to life for second-degree murder.

"The whole thing nearly killed poor Grandpa," Nelda continued after a pause. "He wanted to pull up stakes, sell out, and move somewhere else, some-where far away. We came here looking for a place to move. We went to Prescott for the Fourth of July rodeo and even up to Jerome because he wanted to see a ghost town. But he loved Cottonwood. We both did, and we were thinking about coming here to live when he got sick. Lung cancer. I knew as soon as we got the diagnosis that moving away wasn't an option. Besides, as I told him at the time, what Patsy did or didn't do was no reflection on us, and the people who thought it was weren't worth bothering with anyway."

Ali was struggling to keep track of this long, convo-luted story while wondering how any of it could have contributed to Haley's turning down the scholarship.

"So for a long time, we just tried to keep going. Liam was getting sicker and sicker. It was all I could do to take care of him and Haley and look after the farm, too. Unlike her mother, Haley was good as gold—sweet and loving—and a huge help. When we lost Liam, she was only twelve, but she took care of me more than I took care of her. I don't know how I would have made it if she hadn't been there." Nelda sighed. "I don't know how other people deal with having a child in prison. The way I did it was I pretty much put Patsy out of my mind. I guess I sort of thought they put people in prison to be punished and learn their lessons so they won't make the same kinds of mistakes again. When they come out, they're supposed to be rehabilitated, right? And then two years after Liam died, the year Haley turned fourteen, who should turn up on my doorstep but Patsy. They had let her out on good behavior. And because she was so needy and because she was my child and because I'm a good person, I let her come home."

"Except she wasn't rehabilitated," Ali suggested quietly.

"No," Nelda agreed sadly. "She wasn't."

"Drugs?" Ali asked.

Nelda nodded. "Lots of drugs. She was using them and selling them right there in my house. In my own house. How could I have been so stupid? How could I not have known? Of course, Patsy was never that smart. And when she ran short of money, she paid off her dealer with the only other thing of value she had—Haley."

Ali was dumbfounded. "No."

"Yes," Nelda said. "It was late November. I was trying to get ready for the holidays. A friend of mine and I drove up to Oklahoma City to go shopping. Haley was supposed to go with us, but for some reason she wasn't feeling that well. She was in bed, asleep, when this big guy came waltzing into her room and told her she was his for the day because her mother owed him money. That's how it happened."

"Haley was raped?"

Nelda nodded and whispered as if hoping Liam wouldn't hear. "I came home and found her in bed, bleeding and terrified."

"Where was her mother?"

"Patsy took off. It's a good thing, too. If I could have found her, I would have plugged her on the spot. I took Liam's old forty-five out of his desk drawer and put it in my apron in case she came home. Then I called the cops. And then we had to go through that whole awful rigmarole—the hospital, the testing, the interviews, the photographs. Haley was only fourteen, fourteen and a half."

Ali did the math. Haley would have been fifteen when her baby was born, and she was seventeen now. That meant little Liam was slightly past two.

Nelda dissolved into tears. While Liam patted his grandmother's arm consolingly, Ali looked around the room. Other than their table, the Sugarloaf was empty. Jan Howard was gone. Edie and Bob Larson were evidently hiding out in the kitchen.

Nelda smiled at Liam through her tears while Ali wondered how much of the brutal story was soaking into Liam's agile little brain.

"What happened then?" Ali asked.

"They arrested Patsy and charged her with rape. She tried to get off by turning state's evidence, but that didn't work. They arrested the guy, too. He was a repeat offender, and they're both in prison now. He's not supposed to get out for the next forty years. Patsy's sentence is added on to what's left of her other one. She won't ever get out."

"Then Haley turned up pregnant."

Nelda nodded. "At the time, nobody told us about the morning-after pill. They probably should have, but they didn't, and we didn't know to ask. When we realized she was pregnant, I tried to talk her into having an abortion, but she wouldn't. She told me it was against her religion, and that's reason enough not to have one. But that's also when I decided to sell out and move away. Yes, I know, I had told Liam that what those people thought or said didn't matter, but when it came to Haley and the baby, I didn't want them to have to put up with all that crap. We sold the farm, auctioned everything, and came here. There wasn't much money. We had mortgaged everything to the hilt while Liam was sick. Fortunately, I was able to get work once we got here. It's the perfect job, actually, since I work when Haley's not in school, and she works at Target when I'm home on the weekends." Nelda glanced at her watch. "Speaking of which, I'm going to have to go soon or I'll be late for work."

"What about the scholarship?" Ali asked.

"I know how smart Haley is, and I want her to go on to school, but she won't hear of it," Nelda said. "She thinks that after all the years of looking after first her, then her grandfather, and now little Liam, it's time for me to have some time off."

Ali nodded. "That's pretty much what she told me. That she wanted to move out and live on her own. She's already got a job lined up."

"I know about the job," Nelda said. "At Target, but I want her to do better than that. Look what happened to me. I don't have any education, either. That's why I'm stuck working as a janitor. It was the best job I could get, and I'm glad to have it—at least I have some benefits. But I don't want her to hit my age and be stuck in the same kind of rut. I know you said she's only one of the candidates—one of the finalists—for that scholarship. I hope you'll think about giving it to her and helping me talk her into taking it. I don't want her to end up like me."

Ali reached across the table and took the older woman's hand. "Scholarship or not," she said, "Haley Marsh could do a lot worse than being just like you."

"What in the world was that all about?" Edie wanted to know after Nelda and Liam had driven away and Edie was sweeping up leftover oyster crackers.

"She's the grandmother of one of my scholarship candidates," Ali said.

"My goodness," Edie said. "A senior in high school who already has a baby that old? Are you sure that's the kind of person you'd want to be one of your recipients?"

"Yes," Ali said after a moment's reflection. "I'm pretty sure she is."

Still overwhelmed by the sheer weight of Nelda Harris's story, Ali left the restaurant with only a few minutes to spare. At the stroke of three, she pulled up in front of Marissa Dvorak's modest home in one of Sedona's least fashionable neighborhoods. A homemade wooden wheelchair ramp wound back and forth from the front gate to the side of the large front porch, where a dark-haired girl in a wheelchair sat waiting. She waved shyly as Ali exited the Cayenne.

"Ms. Reynolds?" she asked.

"Yes," Ali answered. "Alison Reynolds."

When Marissa held out her hand in greeting, Ali saw that the fingers were bent at a severe angle. The skin on her wide face was pulled taut across features distended by steroids, but her smile was utterly sincere, and her excitement was only barely under control.

"When Mr. Brooks called to set up this appointment, I went online and did some checking on you," Marissa said. "I think I know what this is about."

"And what would that be?" Ali asked.

"An Askins Scholarship, maybe?" Marissa asked hopefully.

Since Haley had already turned down the scholarship, Marissa should have been the last finalist. Had it not been for Nelda Harris's emotional plea, Marissa would have been the hands-down winner. Now Ali wasn't so sure. "How about if we go inside and talk this over?" she suggested.

The subsequent interview couldn't have been more different from the one with Haley Marsh. Marissa was thrilled beyond measure. She was eager to go on to college. She already had a letter of acceptance from the University of Arizona and had banked several advanced-placement classes, but with two younger children at home—also adopted—Marissa and her family had been worried that her going to college could only come with a huge burden of student loans.

Partway through the interview, Ali made up her mind. Haley Marsh was conflicted. Yes, she was certainly deserving and had been victimized by dreadful circumstances, but was it reasonable to attempt to push her into accepting a scholarship she didn't really want? And even if coercion worked, was it fair to herd her into going to college against her own wishes? On the other hand, Marissa Dvorak was an equally deserving young woman, one who was thrilled at the prospect of receiving a scholarship. She already knew where she wanted to go and would be happy to accept some help in getting there.

"You mean you can just say so?" Marissa asked when Ali told her the scholarship was hers. "You can decide just like that?"

"Actually, I can," Ali said. "Of the three finalists, you're the most viable. If it's all right with you, we'll make the official announcement in a press release sometime in the next week or so. In the meantime, you're welcome to let people know, especially your parents."

"They're not going to believe it."

"You're a remarkable young woman," Ali said. "I think they will."

Ali went on to tell Marissa about the terms of the scholarship—how much she would get and the GPA she'd need to maintain to receive it in subsequent years. When Ali left the house at four-thirty, she felt a real sense of relief and accomplishment. Months earlier, when Arabella Ashcroft had first broached the subject of Ali taking over the administration chores on the Askins Scholarship, Ali had been reluctant. Now, having seen firsthand the tremendous difference the award would make in smoothing the road for Marissa, Ali felt thankful to be involved.

As late as it was, Ali went straight home to Andante Drive, where she was astonished to find Leland Brooks's Mazda pickup still parked there. Several scatter rugs, freshly laundered and hung out to dry, decorated the rail on the front porch. From inside, she heard the wail of a vacuum cleaner. She opened the door and found the furniture pushed to one side of the room while Leland vacuumed where it had once stood. When she shut the front door, he turned off the noisy machine and faced her.

"Why are you still here?" Ali asked.

"Because I'm cleaning," he said simply. "As I told you, I came to get an idea about the kitchen situation—about cooking and serving equipment as well as dishes. Those all appear to be quite adequate. As for the rest of it, your quarters wouldn't pass even the most rudimentary inspection. If you expect to have your home ready to receive guests by Thanksgiving, I'm going to need to spend some time here, whipping it into shape. Vacuuming will do for today, but what this carpet really needs is a thorough shampooing. I've reserved a shampooer for first thing tomorrow morning."

Ali felt a pang of guilt. She and Chris were reasonably neat and conscientious about putting things away, but neither one of them excelled at the kind of deep cleaning required to measure up to Leland Brooks's fastidious standards. That was one of the drawbacks about living with a professionally trained butler. He called the shots in the nicest way imaginable, but he still called the shots.

"How are things at the construction site?" he asked, carefully wrapping up the power cord and attaching it to the vacuum's stem. Ali tended to shove the vacuum cleaner into the broom closet and toss the cord in after.

"When I left," Ali said, "my understanding was that

once the wallboarders finished work today, our job would be shut down until Mr. Forester gives the word."

"That's probably just as well," Leland said. "It also means that it won't be a problem if I'm working over here for the next little while, giving the place some spit and polish."

"About that," Ali began. "It seems to me that Chris and I should be responsible for cleaning up our own mess."

"Madam," Leland said, "for the past several months, while I've been stuck at the construction site, you've barely tapped my potential. I've been quite frustrated. Bored, really, almost to the point of giving notice. I'm sure you wouldn't want that, so let me tackle the work here and get it done. It will give me a chance to show you what I can do—what I'm capable of."

"What about the part where you offered to clean Billy Barnes's clock?" Ali asked with a smile. "Was that part of showing me what you can do?"

"Boasting for its own sake is in very bad taste," Leland said. "But I was trained by the Royal Marines, and I still know the moves. Over the years, I've had to use them more than once."

"The next time Jacky shows up, I might let you use some of those moves on him."

"You think he'll be back?" Leland asked.

"Of course he'll be back," Ali answered. She handed him Marissa Dvorak's file folder. "By the way, I talked to Marissa Dvorak and made up my mind. She's this year's recipient."

"That stands to reason, since Miss Marsh turned it down," Leland replied. "Would you like me to prepare a press release to that effect?"

"Yes, please," Ali said. "I told her you would."

Leland nodded. "Very well." He looked around the room. "I got a start on things today, but since I'm going to be shampooing the carpet tomorrow, I hope you won't mind if I leave the furniture where it is."

Ali knew Leland Brooks was more than capable of pushing the leather couch around, but there was no need for him to do so twice. "Of course not," she said. "This is fine."

"You can expect me here bright and early," he said. "You may want to be out and about. As for your Cayenne, if you'll pardon my saying, that could also use a good detailing."

"Trying to keep me in line must be a real trial for you," Ali said.

"On the contrary, madam," Leland said with a fond smile. "Occasionally, I find it quite stimulating."

{ CHAPTER 9 }

As soon as Chris knew Leland Brooks had left, he ventured upstairs. "Is the cleaning Nazi gone?" he asked. "He was here working up a storm when I got home from school. What was that all about?"

"Thanksgiving," Ali told him. "With everything that's going on with the contractor, we came to the conclusion that there's no chance of having dinner at the new house. Leland came over here to see about whipping this one into shape."

"You're not going to let him clean my studio, are you?"

"He will unless you stop him," Ali said with a laugh. "Since he seems to be a force of nature, I'm not sure that's possible."

Chris took a soda from the fridge and hustled back downstairs. Ali was in the bedroom changing into her comfy sweats when her phone rang. Caller ID told her the number was restricted.

"Ms. Reynolds?"

"Yes."

"It's B."

The B. in question happened to belong to Bartholomew Quentin Simpson. Named after his maternal grandfather, Bart Simpson had been ten years old when the other Bart Simpson first appeared on local TV screens, thereby consigning Sedona's Bart Simpson to a peculiar form of childhood hell. Subjected to unending teasing, he stopped answering to any name but his first initial, since using both of them, B.Q., didn't work for him, either. The one-initialed B. had retreated into the solitary solace that computers had to offer. By seventh grade, he had taken apart his father's old Commodore 64 computer and put it back together.

By eighth grade, B. Simpson had taught himself to write computer code. To his parents' dismay, he had dropped out of high school his junior year after selling his first video game to Nintendo. He had gone to work for them long enough and well enough that he'd been able to "retire" at age twenty-eight. He had returned to the Sedona area, where, although he had never played golf, he bought himself a golf-course-view home. Rather than hitting the links, he had started his own computer security firm called High Noon Enterprises. His company motto was "It takes a hacker to catch a hacker."

Now that B. Simpson was back in town, he easily could have been one of Sedona's most eligible bachelors, except no one really knew he was there. He lived alone and worked odd hours, usually coming into the Sugarloaf for breakfast just as Edie and Bob Larson were closing down for the day. It was Bob who had brought B. Simpson's painful childhood history and the existence of High Noon Enterprises to Ali's attention.

"The way I understand it, he's sort of like an Internet version of an old-fashioned gunslinger," Bob Larson had told his daughter. "As much time as you spend online, you should probably have someone like him in your corner. I wouldn't be surprised if someone shipped you one of those awful viruses. Or worms."

In the end, Ali had signed up with B.'s High Noon Enterprises more to shut her father up than because she was worried about being hacked. In the three months since she'd been a paying customer, it had seemed like a needless expense. As far as she could see, preventing cyber crime seemed about as exciting as watching grass grow.

"Good to hear from you," Ali said now to B. "What's up?"

"You won't think it's good to hear from me when you find out what I have to say," B. warned her. "You've got yourself a Trojan."

"Excuse me?" Ali asked.

"A Trojan horse," B. replied. "In your computer. Twice each day I run a monitoring check on all the computers I have under contract. Today your noon-time analysis came up positive."

"What does that mean?"

"It means that as long as your computer is connected to the Internet, someone else can see everything you do there. He can take over control of your computer. He can gain access to your files and change them. He can also send mail that's ostensibly from you, even though it isn't. You don't use a multiple-computer network, do you?"

"No," Ali said. "I'm usually on my air card."

"That's good," B. said. "If there are other computers

operating on the same network, the bad guy can gain access to those as well. If he's inside your computer, he's also inside your network."

Suddenly, cyber crime sounded a lot more ominous. Ali was surprised to find herself feeling spooked and vulnerable. Knowing that a crook could operate inside her computer made her feel like someone had broken into her house and penetrated her personal safety zone.

"What should I do, then?" she asked. "Turn off the computer? Unplug the damn thing and shut it down?"

"No," B. said. "If you do that, it might tip him off that we're on to him. I want you to leave the computer on. Try to use it more or less the way you usually do."

"Why?"

"Computers that are connected to the Internet are two-way streets," B. explained. "Whoever sent you the Trojan did it over the Internet. I'm going to try to return the favor and send one right back to him. While he's monitoring your every keystroke, I'll be monitoring *his* keystrokes. If he makes a move, I should be able to begin tracking him down."

"Wait a minute," Ali said. "If he has that kind of total access to my computer, shouldn't I cancel my credit cards and shut down my online banking? Should I report this to the police?"

"It's my experience that banks are a whole lot more interested in identity theft than cops are. If there's a murder or even an armed robbery, the cops are all over it. With identity theft, they're not until and unless we can prove that a crime has actually been committed. They'll get on the bandwagon once we've accumulated enough evidence that it's easy for them to make a case without having to expend much effort. Right now the best thing that could happen is that the guy will try to rip you off. In order to catch him at it, you'll need to monitor your credit-card and bank transactions very carefully. Be on the lookout for anything out of the ordinary, but don't use your computer to do it."

"If I'm not supposed to use my computer," Ali objected, "how am I supposed to go about monitoring anything?"

"I have a couple of spare laptops lying around," B. said. "I'll be glad to lend you one of mine to use for the time being. If you don't mind, I can drop off a loaner for you a little later this evening. You can insert your air card and use that for anything you don't want exposed to prying eyes."

"You'll drop it off," Ali murmured. "Does that mean you know where I live?"

"Yup," B. replied, "I'm afraid I do. It was right there in your computer files, plain as day. And I'm not the only one who would know that, either. If I found it out, our sneaky little friend can find it out, too."

"Great," Ali said. "See you when you get here. The sooner the better."

Ali had been planning on taking a look at Bryan Forester's two thumb drives. Heeding her computer security expert's warning, however, she left them in her purse. Under normal circumstances, she might have picked up her computer and checked her e-mail account. But now, self-conscious in the knowledge that her every keystroke might be under observation, she left the computer where it was and went into the bedroom to change into sweats.

Late in the afternoon, Matt managed to get his brain focused on work. When his phone rang, he answered it before the second ring. Yes, he was a bureaucrat—and a lowly one—but that was also why Matt always answered his phone so promptly. He regarded himself as a public servant, and he didn't like to keep the public waiting.

So when he answered, Matt thought it would be someone calling about one of his many accounts. The last thing he expected was a phone call from a detective—a *homicide* detective!

"My name's Dave Holman," the man on the phone announced. "Detective Dave Holman, with the Yavapai County Sheriff's Department. Is this Matthew Morrison?"

Matt's first thought was that it had to be some kind of joke. Bill Baxter was one of Matt's former coworkers at the state auditor's office. Before transferring over to the Department of Weights and Measures, Bill had established himself as a practical joker of the first water. This sounded like the kind of off-the-wall stunt Bill would pull.

"Bill?" Matt asked uncertainly. "Bill Baxter, is this you?"

"No," the caller replied. "It's not Bill Baxter. As I said a moment ago, my name is Dave Holman."

"Sorry," Matt said. "My mistake. You sound a lot like another guy I know, a friend of mine." He glanced guiltily around his cubicle to see if anyone was listening. Bobbie Bacon, his nearest neighbor, was talking on her phone. No one else seemed to be paying the slightest bit of attention. "What can I do for you— Did you say Holman?"

"Yes. Dave Holman. I'm a homicide detective."

"What's this all about?" Matt asked. *Why on earth is a homicide detective calling me?* he wondered.

"I'm working on a case that happened up here in our jurisdiction," Holman explained. "On Monday morning of this week, a woman named Morgan Forester was bludgeoned to death shortly after her children left for school."

"Where was this again?" Matt asked.

"Up by Sedona," Holman answered. "Outside the Village of Oak Creek."

As soon as the detective said "Monday morning," Matt felt his heartbeat quicken, and he went into a state of near-panic. He knew he had a problem. Matt hadn't been anywhere near where he was supposed to be that morning, not even close. In the solitude of his cubicle, he felt his ears turn red. Beads of sweat popped out on what his wife liked to call his "very tall forehead."

"What does any of this have to do with me?" Matt asked. He did his best to keep his tone conversational and even. It would not do to sound upset or panicked. That was critical.

"The car you were driving was reportedly seen in the area shortly before the crime occurred," Detective Holman continued. "I was wondering if I could stop by your office and visit with you about that. We're hoping that perhaps you may have unwittingly witnessed something that could help us in solving our case."

Matt was utterly mystified. "Wait a minute," he said. "What car? You say this happened somewhere around Sedona? I wasn't anywhere near there on Monday morning. What makes you think I was?"

Now it was Detective Holman's turn to be mystified. "You weren't?" he asked. "Where were you, then?"

The easy thing for Matt to say was that he had been at work, but that wasn't true. There was a whole floor of people in his office who would be more than happy to blow a hole in that whopper. Who was this dead woman? And why was the homicide cop calling him? Was he under suspicion somehow? Did he need to have an alibi? The waitress at the truck stop might remember him—he'd left her a nice tip—but if he admitted to having been there, he'd also have to admit why.

Matt's ears burned anew. The cop was saying something, but Matt hadn't been paying attention to anything except the damning sound of his own breath coming in short, anxious gasps. "I'm sorry," he said. "Bad connection. I didn't get that last part."

"According to the people at Hertz, you rented a vehicle from their Sky Harbor facility early that morning and brought it back later in the afternoon."

"Why would I need to rent a car?" Matt asked. His insides lurched. *The car!* That was another problem. Using his fictional early appointment in Tucson as an excuse, he had checked out a motor-pool vehicle on Friday night. He had driven home in it and kept it over the weekend. It was also the vehicle he had driven to his appointment with Susan at the model home in Red Rock. How many traffic cameras along the way might have picked up on that?

He took a deep breath. Obviously, this wasn't a joke. The cop was real. Someone was dead, murdered, and the cops believed that Matt was involved. Then his heart skipped a beat. He hadn't heard from Susan since then—not since the day she had stood him up—though he had written to her time and again, told her he understood completely if she'd had second thoughts. What if Susan Callison was the person who had been murdered? What if that was why she had stood him up and why she hadn't been back online?

"It was rented under your Hertz gold-card number," Holman told him.

"I'm sorry," Matt declared. "There must be some mistake. I don't have a Hertz gold card."

How would he? Why would he? He never went anywhere that he didn't drive himself. Jenny didn't like flying, which meant they didn't fly.

"I see," the detective said.

And Matt was afraid that he did—that Holman saw everything. So Matt didn't demand to know who was dead. That would have counted as making a fuss. And he didn't say again that he hadn't been in Sedona, couldn't possibly have been in Sedona, because he was a third of the state away from there, hoping to get lucky. He just kept quiet.

"So could I come talk to you about this in the morning?" Dave Holman asked. "I could probably be at your office by ten or so, if that would be all right."

"Of course," Matt said. "Ten is fine. You know where we are? We're here in Phoenix, on the capital campus downtown."

"I'm a detective," Dave said with a laugh. "I'm sure I can find it."

Matt wondered if that comment had been intended as a joke, but his first thought was that it sounded more like a threat, and maybe it was.

For a long time after Matt put down the phone, he sat there and considered his options. He could go home and spill the beans to Jenny. He could tell her the whole story, throw himself on her mercy, and hope she would forgive him. Or not.

Around him, other people in the department started leaving the office. A glance at the clock told him that Jenny was still at work. Even if she heard her phone ringing, she wouldn't be able to answer it on the floor. Glad to avoid having to speak to her directly, Matt dialed her number and left a message.

"Something's come up at work," he said. "It's a project that has to be finished in time for a meeting first thing tomorrow morning. So you're on your own for dinner. Sorry about that. And don't bother waiting up for me," he added. "I'll probably be very late."

When Ali returned to the living room, Chris reappeared long enough to say he was leaving. Like his grandfather, Chris had warned her of the dangers of computer worms and viruses. Right at that moment didn't seem like the time to tell him that her computer might have been compromised by an identity thief.

"Where to?" she asked.

"Just out for a burger with the guys." His response seemed a trifle too casual.

"Not with Athena?" Ali asked.

Chris shook his head. "She has papers to grade."

The answer was so quick that Ali wondered if it was true. Was the fact that Chris was on his own for the evening some kind of carryover from the previous night's engagement-party fiasco?

"Want me to bring you something?" Chris added. "I think Mr. Brooks pretty much emptied all the leftovers out of the fridge."

"And probably saved us both from dying of food poisoning," Ali said with a laugh. "Don't worry about me. I'll be fine."

And she was. She turned on her music and fixed herself a container of microwave soup. As she cleared the kitchen, she was careful to dispose of the plastic container in a fashion that would be invisible to her mother, if not to Leland Brooks. As far as Edie Larson was concerned, soup that came in plastic containers wasn't fit to eat.

Ali had just started the dishwasher when the doorbell rang. She went to answer it, expecting to find B. Simpson outside, bringing her a substitute computer. Instead, Athena stood waiting on her doorstep.

"Chris isn't here," Ali said, letting her visitor inside.

"I know," Athena said. "I came to talk to you."

"About last night, I assume," Ali said without enthusiasm.

"Yes," Athena agreed. "It is about last night."

By the time Athena made her way to the couch, Sam was there waiting. As soon as Athena settled down, Sam snuggled up beside her. There was something touching in the way the normally unsociable cat had taken to Athena—as though there was some special connection between these two disfigured beings.

"Look," Ali said. "I'm really sorry about what happened at the party. My mother adores Chris, and she thinks you're terrific. I'm sure she let her natural enthusiasm get a little out of hand, but—"

"I know Chris already bitched Edie out about that," Athena interrupted. "The last thing I want to do is to cause hard feelings between Chris and his grandparents. As far as I was concerned, it wasn't that big a deal—well, maybe it was a little bit of a big deal, but I didn't want him to go to Bob and Edie and make it that much worse."

Time to fess up, Ali thought. "He spoke to my mother at my suggestion," she said. "He told me you were upset, and I thought he needed to get my parents to back off. He may have been less diplomatic than he could have been, but I had said that the two of you should get to do things your way, with nobody else interfering. That goes double for me."

Suddenly, with no warning, Athena burst into tears. "You don't understand," she managed. "Nobody does, not even Chris."

In order to sit down next to Athena, Ali had to pry Sam loose and shoo her out of the way. "What is it?" Ali asked, wrapping a comforting arm around the young woman's heaving shoulder. "What's wrong?"

"How can I explain it to you when I don't really understand it myself?"

"Try me," Ali said.

"You know about Kenny?"

Ali knew a little about Kenneth Carlson, the man who had been Athena's husband. He was also the jerk who had dumped her, filing for a divorce while she had been recuperating from her injuries.

"Some," Ali said, keeping her voice noncommittal.

"We started dating in high school," Athena said. "From our sophomore year on. Our senior year, we were voted most likely to become Ken and Barbie. My folks loved him and still do. As far as they were concerned, Ken was the son they'd never had. His folks loved me the same way, like a daughter. But as we got older, things changed. Or maybe I changed. Ken's a farmer, like his dad. I wanted more than that. I was interested in other stuff, but by then things were already in motion. Both our families—both sides—got all caught up in planning this huge wedding. It was like a moving freight train—the dress, the invitations, the flowers, the whole bit. I knew I was getting cold feet. I wanted to get off the train, to stop it somehow, but I didn't have the nerve. So I went through with the wedding, even though I knew it was wrong. Even though I knew, walking down the aisle, that I didn't really love him the same way he loved me."

Athena paused. Ali, sitting beside her, said nothing. This story was one she recognized all too well. She had allowed herself to be talked into marrying Paul Grayson in much the same way—allowed herself to be persuaded, even though she'd known at the time she was settling for something less than what she'd had with her first husband. Paul had money, position, looks, everything she should have wanted, except for one critical deficit—Paul Grayson wasn't Dean Reynolds. Ali worried that Athena was feeling the same kind of reluctance about her engagement to Chris.

"So I can't really blame Kenny for dumping me," Athena continued finally. "The timing sucked. But he found someone who worships him, someone who's thrilled to be living the farm life the way her mother and grandmother did. I heard a couple of weeks ago that they're expecting a baby. The real problem is, my parents still blame me for everything that happened, including the divorce. They were both dead set against my joining the National Guard, even though that's what paid most of my way through school. My father's old-fashioned. He doesn't think girls should go to war. As far as he's concerned, what happened to me in Iraq is all my own fault. Mom and Dad are both convinced that if I hadn't lost my arm and my leg, Kenny never would have left me for a 'whole woman.'"

"None of us has a problem seeing you as a whole woman," Ali said quietly.

Athena nodded. "I know. Thank you."

"So the only member of your family who's still in your corner is your grandmother?" Ali asked. "The one who flew to D.C. to visit you when you were in the hospital?"

Athena nodded again and wiped her eyes. "Grandma Betsy is my dad's mother, and she's a hoot. You'd really like her."

"What about last night?" Ali prodded gently.

Athena sighed. "That's the thing. I felt like I was back on that same train, the speeding wedding train. Like they say in that old joke, 'Déjà vu all over again.' Chris is great. Your folks are great. So are you, for that matter, but when I saw the food, all I could think about was that huge wedding. My parents were so excited to do it, and they spent money they couldn't afford, because they wanted to do it right. And that's why I wanted the party to be small—why I needed it to be small."

"In case you needed to pull the emergency brake and stop the train, you could," Ali said.

Athena sniffed, blew her nose, and nodded again. "But I didn't mean to make it Chris's problem, and I certainly didn't mean for him to have a big falling-out with his grandparents over it. I mean, the party was more than I wanted, but I know Bob and Edie were only trying to help."

"Don't worry about them," Ali said, patting the back of Athena's hand. "They've had some dealings with temperamental brides in their time. When Chris's father and I were getting married, I was a lot like you. The last thing I wanted was a big wedding. At the time, my mother was determined to 'do the whole thing up brown,' as my father would say. Dean and I responded to all the parental pressure by eloping to Vegas. It wasn't one of those drive-through ceremonies, but close.

"So all these years later, my mother's still walking around singing those 'I missed the big wedding' blues. As soon as Chris admitted popping the question to you, she went off the deep end. She figured this was her last chance at a big production-number wedding. But that's her problem, Athena, not yours. If Edie Larson wants a big wedding, maybe she and Dad should plan a whole formal renewal-of-vows hoopla for their fiftieth—which isn't all that far off, by the way. But for right now, as I told Mom this afternoon, we all need to back off. We're doing things your way. Period."

"You told her that?"

"Yes, I did."

"Is she upset?"

"She was upset," Ali replied. "Maybe still is, but she'll get over it."

"What about your dad?"

"What about him? If Mom is over it, Dad is over it," Ali answered. "That's how they work."

For a moment Athena said nothing. "What about Chris's other grandparents?" she asked. "He never mentions them. What happened to them?"

That was the other problem with our wedding, Ali thought. *My parents wanted a huge wedding. Dean's didn't want any wedding at all—at least not to me.*

"Dean's parents disowned him," she said. "They wanted him to come into the family business. He wasn't interested. My family didn't have any money. His did, and they thought that's what I was after—

his money—so they opted out of their son's life completely. That's the other reason we eloped."

"And they never came back?" Athena asked.

Ali shook her head. "Even though Dean asked me not to, I tried getting in touch with them once after he got sick. They never returned my call. I've never forgiven them for it."

"They don't know Chris?"

"No," Ali said. "Not at all."

Athena gave her a wry and still slightly tearful smile. "So at least I'm not the only one with a screwy family."

The doorbell rang again. Athena leaped off the couch. "Sorry," she said. "How rude. You were expecting company, and here I am, messing things up. I need to go."

"Believe me, you're not messing anything up," Ali began, but Athena wasn't listening. She hurried to the front door and flung it open. With a mumbled apology, she hustled past the visitor waiting outside on Ali's front porch.

"That was Athena, my son's fiancée," Ali explained to B. Simpson, who stood there with a roll-aboard computer case stationed behind him. "They had a bit of a disagreement."

"Nothing too serious, I hope," he said.

"No," Ali said. "I think Athena and Chris both have a case of new-engagement jitters."

"If this is a bad time and I'm interrupting, I could always come back later."

This whole encounter was one Ali dreaded, but it had to be done. "No," she said. "Come on in. Let's get this over with."

One by one, the last few stragglers left the building.

Finally, there was no one left but Matt, who sat there agonizing about Detective Holman's phone call and struggling to understand how this unforeseen disaster had come to pass.

In the movies, earth-shattering events happened with the hero stranded on steep, rocky cliffs overlooking roiling seas. Matt had always loved those black-and-white romances from the thirties in which star-crossed lovers would dine together in high-class restaurants where they could say their bittersweet goodbyes, all the while sipping high-toned cocktails or champagne. But Matthew Morrison was no movie-worthy hero. He was just a regular Joe whose downfall had started months earlier in the checkout line at his neighborhood Lowe's.

He had gone there after work with Jenny to pick up some gardening supplies and flats of annuals, mostly petunias and snapdragons, for the pots she liked to keep blooming out on the back patio. As they left the store, Matt did what he usually did: He scanned through the receipt. When he spotted the error—an eighty-seven-cent overcharge on the bottle of slug bait—he had turned on his heel and marched back into the store and back to the cash wrap to have the clerk set it right. It was an error; it needed to be fixed.

As per usual, Jenny was in a hurry. She had been for as long as Matt had known her and for all of the eighteen years they'd been married. She had followed him back into the store, berating him all the way. Despite the long line of strangers at the checkout, she had kept after him the whole time, bitching him out, screeching at him that "only an anal-retentive auditor would waste his precious time and mine for eighty-seven goddamn cents!"

Matt had prided himself on being a good husband. For the whole time they'd been married, he had been unfailingly faithful to Jenny, even though she'd made it clear from the beginning that no matter what Matt did, he would never measure up to her sainted and mercifully deceased father. Matt liked going to work. Compared to what went on at home, work was peaceful and quiet. He had hired on with the state auditor three years after they married. For fifteen years Matt had kept his nose to the grindstone, doing his important but unheralded work in a quietly efficient manner. It bothered him that when it came time for promotions, he was always pushed aside for someone younger—often someone Matt himself had trained—but he never made a fuss about it. That was something Matthew Morrison didn't do: make a fuss.

In all those years and in all situations, he'd kept a mild-mannered smile plastered on his face and done his best to get along. With everyone. Without realizing it, though, he must have been moving ever closer to the edge. And that fateful night, as the clerk counted out Matt's eighty-seven cents' worth of change and with the people in line snickering at him behind his back, something had snapped. After emptying the trunk and carrying Jenny's flats of annuals out to the back patio, he had locked himself in his home office and gone shopping at Singleatheart, a site for "married singles," which, Matt decided, was what he was.

A month or so later, he had found Suzie Q, also a married single, separated from her husband, not interested in a divorce, but wanting to put some fun and joy back into her life. That was what Matt wanted, too—some fun in his life, although for him, it wasn't so much putting it back in as it was having fun for the first time. Ever.

It hadn't worked. He had never actually seen Susan Callison, had never, as they say, laid a glove on her. But as of this afternoon, his whole nonaffair with her had blown up in his face. He was convinced that Suzie Q was dead, and he seemed to be the prime suspect. Tomorrow morning the detective would be here at his office. Would that be for questioning, or would it be worse than that? Was Holman planning to place him under arrest? Right there? In the office? With everyone around them looking on? Matt's insides squirmed at the very idea.

The janitorial crew swept through the floor. Ignoring Matt completely, they emptied trash cans, vacuumed a little, and then went away. Matt knew what he needed to do, but only when he was left alone once more, only when there was no one left to see, did Matt Morrison reach for his keyboard.

{ CHAPTER 10 }

In talking to B. Simpson on the phone, Ali had forgotten how tall he was—six feet five, at least. He wasn't particularly good-looking. His most outstanding feature was a pair of gray-green eyes that seemed to change color depending on the lighting. There was a hint of natural curl in his short brown hair, and the smile he offered was engagingly shy.

"Can I get you something?" Ali asked.

"Nothing," he said. "I find it's best not to eat or drink around computers." Rather than stopping off in the living room, he headed straight for the dining room table, where he deposited the computer bag. "Mind if we set up shop here?" he asked.

"Sure," Ali said. "Go ahead."

He opened the case and began hauling out two separate laptops as well as a whole series of cables and power cords, which he began connecting.

"Why so many computers?" Ali asked.

"Since we have to assume our friend is monitoring your computer at all times, we'll have to do our own file sharing via cables rather than over the Internet. Oh, and I'll need your computer."

With a nod, Ali went to fetch it. When she came back, she couldn't help noticing that a subtle hint of aftershave had permeated the room. *Good stuff,* she thought. *I wonder what it is?*

B. took the laptop from her. After removing her air card, he placed it on the table, where he began connecting the computer into what was by then an impressive tangle of computer cables.

"So here's the thing," he continued, talking as he worked. "High Noon has been looking after your system for over three months now. Until today, other than some relatively harmless adware programs and cookies, there hasn't been anything out of the ordinary. The Trojan horse wasn't there last night during our midnight scan, but it was there today at noon. So I have to ask you the usual clichéd computer troubleshooting question: What were you doing just before that happened? Had you visited any unusual websites, for example, or did you open any attachments this morning, even an attachment from a regular correspondent, from someone you know?"

"I logged on to something called Singleatheart," Ali said.

"What's that?" B. asked.

"An Internet dating site," she replied.

B. stopped what he was doing long enough to give her an appraising look. "If you don't mind my saying so, it doesn't seem to me that you'd have any reason to go looking at one of those."

To her consternation, Ali found herself blushing at his unexpected compliment. "Thank you," she said.

"But it wasn't for me. I was doing it for a friend of mine."

That sounded lame, she thought. *Totally and completely lame.*

"Right," he said, then returned to his cables.

Bob and Edie had left Ali with the impression that B. Simpson was something of a recluse. She wondered if that was true or if it was simply what he wanted people to believe.

"How much do you know about what goes on in town?" Ali asked.

"Not very much," he admitted with a shrug. "I'm more in tune with what's out there on the Web than I am with what's going on down the street. Why?"

"I have a contractor who's working on my house," Ali said. "My new house. His wife, Morgan, was murdered earlier this week, and now Bryan's fallen under suspicion. I learned that his wife had been involved with this Singleatheart website. That made me curious. I logged on because I was trying to find out why a happily married woman would have signed up on a dating service to begin with. The problem is, you can't go there and look around for free. You have to sign up and log on."

To judge from the puzzled look on B.'s face, Ali wasn't sure he was listening to her. "Did you say Bryan and Morgan?" he asked as though the words had just penetrated his consciousness. "Are you by any chance talking about Bryan Forester and Morgan Deming?"

Ali didn't remember hearing Morgan's maiden name, but clearly, B. Simpson had. "Yes," Ali said. "Do you know them?"

"I knew them both," B. replied after a slight pause.

"It was a long time ago, when we were all still in school. I didn't know they'd gotten married, but that's just as well. As far as I'm concerned, they deserved each other."

So you weren't exactly friends, Ali thought. "What do you mean?" she asked.

Again B. didn't answer right away. "Morgan Deming and Bryan Forester were part of the in crowd," he said finally. "For all I know, you were, too, so maybe you don't have any idea how it feels to be 'out.' The people who are 'in' go through school in a kind of Teflon-coated world. Nothing touches them. They get away with all kinds of outrageous stunts while teachers, parents, and coaches turn a blind eye. Bryan and his best pal, Billy, were the ringleaders of a particularly vicious little gang of thugs. I was still called Bart Simpson when I met them. Once *The Simpsons* showed up on TV, I turned into one of their favorite targets. Bryan and the other creeps made my life so miserable that as soon as I could, I took the only option available to me at the time. I quit school, went to Seattle, and never looked back. The day I left Sedona was the happiest day of my life. I couldn't wait to get out of town."

"You said Billy," Ali pointed out. "Which one? Would that happen to be Billy Barnes?"

B. nodded grimly. "One and the same."

"But you're back here now," Ali observed. "Are your folks still here?"

B. shook his head. "My dad died of a heart attack about ten years ago, and my mother went back to Michigan, where she came from originally. She still has family there. So what brought me back to

Sedona? For one thing, it's a beautiful place. I came back because I loved the red rocks, and I missed them. I loved the blue skies, and I missed those, too. I decided that I wasn't going to let a bunch of school bullies keep me from living wherever I wanted. When I did come back, I did it with a whole pile of cash in my pocket and with the ability to be here on my own terms. By choice, I don't have much to do with local yokels. I probably have more day-to-day dealings with your parents than with anyone else in town, and that's pretty much how I like it."

"What about Bryan Forester?" Ali asked.

"What about him?" B. said with a shrug. "I'm sorry to hear his wife is dead. That's too bad, especially if they had kids. But just because I wouldn't walk across the street to say hello to Bryan Forester doesn't mean I wish him ill."

Ali hadn't anticipated that Bryan Forester and B. Simpson would have such a complicated history, but that was what happened in small towns. Inevitably, everyone knew everyone else, for good or ill. Ali would have liked to tell B. about Bryan Forester's difficulties so she could enlist his help and advice on the two thumb drives. Realizing she had inadvertently poked a stick at a hornet's nest, though, she quickly backed away from that idea. She'd have to deal with the thumb drives on her own.

"Unlike you," she said, "I didn't know Bryan Forester in high school. From what you said, it sounds like he was a complete jerk back then. But he's not a jerk now—at least he doesn't seem like one to me. And he doesn't seem like a possible killer, either. As for Morgan? Maybe she never grew up. Apparently, she liked living on the wild side, otherwise she wouldn't have been messing around in places like Singleatheart. But that's why I went there, to try to find out more about it and see if her being involved in the website might have had something to do with her death."

That comment seemed to get B. back to the problem at hand. "So you went to the site and logged on," he said.

Ali nodded. "And paid money—a hundred bucks—to do it."

"You paid with a credit card?"

Ali nodded again.

"That makes sense." B. nodded thoughtfully. "My guess is that someone who works at Singleatheart is capturing the information that comes in to the website and planting the Trojan horse on the computers of people who sign up. That gives him an unending source of information that he can subsequently use in identity theft scams. He may lift money out of an account here or there, or he may use pieces of real names to create what's called a synthetic identity."

"Synthetic identity?" Ali repeated. "How does that work?"

"The bad guy applies for a credit card under a fictitious name, or else he uses the real name and social security number along with a fake address. That generates a file name and address, as far as the various credit-reporting companies are concerned. Once enough action happens on that name, the guy ends up having a real credit report, which makes him real as far as financial transactions are concerned. It makes him good to go, even though he doesn't exist. The synthetic identity can then be used to empty people's bank accounts or run up thousands of dollars in fraudulent credit-card charges."

Ali was stunned. "That's all it takes?"

"That's all," B. said. "People like that are generally cowards. They don't have guts enough to pick up a gun and go out robbing people face-to-face or holding up banks in person. They'd rather do their stealing second- and thirdhand, hiding behind various virtual camouflages. This is your basic white-collar crime. No blood or guts. That's why the cops generally aren't interested."

Finished with his cable connections, B. punched a series of commands into one of the keyboards. The computer screens came to life with pictures of files floating first in one direction and then another.

"Okay," he explained. "What I'm doing here is making a mirror image of your hard drive on this computer so you'll have access to all your files. If you don't want our bad guy seeing everything you're doing, that one will need to stay off the Internet at all times. We'll leave his Trojan intact on your old computer. I'm loading what I call my stalking horse into your online banking folder and into your e-mail folder as well. Use that one selectively, enough that it looks like business as usual. That way, if he tries to access any of your recent e-mail activity or your banking or credit-card information with his computer, we'll be able to infect him. What goes around comes around."

"In other words, we're turning my computer into a mousetrap, and I'm the bait."

"Exactly," B. said.

"But won't these extra programs slow down my computer—and his, too?" Ali asked. "Won't he notice?"

"Have you noticed any difference?" B. asked.

"Not so far."

"Right. With any luck, he may not notice right away, either. I'm hoping we'll be able to hack in to his system long enough to get a fix on some of his other connections. Even if he wises up and deletes our program, I'll have enough details that I'll be able to track back to him through some of the other people he's targeted. He's most likely hiding behind multiple servers and layers of identities that are strung out all over the globe. This isn't going to happen all at once. It's going to take time to find him. Unfortunately, finding him will be just the beginning."

Ali nodded. "Until we find compelling evidence of some illegal activity, there's no sense in turning him over to the cops. Which means we have to wait until he rips me off before we can do anything about it."

"Not entirely," B. returned after a moment.

"What do you mean?"

"There are really two ways of doing this. The one you've just mentioned—using your computer as bait and waiting for him to do something illegal—is the long way around. First we have to catch him; then we have to bring the cops in on it in hopes that eventually, the justice system will dish out some kind of punishment."

"But we both know that with all the jurisdictional considerations, that's not likely to happen," Ali said. "And even if he is convicted, punishment will be minimal. So what's the other way, a shortcut of some kind?"

"You could call it that," B. said. "It comes under the heading of an eye for an eye, and it bypasses the justice system completely."

"You're talking about some kind of vigilante action?"

B. nodded. "These bad-boy geeks think they're so smart that no one will ever wise up to them, so instead of hitting him with my Trojan, I'll nail him with my other secret weapon. Did you ever watch *Voyager* or *Enterprise* or any of those Trekkie series on TV?"

"I suppose so," Ali answered. "Why?"

"Do you remember tractor beams, the things the bad guys used to grab something and drag it back to their mother ship?"

"I guess."

"My pet worm works the same way. I deploy it by putting it on your computer, the one he's targeted. It sits there until he tries logging on to your system. That carries it into his system, where it's programmed to do two things—retrieve all his files and shoot them back to us while it's trashing them on his end."

"We end up with his files?" Ali asked. "Is that legal?"

"Would whatever we retrieved from there be admissible in a court of law?" B. asked. "Probably not. That's what I meant when I said we'd be bypassing the justice system. But I guarantee you, this is some jerk who thinks he's smarter than everyone else, and when we outwit him, he's going to be annoyed as hell. It'll drive him up a wall."

"Driving him up a wall sounds about right," Ali said. "What's the turnaround time?"

"Once I install the worm program on your computer, all it takes is for him to try opening one of your infected files. As soon as he does, it's kerblammo, and his computer system is toast. So it's up to you. I'm happy to do it either way—fast or slow, through legal channels or not. And until we know we've nailed him—I'll know as soon as the worm is deployed—then you should probably operate on an outside computer."

Remembering her father's gunslinger comment, Ali was glad to have B. and High Noon Enterprises on her side. It didn't take long for her to make up her mind. "I'm all for instant gratification," she told him.

B. grinned at her. "So am I," he said.

Once the file transfers were completed, B. began disconnecting his cables and stowing his gear.

"You'll let me know as soon as anything happens?" Ali asked.

"You bet," he said. "Night or day."

B. left a few minutes later. As he drove his Saab out of the driveway, Chris was waiting to enter.

"Who was driving that 9-7X?" Chris asked. "He's got great taste in cars. Which reminds me, you and Dave don't seem to be spending that much time together lately. Is this a new boyfriend, by any chance?"

"Hardly," she answered. "His name's Simpson—B. Simpson."

"Oh, him," Chris said. "I remember now. He's that friend of Grandpa's who's the computer security guru. I didn't know guys like him made house calls."

"He stopped by because he found a Trojan horse on my laptop."

"Whoa!" Chris said. "If you'll pardon the expression," he added with a laugh. "But a Trojan horse? I've heard of them, but where did you pick one up?"

It wasn't lost on Ali that there were certain similarities between having her computer infected with a virus and picking up an STD after an anonymous one-night stand. Not eager to admit to her son about having logged on to an Internet dating site, Ali shook her head. "I'm not sure."

"Still, he stopped by to help you get rid of it?" Chris asked.

"Not exactly," Ali said. "There may be some kind of identity theft scheme at work. He's planting a couple of countermeasures on my computer, and he dropped off one of his spares for me to use as needed in the meantime."

Before Chris could respond, Ali's phone rang. It wasn't late, but it was after nine. Thinking it might be bad news, Ali hurried to answer.

"Is this Ali Reynolds?" an unfamiliar woman asked.

"Yes. Who's this?"

"It's Beverly Forester," the woman answered. "Bryan's mother." Her trembling voice faltered.

"Is something wrong?" Ali asked. "Are you all right?"

"No. We're not all right," Beverly managed, pulling herself together. "We're still at the Best Western. The cops were here a little while ago. They put my son in handcuffs, loaded him into the back of a patrol car, and drove away."

Ali's heart fell. If Dave had gone so far as to place Bryan under arrest, then the evidence he had collected from the back of the truck must have been damning.

"The girls didn't see that," Bev Forester continued. "But they're dreadfully upset that their father isn't here with them right now, and I don't know what to do. Lindsey's crying like her poor little heart's broken. Lacy's locked herself in the bathroom and won't come out. They've been through so much the last few days, but I can't do a thing with them, and right now I'm at my wits' end!"

"I'm sure if you just talked to them—" Ali began.

"I already tried that," Beverly returned. "So did Harold, Bryan's father. He didn't get anywhere, either. We were wondering if we could convince you to come see them."

"I can't see how that would help," Ali objected. "I don't even know them."

"Oh," Beverly said with a disappointed sigh. "Bryan speaks so highly of you, I thought maybe you knew his girls as well."

"I don't, but it's possible I know someone who does," Ali said. "I met their teacher at a function last night. Her name is Mindy Farber. Her roommate is my son's fiancée. Mindy seemed to be concerned about the girls. Maybe she could help."

"Do you have her number?"

"Let me call her and explain the situation," Ali said.

Once off the phone with Beverly, Ali called Athena's number. While Chris listened with considerable interest, Ali enlisted Mindy's help and made arrangements to come get her.

"Thank you for picking me up," Mindy said twenty minutes later as she buckled herself into the Cayenne's passenger seat. "You didn't have to. I know where the Best Western is. I could have driven there myself."

The truth was, Ali wanted to go, too. Bryan Forester was part of her life; so were his girls. If there was anything she personally could do to help them, she would. As a consequence, on the drive there, Ali filled Mindy in with as much background information as she'd been able to piece together.

At the hotel, Ali drove around the building until she spotted Bryan's Dodge Ram. A man smoking a pipe stood leaning against the front bumper. "Mr. Forester?" Ali asked as she stepped out of her car and into the parking lot.

He straightened. "Ms. Reynolds?" he asked. "Thank you for coming. Bev's not very good at this kind of thing. Completely out of her league. I don't know how much more she can take."

"Where is she?"

"Bryan and the girls were staying in the next room over," he said, pointing toward the adjoining door. "I don't know what we're going to do about that tonight. We can't very well leave them there by themselves."

As Ali walked through the low-lying cloud of pipe smoke, Mindy Farber was already knocking on the door. "Come in," Bev Forester called.

As soon as Mindy opened the door, Ali saw a gray-haired woman sitting on the edge of a bed. A little girl lay on the far side of the bed, crying inconsolably. When the woman reached out to touch her, the girl shrank away. The woman stood up, then, wringing her hands, she hurried to meet Mindy.

"She's been like this ever since her father left," Bev Forester said. "What should I do?"

In answer, Mindy walked past her and took Bev's place on the bed. "Lindsey," she said softly. "It's Miss Farber. Are you all right?"

Without warning, Lindsey sat up and flung herself at Mindy and buried her tearstained face in her young teacher's breast. "Did you hear?" she hiccuped through her sobs. "Our mother is dead. Somebody murdered her. I heard some people talking. They were saying that they think Daddy is the one who did it. I wasn't supposed to, but I was peeking out the window when he left. They put handcuffs on him, put him in the back of a car, and drove away. Oh, Miss Farber, if Daddy's in jail, what's going to happen to us? Where will we live? Who will take care of us?"

"Maybe your grandparents—"

"They don't like us," Lindsey sobbed. "They don't like Lacy."

"That's not true," Bev interjected. "Of course we like Lacy, we just don't understand—"

Just then the bathroom door swung silently open. Without so much as a glance in Bev Forester's direction, Lacy emerged from the bathroom. She went straight to the bed and sat down next to her sister. With a dignity that belied her age, Lacy silently took one of Lindsey's hands and held it tightly with both of hers while two fat tears tumbled down her own cheeks.

Ali knew Lacy to be a troubled child. Her willingness to emerge from the bathroom in hopes of comforting her grieving sister seemed like a display of raw courage.

Mindy Farber was already holding Lindsey. Ali worried that if Mindy tried to draw Lacy into the same hug, she'd once again withdraw. Mindy must have sensed the same thing. She continued to cradle Lindsey but made no effort to reach for Lacy.

"I don't know the answers to any of those questions," Mindy said softly to both girls. "But I do know this much: Wherever you are, I'm sure you'll be together."

Ali held her breath. The words were simple enough to say, but if, for some reason, Bryan's folks were unable to care for the girls and Child Protective Services stepped into the picture, Ali knew that promise might not be easily kept. Where the girls would end up then was anybody's guess.

While Mindy Farber dealt with the two girls, Ali took Bev by the arm and led her outside, where she sank into her husband's arms and burst into tears herself. "What are we going to do?" she asked him. "The girls don't know us, really. Lacy especially refuses to have anything to do with us. How are we going to manage, Harold? And what will become of Bryan?"

"I've got a call in to Mitch," he said. To Ali, he added, "Mitch Gunn used to be our attorney when we lived here. I left him a message. So far he hasn't called back."

"Is Mitch Gunn a criminal defense attorney?" Ali asked.

"I'm not sure what his specialty is. Mitch has handled business agreements as well as our wills—that kind of thing," Harold Forester said. "Up till now, that's the only legal help we've ever needed."

"If your son has been arrested for murder," Ali told the Foresters, "he's going to need a lot more than that."

"If you know someone who would be better, tell us," Harold said. "Whatever it costs, we'll find the money. We have to. He's our son."

In the past several years, a series of tough circumstances had forced Ali to retain a whole series of defense attorneys, all of whom had proved reasonably effective. The first one, however, a local named Rick Santos, had been by far the most affordable. Once Harold Forester was on the line with Rick, Ali went back into the girls' room, where Mindy Farber had somehow convinced Lindsey and Lacy to don pajamas and climb into bed.

"Are you going to stay with us?" Lindsey asked her teacher.

Mindy shook her head. "Not overnight. Your grandparents will be here with you. I have to go home so I can get ready for school in the morning."

"Can we go back to school, too?" Lindsey asked. "I hate being here. So does Lacy. It's boring. There's nothing to do."

Bev Forester had followed Ali into the room. "Of course you can't go back to school," she announced. "Not right now. Not until after the funeral on Friday. What would people think?"

Mindy turned to Bev. "These girls are seven," she said quietly. "It doesn't matter what people think. Let them come back to school, Mrs. Forester. Their whole lives have been disrupted. Going to school will give their days some structure. It will also give them something familiar to think about besides what's happened to them."

"But—" Bev began.

"Please, Grandma," Lindsey interrupted. "Please let us."

"She's right," Harold told his wife from the doorway. "They'll be better off at school than stuck here with us all day long, worrying or else watching CNN."

"What's a funeral?"

At first Ali thought Lindsey was the one who had asked the question, but then she saw Lindsey turn toward her sister in drop-jawed amazement.

"What?" Lindsey said.

"What's a funeral?" Lacy repeated.

Lacy's unprecedented excursion into the verbal world may not have surprised her sister, but it had left all the adults in the room dumbstruck. Mindy Farber was the first to recover.

"A funeral is like a church service," she explained. "Funerals are held when people die. They give the people who are left behind a chance to say goodbye. This one will be for your mother."

"But I don't want to say goodbye," Lacy said. With that, she rolled away from them and covered her head with her pillow, signaling with some finality that her brief conversation was over.

Lindsey was determined. She turned back to her grandmother. "So can we go to school or not?" she asked.

"We'll see," Bev said, but Ali could tell the woman was wavering. So could Mindy.

"Tomorrow, then," Mindy said, patting Lindsey's shoulder as she stood to leave. "See you there."

When Mindy and Ali exited the room a few minutes later, Bev Forester followed. "You had no right to say that," she sputtered. "You had no right to tell the girls that you'd see them tomorrow."

"Did you happen to notice a miracle just happened?" Mindy demanded in return, rounding on the older woman. "Your granddaughter, who has never spoken a single word in my hearing, suddenly said something—something important. She's not ready to say goodbye, and not just to her mother, either. She's not ready to say goodbye to life as she knew it. Please let the girls come to school tomorrow."

"But what if some of the other kids say something to them?" Bev objected. "What if they tease the girls or make fun of them?"

"No doubt the kids will say something," Mindy

agreed. "Ours is a small school, and what happened on Monday was and is very big news. By tomorrow people will probably know that the girls' father is in custody. But Lacy and Lindsey will be better off if they start dealing with comments—kind or unkind—earlier rather than later. That's also part of saying goodbye."

"I'll take them," Harold said, cutting short the discussion. "What time does school start?"

"Eight-thirty."

"All right, then," he said. "The girls will be there. I'll drive them there myself." He turned to his wife. "Now, you go on to bed, Bev. The manager's going to bring down a roll-away bed. I'll be here with the girls in case they wake up."

Shaking her head, Bev disappeared into the other room while Ali and Mindy headed for Ali's Cayenne.

"You were really good with the girls," Ali said. "With both of them."

"Thank you," Mindy said. "But what's going to happen after tonight? If their father ends up going to prison, what will happen to the girls? The grandfather's probably okay, but the grandmother? Yikes!"

"From what Bryan Forester said to me, I doubt his mother is very good with little kids under the best of circumstances, which these definitely are not," Ali said. "Bev's daughter-in-law has been murdered, and her son has been placed under arrest. We should both try to cut the woman some slack."

"And I'll do what I can for the girls when they come to school tomorrow," Mindy added.

"Exactly," Ali said.

When she pulled up in front of Mindy and Athena's apartment, there were no lights on inside, but Chris's

Prius was parked on the street out front. "It looks like the lovers got over their little spat," Mindy said with a laugh as she opened the door to step out of the vehicle. "Thanks for the ride."

"And thanks for all the help," Ali said. "I don't know how Bev and Harold Forester would have managed if you hadn't been there."

Once Mindy had gotten out, as Ali drove on, she found herself thinking about her mother. Ali had always admired and envied Edie's ability to do the right thing in the face of any crisis. Well, almost any crisis. The uproar over the engagement party counted as a major exception to her mother's otherwise unblemished record.

Ali had been operating on pure instinct when she'd invited Mindy Farber into the fray to help deal with Lindsey and Lacy Forester. It had turned out to be the right thing to do. *Maybe I'm my mother's daughter after all,* she thought.

It wasn't until she was back at the house that she remembered the thumb drives. But having just had a serious lesson in computer security, she was no longer willing to insert either one of them into the backup computer B. had lent her. If the virus on her computer had come from Singleatheart, wasn't there a good chance that Morgan Forester's files had also been infected? Before doing something potentially damaging to B.'s computer, she would have to bring him into the picture.

She was in bed and ready to turn off the lights when Chris came home a little after one. He tapped on her door and then entered the bedroom, where he perched on the edge of Ali's bed. "I went to see Athena," Chris said.

Ali nodded without saying that she knew as much.

"We talked," Chris added. "And I think we got some things straightened out; we came to an understanding."

"That's good," Ali said.

"I'm glad you told Athena about you and my father running away to Vegas to get married. She liked that."

"Your grandmother didn't like it," Ali replied. "She still doesn't."

"That's all right," Chris said. "Just knowing about it made Athena feel better, and that made me feel better. So thanks for the good advice, Mom."

"You're welcome."

He glanced at his watch and made a face. "Now I'd better get to bed," he said. "First period is going to come very early."

Ali lay awake for a long time after Chris closed her bedroom door. Athena had told him that she and Ali had discussed the situation with Bob and Edie, but Ali was well aware that in telling the story to Athena, she had neglected to finish mentioning what had gone on with Chris's other grandparents—with Angus and Jeanette Reynolds of Boston, Massachusetts.

For years Ali had managed to keep any remembrance of them locked away. She had never forgiven them for turning their backs on their only son. Even now she couldn't imagine how they could have done such a thing. Angus was an attorney with some big law firm, and he had been offended when Dean had spurned the idea of his going to law school in favor of getting a Ph.D. in oceanography, of all things! That, combined with Dean's decision to marry Ali, had been enough for them to walk away. For good.

Once Dean had been diagnosed with glioblastoma,

Ali had tried to get him to contact them, but he'd proved to be his father's son. He had adamantly refused to take the first step in trying to effect a reconciliation. And after that one abortive phone call, Ali hadn't tried again either.

There were several times while Chris was growing up when he had asked about his "other" grandparents. Ali had told him he didn't have any, and that was the truth. He didn't. But tonight, pondering Athena's complicated family situation, Ali couldn't help thinking about her own. Whatever had become of Dean's parents? *Are they dead or alive?* Ali wondered.

What would Angus and Jeanette Reynolds think if they saw their grandson now, a grown, good-looking man who was almost a mirror image of their long-dead son?

Do they ever regret what happened back then? Ali wondered as she drifted off to sleep at last. *And do I?*

{ CHAPTER 11 }

As usual, Peter had played a round of golf at the Biltmore on Wednesday afternoon with a couple of other docs who also had Wednesday afternoons off. They'd had drinks and dinner afterward. When he'd come home, he had tumbled into bed fairly early— into bed but not into sleep.

The whole time he'd been out golfing and buddying around, thoughts of Ali Reynolds had lingered in the background. Now he found himself tossing and turning and thinking about her again. He was convinced she was a problem. The question was, how serious a problem—major or minor?

It would have helped if Peter had known what had brought Ali Reynolds to Singleatheart in the first place. Had she logged on for the same reasons most other people did—because she was lonely and looking for a date? Sedona was a small town. Peter assumed it was possible that Morgan and Ali were good enough friends that Morgan, as a satisfied Singleatheart customer, had referred this Reynolds woman to the website so she could join in the fun and games. Or was that wishful thinking on Peter's part?

Several things gave him cause for concern: Ali's alleged tendency to be a crimefighter; her license to carry; and most of all, her long-term relationship with Morgan Forester's widower. Since she was one of Bryan Forester's customers, the far more likely scenario was that she had learned about Morgan's involvement with Singleatheart through him. If Bryan was under suspicion for his wife's murder—as Peter most certainly hoped he was—it made sense that Ali had visited Singleatheart while snooping around on his behalf.

It was well after midnight before Peter drifted off to sleep. He did so only after deciding that he would take another serious look at Ali Reynolds first thing in the morning. By logging on to her computer and seeing what she was up to, he'd be able to ascertain whether or not she posed a threat to him. If she didn't, fine. If she did? That was another matter. In that case, Peter would find a way to take care of the problem—forever.

Once Belinda Helwig became Arizona's auditor general, she was determined that she and everyone on her staff would lead by example. Worried that too many state-funded employee hours were being squandered on personal Internet activity, Ms. Helwig had instituted and enforced a comprehensive workplace ban on personal e-mails.

Matt Morrison was someone who always strove to be an exemplary employee. Under normal circumstances, he wouldn't have dreamed of violating that particular rule, but these were desperate times for him. As such, they called for desperate measures.

In their phone conversation earlier, Detective Holman had mentioned the dead woman's name. Unfortunately, Matt had been in such a state of shock that he hadn't been paying close enough attention. It seemed to him now that the name started with an M, but he couldn't remember exactly. Whatever the name was, he hadn't recognized it.

Once he was off the phone, Matt had sat numbly in his cubicle, staring at the shoulder-high walls and mulling his plight. The detective may have called the dead woman by another name, but she had to be Susan Callison.

As the hours passed, Matt called into question everything he knew or thought he knew about Suzie Q. She had claimed to be separated from her husband and had said she lived in Glendale. Now Matt wondered if any of that had been true. According to Detective Holman, the dead woman had been married and living near Sedona. Where did that leave Matt? Out on the end of a limb, while Detective Holman, armed with a chain saw, was ready to lop it off.

From the time Matt's mother had first put a red Crayola in his hand, he had done his best to color inside the lines. Fearing disgrace, he had always played it safe and had never taken chances. Not until Monday. But now disgrace was coming anyway. Matt knew he wasn't guilty of murdering anybody. Surely, with the help of someone, somewhere, he'd be able to prove that, no matter what phony evidence the cop had manufactured about him. But in order to prove his innocence, Matt knew he would end up losing everything else. Jenny would know he had been unfaithful—at least he had tried to be. Their friends at church would know all about it, and so would everyone at work.

That was particularly galling. Work had always been Matt Morrison's safe haven. No matter how tough things were at home, he'd always been able to escape by going to work. Once word about this got out, though, he knew what would happen. Everyone in the office would recognize Matthew Morrison for the loser he was. They'd laugh about him behind his back and whisper about him before and after he left the break room. It would be like the checkout line at Lowe's—only worse.

So Matt set out on a course of action that he hoped would spare him some of that humiliation. It might spare Jenny some ugliness as well. He did it the way Matt Morrison did everything—in a thorough and organized fashion.

First he brought up his folder of Suzie Q correspondence. One at a time, he went through all the e-mails that had come and gone between them, reading each message as he went. The ones that hurt the most weren't the ones at the beginning, when they'd been testing the waters, or the plaintive ones he'd written to her this week after she hadn't written back. No, the ones that made his heart ache were the ones in the middle of their not-quite-affair, the sweet-nothing silly notes from when they had both believed—well, both had *claimed* to believe—in a future that had included the tantalizing promise that somehow, someday, the two of them would be together, living a happily-ever-after existence.

Matt read through the messages and remembered how he had felt when he read those miraculous words the first time—remembered how they had buoyed him and given him hope. Now, once the words had been committed to memory, he deleted each and every one of them. When the messages were gone, Matt went to his buddy list and deleted Suzie Q's name. He didn't doubt that cops, armed with a search warrant, would be able to obtain the deleted messages from the server, but he was hoping they wouldn't bother.

With a sigh, Matt turned off his computer. He put away the files he'd been working on earlier. He straightened his desk. He returned the stapler he'd borrowed from Bobbie Bacon. Once his cubicle was in order, Matt was ready to head home. He knew it was time, but he also knew there was no hurry.

On his way out of the building, he stopped off in the men's room. There, standing behind the closed door of a stall, he removed the condoms and the packet of little blue pills from their hiding place in the back of his wallet. He was dismayed that it took a series of several flushes before the plastic-wrapped containers disappeared down the toilet.

He spoke pleasantly to the security guard at the desk in the downstairs lobby. Out in the parking lot, Matt retrieved his '96 Corolla from the employee lot and then meandered east toward home. Traveling on surface streets rather than hitting the freeways, he stopped at a 7-Eleven on Indian School long enough to fill the gas tank and buy two pint bottles of Baileys.

He opened one of the bottles while he was still parked at the gas pumps. Swallowed straight, the stuff was so cloyingly sweet that he almost gagged, but he managed to keep it down. He hadn't had anything to eat since lunch, so the booze hit him hard. Not wanting to be picked up on a DUI, he waited until he was at Scottsdale Road and North Chaparral before he took his next big swig. It was important that there be enough booze in his system to blur the lines between deliberate and accidental. The trick was being able to show an intent to get drunk without an intent to do anything else.

When Matt pulled up in front of his house, he was relieved to see that all the interior lights had been turned off. Jenny wasn't the kind of person who would leave a porch light burning on those rare occasions when he came home later than she did. The darkness inside meant she was fast asleep. Considering her snoring problem, he doubted that his opening and closing the garage door would disturb her in the slightest.

He drove into the painstakingly neat two-car garage and parked the faded blue Corolla next to Jenny's much shinier '05 Acura. Once the garage door had closed behind him, he put the car in park and engaged the emergency brake. Leaving the engine running, he reached for the bottle again and took several more quick swallows, one after the other. As the stuff slid down his throat, he started to feel the buzz. That was good. So was having a full tank of gas.

Leaning against the headrest, Matt wondered how long it would take. It would be better for all concerned if it was over long before Jenny woke up. She usually staggered out of bed around seven or so and came scrounging out to the kitchen in search of her first cup of coffee. Matt knew there would be far less fuss and bother if there was no chance of reviving him when she opened the door and found him. Things were going to be bad enough for her that Thursday morning. He didn't want to make the situation any worse.

The first bottle of Baileys was entirely empty, and the second was mostly so by the time he started feeling more drowsy than drunk. It took several tries before he was able to twist the cap back on the bottle, but he managed it.

Good, he thought dreamily. *No sense in spilling what's left and making a mess.*

Ali's phone rang at five to six, dragging both her and the cat out of a sound sleep. Samantha left the foot of the bed in a huff while Ali groped for her phone.

"We have a bingo," B. announced triumphantly. He sounded wide awake and amazingly chipper.

Ali was not. "A what?" she grumbled.

"A bingo," he repeated. "Our bad guy tried logging on to your e-mail account a little while ago. I'm pretty sure we nailed him."

"And you collected all his files in the process?"

"I think so," B. said. "And if he had to sit there and watch his computer die, he's probably not a happy camper at the moment."

Ali made the effort to sound a little less grumpy. "That's great," she said. "So does that mean I can use my own computer again?"

"Probably," B. said. "If I were him, I'd have learned from my mistake. I doubt very much that he'll be trying to invade your computer files again anytime soon. He won't want to risk damaging a second computer."

"So we're done, then?" Ali asked.

"Not by a long shot," B. said. He sounded focused and energized. "I'm a little surprised it was that easy. I would have thought he'd do more about securing his own equipment. He does have a fairly sophisticated encryption code. I'm working on breaking that in hopes of getting a look at his files."

"What are you hoping to find?" Ali asked.

"We managed to stop him before he could do any real damage to you, but there may be others who weren't as lucky—people who maybe don't yet know they've been victimized. If we can find them and let them know what's going on, we may be able to bring law enforcement in on this after all."

Now that the crisis with her own computer had been averted, Ali found that idea appealing. "In other words, now that we've had our immediate gratification, we'll let someone else take a crack at him."

"Exactly," B. agreed. "In the meantime, I'm hoping that having access to his files will give us some clues about who this guy is and where he lives."

"Any ideas on that?" Ali asked.

"My first guess would be that he's one of the employees on the Singleatheart server farm in South Dakota—some low-level minimum-wage guy who figured out how to circumvent the system. I'll start by doing some unofficial background checks on a few of those folks and see if anything jumps out at me."

"How?" Ali asked. "Will you ask the cops for help?"

B. chuckled. "Are you kidding? There are background checks, and then there are underground background checks. For what I do, the second one is far more useful, and those will have to wait until later. Right now I have all my computer power working on breaking that encryption code. And since my computers can churn out algorithms without any help from me, I'm on my way to bed."

Having just abandoned her own, Ali was a little

surprised. "You're going to bed at six o'clock in the morning?"

"What I do crosses international datelines, so local time zones tend to fade into the background," he replied. "I sleep when I'm tired, eat when I'm hungry, and don't punch a time clock."

"Luckily for me," Ali said. "And thank you for this good news, but are you sure it's safe to use my computer?"

"Relatively safe," B. told her with a laugh. "From that one source, at least. It doesn't mean someone else won't try to pull the same stunt, but you can rest assured that if there's another problem, it'll show up on my system as well."

"Good night, then," Ali said. "Or should I say good morning? Sleep well."

Fully awake, she scrambled out of bed and reached for her robe. Out in the kitchen, the coffee grinder howled into action as Chris started brewing fresh coffee. She followed the heady aroma into the kitchen, where she found her son looking questioningly at the two computers and the two thumb drives that still littered the dining room table.

"What happened with all the computer drama?" Chris asked.

"Thanks to B. Simpson, good has prevailed," Ali replied. "When whoever it was tried to access my e-mail account early this morning, our worm knocked him out and collected all his files in the process."

"Way to go," Chris said admiringly.

While Ali waited for the coffeepot to finish, she sat down at the table. Her old computer, left on as bait, clicked with a new mail announcement. Reassured that whoever had been spying on her had been taken offline, Ali was relieved to see a familiar name in the address line—Velma T, her longtime correspondent from Laguna Niguel.

Dear Babe,

I've had the most wonderful surprise, but now I'm in a bind and don't know what to do about it. You maybe remember that earlier this year, when I went on that long trip, I met up with a wonderful lady from Oak Harbor, Washington, Maddy Watkins. She just sent me an e-mail that she wants to come down to see me over Thanksgiving. I think she's really trying to get away from her kids, but that's another story.

The problem is, I had just told you that I'd come to your place for Thanksgiving, and now I don't know what to do. I've never been to Sedona, and after you brought it up, I had my heart set on coming to see you. Should I e-mail Maddy and tell her not to come or what?

Velma T in Laguna

Ali sent off an immediate reply.

The more the merrier. Invite her to come here. Will she be coming from Seattle, or will she be coming with you? Please let me know so I can make suitable travel and room arrangements for you.

After punching send, Ali reached over, absently picked up one of Bryan Forester's thumb drives, and held it in her hand. She had fallen asleep the night before while still wondering what to do about them. Now that B. had cleared the way, Ali felt she could risk looking at them on her own computer. If there happened to be another computer virus lurking in the background of Morgan's files, Ali could be reasonably sure that she wouldn't be putting B.'s equipment at risk. And since there was no love lost between Bryan Forester and B. Simpson, it was a relief to Ali that she wouldn't have to ask for B.'s help in dealing with the Foresters' situation.

She was about to insert the drive when the doorbell rang. *Company?* she thought. *At six-thirty in the morning?*

Except what she found waiting on her front porch wasn't company at all. It was Leland Brooks, lugging a humongous carpet-cleaning machine. "What are you doing here so early?" she wanted to know.

"Sorry," he said apologetically, wrestling the machine through the front door. "I thought I mentioned it to you last night. It turns out everyone else is trying to get ready for Thanksgiving company, too. They told me I could use this today on the condition that I have it back by nine A.M., when it's booked to go out again."

Sam took one look at the load of equipment and bolted for the relative safety of the laundry room, where she would no doubt squeeze herself behind the dryer and then need to be coaxed out with offers of food. For right now, however, it was a good place for her.

Chris emerged from his room dressed for school. He paused in the kitchen long enough to fill his coffee cup. "Good morning, Leland," he said. "I hope you're not planning on doing any cleaning down in my studio."

"Let's see," the butler said. "Would your studio happen to be the source of all the metal filings and BBs I vacuumed out of the carpet yesterday afternoon?"

Chris's metal sculptures did leave behind a certain amount of debris. He looked slightly crestfallen. "Yes," he admitted. "I suppose so."

"In that case," Leland replied, "since I expect to do a thorough job of cleaning the carpet, you can also expect that I will clean your studio. There's not much sense in doing one without the other. You can also rest assured that I'll put everything back where I found it, which won't necessarily be where it belongs."

It was a statement that brooked no disagreement. "Right," Chris said, backing down. "I'll get out of your way, then."

Ali concealed a grin behind her coffee mug. She had already learned that when it came to cleaning, Leland Brooks was not to be denied. Chris was coming to that same conclusion.

"Why don't I get out of your way, too?" Ali offered. "I'll get dressed and go have breakfast with my parents."

As someone accustomed to taking full advantage of other people's lax computer security measures, Peter Winter was surprisingly blasé about his own. His dealings with Singleatheart were concealed through multiple layers of identity that protected him. For his personal computer, he employed a sophisticated encryption routine, but for the most part, he didn't worry about it. People like Matt Morrison and his ilk were nothing but chumps, and Peter was willing to bet this Ali Reynolds woman was the same—stupid beyond bearing.

By five A.M. on Thursday morning, after a restless night, Peter took his cup of coffee over to the desk and sat down at his computer. The little notes people sent back and forth to their friends and relations often gave away much more than they knew. And that was where he went—straight to Ali Reynolds's computer and her e-mail records.

The moment he tried to log on to Ali's e-mail account, however, something strange happened. The egg timer showed up and stayed there. After a moment or two, he tried control/alternate/delete, but nothing happened. The egg timer wouldn't go away. And that was when he knew he'd been hacked. His computer froze up. He knew that even unplugging the damn thing would accomplish nothing. As soon as the power was restored, the inevitable destruction would continue. For the next three minutes, unable to stop the slow but inexorable process, he sat and watched helplessly to the end, until the words FATAL ERROR flashed across his screen.

Full of impotent fury, Peter watched his computer's death throes and worried that his whole house of cards was about to tumble down around him. It wasn't just his computer. He could replace that. Though it would take time, eventually, he'd be able to reconstruct the passwords and most of the files. But he couldn't do it right then. What left him feeling half sick was that someone—a woman, no less—had been smart enough and had gotten close enough to him to do this kind of damage. And she'd had balls enough to hit him where he lived. Yes, Peter hacked in to other people's systems all the time, most recently, that hopeless asshole Matt Morrison's. But to Peter's knowledge, this was the first time anyone had ever hacked him. Turnabout definitely wasn't fair play.

Who the hell is this bitch? he wondered. *How dare she do this, and what makes her think she can get away with it?*

Slamming away from his desk, Peter headed for the shower. Trying to harness his outrage, he stood under the stream of hot water and considered the problem. Nothing Peter had read about Ali Reynolds had indicated that she was any kind of computer genius. In order to take on the unassailable Peter Winter, he knew she must have had help of some kind—talented and very capable help. That detective friend of hers, maybe? What Peter found most disturbing was that the woman had made no effort to conceal her identity, although clearly the attack had come from her. What did that mean? Was she letting him know she knew everything? And what if she and her helper had somehow managed to gain access to his files or break his encryption code? That would spell utter disaster.

By the time Peter stepped out of the shower, he had settled on a course of action—he'd have to go to Sedona and find her and her helper, too. Fortunately, even without access to his computer, Peter had a good idea where to start looking. He had scanned through a surprising amount of Internet-based Ali Reynolds material the day before and had read about her restoration project on Manzanita Hills Road, which also happened to be where he had located Bryan Forester's truck. If the house was under construction, she probably wasn't living there at the moment, but with any kind of luck, Peter thought he'd be able to decoy her into coming there—alone.

And once he found her? It was pretty clear to him that he'd have to put her out of her misery. After that, it would be time for Peter Winter to exit stage left. He'd had that game plan set up and waiting for a long time, along with several suitable alternate identities. The problem was, he hadn't intended to make use of any of them yet.

Moving deliberately, he dragged two suitcases out of the hallway closet. He packed one with nothing but computer gear—the still-working laptops as well as the dead one. In the other bag he packed clothing, and not much of that, either. Depending on where he ended up, he'd buy whatever he needed. Right now it was important to travel light. He opened his brief-case and made sure he was fully equipped with gloves, scrubs, and duct tape. The last items he placed in the briefcase were the several vials of Versed that he kept at home and at the ready. Experience had taught him that unconscious victims were far less troublesome than those who were able to fight back.

Just before leaving the house, he emptied the safe. The DVD and his collection of false documents went into the briefcase. The key ring went into his pocket. With Alison Reynolds rocking the boat, carrying a cache of phony IDs and precious mementos could prove dangerous, but leaving them behind was even more so. He might find himself in a position where he'd need access to one or more of them. As for the DVD and his collection of rings? He'd carry those with him until he once again had a secure hiding place.

By eight o'clock, Peter was driving north on I-17,

heading toward Sedona. When he called the hospital to let them know he wouldn't be coming in to work that evening, he was already north of Black Canyon City. Careful to keep the right measure of hesitation and concern in his voice, he explained to Louise Granger, the administrator on duty, that he'd just received a distressing phone call from his mother's physician in upstate New York. "My mom's in the ICU in Buffalo," he said. "She may not make it through the day. I'm on my way to the airport right now."

Louise was nothing if not sympathetic. "I'm so sorry to hear that, Dr. Winter," she said. "Is there anything we can do?"

"Cover my shifts in the meantime," Peter said. "I'll be back as soon as I can, but there's no way to tell how long I'll be gone."

"Of course, Dr. Winter," Louise said. "Don't give it another thought."

Thanks, Mom, Peter said to himself as he put down the phone. He hadn't spoken to his mother in over fifteen years, not since she had caught on to the fact that he'd been using forged checks to take money from her account. That tardy discovery had come years after he'd forged her name to countless excuses and permission slips all through junior high and high school. When the subject of families came up, he usually told people that his mother bounced back and forth between her condo in Florida and her home in upstate New York. That wasn't true, of course. She'd been dead for a long time.

He'd seen to it.

By the time Ali emerged from the bedroom, Leland had the noisy carpet cleaner up and running. Ali grabbed her computer, the power cord, and the two thumb drives and headed for the Sugarloaf Café. It was cold and spitting snow as she started down Andante Drive. When she reached the Sugarloaf parking lot, her nose was assailed by the unmistakable aroma of freshly baked sweet rolls.

Edie met her at the door. "You're up bright and early," she said.

In answer, Ali held up her computer. "I'm looking for office space," she said. "Leland Brooks is cleaning carpets."

Edie generally disapproved of people who used her tables for anything other than eating, but the restaurant wasn't crowded, and she cheerfully led Ali to a booth in the back.

"I know the drill," Ali said. "I'll close down and move along if it gets too crowded. In the meantime, I'll settle for coffee."

Once the computer booted up, Ali extracted the two thumb drives from her jacket pocket. The two drives looked exactly alike, and neither of them was labeled. The first one she inserted into her computer turned out to be Bryan's. Ali had no difficulty searching through his various files and folders. The internal passwords that had been installed in his programs worked as though the files were being opened by Bryan on his own computer.

As far as Ali could see, everything was work-related and as dry as dust. There were immense files that held nothing but computerized architectural drawings. The saved e-mail file consisted mostly of back-and-forth correspondence between Bryan and his various suppliers or customers. Some of the e-mails concerned projects that were still at the planning or construction stage, along with others that had been completed.

Ali remembered Morgan's video complaint about her husband—that the man worked too hard and wasn't any fun. From what Ali could see, he appeared to be guilty as charged. If he had any interests or pursuits outside work, they weren't apparent in his computer files.

"Okay if I sit down?" Dave Holman asked. "Your mother thought you might not mind sharing."

Having lost track of time, Ali looked around and was surprised to find that the restaurant had filled up while she was perusing Bryan's files. Dave Holman, coffee cup in hand, was standing next to her booth.

"Of course," she said, closing the computer and setting the Mac down on the banquette next to her. "Have a seat."

Dave slid into the booth opposite her. "I stopped by your place earlier, looking for you," he said. "Mr. Brooks told me I could probably find you here."

"You stopped by before seven A.M.?" Ali demanded.

"Before eight," Dave corrected. "But I need to talk to you, Ali." His serious expression worried her.

"What about?" Ali asked.

"I know that when it comes to the Forester situation, the two of us are on opposite sides of the fence," he said. "I hope you'll consider this more of a courtesy call than anything else."

"What do you mean?"

"Look," he said with a sigh. "Morgan Forester is dead, and it's my job to find out what happened to her, even if I end up having to step on your toes."

"My toes?" Ali asked. "What are you talking about?"

"It's been brought to my attention that Bryan Forester maintains a storage facility of some kind at your place up on Manzanita Hills Road."

Ali nodded. "He has one of those Mini-Mobile things. He keeps supplies and equipment in it. Why? What does that have to do with me?"

"Now that we know about it, we'll have to search it," Dave said. "And probably the rest of the construction site, too."

"Wait a minute. You're planning on searching my house? Why? What are you looking for?"

"I'm not at liberty to say," Dave said. "To anyone. This is an active investigation."

Before Ali had a chance to say anything more, Edie Larson bustled up to their booth with her order pad in hand. "Ali appears to be drinking coffee and using her computer. Are you here to order, or are you just talking?" Edie asked.

"A little of both," Dave told her. "We'll have breakfast, and when it's time for a bill, give it to me. I'm buying."

{ CHAPTER 12 }

After Edie Larson had finished taking their order and left, Dave picked up the conversation. "I wanted to see you before I left town," he said. "I'm on my way to Phoenix in a couple of minutes. With your help, we've located a possible witness down there."

"My help?" Ali asked.

Dave nodded. "The driver of that vehicle whose license you had Bryan call in to me the other day."

"The car Lacy saw?" Ali asked.

"That's the one," Dave said. "A rental from Hertz. The guy who rented it was from Phoenix. I have an appointment to interview him later on this morning. It could turn out he saw nothing at all, but he played so coy with me on the phone, and that got my attention."

"If he was evasive on the phone, are you thinking he might be involved?" Ali asked.

Dave shook his head. "Forget it," he said. "I probably shouldn't have mentioned him. Right now he's nothing but a potential witness. But after my meeting with him, I'll be stopping by Prescott on the way home. That's when I'll pick up a warrant to search your place on Manzanita Hills Road. We'll be executing it later this afternoon."

"Why are you telling me about this in advance?" Ali asked. "Isn't that a little unusual?"

"It's a lot worse than unusual," Dave admitted. "The sheriff would have my badge if he ever found out about it, but the two of us go back a long way, Ali. I'm letting you know in advance so you can be on-site when we do it. There'll be a lot less chance of damage if someone—you or Mr. Brooks, perhaps—is there to unlock doors with actual keys."

"As in unlock the doors to my house," Ali said.

"It may be your house, but it's also a construction site," Dave explained. "A construction site where our homicide suspect may have concealed evidence of his crime."

"But it's still my house," Ali insisted.

"I know," he said. "I'm sorry."

Dave's regret sounded genuine, but Ali didn't much notice. "Aren't you afraid I might go there before you do and try to get rid of anything incriminating?"

Her sarcasm wasn't lost on him. Dave looked at Ali sadly and shook his head. "No," he said, "I'm not. To begin with, you wouldn't know what to look for. Besides, that's not who you are. You'd never conceal evidence."

Stealing a look at the computer beside her, Ali wasn't so sure about that. She was about to tell him about the two thumb drives when Edie arrived at the booth with their breakfasts—ham and eggs for Dave and French toast for Ali for the second day in a row.

"So will we be seeing you and your girls at Ali's for Thanksgiving?" Edie asked.

Dave looked at Ali. "As far as I know, we haven't been invited. Besides, the girls will be in Vegas with their mom for Thanksgiving. I get all three kids for Christmas."

Knowing she had stepped in it, Edie beat a hasty retreat, leaving Ali to sort out her mother's unintentional gaffe. "Sorry, Dave," she said. "We've both been so busy, and I was waiting to figure out where the dinner would be. But now that we know the new house won't be ready, it'll be at the old one. And you're definitely invited. Are you coming?"

Dave looked at her and grinned. "Depends on who's doing the cooking," he said.

Ali's lack of cooking credentials was well known, but having people continually pointing it out was also a bit tiresome. "That's not fair," she said. "Accurate but not fair. And Leland will most likely be overseeing the food, so no one should die of food poisoning. Will you come, then?"

"I doubt I'll get a better offer," he said. "Count me in."

Lighthearted banter had fixed the momentary awkwardness left behind by the warrant discussion. They started into their food. Dave had managed only a bite of his ham and eggs, and Ali was about to tell him about the thumb drives, when his phone rang.

He put down his fork and answered. "Holman here." Then he listened for a long time while someone else spoke. "What do you mean both hard drives are ruined?" he demanded at last. "How is that possible? You're telling me somebody deliberately crashed the computers before we could execute our warrant?" There was another short pause before Dave went on. "But crashed or not, surely we can find someone smart enough to retrieve the data."

As Dave listened again, Ali tried to make sense of what she had overheard. She was sure that the damaged computers in question, picked up as a result of a search warrant, were the ones that belonged to Bryan and Morgan Forester.

"You're right," Dave was saying. "I can see how writing over the files is worse than just erasing them. Cute. Well, we'll see how funny Mr. Forester thinks this is once I finish up with him. Do you remember that computer-science professor up at Northern Arizona University, the guy we asked for help on that other case a couple of months ago? Yes, that's it. Professor Rayburn. Check with him and see if he has any ideas on how we can go about recapturing the data. With any luck, Bryan Forester isn't nearly as smart as he thinks he is. There's always a chance he missed something."

Shaking his head in disgust, Dave slammed his phone closed and jammed it into his pocket. "What do you know about that!" he muttered. "It seems someone has written over all the files on the Foresters' computers. And whoever did it thought he was being incredibly cute—he wrote the same letters over and over: H-A, as in ha, ha, ha. That's funny, all right. Funny as hell. You probably think your friend Bryan is downright hilarious."

"Bryan wouldn't do that," Ali said quietly. She realized as soon as she'd said it that it was absolutely true. Why would Bryan go to so much trouble when he knew there were perfectly usable and readable backup copies available, copies that were, even now, within arm's reach of Dave Holman? Someone else might have done that, but not Bryan.

"You might believe it, but I don't," Dave returned abruptly. "Trust me, there was something incriminating in those files, and I intend to find out what it was."

"I have them," Ali said. "I can show them to you."

Dave stared at her, thunderstruck. "You what?"

"I have Bryan's files, and I've looked at them," she added. "The ones from his computer, anyway. Believe me, Dave, they're all business-related."

"And how is it that you happen to have them?" Dave asked.

"Because Bryan gave them to me. For safekeeping."

"Sure he did," Dave said. "Once he took out whatever it was he didn't want you or anybody else to see. What the hell do you see in the guy, Ali? Don't you see what he's up to? He's playing you for a fool."

For the first time, Ali wondered if Dave Holman was jealous. "I can give you copies," she offered.

"Right," Dave said. "Sure you can. Copies of copies with everything he wanted deleted already deleted. Don't bother! It'll be a waste of your time and mine." Shaking his head, he once more yanked his phone out of his pocket and punched in a series of numbers. While he waited for his call to be answered, Ali concentrated on her French toast. She had offered the drives to Dave, and he had turned her down. Now, though, she was thinking about her computer, where Bryan's contaminated thumb drive was parked in her USB port. If a delayed-reaction worm of some kind had corrupted the files on Bryan's and Morgan's computers, would hers be next?

"Yes," Dave was saying into the phone. "This is Dave Holman of the Yavapai County Sheriff's Office. I'm calling for Mr. Morrison. Mr. Matthew Morrison."

That statement was followed by a long pause and a deep frown. "What do you mean, he won't be in today? Is he sick or what? I have an appointment with him scheduled for this morning, and I was calling to see if I could move it to a little later."

There was another pause. "Look," Dave said curtly. "I already said who this is. I'm *Detective* Dave Holman with the Yavapai County Sheriff's Department. And it's urgent that I speak to Mr. Morrison today. No, I don't need to speak to his supervisor, I need to speak to him. All right, then. I'll wait."

While he sat on hold, Dave managed another few bites of breakfast. Then, covering the phone mouthpiece with his hand, he spoke to Ali. "Guess what? It seems that Mr. Morrison, our reluctant witness, has unexpectedly taken the day off work. I wonder if the prospect of having to see me has anything to do with his going AWOL."

Dave turned his attention back to the phone as someone came on the line. "Yes, Mrs. Helwig. I'm not sure why they brought you into this, but yes, that's correct. I'm a homicide detective with the Yavapai County Sheriff's Department. Mr. Morrison is a potential witness in a case I'm investigating . . ."

The person on the other end of the line did some talking, and Dave's face took on a distinctly reddish hue.

"Mrs. Helwig, please slow down. Are you telling me Mr. Morrison is dead?" Even across the table, Ali could hear snippets of a woman's voice—an almost hysterical woman—talking at warp speed.

"When?" Dave asked at last. "And how did it happen?" Finally, he added, "Can you tell me who's doing the investigating?"

Holding his phone between his chin and his shoulder, Dave dragged a tattered notebook out of his shirt pocket and began scribbling in it. "Yes, I have it," he said. "Detective O'Brien with the Scottsdale Police Department. And what's that address again?"

Seconds later, when Dave closed both his phone and his notebook, he looked at Ali and shook his head. "So much for my potential witness," he said. "Matthew Morrison is dead. Sometime overnight he drove his vehicle into his garage, closed the door, and left the motor running. His wife found his body this morning. Just before I called the office looking for him, she had phoned to let them know that he wouldn't be coming in ever again."

As he spoke, Dave was already dialing the next number. "Someone else will have to go to Prescott to pick up that search warrant," he said into his phone. "I'm on my way to Phoenix. Scottsdale, actually. It seems our possible witness or suspect in the Morgan Forester homicide offed himself overnight. Well, so far it seems like suicide, anyway. Right. It's probably a good thing for Bryan Forester that we've still got him under lock and key. Otherwise he might be declared a suspect in a second homicide."

There was another long pause. "No!" he exclaimed. "You can't be serious. They're actually thinking about cutting him loose? Who came up with that lamebrained idea? All right, then, if they do let Forester out, I want someone on his tail every step of the way. I want to know where he goes and who he talks to. I also want you to amend that warrant request to include his telephone records. If there's any kind of connection between him and the guy who's dead down in Phoenix,

I want to know about it. He may have been able to do a clean sweep of his computer, but his phone records won't be as easy to destroy."

Dave hung up and took one last slug of coffee. Between phone calls, he had eaten very little. Leaving most of his food, he slapped a twenty-dollar bill down on the table. "Tell your mom to keep the change," he said. "I've gotta go." With that, he dashed out the door.

Edie came back over to the table after he left. "Sorry about the Thanksgiving thing. I really stepped in it. Is that why Dave went racing out of here like that, or was there something wrong with the food?"

"The food was fine," Ali said. "And there's no problem about Thanksgiving. Dave's on his way to Phoenix. Something happened to one of his potential witnesses."

"I wonder if they've had any luck in finding Morgan's ring," Edie said.

"What ring?" Ali asked. "What are you talking about?"

"Morgan's wedding ring," Edie answered. "And the three-carat diamond engagement ring that was with it. I heard they're both missing."

"They weren't found on the body?"

Edie shook her head. "Nope. One of the cops was asking Cindy Martin about them last night. Cindy always did Morgan's nails, and the cops wanted to know if Morgan was wearing her rings the last time she came into the salon—which she was, by the way. Cindy said she never went anywhere without them."

"So people are thinking that the killer stole her rings?"

Edie shrugged. "Cindy says she's heard that Bryan is really hard up for cash right now."

"So now she's suggesting that Bryan made off with his wife's rings in hopes of what—pawning them and realizing some quick cash?"

"It's just a theory," Edie said. "People are entitled to their opinions."

"And I'm entitled to mine!" Ali returned. "What else are people saying?"

"There's evidently some talk about possible drug use. I guess there was a puncture wound of some kind found on the body. The cops asked Cindy if Morgan Forester ever used drugs of any kind. Cindy said that if that had been the case, she for sure would have known about it."

Did she know about Singleatheart? Ali wondered. *If she had, she would have spilled her guts about that, too. Remind me never to set foot in Cindy Martin's salon.*

"Look, Mom," she said. "I don't think we should be discussing any of this."

"Why not?"

"For one thing, these sound like confidential details of a homicide investigation."

"But Cindy—"

"Cindy talks too much," Ali declared.

As Edie went to deliver coffee to another table, Ali was left thinking about the series of ha-has that had been written over every one of Bryan Forester's computer files. If Bryan wasn't responsible for destroying his own computer files, who was? Someone who had no idea Bryan had backups. Ali was equally sure Dave was right about one thing—the culprit, whoever it was, had something to hide. And that was when it came to her for the very first time that there might be some connection between the guy who had infiltrated Ali's computer and Morgan Forester's killer.

Maybe what Ali and B. had been dealing with was something far more deadly than a simple identity thief. Lost in thought, Ali removed Bryan's thumb drive from her computer. She needed to warn B. about that, and much as she had wanted to avoid doing so, she also knew that she would have to ask him for help with the possibly contaminated thumb drives.

Ali glanced at the clock on the far wall. She had spoken to B. on the phone under three hours earlier, and he'd been on his way to bed, but the urgency of the situation meant she needed to talk to him sooner than later. When she called, though, his line went straight to voice mail, so she left a message. When her cell phone rang a few minutes later, she more than half expected to hear B.'s voice on the line. She didn't.

"This is Haley Marsh's grandmother," Nelda Harris said. "Is this Ms. Reynolds?"

"Yes, it's Ali. What's going on?"

"I'm sorry to bother you so early in the morning, but I need your help."

"Why?" Ali asked. "What's wrong?"

"It's Haley. I told her about our conversation when I got home from work last night. I wanted her to reconsider turning down your scholarship offer. She was very upset with me. She claimed I had no right to go behind her back and talk to you. We had a terrible fight about it. This morning she's shut herself up in her room with the baby and is refusing to come out, refusing to go to school. What if she drops out completely, Ms. Reynolds? What will happen to her then? In all the years we've been together, we've never had this kind of difficulty. I can't imagine what's gotten into her. I'm at my wits' end."

"Do you think my talking to her directly would do any good?" Ali asked.

"I don't know," Nelda said. "Maybe. Right now she won't listen to a word I have to say. Like I said, she won't even come out of her room."

Ali finished putting away her computer. "All right, then, Mrs. Harris. If you think I can be of assistance, I'll come right over. I'll be there as soon as I can."

"Thank you so much."

Halfway between Sedona and Cottonwood, Ali's phone rang again. This time, when she answered, the caller was Leland Brooks.

"Do you remember hearing anything about a tile delivery scheduled for today?" he asked.

Ali didn't. What she did remember was spending what had seemed like weeks of her life narrowing her choices down to the particular kind of Italian limestone tile that was to be laid in all three baths.

"What about it?" Ali asked.

"A driver from Contract Transportation just called here looking for Mr. Forester. He's bringing a load of tile up from Phoenix and is on his way to Manzanita Hills. He says he can't unload it without having someone on hand to sign for the delivery. He's currently unable to locate Mr. Forester."

"Because Mr. Forester happens to be in jail at the moment," Ali supplied.

"Yes," Leland agreed. "I thought it best not to mention that. The driver told me that since your name is on the invoice, along with Mr. Forester's, you can okay the delivery in his stead."

"I can," Ali agreed. "Unfortunately, I'm halfway to Cottonwood right now. What about you? Could you sign for it for me?"

"If that's what you'd like, I'll be happy to do so," Leland said. "But I'll have to drop off the carpet shampooer first. It's due back before nine. The carpet is quite damp at the moment, so it's just as well that I'll be out of the house for a while. That'll give it a chance to dry a bit. Is there anything else you need me to do?"

"Not right this minute, but I'll need your help this afternoon. We should probably both plan on being back at Manzanita Hills later on today. Detective Holman told me that someone from the sheriff's department will be executing a search warrant there, looking for incriminating evidence they believe Bryan Forester may have hidden somewhere on the property. We'll need to be there to let them in."

"Very well," Leland said. "I have all the keys. I'm more than happy to handle that for you as well."

"Thank you," Ali said. She was incredibly grateful to have the unflappable Mr. Brooks backstopping her every move. "Depending on what happens in Cottonwood, I should be back in plenty of time for the search warrant."

A few minutes later, when Ali stopped in front of Nelda Harris's duplex, the woman herself hurtled through the front door and came rushing to meet her.

"We're not having a good morning," she said, gripping Ali's hand. "Not at all. Thank you so much for coming."

"Where is she?"

As Nelda led the way into the house, Ali's ears were

assaulted by the sound of wailing. Liam was clearly unhappy. "They're both still in her room," Nelda said, pointing toward a closed door. "She won't come out."

Ali went over to the door and tapped on it. When nothing happened, she tapped louder. "Haley?" she said. "It's Ali Reynolds. I'm here with your grandmother. We need to talk."

"Go away," Haley said, raising her voice to be heard over Liam's screeching. "I don't want to see you, and I don't want to talk."

"What's wrong with Liam?" Ali asked. "He sounds upset. Is he all right?"

"He's tired. He needs a nap. He didn't sleep last night, and neither did I. Now go away and leave us alone."

Ali felt her heart constrict. She remembered those early years when Chris had been little and when everything to do with him had fallen on her shoulders. She'd had some help from babysitters during the day, but she also recalled those long sleepless nights when Chris had cried for hours on end and hadn't cared at all that his weary mother needed to stagger off the next day to school where she'd had to fight to stay awake during class.

"Please come out, Haley," Ali pleaded. "Let's all talk about this. Your grandmother is here to help you, and so am I."

There was a pause filled only by Liam's plaintive wailing. At last the bedroom door inched open to reveal Haley standing there in a pair of sweats with her sobbing child perched on one hip. Without a word to Ali or her grandmother, Haley marched into the kitchen, filled a sippy cup with milk, and then went over to the couch. When she sat down, Liam reached for the cup.

"Help me with what?" Haley demanded as Liam settled back against her. "With him? Have a ball. Welcome to my stupid life. And you think we should talk? What's there to discuss? I thought the two of you had it all figured out, that you'd decided everything about my future without bothering to consult me."

As Liam drank from the cup, a sudden silence filled the room. He hiccupped a little and then handed the cup back to his mother. Exhausted, he leaned against her and stared up at her chin. Within a matter of moments, he fell fast asleep.

"Great!" Haley exclaimed. "Maybe I can sleep now, too." She slammed the still-full cup down on the end table beside her, whacking the cup hard enough that a few drops of milk spurted out, but the noise wasn't loud enough to disturb the sleeping baby. Without a word, Nelda picked up the cup and put it in the fridge, then went back over to the table and sponged up the spilled milk.

"So talk," Haley muttered defiantly, staring at Ali. "Isn't that what you came here to do—to tell me what a terrible mother I am and order me around?"

"I didn't come here to tell you anything," Ali said. "I came here to help. And believe me, I know how hard it is to think about going to school when you've been up all night with a fussy little one."

"Sure you do," Haley retorted. "Other kids get to go to football games and basketball games and dances. I get to come home, do homework, and take care of Liam. That's it."

"Once you go to work, it'll be the same thing," Ali

pointed out. "You'll go to work. You'll come home. You'll take care of your baby. How will that be different from what you're doing now? And how would it be different if you were going to school instead of going to work?"

"I wouldn't have to do homework, for one thing," Haley said. "And I wouldn't have to put up with all the other kids at school. You don't have any idea what it's like. Neither does Grandma. School is hell. The kids treat me like I'm some kind of freak because I have a baby. They're all busy talking about what it'll be like when they go off to school—what school it'll be, what dorm they'll live in, what clothes they'll take along, who their roommates will be, stuff like that. As far as I know, none of the schools have dorms for girls with babies."

That one exchange was enough for Ali to get it. Haley Marsh's disinclination to go on to school or accept the scholarship had far less to do with ability or ambition than it did with her having been treated as a social outcast in high school. She had claimed she wanted to stop going to school and to get a job in order to give her grandmother a break. Maybe that was partially true, but it wasn't the whole story. Haley wanted to give herself a break as well.

Meanwhile, Haley turned away and ducked her head, letting a screen of long blond hair obscure her face. Ali wondered what else the girl was hiding.

"High school is hell," Ali agreed quietly. "There's nothing as mean as high school girls when they turn on someone who doesn't fit in."

Ali paused, waiting for Haley to respond. She didn't. Instead, she ducked her head even lower, but Ali caught sight of the single tear that rolled down Haley's cheek and dripped onto her shirt. Ali saw it; Nelda didn't. And in that moment, Ali understood something else about Haley Marsh. During the last two years, she had somehow managed to conceal her desperate social status from her caring and loving grandmother.

"The kids at school treat you like crap?" Ali asked.

Haley looked up and met Ali's gaze. "Pretty much," she admitted.

"College is different," Ali said. "For one thing, not everyone is the same age. It's a bigger pond with a lot more fish, so it doesn't matter so much if you don't fit in with one group, because there are plenty of others. And some of the people you meet there will already have kids. I did."

"But you were married, weren't you?" Haley asked. "That's a lot different."

"Not as different as you might think," Ali told her. "By the time my son was born, my husband had been dead for two months. He died of a brain tumor. Admittedly, I wasn't a freshman at the time. I already had my B.A. and was working on my master's, but still, going to school and looking after a baby was desperately hard. Going to high school with a baby must have been awful, and going to college would be tough. I won't try to pretend otherwise."

Haley nodded. "But at least you *had* a husband," she said wistfully. "You weren't doing it all alone."

"You're not alone, either," Ali pointed out. "You have a grandmother who would do anything for you and has been doing it all along. You also have your son. Regardless of how Liam came into being, you chose to have him, didn't you?"

There was a pause before Haley nodded.

"You could have had an abortion," Ali added. "Under

similar circumstances, I think many people would have, but you didn't. Why not?"

"Because I don't believe in abortion," Haley said quietly. "It's against my religion."

"You also could have given him up for adoption," Ali suggested. "But you didn't do that, either, and why not? Because no matter what, he's your baby, and you love him, all of which means that you really are a good mother."

Haley ducked her head again, and another tear dribbled onto her shirt.

"But part of being a good mother is being good to yourself, Haley," Ali continued. "I didn't come here today to tell you what to do about going on to school or to beg you to accept a scholarship you don't want, but I did come to tell you something important. Your grandmother came to see me yesterday for one reason and one reason only. She loves you. She wants you to have a chance to live up to your potential. And why does she want you to do that? Because she wants you to give your son a better life than her daughter—your mother—gave you. By being good to you, your grandmother is being good to herself."

"You know about all that, then?" Haley asked. "About my mother? Grandma told you about what happened?"

"Yes," Ali said with a nod. "She did. She also told me that you have Liam because you chose to have Liam. Having him and keeping him were the only possible decisions open to you, but you need to remember that was a choice, Haley, a conscious choice made by you and nobody else. I'd like you to feel empowered by that decision instead of feeling trapped by it. I don't give a rat's ass what the girls at Mingus Mountain think about you. What's important is what you think about yourself."

"But you still want me to go to college."

"No one is telling you to do anything, but I am asking that you think about it—that you think about the kind of life you want to live with that little boy of yours. And when you make up your mind, let me know."

Ali stood up and collected her purse. Haley didn't move to accompany her; neither did Nelda. At the door, Ali turned back. "Regardless of what you decide, Haley, I want you to know that I think you're a pretty remarkable human being. And so is your grandmother. Your bitchy classmates may not be impressed, but I am."

Outside in the bright winter sunshine, Ali started her vehicle with the clear knowledge that if Haley changed her mind and accepted the scholarship offer, Ali had just committed to doing two scholarships as opposed to one.

And if that's what happens, so be it, Ali thought. *If I decide to do two, it's entirely up to me.*

Turning on her Bluetooth, Ali punched Leland Brooks's number into her phone. When the call went directly to voice mail, she left him a message. "You must be busy. I'm on my way back from Cottonwood," she said. "Just checking on that load of tile. Hope you got it signed for and unloaded. If you need anything, call me."

She was still driving when her phone rang. This time, when she expected to hear Leland Brooks's voice, the caller turned out to be B. Simpson. With the flip of a switch, Ali moved from Haley's difficulties to her own.

"What are you doing up already?" she asked.

"Fortunately, I don't need much sleep. What was keeping me awake was you."

"Me?" Ali echoed. "How come?"

"I Googled you," B. said. "And now I've got a question."

Ali cringed. There were any number of things a Google search of Ali Reynolds might bring to light. "What's that?" she asked.

"Who's the big baseball nut in your family?"

Ali knew at once where that was going. Being teased about the "other" Allie Reynolds, a famed New York Yankees pitcher from the late forties and early fifties, was something that had plagued Ali for a very long time, from the moment she'd first married Dean. From even before she had married Dean.

"I'm a one-L one-I Ali," she pointed out. "The other one happens to be a two-L and an IE Allie. Besides, Reynolds is a married name, not a maiden one, so even though my father does happen to be a baseball nut, his preferences had nothing to do with it."

"I thought maybe it was your first husband—that he married you because he was a fan."

"What else did you find out?" Ali asked.

"That you carry a gun," B. said. "One of the articles I read, or maybe even a couple of them, mentioned something about that. Is that true?"

"Yes, it is," Ali said. "I carry a Glock. I have a license to carry it, and I know how to use it, and maybe that's not such a bad thing. What if the guy who killed Morgan Forester is also our identity thief?"

That question was followed by a quiet intake of breath on B.'s part. "What makes you think that?" he asked.

Over the next few minutes, she brought him up to date with everything that had gone on over the course of the morning. In telling B. about the possible connection between Morgan's killer and the Foresters' destroyed computer files, Ali succeeded in convincing herself as well.

"If you're right about this, the killer already knows way too much about you," B. said when she'd finished. "And it probably is a good thing you're armed and dangerous, but we have to bring Detective Holman in on all this."

"We don't have any real proof that the two bad guys are one and the same."

"We don't have any proof that they're not," B. insisted. "And if we even suspect that there's a connection, we need to let him know."

"All right," Ali agreed. "I'll call him as soon as I get off the phone with you. But what about those two thumb drives? I offered them to Dave, and he dissed them, assuming that Bryan had already gone through them and deleted whatever he didn't want seen. But what are the chances that they're also infected and something will overwrite all the files on the next computer someone uses to try accessing them? I was looking at Bryan's files earlier, and there didn't seem to be any problem, but . . ."

"Were you off-line at the time?"

"Yes."

"I should probably take a look at both of those drives," B. said. "If there's a Trojan lurking in them, maybe I can disable it before it does any damage. Right now, though, I'm still working on that encryption problem. I think we're getting close, and I don't want to walk away from it. Could you maybe drop the thumb drives off here at the house?"

"Where is that?" Ali asked.

"The Village of Oak Creek," he said. "Overlooking a golf course."

"Which one?"

"The one by the Hilton."

"Okay," Ali said. "I'm on my way."

"Right now?"

"Yes, right now."

"So where are you?"

"Just coming into Sedona from Cottonwood. Why?"

"Do me a favor," he said. "I'm famished. I haven't taken the time to go have breakfast, and there's no food here—plenty of coffee but no food."

"What do you want?" Ali asked.

"One of your dad's meatloaf sandwiches."

"Done," Ali said. "Meatloaf it is."

CHAPTER 13

On his way down from Sedona, Dave Holman had notified the Scottsdale police of his impending arrival and of the possible connection between their case and his. Driving to the address he'd been given in the far northern reaches of Scottsdale, Dave was surprised to find himself in a neighborhood of relatively modest tract homes that had been built years before far more affluent housing had grown up around them. The garage door of the house stood open, but the opening was strung with yellow crime-scene tape, and a pair of uniformed officers were stationed outside.

Led inside by one of the uniforms, Dave introduced himself to Scottsdale homicide detective Sean O'Brien and to Matthew Morrison's widow.

"I still don't understand why you won't let me use my car," a surprisingly poised and dry-eyed Jenny Morrison was saying. "After all, since Matthew died in his Toyota, I don't see what any of it has to do with my Acura. How can I go about planning a funeral if I can't even drive my car?"

An aggrieved widow rather than a grieving one, Dave

thought. *Someone who's far more concerned about being able to drive her car than she is about finding out what happened to her husband.*

"As I explained earlier," Detective O'Brien said, "for right now, the entire garage is considered part of the crime scene until we have a chance to have our CSI team process it—"

"But there wasn't any crime," Jenny insisted. "I'm telling you, what happened to Matt has to be an accident. He would never commit suicide or do anything at all that would attract this kind of attention. Not on purpose. It's totally out of character."

"So what do you think happened?" Dave asked.

"Who the hell are you?" Jenny asked.

"Detective Holman," Dave said, handing over his ID. "Yavapai County Sheriff's Department. We're working on a related case. Now, getting back to your husband—"

Jenny shrugged impatiently. "He called me yesterday afternoon at work and left me a message. He said there'd been some kind of problem at work and that he would be late getting home. Once he got it straightened out, he must have had a drink or two with a colleague on his way home. He passed out in the car without ever turning off the engine."

"Was that something he did often?" Detective O'Brien asked. "Have 'one too many' on his way home from work?"

"No," Jenny said. "But there's always a first time, isn't there?"

And a last time, Dave thought. "Had your husband been upset about anything recently?" he asked.

Jenny turned back to Detective O'Brien. "I already

went over all this with you. Do I have to repeat it to him?"

"Please answer the question, Mrs. Morrison," O'Brien said. "Believe me, the more information we all have, the easier it'll be to get to the bottom of this."

Jenny Morrison gave an exaggerated sigh. "All right, then," she said. "In answer to your question, no, Matthew didn't seem particularly upset. If anything, he seemed pretty cheerful."

"Not what you'd call depressed," Detective O'Brien offered.

"No more than usual," Jenny replied.

"What do you mean?"

"My husband was never what you'd call a wild and carefree guy. He was an auditor. The only thing he would have liked more than working for the state would have been working for the IRS. In other words, he wasn't ever a bundle of laughs. In fact, he may have known a joke or two, but I never heard him tell one. He was just a regular guy who wore a suit and tie when he went to work every day. After work, he came home, ate dinner, watched TV or messed around on his computer, and then went to bed. Mr. Regular-as-Clockwork."

"Did he have dealings with anyone in or around Sedona?" Dave asked.

"Probably. Matthew had dealings with people from all over the state," Jenny said. "Like I said, he worked for the auditor general. I'm sure she can tell you which accounts he was working on."

"Did he mention anything to you about maybe going to Sedona this past Monday morning?"

"I'm sure you're mistaken about that," Jenny said.

"He told me he had a Monday-morning meeting in Tucson. He brought home a motor-pool vehicle on Friday so he'd be able to leave for Tucson bright and early on Monday."

On his way to Scottsdale, Dave had already checked on Matthew Morrison's supposed Monday-morning appointment in Tucson and had found it totally bogus. No record of any scheduled Tucson appointment existed. Period. The car-rental agreement, however, did exist.

"You're saying your husband was driving a state-owned vehicle on Monday morning when he left here, and not a Hertz rental?" Dave asked.

"Isn't that what I just said?"

"My understanding is that he used his Hertz gold card to rent a vehicle that was seen near Sedona—"

"You think Matthew rented a car? Never. He didn't have a Hertz gold card," Jenny declared flatly. "He never rented a car in his life, not once. For one thing, we never went anywhere. Besides that, he was too cheap."

"You mentioned your husband's computer. Was it here at home?"

Jenny nodded.

"And did he use it for work?"

"I don't know. The last few months he was on it almost every evening. But it doesn't really matter what he did with it. It's broken."

"Broken?" Dave asked.

"Yes. To begin with, I thought the same thing you did—that he had done himself in and he might have left me a note. But when I tried to turn on the computer, it wouldn't even boot up. It was several years old, though. It probably died a natural death and he didn't want to tell me about it."

Dave's phone vibrated in its holder on his belt, but the news about another broken computer made the call easy to ignore. Both Bryan and Morgan Forester's computers had been tampered with. He tried to keep any sense of urgency out of his voice when he spoke. "Would you mind if we took a look at it?" he asked. "If someone at the crime lab could reinstate some of the data, it might give us a better idea of what was going on with your husband."

"By all means," Jenny Morrison said. "Knock yourselves out. You can take it right now if you want to. The sooner you get to the bottom of all this, the sooner I'll be able to drive my car."

"What about a photo?" Dave asked. He caught the raised eyebrow that Detective O'Brien gave him. Dave knew that eventually, they'd be able to retrieve Matthew Morrison's photo from the DMV, but that would take time and going through channels. Right this minute, Detective Holman was looking for speed.

"That one," Jenny said. With a careless shrug, she pointed to a gold-framed eight-by-ten photo sitting on an end table next to the couch—a photo of both of them together, Jenny with her hard-edged, fashion-plate good looks and beefy Matthew with a bad comb-over and a bulky sport jacket.

"It's not brand-new," Jenny said. "It's from last year's church directory."

"Would it be possible to borrow it?" Dave asked.

"Sure," Jenny told him. "You can keep it if you like. If I need a copy, I can always order another."

Somehow, listening to Jenny Morrison talk, Dave doubted she'd be ordering another copy.

Half an hour later, he helped Detective O'Brien load Matthew Morrison's dead PC and old-fashioned CRT into the back of his sedan.

"I'm not sure why we're even bothering to drag this old computer out of there," Sean said as he slammed the car door shut behind it. "Sounds as though it's as dead as he is, poor guy. Maybe Morrison's death really will turn out to be an accident, although, if I had to be married to a coldhearted witch like her, I'd have blown my brains out long ago."

"Yes," Dave agreed. "Jenny Morrison is definitely bad news, but I don't think her husband's death was an accident, and maybe not suicide, either."

"What makes you say that?" Detective O'Brien asked.

"What if I told you I've learned about three dead computers connected to this case so far this morning?"

Once Dave explained, O'Brien nodded. "I see what you mean," he said. "Sounds like at least two too many. I'll drag this one back to the crime lab and see if anyone there can extract any data from it. What are you going to do with that photo?"

"Go see Hertz," Dave said. "Matthew Morrison rented a car there on Monday. I want to see if anyone remembers him."

Ali arrived back at the Sugarloaf during the late-morning lull. The parking lot was empty, and when she stepped inside, the place was deserted except for Jan Howard, who was grabbing a quick cup of coffee. Edie's laptop sat open on the counter, but what should have been a pre-lunch quiet was punctuated by the sound of raised voices from the kitchen.

"I don't care what I said about not minding," Bob Larson was telling his wife. "The reason I didn't mind is I never thought you'd do it. I thought you'd have better sense. No matter, you're not bringing that damn thing into our house. I won't have it. The last thing this world needs is a bunch of hysterical little old ladies going around zapping everything in sight."

"I'm not hysterical," Edie returned. "And I haven't zapped anyone, not yet. And I certainly haven't zapped you, now, have I?"

"What's going on?" Ali asked Jan.

Bob and Edie's longtime waitress rolled her eyes and shook her head. "You know how your parents are, Ali. They're always squabbling like cats and dogs about one thing or another."

That was true. For Bob and Edie, a day without a verbal skirmish was like a day without sun.

"What about this time?" Ali asked.

"Your mother's Taser," Jan returned.

Ali was aghast. "My mother's what?"

"Her Taser," Jan repeated. "FedEx delivered it a little while ago. She went out into the kitchen to load and authorize it, and your father started pitching a fit. Are you here for lunch?" she added, pulling out her order pad. "It's early, but what can I get you?"

"You're telling me my mother has a Taser, like on *COPS*?"

"Not exactly like on *COPS*," Jan said. "Theirs are black. Edie's is that pretty metallic pink. She got one that matches her cell phone."

Pink? Ali marveled.

"And what happens when you hit some poor little

old guy with a pacemaker and he flops over dead?" Bob's tirade continued. "What happens then?"

"You need to watch the video," Edie said patiently. "It goes into all those details. The amount of charge in the Taser doesn't do anything at all to pacemakers. Besides, how many crooks that are robbing banks or doing carjackings already have pacemakers?"

"And how many carjackings have you been involved in?" Bob demanded.

"None so far," Edie replied. "But if I ever am, the guy doing it will be in for a big surprise."

Walking around the end of the counter, Ali stepped into the kitchen. Her father stood leaning against the kitchen sink with his arms folded belligerently across his chest. Edie, frowning in concentration, was holding and manipulating a metal object of some kind in one hand while consulting a piece of paper in her other hand. The pink metallic object was about the same size and shape as an ordinary office stapler, and the color did indeed match Edie's hot-pink cell phone.

Intent on their argument, neither Bob nor Edie registered Ali's arrival on the scene. Since bickering was a way of life for her parents, Ali didn't hesitate before stepping into the melee. "What's going on here?" she demanded.

"Your mother's gone off the deep end this time," Bob replied. "Bought herself one of those Taser outfits from that Frieda Rains woman. With her packing that thing around, God help me if she ever goes on the warpath."

None of this made much sense, but Ali plucked a familiar name out of her father's diatribe: Frieda Rains was a local woman somewhere in her mid- to late seventies who had been left virtually penniless by her husband's long bout with numerous health issues, including his eventual death from complications related to Alzheimer's. In order to keep a roof over her head, Frieda had taken over as manager of a trailer park somewhere farther up Oak Creek Canyon. In addition to that, she eked out a meager living by doing other various odd jobs, including working as a food demonstrator and selling Tupperware.

"What's Frieda doing with Tasers?" Ali asked.

"Selling them," Edie Larson answered. "She can make a lot more money selling Tasers at a party than she can make selling plastic dishware."

"My point exactly," Bob said. "Once she sells them to everyone she knows, we'll all be at risk. No one in town will be safe."

"You should be grateful," Edie said. "With the women in town prepared to defend themselves, you'll be a whole lot safer than you were before."

"You're saying Frieda Rains is an authorized dealer, then?" Ali asked.

"Yes," Edie answered. "She's a fully authorized dealer. I went to one of her first parties here in town last week. Your father knew at the time that I was going. I told him well in advance."

"Yes," Bob grumbled. "But when you came home, you neglected to mention that you actually bought one. You seem to have left out that important detail."

"Because I knew you'd pitch a fit five ways to Sunday when you found out," Edie shot back. "Which is what you're doing right this minute, in case you haven't noticed. Since I knew having this argument was inevitable, I decided to postpone it until my C2 actually got here and it came time to activate it. Which I've done, by the way, by putting in the authorization code."

"You're saying that now it's loaded?" Bob asked warily. "Are you telling me all you have to do is shoot the damn thing? Shouldn't there be some kind of training program before you're allowed to go around with it in your hand?"

"It isn't a lethal weapon," Edie returned. "And I've already done the training. Frieda gave me a copy of the video. I've watched it several times. Running this thing is as easy as pie."

"What about a license? Shouldn't you have one of those?"

"A license isn't required," Edie said. "I brought the computer over from the house so I could answer the questions on the felony check. Obviously, there weren't any of those. Now that it's activated, I'm good to go."

"How about if you go out of my kitchen, then," Bob suggested. "And take that blasted thing with you. What if it goes off accidentally and messes up my microwave?"

"It doesn't go off unless you move back the cover and push the red button," Edie said. "And it's not going to hurt your microwave."

"I don't care," Bob said. "I want it out of here!"

With a glare in her husband's direction, Edie stuffed the Taser in the pocket of her apron and headed for the dining room. Bob turned on his daughter. "As for you," he said, "if you're looking for lunch, we don't start serving for another five minutes. No exceptions, not even for you."

Ali followed Edie back into the dining room. "Can I see it?" she asked. "Please?"

Edie sighed. "As long as you don't give me any grief about it. See? This is how it works." She held out the sleek little instrument and pulled back the plastic cover that served as a trigger guard. As soon as she did that, a bright red laser light appeared on the opposite wall.

"A lot of the time, just having that light aimed at his chest is enough to get a crook to back off. If he doesn't, you press this button, the one with the lightning on it. You've got to keep the Taser vertical. The darts shoot out about fifteen feet, and they say you should always aim for the chest. The second dart hits about a foot lower than the first one. If he still doesn't go down, you can use this as a stun gun in close physical combat, but that's a lot harder."

"You seem to know a lot about this," Ali said.

"You bet," Edie replied with a grin. "Like I said, I've watched the video."

The bell rang over the door, signaling arriving customers. Without another word, Edie stowed her Taser in the locked compartment under the cash wrap next to her purse. While Jan went to seat the new arrivals, Edie busied herself with brewing a new pot of coffee. "I swear," she said, "I think your father would be happier living in the twentieth century—the *early* twentieth century. The moment something new comes along, he digs in his heels. That's why he's still driving that old wreck of his."

Bob Larson's 1972 Bronco was his pride and joy. It was also his sole means of transportation. Refurbished after being stolen and stripped sometime earlier, it now sported a brand-new coat of paint and newly acquired copper-plated antique-vehicle license plates.

Ali wasn't about to be deflected from the subject at hand. "But why a Taser?" she asked.

"Why not?" Edie returned. "Not everybody has what it takes to be a martial-arts expert, and we can't all be like you and carry a loaded Glock around."

Both of Ali's parents had objected to her having a gun and a concealed-weapon permit, although the criticism had pretty much gone away after an almost fatal shoot-out in a Phoenix-area hospital waiting room. On that occasion, the presence of Ali's weapon had played an important part in saving countless lives.

"I used to think Sedona was the safest place in the world, but not anymore," Edie continued. "I'm the one who takes the receipts to the bank every day. When I'm walking around with that bag of cash in my purse, I can tell you, I feel mighty leery about it. I'm the one at risk, you know. Who's to say some would-be thief might not take a look at me and decide I'm an easy mark?"

"But Mother," Ali began.

"No buts," Edie said. "It's not a lethal weapon. If someone was coming at me and I had a gun in my hand, I'd probably think about it for a minute. Do I want to kill this guy or not? And by the time I made up my mind, it would be too late. With this, I pull the trigger. And what happens if there's a struggle and he takes my weapon away and shoots me instead? Same thing. I may be tased, but I won't be dead. I may fall down on the ground and wet my pants in public, which would be embarrassing as all get out, but again, I won't be dead. Big difference."

"Let's suppose you end up tasing a bad guy," Ali

said. "What if he gets up and comes at you anyway? What do you do then?"

"That's the beauty of it," Edie said. "You've got the thirty seconds while he's helpless on the ground to call for help and get out of Dodge. You take off and leave your Taser right there with the darts still in him. Afterward, you submit a police report about the incident to Taser International, and they replace your Taser, no questions asked. So it comes with a lifetime guarantee."

"Interesting," Ali said.

"Look what happened to Morgan Forester," Edie continued. "Whoever killed her did it right there in her own front yard, and she was completely defenseless. If she'd had a Taser, maybe she could have gotten away. Frieda told me that she booked three parties for next week based on that incident alone."

Ali had to concede that Edie had a point. Sedona wasn't nearly as crime-free as it had once been. That lethal weapon/shoot/don't shoot pause in the action, the critical seconds of wrestling with the decision of pulling the trigger and possibly killing an attacker, had proved fatal for countless police officers and civilians alike over the years. And how many people died when, in the course of a struggle, their own weapons were used against them? Maybe Edie and Frieda were right—that having access to a nonlethal alternative wasn't such a bad idea.

Edie glanced at the clock. "It drives me nuts when your father starts acting like a prima donna, but it's after eleven now. If you want lunch, I can take your order, but didn't you just have breakfast?"

"I need a meatloaf sandwich," Ali said. "To go."

"With everything?"

Ali nodded. She didn't mention that she would be delivering it to B. Simpson at his home. That would spin off another whole set of questions, to say nothing of rumors.

Once Ali's order was up on the wheel, Edie turned back to her daughter. "Frieda asked me if I thought you'd be interested. Next week's parties are booked, but she said she'd be able to squeeze you in to one of them if you'd like to attend."

"No, thanks," Ali said. "For right now I believe I'll stick with my Glock."

Gradually, the Sugarloaf's lunch crowd began to filter into the restaurant. From the sounds of banging pots and pans in the kitchen, Ali knew her father wasn't yet over his snit, but he would be. He and her mother had their various differences of opinions, but they always got over them one way or the other.

While Ali waited for the sandwich, she tried calling Leland Brooks, hoping to see how he had fared with the tile delivery. She was a little surprised when he still didn't answer his phone; he usually picked up after only one ring.

"Back in town now," she said, leaving another message. "Give me a call when you get this."

As the booths filled up, so did the stools at the counter. Blanche Sims, a teller from Wells Fargo, slipped onto a stool one down from Ali. "I heard they let Bryan Forester out of jail this morning," Blanche said as Edie filled her coffee cup. "Someone told me they saw his truck parked in front of the funeral home. Probably there making arrangements for tomorrow's funeral. Under the circumstances, I don't think the man has any business arranging a funeral, much less attending it."

The comment was addressed to Edie. Ali had no business involving herself in the discussion, but she couldn't help it. She couldn't sit idly by while people who had no idea of what had happened sat around proclaiming Bryan's guilt.

"Why wouldn't Bryan show up for the funeral?" Ali demanded sharply. "Morgan was his wife and the mother of his children. He has every right in the world to be there."

Everyone within hearing distance, including Blanche, seemed taken aback by Ali's outspoken response.

"Your order's up," Bob said from the kitchen.

Hurriedly grabbing Ali's to-go bag from the pass-through, Edie handed it to her daughter. "Go ahead," she said. "We can straighten this out later."

"Yes," Ali declared, standing up and favoring Blanche with a cold-eyed stare. "We certainly can." With that, she stomped out of the Sugarloaf and headed for the Village of Oak Creek.

Unconvinced that Matthew Morrison's damaged computer would provide any answers, Dave Holman left the crime scene in Scottsdale and headed for Sky Harbor airport. Shortly after noon, armed with the formerly framed photo of Jenny and Matthew Morrison, Dave arrived at the Hertz car-rental facility at Sky Harbor. Not that it did him much good.

Once Dave showed his ID, Jim Henderson, the young branch manager, was polite and eager but less than helpful. A check of their records showed that the vehicle in question—a blue Ford 500 with Colorado plates—was out on another rental and wasn't scheduled to be returned again until Sunday evening. As for Morrison's rental agreement? It had been done through their online facility. Since Matthew Morrison had a valid gold card, he didn't have to stop at a rental counter. All he had to do was step off the shuttle, climb into his waiting vehicle, and then drive through the guarded gate, showing his paperwork as he went.

"That's all there is to it?" Dave asked.

Henderson nodded. "It's a service for our repeat customers. We maintain profiles on each of them. We know what vehicles they like and their insurance preferences. We also have their license information on file, along with their preferred credit card. That's all we need. It streamlines the process for everyone."

"What happens when the vehicle is returned?"

"Customers drive up to one of our drop-off lanes. An attendant checks the car for damage, verifies the mileage and fuel readings, and makes sure nothing's left in the vehicle."

"Can you tell which attendant that would have been?"

"Sure. Just a second. Attendant 06783. That would be Bobby Salazar. He's out on the line now."

"Do you mind if I talk to him?"

"You can try, but I wouldn't hold my breath, if I were you," Henderson said. "These guys check in hundreds of vehicles in a week's time. Bobby's one of our best, but this is Thursday. He's not going to remember a vehicle that was turned in on Monday."

Dave arrived at Bobby Salazar's station and waited on the sidelines while the attendant finished checking in two very sunburned guys in shorts and Hawaiian shirts who came equipped with a mountain of luggage and two sets of golf clubs. As they piled their stuff onto a rolling cart, Bobby turned an appraising gaze on Dave. "What can I do for you, Officer?"

Wordlessly, Dave handed over first his ID and then the photo of Jenny and Matthew Morrison. "Have you ever seen this guy?"

Bobby studied the picture carefully, then shook his head. "Nope," he said confidently. "I've never seen him before."

"That's funny," Dave said. "According to the check-in records, he came through your line on Monday—late in the afternoon."

"Driving what?" Bobby asked.

"A blue Ford 500 with Colorado plates."

Dave caught the subtle tightening of Bobby Salazar's jaw. He looked down at the photo and then handed it back. "I remember the vehicle, but this guy wasn't the one who was driving it. Why? What's this about?"

"I'm investigating a homicide that occurred outside Sedona on Monday morning," Dave answered. "This vehicle was seen in the area and—"

"There was blood in it," Bobby said. "On the floor-board of the passenger seat. At least it looked like blood."

"And you didn't report it?"

"My shift was almost over," Bobby said. "I didn't want to be late for class. There wasn't any other damage to the vehicle. Besides, it wasn't that big a stain. Carpets get dirty over time. The detail guys clean them up as best they can."

"I'm sure they do," Dave said. "But this is the man

whose name was on the rental agreement." He held up the photo. "You're sure this isn't the man who was driving?"

"I remember the guy very well," Bobby said. "He was rude to me—a first-class asshole, but not this asshole. This isn't him."

When Ali arrived at the address she'd been given, she found herself in front of a sprawling piece of stucco-covered architecture stacked on top of a three-car garage. Looking at it, she knew the modern-looking affair would total up to be well over a million-dollar property, especially since it was built on a steep hillside lot that backed up to a large swath of undeveloped and probably undevelopable open space. In the Sedona area, that kind of privacy meant big bucks.

She parked in the driveway and stepped out of her Cayenne to admire the view. The house overlooked the ninth fairway of a well-kept eighteen-hole golf course, with Sedona's fringe of deep red rocks dominating the horizon.

B. hurried out to meet Ali as she gathered her purse and the take-out bag containing his sandwich. Ali handed the bag to him and then reached back into the Cayenne to retrieve her laptop. B. led her up the steep driveway and under a covered portico on the south side of the house, where two double doors—either antique or suitably distressed—created an impressive entry.

"For real?" Ali asked, fingering the rough-hewn wood.

B. grinned and shook his head. "Nope," he replied. "Well done but absolutely fake. There's a door factory down in Mexico that's made a real name for itself manufacturing reproduction doors. The doors were going to be part of a whole Mexican-hacienda motif. I had planned on hiring a decorator and really doing the place up in spectacular fashion, but it turns out I've had a few other things on my plate. In other words, I haven't quite gotten around to redecorating. You'll have to take the house as is."

The tall wooden doors opened onto a soaring two-story foyer with an exquisitely tiled floor. After that impressive entry, things pretty much went downhill. The living room was huge, with a massive black granite fireplace at the far end. What should have been a spectacular focal point for the home suffered from the furnishings—an oddball collection of mismatched tables, desks, and benches, all of which held one or more computers. The only concession to comfort came in the guise of two rolling desk chairs that evidently migrated as needed from one computer station to the next.

"Why do I feel like I just ended up at a computer garage sale?" Ali asked.

"It's not," B. said with a chuckle. "For one thing, not one of these computers is dead. They're all hard at work doing their own little part of solving our encryption problem. I'll admit, I probably shouldn't have set them up in the living room, but there was more room here than anywhere else. The kitchen's on through there," he added, pointing and leading the way. "I put on a new pot of coffee, and if you're hungry, I'll be happy to share some of my sandwich."

Taking the hint, Ali followed B. into the kitchen. "Yes on the coffee," she said. "I already had breakfast, so I'm not hungry. Don't let that stop you. You go ahead."

She watched while he dished the sandwich out onto a paper plate and set the table with an assortment of plastic utensils. *A confirmed bachelor,* Ali concluded.

B. seemed to read her mind. "I was married once," he said as he poured freshly brewed coffee from a state-of-the-art Krups brew station into a pair of mugs that were covered with fading Nintendo logos. "Briefly and badly," he added. "She wanted to fix me and turn our house into something out of *House and Garden.* I'm more into retro *Star Wars.* She also wanted me to work regular office hours with nights and weekends off. I took the position that as much money as I was making, I didn't need to be fixed. We decided to go our separate ways. She lives the way she lives, and I live like this." He paused and looked at Ali expectantly, as if waiting for her to fill in the blanks of her own life.

"If you've Googled me," she said, "then you already know I got turned in for a newer model. Or two."

"Yes," B. agreed. "I believe there was some mention of that. I also read that before all was said and done, you ended up being accused of knocking him off. Is that what got you so bound up in trying to help Bryan Forester?"

It was a fair question, especially in view of the fact that Ali's involvement had drawn B. into the equation as well. "I suppose," Ali admitted. "And considering your past history, I really appreciate that you're willing to help out."

B. grinned at her before taking a bite of the oversize sandwich. "You're a paying customer," he said, when he finished chewing. "And the customer is always right. You brought the thumb drives?"

"Yes." Ali reached into her purse, pulled out the drives in question, and put them on the table. "I already tried using one of them in my computer," she said, patting her computer case. "Nothing happened, but as you said, I wasn't online at the time."

B. nodded. "Thanks for dropping them off. As soon as I'm done with my sandwich, I'll check them out. The drives and the computer."

"Thank you," Ali said.

"And what about Dave Holman?" B. asked. "Did you tell him about the possible connection between his case and our identity thief?"

"Not yet," Ali said. "I've tried calling him several times. He must be busy. The calls go straight to voice mail."

"Keep trying," B. urged. "The more I think about it, the less I like it."

Ali stayed long enough for B. to polish off the sandwich. Once he reached for her computer, she stood to leave. She still hadn't heard back from Leland Brooks, and she wanted to make sure someone was at the Manzanita Hills house in advance of the deputies with their search warrant.

"You're welcome to stay if you want to," he said.

Ali shook her head. "I've already seen you working on computers," she said. "It's about as much fun as watching grass grow."

"That's funny," B. said. "It's almost the same thing my ex-wife used to say."

{ CHAPTER 14 }

Leaving the village, Ali tried calling both Dave and Leland again. To no avail: Neither of them answered. On the way, she drove up to the Manzanita Hills house, expecting to see a pallet or two of tiles sitting in the driveway. There wasn't one, and Leland wasn't there, either.

Exasperated, Ali called B. Simpson back. "Have you taken a look at either one of the thumb drives?" she asked.

"Both of them," he said. "And you're right. They were both infected, but now that I know how this guy works, it wasn't hard to disable the worm. I just finished working on Morgan's. Why?"

"Someone was supposed to deliver a tile order today," Ali said. "But there's no sign of it here, and no sign of Mr. Brooks either. I'm wondering what happened."

"Would you like me to check Morgan's address book and see if I can find a phone number for you? Do you happen to remember the name?"

"Tile Design," Ali answered impatiently. "Something like that."

"Import Granite and Tile Design?" B. returned a moment later. "On Buckeye Road?"

"That's the one," Ali said. "Can you give me the number?"

"And down here on the notes, there's a whole series of invoice numbers," B. said. "Would you like those as well?"

Ali noted them. Once she dialed the number, she spent the next several minutes on hold before someone from customer service came on the line.

"My name is Alison Reynolds," Ali told the woman. "My contractor is Build It Construction here in Sedona. I was told my order of limestone tile would be delivered today, but it hasn't shown up."

"You were expecting an order today?" the woman asked. "Where again?"

"In Sedona. At my construction site on Manzanita Hills Road. The contractor is currently unavailable, and I was told I needed to have someone on-site to sign the invoice and accept delivery."

"I'm so sorry, Ms. Reynolds," the woman said. "I see the order right here, but there must be some kind of mistake. We don't make deliveries in Sedona on Fridays. And your tile is in transit, but it isn't due at our warehouse here in Phoenix until late next week at the earliest."

"But I was told it would be here today."

"Perhaps it's an order from another company," the woman said cheerfully. "It's possible that the contractor ordered from more than one supplier. You should probably check with him."

I would, if I could find him, Ali thought grimly. *If he really is out of jail.*

She was still fuming when she pulled into the driveway at Skyview, where she was relieved to see Leland Brooks's pickup parked right outside the house. That meant he was back here. Maybe he was vacuuming or doing some other noisy chore that made hearing the ringing of his telephone impossible. If nothing else, he might be able to unravel the puzzle of that missing load of limestone tile.

"Hi," she called, coming inside. "Leland? Anybody home?"

There was no answer as she closed the front door and turned to deposit her keys and purse on the burled-wood entryway table. When she looked up from doing that, she was astonished to find herself faced with a complete stranger. A dark-haired man with a grim expression was seated directly across from her on the leather couch. In one hand, he held a gun—an enormous handgun—that was trained on her. Both that hand and the other one, the one resting casually on his knee, were covered by latex surgical gloves. That was definitely a bad sign—a very bad sign. The man was dressed all in green, like one of the doctors on *Scrubs,* and he wore a pair of surgical booties on his feet.

"Who are you?" she demanded. "What the hell are you doing in my house? Who let you in? And where's Leland Brooks?"

The man's face twisted into a sardonic grin. "So many questions," he said, "and from someone who no doubt thought she already had all the answers. First let me see that Glock of yours. I understand you never leave home without it. Take it out from wherever it is you carry it. Take it out very carefully and put it right there on the floor in front of you. Then move back to the door and sit there. No heroics, Ms. Reynolds. One false move, and I promise you, I will pull the trigger."

He spoke so calmly, so deliberately, that Ali had no doubt he meant every word. With her heart slamming wildly inside her chest, she did as she'd been told: She carefully removed the Glock from its small-of-back holster and put it on the floor. Then, as directed, she moved back to the door and slid down to the floor in front of it.

How can this be happening to me? she wondered. *Why didn't I see it coming?*

There had been no warning. None. One moment things had seemed completely normal. She had been performing the perfectly ordinary tasks of stepping into her house and closing the door behind her. The next moment her life was on the line: There was a stranger in her house, and she was staring down the barrel of a deadly weapon.

"You still haven't told me who you are," she said. With her whole body quaking, she struggled to steady her voice. She needed to put up a good front and to sound less threatened than she felt.

"Why don't you tell me who I am?" the man returned.

Just then Ali heard a car pulling up in the driveway. A car door slammed shut. Hearing it, she was terrified that school had let out early for some unknown reason and her son, Chris, was about to walk into a trap. But then a second door slammed as well. She heard the sound of approaching voices, of two men talking. Her captor heard them, too.

"Whoever it is, get rid of them," he whispered urgently. "Now! And no tricks, either."

When the doorbell clanged right above Ali's head, the sound was so loud it took her breath away. She knew that she needed to call for help. Someone was right there, on the far side of the door, but if she did call out and sound an alarm, what would happen? She would be dead, and so might the unsuspecting people outside. For a long time, she didn't move and didn't speak.

"I said get rid of them," the man hissed.

The bell rang again. "Ali," Jacky Jackson said. "Your car's parked right outside. We know you're in there. Why aren't you answering the door?"

"What do you want?" Ali croaked, her voice cracking with a combination of fear and raw emotion. She tried to pull herself together. *I can't let him know how scared I am,* she told herself. *I can't.*

"It's Jacky," the agent said, as if she couldn't recognize his voice. "I've brought someone along who wants to meet you. You need to meet him, Ali. It's important. He wants to talk to you about that offer we discussed yesterday. We've been looking for you all morning long, traipsing all over hell and gone."

The only thing that was important right then was survival. Ali knew that in a fair fight, Jacky Jackson would be no help at all—in fact, he'd be less than no help. But his unexpected and unwelcome presence right outside her door at this exact moment did serve one useful purpose. It made Ali mad as hell, and that helped clear her head and made her focus.

"Go away," she ordered. "Leave me out of it. I already told you, I'm not interested."

"But you don't understand," Jacky wheedled. "This is one of the major players in this deal. He flew in last night for the express purpose of seeing you. He wants to be sure you understand what's at stake here—what kind of an offer you may be turning down."

And what I'm keeping you from walking into, Ali thought.

"You could be here with the pope himself, for all I care," Ali returned. "I'm not interested. My answer was no yesterday, and it's still no today. What part of N-O don't you understand, Jacky? Go away and leave me alone."

"If you let us walk away from here, you're going to live to regret it," he said.

Yes, that may be true, Ali thought, *but only if I'm alive long enough to care.*

She waited until the car doors slammed again and the engine turned over. Tires crunched in the gravel of the driveway. By sending Jacky and his friend away, Ali knew that she had saved his weasely little life and that of his friend as well. Now she needed to save her own.

"Who are you?" she said to the man. "What do you want?"

"You tell me," he replied. Obviously, he was enjoying this dangerous game of twenty questions.

On the trail of a possible identity thief, Ali and B.'s amateur sleuthing had led them to Singleatheart. This man had evidently doubled back on the same trail and had come looking for them in return—looking for Ali. Devoid of her Glock, all she could do was bluff.

"You're from Singleatheart," she said.

He smiled again—a chilling grimace that filled Ali's soul with dread. "I'm not just *from* Singleatheart," he told her deliberately. "I *am* Singleatheart. Who helped you find me? Who helped you destroy my files?"

"Does it matter?" she said. "And what makes you think I had help?"

"I *know* you had help," he returned. "You may be a lot of things, Ms. Reynolds, but you're no computer genius. I saw what equipment you have lying around here. There's a Mac down in the basement—one your son evidently uses—but that's it. Less than basic."

"And I suppose you consider yourself some kind of self-styled computer genius?" Ali replied. "Maybe you are, but once we break your encryption code, we'll have all your secrets."

She knew it was dangerous to taunt him, just as it was dangerous to taunt a coiled rattlesnake, but she couldn't help herself. She needed to do something to unsettle him. Words were the only weapons at hand.

"So you didn't only destroy my files," he snarled at her. "You stole them."

Without warning, he sprang from the couch and crossed the room, brandishing the gun like a club. Before she could raise her hands to defend herself, the blow fell. The weapon slammed into the flesh of her cheek with a tooth-jarring intensity that sent her sprawling, bouncing off the door and sliding across the tiled entryway. As stars exploded in her vision, she came to rest against the legs of the burled-wood table. The room spun and swam around her. Blood spilled from the cut on her cheek and slopped into her eye, blurring her vision that much more. She tasted blood in her mouth as well, and the pain was more than she could imagine. But by then he had grabbed the crewneck of her sweatshirt and was hauling her to her feet.

"Who helped you?" he snarled.

He was mere inches away. She could feel his hot breath on her face.

"No one," she managed. "I didn't need any help."

"That's a lie," he said, shaking her as though she were a rag doll. "You just said 'we.' Who's we?"

With that, he let loose of her shirt and gave her another powerful shove, one that sent her careening across the room. She landed backward onto the couch, hitting the back of it hard enough that her head snapped whiplash fashion. The room spun around her again. When it stopped spinning, he was looming over her once more.

"Who helped you?" he repeated. "It sure as hell wasn't that useless little Brit."

For the first time since the confrontation had begun, Ali put it together. This guy was here, in her house. He had driven here in Leland's truck and let himself in with Leland's keys. For all she knew, Leland Brooks was lying dead in the basement.

"What did you do to him?" she managed. "Where is he?"

"Indisposed at the moment, I'm afraid," the man replied. "He refused to tell me what I wanted to know. Maybe he didn't say because he didn't know. But you do know, and you're going to tell me!"

"Where is he?" Ali demanded. "Is Leland hurt?"

It was all she could do to force the words out past her already badly swollen lips. She wondered in passing if her jaw was broken, but the pain was so intense that it was almost as though she were observing someone else's battered and bloody body and hearing someone else's labored voice.

Staring down at her, he said nothing. The fact that

he wouldn't answer her questions was answer enough. In a moment of appalling clarity, Ali knew that whatever horrors had already been visited on poor Leland Brooks would also be coming to B. Simpson as soon as this monster knew who B. was. And when that happened, Ali knew it would be her fault for dragging Leland Brooks and B. Simpson into this nightmare along with her.

"Tell me what I want to know!" her tormentor ordered. "Tell me now or else."

"Or else what?" she spat back at him. "Go to hell!"

He reached for her then. She thought for a moment he was going to hit her again, but just then a bell sounded, and it was enough to make him hesitate. The ringing seemed to be coming from the far distance, like the bell signaling the end of a round in a boxing match. It took a moment for her to realize that the sound was coming from her cell phone. It was ringing from the spot inside her bra where she sometimes stowed it. The same place Edie Larson carried hers.

"Don't answer that," her attacker ordered in a hoarse whisper. "Don't even think about touching it."

It wasn't until he was headed back up I-17 that Dave Holman realized he'd never bothered to turn his phone back on when he'd left the Morrisons' house after the interview with Jenny. As soon as he turned it on, he saw he had six messages. Four were from the office, telling him with increasing urgency that his warrant was ready, and did he want to be on hand when they went to search Ali Reynolds's house? Two of the voice mails were from Ali herself. After calling in to the office and letting them know he was on his way, he tried calling Ali back. When she didn't answer, Dave felt a small surge of relief. He knew that she'd been pissed at him this morning when he'd told her about the search warrant, and she probably still was. He'd talk to her later and try to smooth her ruffled feathers. She had offered to show him files purported to be from Bryan Forester's computer. And even though he had turned her down, he should probably attempt to revisit that decision. In the meantime, he had another problem.

Dave now suspected that Bryan Forester had at least one accomplice in the plot to murder his wife. Dave was also thinking that one of those accomplices could have been Matthew Morrison. Sure, Bobby Salazar had sworn that Morrison hadn't been behind the wheel of the car turned back in on Monday, but if Matthew wasn't involved in the Forester homicide, why had he killed himself? Jenny Morrison had taken the position that her husband's death was accidental. Dave's homicide-detective gut told him it was definitely deliberate.

This wasn't just idle speculation. Dave sensed there was some kind of connection between Matthew Morrison's dead computer and Bryan Forester's overwritten files. Someone had made a concerted effort to obliterate the information on three different computers. That meant the data from one of those held an important clue, a key to everything that had happened. All Dave Holman had to do was find it.

Neither Ali nor the intruder said a word while the phone continued to ring. It was maddening for Ali to know there was someone on the other end of the line.

If she answered, there might be enough time for a desperate scream for help. But she knew better. By the time she flipped the phone open, she would be dead. If help came at all, it would come too late.

After ringing five times, the phone subsided into silence. The man was still standing over her, holding the gun.

"Who helped you?" he demanded again. "And where the hell are your real computers?"

Ali didn't answer. A trickle of coppery-tasting blood ran across her tonsils. As she fought off her gag reflex, her phone jangled again. This time she knew it was announcing a voice mail—a message she didn't know if she'd ever have a chance to hear, much less return.

"Get up," he ordered.

Ali didn't move. She couldn't. After a moment he grabbed her sweatshirt again. Holding it so tightly against her throat that she could barely breathe, he jerked her to her feet and propelled her across the room and into her bedroom. As she stumbled into the room, she caught a glimpse of poor Sam dodging for cover under the bed. That was also when Ali caught sight of Leland Brooks. Duct tape pinned his arms to his body and bound his legs together. From the knees up, he appeared to be soaking wet, and so was the carpeted floor all around him. Trussed, helpless, and absolutely unmoving, he lay on the floor between the bed and the dresser. As far as Ali could tell, he wasn't breathing. Was Leland unconscious, or was he already dead?

She struggled and twisted, trying to escape her attacker's iron-fisted grasp. "What have you done to him?" she demanded. "Is he dead?"

"Not yet, but he will be soon if you don't give me what I want."

She knew from the way the man said it that he wasn't making idle threats. She knew instinctively that he was a killer who would kill again. He would murder Ali and Leland Brooks in cold blood without a moment's hesitation.

"What do you want?" Her lips were almost swollen shut. She could barely speak.

"I already told you," he said. "You didn't just destroy my files, you stole them. How else would you know they were encrypted? I want them back, all of them."

Ali said nothing.

"Even more than my files," he added, "I want the bastard who did this."

And there it was: the automatic and arrogant assumption that whoever had managed to do this to him—to outwit him—had to be a man. In his distorted view of the universe, only another male would be smart enough to catch him.

By then he had muscled Ali through her bedroom and into the bathroom beyond it. Still holding her sweatshirt bunched at the front of her neck, he reached down long enough to put the gun down on the side of the tub. The bathroom floor was slick with water. The room reeked of vomit, and the bathtub was full almost to overflowing with vomit-spattered water.

Ali knew then what was coming. "That's what you did to Leland Brooks?" she gasped. "You forced him underwater?"

The man nodded grimly. Letting go of her shirt, he twisted her around so her back was to him. "Believe me, if he'd known anything, by the time it was over, he would have told me. The same way you will."

"No," she said, trying desperately to pull away from him. "You can't do this. Please."

"Of course I can do this," he returned calmly. "I can do anything I want. Surely you've heard of water-boarding. Everyone has these days. If it's good enough for Islamic terrorists, it's good enough for you, and it's pretty much foolproof. When we're done, it'll work the same way for me that it does for the CIA. In order to keep from drowning, you'll tell me everything I want to know."

"You'll never get away with it," Ali said. "They'll find you. They'll put you away."

"No, they won't, my dear. I'll be long gone before anyone ever finds you or your friend out there. Long gone."

Staring down at the bathtub full of water, Ali Reynolds knew one thing that her captor couldn't possibly know: She was petrified of water; terrified of drowning. As a teenager, she had nearly drowned on an outing to Oak Creek's Slide Rock. She had knocked herself out on a rock and gone under. She had been unconscious when one of her friends pulled her from the water and pumped the water out of her chest. She had awakened coughing and choking.

All her adult life, she had avoided swimming pools and hot tubs, and wading in the ocean was totally off limits. She simply couldn't bear the idea of being at the mercy of those unpredictable waves. She had enrolled Chris in swimming classes early because she had wanted him to be water-safe. She had wanted him to be able to save himself rather than looking to her for help. Only in the last few years, in the safety of this very room, had she forced herself to overcome that fear by facing it—by trying the occasional bubble bath.

But now the tub had turned into Ali's worst horror. Staring down at it, she knew what would happen. Once he forced her head underwater long enough for the water to gush into her lungs, she would tell him whatever he wanted to know when she came back up. She would do anything to keep it from happening again—to keep him from doing to her what he had already done to Leland Brooks.

Who could already be dead, she reminded herself. *Who told this monster nothing because he had nothing to tell.*

She knew that Leland Brooks's fate should have been enough to make her capitulate right then. Maybe that was what her captor had in mind—that simple dread would make her weaker. To her astonishment, it had exactly the opposite effect. A pulse of absolute abhorrence shot through her, filling her body with a physical strength she didn't know she had.

Ali fought him then, fought him tooth and nail, biting and scratching in a desperate attempt to maim him, to knee him in the groin or gouge out his eyes. He outweighed her, though. He was taller and far stronger. She knew going in that no matter how hard she fought, eventually, she would lose. That was inevitable.

Yes, Ali thought as he forced her down on her knees beside the tub and pressed her face toward the water. Dreading what was coming, she took one last desperate gasp of air, filling her lungs as he grabbed the back of her neck and plunged her head underwater.

Dave Holman's phone rang again as he approached the exit at Cordes Junction. "Is this Detective Holman?"

"Yes. Who is this, and how did you get my number?"

"My name is Simpson—B. Simpson. I run an Internet security firm called High Noon. Ali Reynolds is one of my clients, and I have access to her files. I found your numbers listed in her contact list. Have you heard from her?"

"From Ali? Not in the last little while," Dave replied. "I missed a couple of calls from her earlier this morning, but when I tried calling back, she didn't answer. Why? What's up? Is something wrong?"

B. paused before he answered. "I know the two of you have a lot of history," he said tentatively. "And this would probably be better coming from her, but . . ."

"What would be better coming from her?" Dave asked impatiently. "What are you talking about?"

"I have a name for you," B. said. "A name for the case you're working on. The man's name is Winter— Dr. Peter Winter. I just Googled him. He's an ER physician at Phoenix General."

"Which case would that be?" Dave asked.

"Morgan Forester's murder," B. answered.

"And how exactly is this Dr. Winter supposed to be related?"

"Earlier this week I discovered that a worm had taken up residence in Ali's computer. I was able to neutralize it before it could do any irreparable damage, and we assumed it was just a case of attempted identity theft. A little while ago, Ali brought me a pair of thumb drives Bryan Forester had given her for safekeeping. They contained copies of files from his computer and from Morgan's as well. The same worm had been planted in the thumb-drive files. If they had been opened on a computer with access to the Internet, those files would have been destroyed, the same way the files were destroyed on the two computers you picked up on your search warrant. Once again, I've neutralized the worm before it was able to do any damage."

"Wait," Dave said. "You're saying the same worm that was on the Foresters' computers was also on Ali's? How can you be sure?"

"How does an epidemiologist know one strain of flu from another?" B. returned. "By analyzing the makeup of the virus that causes each individual case. This is the same thing. All three worms come from the same basic source—in other words, from the same programmer. Had the worm actually been unleashed, the end result would have been slightly different. For instance, the Trojan in Ali's system was set to simply crash the computer. The worm on the Foresters' computers was set to overwrite files. But it's still the same guy."

Dave's heartbeat quickened. The guy was a doctor? That might explain the single unexplained needle mark the ME had found at the back of Morgan Forester's neck, in a spot where it couldn't possibly have been self-administered. And now there was another crashed computer? Anxious not to give anything away, the next time he spoke, Dave was careful to keep his voice and his questions firmly neutral. "What does this Winter character have to do with any of this?"

"That's the thing," B. said. "I gave Ali a choice. I told her we could pursue legal recourse, or we could go after the guy on our own."

"Don't tell me," Dave said. "I already know where Ali Reynolds came down on that one."

"Yes," B. agreed, "you do. So we sent the guy a worm of our own and picked up all the files from his PC in the process."

"In other words, you used an illegal wiretap. Evidence from that wouldn't be admissible in a court of law."

"Maybe not," B. agreed. "But it's good enough for an anonymous tip. Most of Winter's files are encrypted. I'm working on breaking the code. So far I haven't had much luck, but I did come across one unencrypted file—one he somehow missed: his initial licensing agreement with Microsoft from back when he first purchased the computer. That's where I got his name. He's apparently connected to an Internet dating site called Singleatheart. Ali's computer was infected after she registered at that site. I believe Singleatheart may also have some connection to the Forester murder."

Listening intently to every word, Dave fought to avoid betraying his eagerness. Maybe the files Ali had offered him were the Foresters' real files after all. If someone besides Bryan had tried to destroy them, maybe Dave had missed something. It was possible that this Winter guy was in on everything with Bryan Forester. It was also possible Dave was wrong.

As the Cordes Junction exit came up, Dave switched on his turn signal. "All right," he said. "I'll see about looking into all this, Mr.—" He paused. "What did you say your name was again?"

"Simpson. B. Simpson."

Once he was off the exit ramp, Dave pulled over. "And how do I get back to you?"

B. gave him a phone number. After ending the

call, Dave wasted no time putting in another one—to Phoenix General Hospital. His first call, to the ER, came up empty. Dr. Winter was not due in today, and the person who took the call said he was expected to be away for an indefinite period. Dave's next call was to the hospital's administration office. It took a while before he managed to work his way up the chain of command and found someone who seemed to know what was going on.

"Yes, Dr. Winter is on staff here," a woman named Louise Granger told him. "But he's currently on leave. His mother was taken ill overnight and was transported to an ICU. Dr. Winter flew out to be with her first thing this morning."

"Did he say where?" Dave asked.

"I don't remember the exact location. He may not have even mentioned it to me, but I believe it was somewhere in upstate New York. Buffalo, maybe."

Dave ended the call and then looked at his watch. He wanted to go back to Phoenix and start following up on this lead, but he had told the people at the office to wait for him—that he wanted to be on the scene when it came time to execute the search warrant. Since it wasn't possible to be in two places at once, he picked up the phone and punched in the number for Detective Sean O'Brien of the Scottsdale PD.

"Hey," O'Brien said once Dave had identified himself. "Have I got some hot news for you. Mr. Morrison's got nothing to do with that homicide case of yours."

"What makes you say that?" Dave asked.

"After you left, I went back to Jenny Morrison. I convinced her that with Mr. Morrison's computer broken, and in order to ascertain that her husband hadn't committed suicide, we needed access to his e-mail accounts, which she was happy to give me. It turns out that the day before he died, Mr. Morrison went through his mail account and deleted a large number of messages. Unfortunately for him, the deleted messages were still stored on his ISP. He wasn't in Sedona on Monday morning. He was actually down in a new development called Red Rock, where he was hoping to meet up with a sweet little real estate babe he met over the Internet. He was all hot to trot and hoping to get lucky, but she stood him up."

"What real estate agent?" Dave asked.

"A woman named Susan," O'Brien answered. "From an Internet dating site."

"Was it a place called Singleatheart, by any chance?" Dave asked.

"As a matter of fact, it was," O'Brien replied. "How did you figure that out?"

"Luck," Dave said. "Combined with an anonymous tip. But now I've got someone else I need you to track down. An ER doc from Phoenix General. His name's Peter Winter, and he supposedly flew out of Sky Harbor this morning on his way to visit his ailing mother in upstate New York."

"That's all you know about him?"

"So far. Except that I've been told he's also involved in Singleatheart, and I need you to find him."

"What do you want me to do with him once I find him?"

"Just let me know where he is. I'll take it from there."

"Anything else?" said Sean O'Brien.

"If you can locate a photo of Dr. Winter, I need you

to take a copy of it over to the Hertz facility at Sky Harbor. Show it to a guy who works the vehicle check-in line—a guy by the name of Bobby Salazar—and ask him if it looks familiar. Let me know what he says."

"Will do," Sean said. "Glad to help out."

Ending the call, Dave steered his vehicle back onto the freeway, heading north. He knew he had just learned something important. One way or the other, Peter Winter was involved, and without Ali and B.'s efforts, that connection wouldn't have come to light— at least not this soon.

Wanting to say thank you, he tried calling Ali one more time. Once again, she didn't answer.

Why leave word for me to call if you're not going to pick up? Dave wondered.

He hung up without leaving a message.

{ CHAPTER 15 }

Ali was falling—falling through space and time. The ground was coming up at her fast. It was reddish, rocky dirt punctuated by a few scrubby bushes, a lot like the ground around Sedona. As she fell to earth, she realized she was supposed to pull the cord on her parachute, but she couldn't find the cord, and she didn't have a parachute. Someone had told her that she should pack it, that she should keep it with her at all times, but she didn't have it now, and when she hit the ground, she was going to die.

Suddenly, she came out of the water. He grabbed her by her hair and pulled her out of the tub. He flung her gasping and wheezing and choking onto the bathroom floor. The water and other things as well gushed out of her—out of her nose and her mouth—as she choked and heaved. Her whole body shook with terrible spasms as she tried desperately to clear her lungs and find a way to breathe again. To find a way to live.

How many times had he shoved her under? She didn't know and couldn't remember. The only thing that mattered now was would he do it again? And when? And where was he? He seemed to have left her alone on the bathroom floor. Why? Not that being left alone offered any particular advantage. Ali was helpless. She couldn't move. The racking spasms of choking and coughing left her weak and dizzy and almost paralyzed. She knew she couldn't stand up. She couldn't even crawl. All she could do was pray—for wisdom, for strength, for grace.

Then her tormentor was back. She saw his bootie-clad feet next to her face and heard his voice speaking to her from very far away. "Had enough?" he asked.

Ali tried to answer, but another set of body-racking coughs rocked her. She tried to say "Enough," but she couldn't speak. All she could do was nod.

He dragged her up off the floor and pulled her sopping-wet body into the bedroom. Grasping her under her shoulders and knees, he lifted her and then dropped her on the bed. The movement dislodged more water from her lungs and set off another spasm of choking. Turning her head to cough, she noticed Leland's body wasn't exactly where it had been. He was still and unmoving again. Either Leland had moved himself or he had been moved.

Maybe Leland's alive, Ali thought. *Why else would he be duct-taped? Maybe I'm not alone in this after all.*

"So tell me," her tormentor urged. "I'm waiting."

She looked up at him. He was no longer training his gun on her. Instead, he was using a towel to dry it. Evidently, in the course of their epic struggle, she had managed to knock the weapon—a .357, from the looks of it—into the tub. Ali knew that didn't count in her favor. Just because the gun had gotten wet didn't mean it wouldn't work. If he aimed it in her direction and pulled the trigger, it would fire, and she would be dead.

"Well?" he pressed. "Who was it?"

And that was when the answer came to her. It was an answer to her prayer, and it came to her out of the blue. *He's waiting for me to tell him something. But I don't have to tell him the truth.*

The truth would mean divulging B. Simpson's name and address, but Ali already knew that B., by his own admission, wasn't armed. He was tall and imposing and could probably defend himself under most circumstances, but not against a determined killer armed with a .357.

If she told the man that the cops had helped her, it would be over. He'd kill her and be done with it. What Ali really needed was a bargaining chip, something she could use to divert him long enough to get help. And where would she find that? She needed an ally who was armed to the teeth and who would be utterly fearless when it came to fighting back.

With a start, Ali realized she knew just such a person.

"My mother," she whispered aloud.

"Your what?"

"My mother," she repeated.

"You're saying your mother did this? No way!" he blurted. "I read all about your parents in some of those articles on you. Don't they run some stupid restaurant or something?"

That he could so easily dismiss her parents and their life's work made Ali that much more determined. She had paid a huge price to be able to lie to this man. Now her very life depended on making sure that lie was believable.

"It's true," she insisted between coughs. "All of it. Mom helped me grab your files. It's her hobby. She does it for fun."

The disbelief on his face was clear. He simply couldn't get his mind around the fact that he might have been bested by a woman or, rather, by two women—Ali and her mother. That was absolutely unacceptable.

"For fun? No!" he exclaimed. "You can't tell me that an old woman who makes her living cooking in some dinky restaurant is some kind of computer genius. That's not possible. It makes no sense."

"It's true," Ali said again.

"Where did she go to school, then?"

Ali knew that in order to convince him, she would need to come up with a whole series of telling details.

"Mother's family was poor. When it was time for her to go off to college, there wasn't any money, especially since she wanted to become an engineer. Back then engineering schools weren't interested in enrolling women, so she taught herself."

That bit was taken from B. Simpson's nonstandard education. He didn't have an engineering degree, either.

"But she was always curious about how things work," Ali went on. "She was forever taking stuff apart and putting it back together and improving whatever it was in the process."

That, of course, was more like Ali's father. It was how Bob Larson had kept his beloved Bronco in working order all these years.

"She taught herself programming, too," Ali said, warming to her story. "A couple of years ago, when a friend's computer got taken down by a virus, Mother made it her business to become a self-taught expert in worms and viruses."

That last whopper may have been a step too far.

"I suppose next you're going to tell me she's also an expert at encryption?" the man asked sarcastically. "Is that another of your remarkable mother's spare-time specialties?"

"You're right," Ali said. "Mom doesn't know anything about encryption, but she has a friend who does, an elderly friend who specialized in code-breaking during the Cold War. He and his new wife have a winter home in Yuma. Mother asked him to come help out. They'll be driving up later on this afternoon."

The man's momentary expression of dismay was immediately replaced by something cold and calculating. Once again the gun was aimed squarely in Ali's direction.

"Where are my files, then?" he asked. "Who has them right now, and who has access to them?"

"They're on my mother's computer," she said. "At her house."

"Where's that?"

"Here in Sedona. Down by the highway."

"And where's your mother?"

Ali glanced at her watch. It wasn't waterproof, so the glass was covered with a layer of steam from being dunked in the tub, but the watch was still running. It was two o'clock. Soon the restaurant would be closing for the afternoon. Her father and Jan would be cleaning up and putting things away. Her mother, having arrived early to do the Sugarloaf's morning baking, would have gone home to rest, to put her feet up and have an hour or so of peace and quiet before her husband came in for the evening.

"She's home now, too," Ali said.

"Call her, then," the man ordered. "Have her come here and bring her damn computer with her."

Ali knew that wasn't going to work. Asking Edie to bring over her computer with its nonexistent files would provoke an immediate storm of difficult and impossible-to-answer questions. Fortunately, when Ali reached for her phone, it wasn't there. It had disappeared from under her bra strap during the struggle in the bathroom. It was probably sitting on the bottom of the tub.

"I can't," she said. "I lost my phone."

The man checked his own watch and abruptly changed his mind. Turning away from Ali, he rummaged in her closet, found a jogging suit, and tossed it in her direction.

"Get out of those wet clothes and put these on," he ordered. "We won't have your mother come here. We'll go see her instead."

Dave had put himself out on a real limb by letting Ali know in advance that the search was coming. Having run that risk, Dave was annoyed when he arrived at the Manzanita Hills house and found that his officers were on the scene and armed with their search warrant but Ali hadn't bothered to show up. She hadn't sent Leland Brooks, either. With no keys available, Dave had no choice.

"Cut the padlock on the Mini-Mobile," he ordered. "If you can jimmy the lock on the front door, do it. Otherwise, knock it down."

The uniformed officer had just swung open the

door on the metal storage unit when Bryan Forester's Dodge Ram pulled into the driveway. He jumped out of the cab and came running over to the officers, who were about to step inside.

"What the hell do you think you're doing?" he demanded.

So Ali did tell him, Dave thought grimly. *Too bad for him, he got the news too late.* "Back off, Bryan," he ordered. "My officers have a warrant to search this site."

"There are valuable tools and equipment in there," Bryan objected. "I don't want people messing with them."

"I said back off," Dave repeated. "We're doing a search. We're not going to bother your equipment. I don't see any of your guys working today. What brings you here?"

"The tile company in Phoenix called me about some kind of delivery mix-up. Supposedly, someone was on his way here to drop off a load of tile that isn't mine. I came by to check it out."

Dave glanced around the driveway and saw nothing. *Likely story,* he thought. "What tile?" he asked. "I don't see any tile."

"I don't see any, either," Bryan said. "Like I said, it was a mix-up of some kind—probably someone else's order. I just didn't want it to be delivered here by mistake and then have to make arrangements to ship it back."

"This is going to take some time," Dave said. "If you want to hang around, how about if you and I go have a seat over at the picnic table and give these officers a chance to do their jobs."

Nodding, Bryan headed for the table, shaking a cigarette out of a pack as he went. "You let me out this morning," he said once he was seated and had lit up. "So how come you're searching my stuff this afternoon? What changed?"

Nothing, except the prosecutor lost his balls, Dave thought. He said, "Letting you out was someone else's call, not mine."

"So you still think I did it?" Bryan asked. For a moment the two men glared at each other in charged silence. "Go to hell, then," Bryan added when Dave didn't respond. "I shouldn't be talking to you, not without my lawyer." He stood up as if to go.

"Sit," Dave said.

Bryan sat.

"Who's Peter Winter?"

"Peter who?"

"Winter. Dr. Peter Winter."

Bryan shrugged. "I have no idea. Never heard of the man."

"We believe he had some connection with Singleatheart," Dave said.

"So?" Bryan asked, blowing a cloud of smoke skyward. "What does that have to do with me? Morgan was involved in all that garbage, not me."

"Maybe you both were," Dave suggested.

"Like I said before, go to hell," Bryan told him. "Everyone in town knows your ex screwed around on you while you were off in Iraq. You didn't kill her."

"How kind of you to mention that," Dave returned. "But it turns out my ex isn't dead. Yours is."

"Yes, Morgan was screwing around on me, but that doesn't mean I killed her."

"If you knew what was going on, why didn't you divorce her?" Dave asked.

"Why do you think? The first time it happened, it broke my heart. But I got over it. After a while I just didn't care anymore. I hung in because of the kids, because I didn't want to lose my girls."

This was far more than Bryan had said during all the hours Dave had spent with him in the interrogation room. "You knew about Singleatheart, then?" Dave asked.

"Not until Monday night, when I went through Morgan's computer files."

"How could you do that?" Dave asked. "Her computer was at the house. It was under lock and key as part of the crime scene."

"There's a backup system," Bryan said. "It was all there—her own little black book. Morgan kept a detailed account of all her conquests: where they went, what they did, when she dumped the poor guy, and how. And if you want to find someone who was pissed about being dumped, maybe you should talk to my old pal Billy Barnes. That two-faced SOB, my good buddy, a guy whose ass I saved by giving him a job, was more than happy to screw around with my wife behind my back. And when she dropped him for that new guy, somebody named Jimmy, Billy went all to pieces. Sent her whiny, pleading messages, begging her to take him back. But by now you've been through her files, and you already know all this stuff. You've seen it."

"No, I haven't," Dave said. "The files on Morgan's computer had all been destroyed. So were yours."

The undiluted surprise on Bryan Forester's face would have been tough to fake. "Destroyed?" he demanded. "What do you mean, destroyed? How's that possible?"

"Someone overwrote the files. There's nothing left."

"Nothing?" Bryan repeated, shaking his head. "That can't be. No way. My whole business is on those two computers—all my contracts and sales records; my tax and insurance information." He paused. "You don't think I did this—that I deliberately set out to destroy the information. Besides, I made copies on two thumb drives. I gave them to Ali, but maybe they're wrecked, too. Crap. If they are, then I'm done for. Out of business. That's what this is all about, isn't it? Somebody's out to destroy me."

From Monday afternoon on, from the moment Dave had seen Morgan Forester's lifeless body in the porch swing, he had been convinced that her husband had done the deed. And when he'd first learned of the damaged computers, he'd been even more certain that Bryan was responsible for those as well. B. Simpson had tried to tell him otherwise, but Dave hadn't really believed it. Now maybe he did, and for the first time it occurred to him that there might be two victims here—both Morgan Forester and her husband.

Ali felt self-conscious peeling out of her sodden clothing and putting on the jogging suit under the watchful eye of her captor. As she did it, she seesawed back and forth, second-guessing her strategy. She kept hoping that somehow she'd find another way out of this awful mess—a way that wouldn't require involving her mother in a desperate life-or-death gambit.

Ali knew she should leave Edie out of it, even though her mother and her newly activated Taser held the key to evening the odds. What if it all went bad—if one or both of them died? Ali knew in advance that no matter what happened, her mother would forgive her, and so would her father. There was no question about that. The problem was, if something awful happened to Edie and her daughter somehow survived, would Ali ever be able to forgive herself?

Even so, Ali knew several important things about Edie Larson that the bad guy didn't. For one thing, Ali understood that her mother would fight to the death to help protect her child, in the same way Ali would fight for Chris if the situation called for it. Ali knew, too, that her mother was stubborn. Having gone to war with her husband over whether she should have a Taser, Edie would be damned rather than leave the restaurant without it. Just to show her husband, she would have taken it home with her. It would be someplace close at hand—in her pocket or her purse.

Ali's captor wouldn't consider the possibility that Edie Larson would be armed for bear. This arrogant jerk would automatically assume that Edie—a harmless-looking gray-haired, hearing-aid-wearing old lady—would pose no threat to him at all. Ali understood instinctively that he would totally "misunderestimate" her mother.

Edie Larson's stubborn streak was much like Ali's own, and Edie would fight like crazy once she knew what was going on—if she knew what was going on. That was the problem. How could Ali manage that feat of mother/daughter communication? How would she let Edie know what was at stake without alerting the gunman?

At last Ali was dressed. When she stood up, she was woozy. Clutching at the dresser for support, she looked around for her shoes, which were nowhere to be seen. The cut next to her eye was still bleeding. She looked down at her bare feet just as a drop of blood trickled off her chin and dripped onto the top of her foot. Her cheek ached, her mouth was close to being swollen shut, but seeing the blood—her own blood—shocked her.

I could die today, she thought. *It could all be over.*

Meantime, her captor pointed the gun at Leland Brooks, who lay motionless on the floor. "Drag him into the other room," he ordered Ali. "We'll load him into the back of his truck and take him with us when we leave."

To go where? Ali wondered. *Where are you taking us?*

She didn't ask that question aloud, though. She knew better. Wherever he planned to take them, it wasn't going to be good.

When she bent down to lift Leland, she was relieved to find him soaking wet but warm to the touch. He was breathing and probably heavily sedated, but at least he wasn't dead. He was deadweight, however. Grunting with effort, she managed to drag him out of the bedroom, through the living room, and over to the front door. He moaned softly as she wrestled him out the door and onto the front steps.

She hoped briefly that one of her neighbors might see what was going on and summon help. Ali's Andante Drive house sat at the top of the hill with an unobstructed view of the surrounding countryside, but that also meant the house next door shielded her place from all the others farther down the street. As for her next-door neighbor? She was a single mother who was most likely at work, and her kids were at school. Looking at that deserted street, Ali had never felt more isolated or more alone.

At the edge of the porch, she stopped, panting with effort. "He's too heavy," she gasped. "I can't do this alone."

With a sigh of disgust, the man shoved the .357 into the top of his pants. Bending over, he effortlessly lifted Leland off the porch and flung him over his shoulder. Ali thought briefly about making a grab for the gun while both of the man's hands were occupied. She thought about it, but she didn't even try. She was too spent to make it work.

"Open it," he ordered.

Months earlier, Leland Brooks had installed an aluminum camper shell on the back of his truck. The tailgate on the camper shell flipped up while the tailgate on the truck flipped down. Ali wrenched both of them open and then stood back while her captor tossed Leland's helpless body onto the floor of the pickup as casually as if he were a bag of potatoes.

"So much for him," the man said, closing the tailgates. "We can finish this later. Time to go. You drive."

But Ali didn't move right away. The water was finally clearing from her lungs, and the crippling fog was lifting from her brain as well. She stared up at him. He was still wearing his latex gloves. Why? Because he didn't want to leave any prints behind. He claimed this was all about his stolen files—that he wanted his files back. But there had to be more to it, had to be more at stake. In a moment of insight, Ali understood what it was—the only thing that made sense.

"You murdered Morgan Forester, didn't you?"

He gave a mirthless chuckle and shrugged. "Brainy as you are, you're just now figuring that out? Morgan thought she was smarter than I am, but she wasn't. Neither are you, and neither is your mother."

"And now you're going to kill us, too?"

He nodded. "More than likely," he said. "Get in."

"But why?" Ali objected. "Why are you going to kill us?"

"Because I have to," he said reasonably. "Because you have no idea who you're messing with or what you've done. Now let's go. I don't have all day."

When Ali climbed into the pickup, she found Leland's car key already in the ignition. She turned it, and the engine roared to life. A lightweight windbreaker had been lying on the seat. As they started down Andante Drive through Skyview, her captor put on the jacket and then slipped the .357 into his pocket.

"You still haven't told me why you killed Morgan," Ali insisted. "What did she do wrong?"

"I killed her because she asked too many questions, and so do you. Now shut up and drive."

When they reached the highway, there were still a few cars in the parking lot at the Sugarloaf Café. Ali knew her father and Jan would be fully occupied with shutting down for the day. While they were driving down the hill, Ali had half hoped her mother's Oldsmobile Alero wouldn't be parked there. Maybe Edie would have gone off to run an errand, to pick up some groceries for dinner or to have her hair done. Then whatever happened—whatever this maniac had in mind—would happen to Ali alone. Her mother wouldn't be involved.

But Edie's Alero was there, parked right next to her husband's venerable Bronco. Ali expected that her mother was safely ensconced in her cozy living room, where she could indulge in her one guilty pleasure—watching TiVoed episodes of the previous day's *Dr.*

Phil and *Judge Judy.* That was what she often did in the afternoons before her husband walked in from the restaurant and switched over to nonstop cable news.

The man was right behind Ali with his hand in his pocket as she walked up to her parents' front door. She could hear the television set blaring from inside. As soon as Ali tapped on the door frame, her mother muted the volume.

"Just a minute," she said. "I'm coming. I'm coming. I can't do everything at once." A moment later, Edie, with a phone in one hand, opened the front door and caught sight of Ali. "Why aren't you answering your phone?" she demanded. "I've been trying to reach you, and so has B. I was waiting for your father to finish cleaning up so we could both come check—" She stopped abruptly. "Ali, you're bleeding!" she exclaimed. "And your hair's all wet. What happened? Are you all right?"

Only then did Edie catch sight of the man standing behind Ali. "Who's this?" she asked.

"It's the man whose files we stole this morning." Ali spoke quickly, hoping to stave off any comments that would give the game away. "He's dangerous, and he's got a gun. He wants his files back, Mom. I told him they're on your computer."

Edie peered up at the man. "Oh, yes," she said, dropping the phone into the sagging pocket of the worn cotton sweater that was her preferred around-the-house attire. "The files. That means you would be Peter Winter, then, correct? Dr. Peter Winter, I believe."

Edie's question may have astonished her daughter, but it floored the man behind her. He took an involuntary step backward.

His name is Winter? Ali wondered. *How on earth did Mom know that?*

By then he had recovered enough to press the barrel of the gun into the small of Ali's back. "Move," he ordered. "Get inside. Both of you. Now."

Still mystified by her mother's reaction, Ali stumbled over the threshold and into the comfortable, crowded clutter that was Bob and Edie Larson's tiny living room. There was the recliner her mother occupied only when Bob wasn't home, as well as a sagging cloth-covered couch with a colorful crocheted afghan covering the spot on the back where aging material had given way.

Both couch and chair were situated within easy viewing distance of an old-fashioned console TV, one that was far too big for the room. The television inside the shiny cherry cabinetry had been dead for years, but the piece of furniture served as a handy base for a newer, slimmer model as well as a collection of cable boxes, receivers, and recorders, everything from an old-fashioned VHS model up through the spanking-new DVR Chris had given his grandfather for his birthday.

Glancing at the TV screen in passing, Ali expected to see a frozen image of Judge Judy preparing to pass judgment on some hapless pair of feuding dimbulbs. Instead, she saw a Taser, one that was improbably decked out in a leopard pattern. Ali knew then that, rather than watching a television program, Edie had been reviewing her training DVD. As for Edie's metallic pink Taser? That one lay on the hassock that served as her parents' joint footstool, hidden in plain sight among a scattered collection of remote controls. It was tantalizingly close but out of Edie's reach and certainly out of Ali's.

Edie had backed away from the door in order to let them in, but Ali noticed that her eyes remained locked on the man—a man whose name she somehow seemed to know. How was that possible?

"The computer's in the office," Edie said to him. "Do you want to go get it, or should I?"

Calling the room that had once been Ali's bedroom an "office" was vastly overstating the case. Every bit as cluttered as the living room, the second bedroom was actually a catchall storage room. It contained the entire collection of holiday decorations for every conceivable occasion that went up inside the Sugarloaf Café with absolute predictability. It was also a resting place for Bob and Edie Larson's various short-lived hobbies.

A rickety table in one corner held Edie's Singer sewing machine, while the flower-patterned spread on the twin bed had long since disappeared under stacks of material and patterns, as well as Edie's many half-completed sewing projects. One wall of the room was stacked with boxes of books Bob had gathered up in preparation for retirement reading in case retirement ever became a viable option. Another jumble of boxes held the latest assortment of cast-off clothing and household goods that Bob Larson routinely collected and then passed along to anyone who happened to be in need. If a computer—even Edie's laptop—had somehow been shoehorned into all that mess, Ali had no idea where it would have gone.

Winter, if that really was his name, pulled the .357 out of his pocket and waved it in Edie's direction. "You go," he said. "And remember, since your daughter's here with me, you'd better not try anything."

Shaking her head in apparent disgust, Edie disappeared into the bedroom/office. Ali was torn. She wanted to edge closer to the hassock, but she didn't want to risk drawing the man's attention to either the Taser image on the television screen or the real Taser resting just beyond her reach.

What if she somehow managed to retrieve it? Her mother had shown her how to push the switch cover out of the way, and which button to depress, but would it work? And if Ali did get off a shot, would the darts penetrate the man's jacket?

A moment later, and much to Ali's amazement, her mother emerged from the bedroom carrying what looked like part of a very old desktop computer. She lugged it over to the table and set it down. "There you are," she said.

"What's that?" Winter asked.

"My computer," Edie said brusquely. "You said you wanted my computer. I'm bringing it to you."

"But that thing is ancient," Winter objected. "You're telling me that's what you used to steal my files? Does it even still run?"

"Of course it still runs," Edie assured him archly. "A computer's a computer, isn't it? It takes a while to boot up, but once it does, it's good to go. If you'll wait just a minute, I'll go get the rest of it—the keyboard, the CRT, and the power cords."

While she returned to the bedroom, Winter moved closer to the table. Clearly expecting the latest and greatest, he seemed both fascinated and appalled by the appearance of this old machine. Taking advantage of his momentary lapse in focus, Ali moved closer to the hassock.

He reached down and touched the computer. "It's

dead cold," he said when Edie returned with the oversize monitor. "This thing probably hasn't run in years."

"Of course it's cold," Edie told him. "I'm not the kind to leave something plugged in and wasting electricity when I'm not using it."

And that was when Ali understood what was going on. Somehow—through B., in all likelihood—Edie had learned that the man's name was Winter, but the rest of it was all bluff. Edie was making a huge production of dragging this computer equipment from the other room. But Ali knew for sure this wasn't her mother's computer and never had been. It was probably an ancient model someone had donated to Bob, one that was so out of date even he couldn't give it away. And Winter was probably right when he said that if Edie ever did plug it in, it wouldn't boot up.

A telephone rang. Edie pulled it out of her pocket, answered, and then listened. "I'm really very busy right now," she said finally. "And I'm certainly not in the market for aluminum siding."

Sticking the phone back in her pocket, she handed her daughter a tangled power cord. "Here," she said. "Plug this in. If it'll reach that far, we'll have to use the outlet over by the TV set. The one next to the table burned out. And you'll probably need to unplug the lamp or the TV to make it work."

Without a word of objection, Ali took the cord and turned toward the television set. Dropping to her knees next to the hassock, she crawled close enough to the wall to reach the outlet. First she unplugged the TV; she was relieved to know that the Taser with the leopard pattern would now have disappeared. She plugged in the cord, then turned back to the table, where Edie was in the process of reassembling the computer equipment.

Winter, engrossed in watching Edie's every move, was no longer concentrating on Ali. It took only a moment for Ali to pluck the brightly colored C2 out of the cluster of remote controls. As soon as she pulled back on the switch-plate cover, the infrared dot appeared silently in the middle of the man's back. Ali didn't shout out a warning to him. Instead, she simply pressed down on the switch. Winter immediately crumpled to the floor, screaming as he fell. The gun fell, too. It landed on the hardwood floor and went spinning away from him. Edie pounced on the .357 before it ever came to rest. "Got it!" she crowed. "Now open the door. I called nine-one-one. They should be here any minute."

Dropping the Taser, Ali raced to the door and flung it open. As soon as she did, she could hear an approaching siren somewhere in the background.

"I'll go get them," Edie said. "You take the gun. If he tries to get up, I'm sure you'll know how to use it."

Yes, Ali thought savagely. *I sure as hell will!*

{ CHAPTER 16 }

Arriving officers burst into the house while Peter Winter still lay twitching and helpless on the floor. Seeing Ali with the weapon in her hand, they immediately misread the situation.

"Drop the gun," one of them shouted at her. "Get on the floor."

After having her head held underwater, dropping to the floor was no problem. Ali was only too happy to comply.

"That's my daughter," Edie screeched from behind them. "Get him! The guy on the floor. He came in here with a gun. He was going to kill us."

Just then Bob Larson appeared in the doorway behind his wife. Taking in the room, he paused when he saw the man on the floor. "Oh my God, Edie!" he exclaimed. "What have you done? Did you shoot him? Is he dead?"

But by then the thirty-second burst from the Taser had run its course, and Peter Winter lay whimpering on the floor in a puddle of his own making. Moments later, a pair of uniformed Sedona officers fitted him with a pair of Flex-Cuffs and then hauled him to his feet. The jolt of electricity seemed to have turned his legs to rubber.

While the one officer held him upright, the other turned to Edie. "What happened here?" he asked.

"He came to the door holding my daughter at gunpoint," she said. "He thought we'd stolen some of his computer files."

Dave Holman was the next man who darted through the front door and into the crowded room. "What's going on?" he wanted to know. "What's happened? Is anyone hurt?"

By then Bob was helping his daughter to her feet. "Leland Brooks may be," Ali said. "He's outside, unconscious, in the back of his truck."

Nodding, Dave turned. "I'll call the EMTs," he said on his way out.

Meanwhile, two more Sedona officers edged their way into the room. "Whose Taser?" one of them asked.

"Mine," Edie said. "My daughter fired it, but it belongs to me."

Leaving the crowd inside to sort things out, Ali followed Dave. She found him on his hands and knees in the back of the camper shell. By the time she got there, he had pulled Leland to the end of the pickup and was loosening his restraints.

"Is he all right?" Ali asked.

Dave shook his head. "I can't tell," he said. "Looks like he's out cold, but he's got a pulse, and he's breathing on his own." He glanced up at Ali. "And what about you?" he asked. "That looks like a pretty bad cut."

"It's nothing," Ali said. Compared to what it might have been, the injury to her face really was nothing.

A fire truck with a blaring siren arrived in a cloud of dust, followed by an ambulance. As a pair of EMTs raced forward, Ali motioned them toward the pickup. "He's in there," she said. She meant to be there with them, but suddenly, her legs were no longer cooperating.

Dave turned to Ali with a look of concern. "Are you all right?"

"I'm fine," she said, but not too convincingly. Taking her arm, Dave led her over to the back of the Sugarloaf and eased her down on the set of cement steps that led up to the back door.

"I should be there with Leland," she objected.

"Sit," Dave said.

When Ali looked down at her feet, she was surprised to see that she was barefoot. It was November and cold, but until she saw her feet, she hadn't been aware of being without shoes.

"How did the cops get here?" Ali asked. "Who called them?"

"Your mother," Dave replied. "She evidently placed a nine-one-one call and then hung up. When they tried calling back, she yelled at whoever was on the line and accused him of being an aluminum-siding salesman. Luckily, the operator was smart enough to realize something was amiss. He went ahead and dispatched units."

"What about you?" Ali asked.

"B. Simpson had already told me that he'd plucked Peter Winter's name out of the computer files he had lifted. When I tried to check on Winter myself, I was told he was off duty for the foreseeable future. That worried me. It worried me even more when Simpson told me he had been trying to reach you and couldn't get through. I left my guys to execute the warrant at Manzanita Hills and was on my way to your other place when I heard the radio transmissions. I came here instead."

"B. may not have been able to reach me, but he talked to my mother," Ali said. "You should have seen her, Dave. She was amazing. I show up with my face dripping blood and with a guy who's holding me at gunpoint, but she's cool as a cucumber. 'You must be Peter Winter,' she says, as calm as can be. The next thing I know, she's dragging some old discarded heap of a computer out of Dad's trash pile and convincing the guy that was what she had used to hack in to his files. And he believed her. While he was busy watching her hook it up, I managed to grab the Taser and nail the guy."

"Taser?" Dave asked. "What Taser? Where did you get one of those?"

"It's Mom's," Ali answered. "She bought it at one of Frieda Rains's parties."

Dave shook his head and rubbed his forehead. "Remind me not to make your mother mad," he said.

By then the EMTs had loaded Leland Brooks onto a gurney and were headed for the ambulance. "Where are you taking him?" Dave called after them.

"Yavapai Medical Center," the driver returned. "Do you want us to come back for the guy with the darts once we get this one transported?"

"Don't bother," Dave told them. "We'll be able to handle him."

In the meantime, someone—Jan Howard, maybe— had brought a chair from the restaurant and set it down near the steps where Ali was already sitting. While Ali watched, Bob led a pale and shaken Edie out of their house. Holding his wife's arm as though afraid she might break, he led her over to the chair and helped her sit down.

"I'm fine, Bobby," Edie was saying. "Really, I am."

But she didn't look any finer than her daughter did. Like Dave, Bob Larson didn't believe a word of it.

Just then Chris's Prius raced into the parking lot. Jumping out and slamming the door behind him, he ran over to where Ali was sitting. Athena was hot on his heels.

"Mom, are you all right?" he gasped. "What's going on?"

"I'm okay," Ali assured him. "So's Grandma." But Ali was surprised to notice that at the same time she was uttering those supposedly reassuring words, she was also shivering uncontrollably. She didn't know if the shakes were coming from being outside barefoot in the November cold or from realizing that the worst of the crisis was past.

Chris responded by whipping off his sport jacket and throwing it over his mother's quivering shoulders. "Someone called the principal at school and said there was a problem at the Sugarloaf. He took charge of my class so I could get over here. What the hell happened?"

"It would appear that your mother and grandmother have succeeded in apprehending a possible homicide suspect," Dave said, getting to his feet. "Now, if you and Athena will look after your mother, I'll check out what's going on inside the house and make sure the guy they tased is okay."

"They tased somebody?" a baffled Chris asked. "As in a Taser? Who did that?"

"Your mother was the one shooting it," Dave observed with a tight smile. "But it isn't hers. I believe she used your grandmother's Taser."

Chris looked questioningly at his grandmother. She nodded in return. "That's right," she said. "It's mine."

"But you're all right?" Chris asked.

Edie was getting a grip. "Couldn't be better," she replied stoutly, as if daring her husband to say otherwise.

Chris turned back to his mother and paused when he saw her bloodied face. "Then who was in the ambulance?" he asked. "They almost took us out back at the stoplight."

"Leland Brooks," Ali replied, struggling to her feet. "He's hurt. They're taking him to the hospital, and I'd like to go, too. If you and Athena would be kind enough to give me a ride . . ."

But before she could finish the sentence, a strange procession emerged from Bob and Edie Larson's house, and everyone who had gathered in the Sugarloaf's parking lot stopped to watch. Two cops, each of them holding a handcuffed Peter Winter by an arm, led the way. The three of them were followed by a third cop who trailed behind, carrying Edie's Taser. With the darts still stuck in the middle of Winter's back and the strings attached to the Taser trailing along behind him, the whole thing resembled a bizarre bridal procession.

Ali was relieved to see that Peter Winter appeared to be much the worse for wear. Even though electricity was no longer flowing through his body, he still seemed to need help remaining upright. The shaming telltale marks of urination stained his clothing. In order to reach the waiting patrol car, the cops had to lead their prisoner past both Ali and Edie. When he saw them, he ducked his head and turned away.

"See there?" Edie said to her husband. "I told you he's fine."

Bob Larson shook his head. "The poor guy doesn't look fine to me," he said. "And like I said earlier, don't you go shooting that thing off at me. If it made him piss his pants, it would probably kill me."

"Would you stop harping about it?" Edie returned. "Please. If we hadn't had that Taser, Ali and I would probably both be dead by now. Would you like that any better?"

Chris left Ali's side long enough to give his grandmother a brief hug. "I wouldn't," he said. "Tase away, Grandma. Way to go! But will you be all right if I take Mom to the hospital? She wants to check on Mr. Brooks."

"I just wish everyone would quit worrying about me," Edie said. "You take care of your mother. If Grandpa ever finishes complaining, he can look after me."

Athena piled into the front passenger seat of the Prius while Ali sat crammed in the back. With Chris at the wheel, they headed for the hospital.

Yavapai Medical Center operated more as a stand-alone emergency room than it did a full-service hospital. Although it had rooms that could accommodate the occasional overnight stay, the medical center's physicians specialized primarily in stitching together minor cuts, setting broken bones, and delivering the occasional fast-arriving baby. Patients requiring more comprehensive care or longer stays were routinely transported to hospitals in Cottonwood, Flagstaff, or Phoenix. The fact that the EMTs had opted for local treatment gave Ali cause to hope they didn't regard Leland's situation as life-threatening.

"Do you know anything about Leland's family?" Athena asked. "Is there someone we should call?"

If he had relatives living anywhere in the States, Ali was unaware of them. Even so, there was someone Ali was quite sure would want to be notified about Leland's condition. Without thinking, she reached for her phone, only it wasn't there—or rather, it *still* wasn't there because it was still at her house, still sunk at the bottom of that tubful of water.

"Can I please borrow a cell phone?" Ali asked.

Without a word, Athena passed one back. With the help of directory assistance, Ali was connected to the Yavapai County courthouse in Prescott, where she asked to speak to Judge Patrick Macey.

"I'm sorry," his secretary told Ali. "It's impossible to reach Judge Macey just now. He's conducting a trial."

"This is urgent," Ali insisted. "Perhaps his bailiff could let him know I'm on the phone."

"What's your name again?"

"Ali," she said. "Ali Reynolds from Sedona."

The woman sighed. "One moment, then," she said.

Ali waited. She knew that Leland and Judge Macey had been involved for quite some time. She remembered hearing that the judge's wife, after years of being confined to a nursing home, had succumbed to the ravages of Alzheimer's. Prior to the wife's death, there had been some need to keep the relationship under wraps due to objections from the judge's grown children, but with their mother gone, Ali had assumed that—

A man's voice came on the phone. "Why are you calling me?" Judge Macey asked.

The brusque response caught Ali off guard. "I'm sorry to disturb you," she said. "It's about Leland Brooks. I thought you'd want to know that there's been a problem, and he's been taken to the hospital in—"

"You had no business interrupting a trial," Macey interrupted. "Do not call me about this matter again!" With that, he hung up.

Staring at the words CALL ENDED on the phone, Ali couldn't help feeling sorry for Leland Brooks. From the way it sounded, far more than a phone call had been disconnected.

By then Chris had pulled up at the entrance to the medical center, where an empty Sedona patrol car was parked right outside the front entrance. With a start, Ali realized that Leland Brooks was being treated here, and so was the man who had attacked them. No doubt Peter Winter had been brought here to have the darts removed from his back.

"Go on in, Mom," Chris suggested. "Athena and I will park and be there in a few minutes."

When Ali stepped into the lobby, she was relieved to see that Dr. Peter Winter was nowhere in sight. She approached the reception desk, fully expecting to be rebuffed. After all, Ali was no relation to Leland Brooks; she was sure HIPAA rules would prevent hospital personnel from giving her any information concerning his condition. They might not even acknowledge that he had been admitted as a patient.

When Ali gave her name to the receptionist, however, the woman nodded knowingly. "Of course, Ms. Reynolds. Dr. Langston, one of our in-house doctors, is with Mr. Brooks right now and assessing his situation. If you'll have a seat, I'm sure he'll be with you shortly."

Stifling her surprise, Ali did as she was told—she took a seat and waited. Because she still had Athena's phone in her hand, she used those few moments to attempt to contact B. Simpson. There was a problem, however: This wasn't her phone. She was used to dialing B. by simply using her directory. Without access to her cheat sheet of numbers, she was unable to recall B.'s. She had already dialed two wrong numbers by the time Athena and Chris came into the waiting room.

"Any word?" Chris asked.

"Not yet." Ali started to hand the phone back.

"You keep it until we find yours," Athena said.

"Thanks." Ali stuffed the phone in her pocket.

"I just talked to Dave again," Chris said to his mother. "He told me that both our house and Grandma's are currently considered crime scenes. That means until they can get them processed, we'll need to stay somewhere else. I can stay with Athena, but do you want her to find rooms for you and Grandpa and Grandma?"

Nodding, Ali leaned her head back against the wall and closed her eyes. "We'll need a place for Sam, too," she said. "Assuming anyone can catch her, that is. She's probably petrified."

Athena collected Chris's phone and went to the desk to find a phone book while Chris turned to his mother. "Why?" he asked. "What happened there?"

Just thinking about it was enough to make Ali feel sick again. "He filled the tub with water, shoved my head under, and held it there. Repeatedly," Ali said. "He did the same thing to Mr. Brooks."

Chris knew all about Ali's fear of water, and he was obviously appalled. He reached over and took his mother's hand. "But who is this guy?" he asked. "And why would he do such a thing? Is he really a killer, like Dave said, and how did you and Grandma and Leland Brooks get mixed up with him?"

"Do you remember that identity thief B. and I were tracking?"

Chris nodded. "What about him?"

"B.'s a very smart man," Ali said. "The man's name is Peter Winter. We were actually able to lift his files right off his computer. It turns out they're encrypted, so we still don't know what's on them, but whatever it is must be really incriminating. He was worried enough that he came here looking for me in hopes of getting them back."

As if speaking of the devil, a pair of swinging doors opened, and there was Peter Winter himself. He was sitting in a wheelchair being pushed by a nurse, while the same two uniformed officers flanked the wheelchair. Winter wore the cuffs, but his clothing was gone. Instead, he was clad only in a skimpy hospital gown, with a single sheet thrown over his bare legs. The moment he saw Ali, his eyes sparked a look of pure fury.

"Bitch!" he muttered under his breath as the chair rolled past her. "You incredible bitch!"

To her surprise, Ali burst out laughing. She couldn't help herself, and she was still laughing when the automatic outside door whirred shut behind him. Before she managed to get back under control, the swinging doors opened once more. A man dressed in scrubs strode into the lobby.

"Ms. Reynolds?" he asked, glancing around.

Stifling her laughter, Ali got to her feet and hurried forward. "Yes," she said, "that's me. Is Mr. Brooks going to be all right?"

"I'm Dr. Langston," he said, "Mr. Brooks's attending physician. We believe he'll be fine. He's very heavily sedated at the moment. That means that his blood pressure and heart rate aren't entirely normal. We found two separate puncture marks on Mr. Brooks's arm, marks that might possibly indicate he had been dosed with some kind of medication. Do you have any idea what drugs might have been administered?"

Ali closed her eyes. She thought about lying helpless on the bathroom floor while her captor temporarily disappeared from view. She remembered that when she'd come back into the bedroom, Leland's body had apparently been moved.

"The man who was just here," Ali said. "The one they just took away in the cop car—"

"The one who was hit by a Taser?" the doctor asked. "What about him?"

"He was dressed when they brought him here. What happened to his clothes?"

"I believe the police officers who were with him took charge of all his personal property, clothing included. Why?"

"Have them check his pockets," Ali suggested.

Dr. Langston looked at Ali for a moment, then nodded. "All right," he said. "I'll do that. And I should probably take a look at your face, Ms. Reynolds. Apparently you got hit pretty hard. In the meantime, if you'd like to go wait in Mr. Brooks's room . . ."

The whole time they had been in the hospital lobby,

Athena had been on the phone. "The Majestic Mountain Inn has two rooms," she reported now. "And they take pets. Do you want me to book them?"

Ali nodded. Automatically, she reached for her purse and her credit card, but she didn't have those, either.

"Don't worry, Mom," Chris said. "I'll put the rooms on my card."

Leaving Chris and Athena to make the room reservation, Ali followed Dr. Langston through the swinging doors and into the interior of the building. "He's in there," Dr. Langston said, motioning Ali toward a room two doors down the hall.

Entering Leland's room, she was more than a little gratified to have been given such unlimited access. He lay on his back with his hands folded peacefully across his chest. He was sleeping soundly and snoring with window-rattling volume. The thought that such a small man could make so much noise would have been humorous under any other circumstances. Today it wasn't funny.

Ali studied his sleeping face. His lips were cut and swollen. One eye was black, and the rest of his face was mottled with bruises and abrasions. One arm was in a sling, and both hands showed signs of having been in a serious physical altercation. Neither he nor Ali had won, but they had gone down swinging.

There was a single chair near the head of the bed. Ali slipped gratefully onto that and settled in to wait. The doctor reappeared within a matter of minutes. "You're right," he said. "They found two empty syringes of Versed in his pockets. Where the hell did he get those?"

"I think Winter is a doctor," Ali said. "That's what I was told."

"A doctor!" Dr. Langston repeated, shaking his head. "In that case, it'll take time for the medication to wear off. Fortunately for someone Mr. Brooks's age, he doesn't appear to be in any kind of distress at the moment. Other than bruising and battering, he has a dislocated shoulder and possibly a torn rotator cuff. We're capable of monitoring his progress here, but if you'd prefer to have him moved to another facility . . ."

It was one thing to be allowed into Leland Brooks's room, but Ali was surprised to be given so much information about his condition, and she certainly hadn't expected to be consulted about the kind of care provided.

"Look," Ali said. "I need to tell you that I'm not a blood relation and probably shouldn't have any say."

"Mr. Brooks has an unusual blood type— O-negative—and wears a MedicAlert tag that gives emergency personnel access to his information. You're listed as the person to be notified in case of an emergency. You've also been designated the decision maker regarding his treatment options."

"He's given me his medical power of attorney?" Ali asked.

"Do you mean to say that you didn't know?" Dr. Langston asked.

"I do now," Ali said. "And we'll wait here until he wakes up," she added, making the decision as she spoke.

"Let's go take a look at you in the meantime," the doctor said.

An X-ray revealed that her aching jaw wasn't broken,

but the cut next to her eye required two stitches. In another time and place, she would have been concerned about scarring. Now she was just glad to be alive.

After leaving the examination room, Ali returned to the chair next to Leland Brooks's hospital bed, where she remained for the next several hours. She couldn't help being sorry about keeping that solitary vigil. He was a wonderful human being, she had worked with him for months, but she didn't know him that well. She had known nothing about his snoring, for instance, or the breakup of his romance, but she was the only person he had trusted to make life-and-death decisions about his medical care. How could that be?

Somewhere along the way, she fell asleep. When she awakened, it was dark outside, and someone had turned on a night-light on the far side of Leland's bed. When she opened her eyes, she was surprised to see he was awake, too, and staring at her intently.

"I'm sorry," Leland murmured. "So very sorry."

"Sorry?" Ali repeated, straightening up and rubbing her eyes. "What do you have to be sorry about?"

"I let you down," he said. "He was there in the driveway waiting for me, and I simply didn't see it coming. He had brute force and surprise working in his favor. I never had a chance. I'm so sorry if he hurt you."

It was entirely predictable that Leland's first thought would be for someone else rather than for himself.

"He didn't hurt me," she said reassuringly. "Not really."

"There's a cut on your face—with stitches," Leland objected.

"It's nothing," she said. "I'm fine."

"Who was he?" Leland asked. "Do you know his name?"

"Winter—Dr. Peter Winter."

"And did he get away?"

"No," Ali said. "We got lucky. He's in custody."

"He was a big man," Leland said. "Who caught him and how?"

"My mother has a Taser," Ali said simply. "We used that."

"I see," Leland said with a nod, as though the idea of Edie Larson having a Taser were the most natural thing in the world. "What about Mr. Simpson?" he added. "Winter didn't find him, did he? I hope he's all right."

That stopped Ali for a moment. Winter had claimed Leland had said nothing because he'd had nothing to tell. Evidently, that wasn't the case. "Are you saying you knew about my involvement with Mr. Simpson?"

"Of course I knew about it," Leland answered. "I'm your butler. I didn't know the details, but I knew it had something to do with computers. So when this man, this Winter person, kept raving about someone who had wrecked his computer files, I assumed it had to be Mr. Simpson."

"But you didn't give him Mr. Simpson's name," Ali said.

"No," Leland replied. "Of course not. That's not something I would do."

"Thank you," Ali said quietly. She meant it.

She wanted to say more, but just then a nurse stuck her head into the room. "We don't have a kitchen here," she said. "If you'd like something to eat, I can order in."

They settled on Subway sandwiches. Once the nurse was gone, Ali turned to what had been bothering her while she'd been sitting awake and watching Leland sleep.

"I called your friend," she said. "Your friend from Prescott. I'm sorry if that was the wrong thing to do, but I thought he'd want to know what had happened."

"I assume he didn't," Leland said sadly.

"That's correct," Ali agreed. "He didn't."

"We broke up," Leland said. "His children don't approve of me, you see. I guess that means they don't approve of him, either, but he's their father. He doesn't want to lose them. They gave him a choice of them or me. He chose them, and who can blame him?"

It struck Ali that this was almost the same thing Bryan Forester had said about not wanting to lose his girls. Although the situations were very different, they were also surprisingly similar—a father choosing to live a lie rather than risk losing his kids.

"I'm sorry," Ali said.

"I am, too," Leland admitted. "I thought that once Patrick's wife was gone he'd find the courage to live his own life and be who he really is, but it turns out he can't. I suppose I should have mentioned it to you."

"No," Ali said. "There was no need to tell me. Your personal affairs are none of my business."

"Not telling you was rather cowardly on my part," Leland Brooks said thoughtfully. "I just didn't want to get into it."

Ali reached over and took one of his hands in hers. "No, Mr. Brooks," she said quietly. "That's not it at all. I don't think you could ever be a coward. That's not who you are."

A while later, once Leland had drifted back to sleep, Ali ventured out of the room long enough to use the restroom. Studying her face in the mirror, she was shocked by what she saw. The stitches were the least of it. An ugly bruise stretched from the corner of her left eye and down across her jawline. It ended halfway down her neck.

Not a pretty face, Ali thought ruefully. *If Jacky Jackson sees me now, it'll all be over between us.*

A nurse came through the doors at the end of the hallway. Before the doors swung shut again, Ali heard the sound of familiar voices and caught a glimpse of her mother's steel-gray pageboy. Hurrying into the lobby, she found it packed with people she knew—both her parents and Athena and Chris were there, along with several concerned neighbors from Andante Drive. All of them were worried about her.

"Oh my," Edie Larson said tearfully, rushing over to her daughter. "Look at you. If you aren't a sight for sore eyes, or should I say, a sight *of* sore eyes! They said you were in with Mr. Brooks and that he couldn't have any more visitors, but I was so afraid that animal had hurt you."

Bob Larson stepped between Edie and Ali and engulfed his daughter in a crushing bear hug. "You and your mom are quite the tag team," he said. "But what about Mr. Brooks? Is he going to be all right?"

"He's a little worse for wear," Ali said. "But he's sleeping now. The doctor says he'll be fine."

"Too bad he didn't have a Taser," Edie said. "Maybe you should give him one for Christmas."

That broke the tension in the room, and everyone laughed. For the next few minutes, Ali told her collection of well-wishers as much of the story as she and Leland had managed to put together. Peter Winter had expected Ali to show up in response to his tile-delivery ruse rather than Leland Brooks. Once again, as she had with Chris and Athena, Ali recounted for everyone what Peter Winter had done to her and to Leland Brooks, shoving them under the water in hopes of their telling him who had taken his files.

"Those files were the tip of the iceberg," Edie said. "Dave thinks Winter is the one who killed Morgan Forester."

"He did," Ali confirmed. "He told me so himself."

"That means Bryan is off the hook, then?" Bob Larson asked.

"I hope so," Ali said.

An hour or so later, a nurse shooed everyone out of the lobby, and Ali returned to her spot next to Leland's bed. She had dozed off briefly when someone touched her shoulder. She awakened to find Dave Holman standing next to her chair and beckoning for her to follow him.

"I know you're tired," he said once they reached the lobby. "And this probably isn't the best time to do this, but we need to take your statement as soon as possible."

"We?" Ali asked.

"This is Detective Marjorie Hill from the city of Sedona," Dave said, as a woman who had been seated near the windows rose to greet them. "She's here because the attacks on you and Mr. Brooks occurred inside the city limits. I'm here because of Morgan Forester."

"So you believe me, then?" Ali asked, glad of the confirmation.

Dave nodded grimly. "We found Morgan's missing wedding and engagement rings on a key ring in Peter Winter's pocket. But there's a problem with that."

"What kind of problem?" Ali asked.

"There are four other sets of rings there, which leads me to think there are at least four other victims. We just don't know who they are. One of them may have been his wife, Rita."

"You're saying Peter Winter is a serial killer?"

"Most likely," Dave said. "It also means you and your mother had a very close call."

{ CHAPTER 17 }

It was after midnight when Dave drove Ali to the Majestic Mountain Inn. "You'll be all right?" he asked.

"Yes," she told him.

When she got out of Dave's Nissan, Ali was gratified to see that someone had driven her Cayenne to the hotel and parked it there. She limped toward the door of her room, still wearing the jacket Chris had placed on her shoulders much earlier in the afternoon. On her feet were ill-fitting bedroom slippers that the nurse at the hospital had produced for Ali's use.

Ali opened the door, expecting to find the room empty. To her surprise, both Chris and Athena were there waiting for her. Chris was asleep on the bed, while Athena dozed in an armchair with Sam curled comfortably in her lap.

"She was hiding behind the dryer in your laundry room," Athena explained. "Chris dragged her out of there, and we brought her here, but we couldn't leave her in this strange place all by herself."

In actual fact, Sam didn't seem all that upset. She opened her one good eye, gave Ali an appraising glance, and then closed it again.

"Thank you," Ali said.

"We packed a suitcase for you," Athena added. "It's there in the closet. We brought your robe and nightgown and some clothes for you to wear tomorrow. No toiletries, though—the cops said your bathroom was off limits—so we stopped by the drugstore and picked up a hairbrush, a toothbrush, and some toothpaste. For makeup, you're on your own."

The idea that Chris and Athena had managed to talk their way into bringing anything at all from the crime scene was impressive. "They let you into the house?" Ali asked. "That must have taken some convincing."

"A little," Athena agreed. "One of the CSI guys helped."

Grabbing her nightgown and robe, Ali went to the bathroom to change. In addition to the bruises on her face and neck, there were bruises on her legs and arms. She had been in a fight for her life, and it showed.

When she came back out of the bathroom, Chris was sitting up on the side of the bed, and Sam was stretched out on one of the pillows.

Chris stood up. "Mom," he said, giving Ali a hug. "You've got to stop doing stuff like this. You scare me to death."

"It scared me, too," she admitted.

"It's late," he said. "I'm going to Athena's. If you need anything, Grandpa and Grandma are right next door. And here's Athena's cell phone. You can use it until we can get you a new one. According to the cops, there's one sitting at the bottom of your bathtub at home. I think that one's a goner."

Ali let Chris and Athena out and then locked both the deadbolt and the security chain behind them. Crawling into bed a few minutes later, she was grateful to feel Sam's stolid presence snuggled up next to her. She fell asleep almost immediately, but three times she was awakened by the same recurring nightmare: Someone was holding her head underwater, and Ali was drowning.

She was awakened shortly after sunrise by someone knocking sharply on her door. It took a moment to gather her wits and figure out where she was. Meanwhile, Sam skittered away and disappeared under the bed.

"Who is it?" Ali asked, pulling on her robe and slippers.

"It's B.," B. Simpson said. "I'm sorry to wake you, but I need to talk to you. I need to see with my own eyes that you're all right."

"Maybe not one hundred percent," she said as she unlatched the security chain and the deadbolt to let him in. Catching sight of her stitched and battered face, he took a step back.

"Come on in," Ali said. "How did you know I was here? Is something the matter?"

"I just dropped off copies of the files with Dave Holman. He told me where to find you," B. answered. He looked haggard and careworn, as though he hadn't slept in days. "As for what's the matter?" he continued. "Hell yes, there's something the matter! Look what happened to your face. I almost got you killed."

"Wait a minute," Ali said. "You just said you dropped

off the files. If you gave them to Dave, does that mean you broke Winter's encryption code?"

"If Winter turns out to be his real name, I'll be surprised," B. said. "But it does mean I broke his damn code. Just a little while ago, as a matter of fact. And now I know why the bastard was so desperate to get those files back. He had his whole world tucked away in them. He's so friggin' arrogant that it never occurred to him someone else might be smart enough to take him down. When it happened—when we hacked in to his system—it pushed him over the edge.

"But he's not the only one with an arrogance problem, Ali. What about me? I thought he was just your run-of-the-mill identity thief. I had no idea how dangerous this creep might be or what he might do. If something had happened to you and your mother, if one or both of you had died because of my actions, I don't know what I'd do or how I'd live with myself. I'm so sorry about all this, I just—"

"Stop," Ali said, interrupting B.'s bout of self-recrimination. "None of this is your fault. You gave me a choice about what to do, remember? You said we could either turn the guy over to the cops and let them deal with him, or we could smack him down by taking his files. Since it seemed likely the cops wouldn't do anything, I was the one who said turnabout is fair play, let's rattle his chain and take his files."

"The cops have them now," B. said somberly. "I turned everything I had over to Dave Holman. Those files and the Foresters' thumb drives as well. Bryan told me it was okay to turn them in."

"You've done everything you can, then," Ali said. "It's up to the cops now. Go home and get some rest."

Apparently, B. Simpson was too tired to object. He left, and Ali set about getting dressed. Chris and Athena had brought along underwear, jeans, a sweatshirt, and a pair of running shoes so she had something to put on that wasn't the jogging suit, which had already been deposited in the trash can in the bathroom.

Ali used fresh food to coax Sam out from under the bed. Once she emerged, Ali scooped her up and stuck her in her crate. She didn't want Sam exiting the room when an unsuspecting maid came by to clean.

By seven A.M. Ali was at the counter in the Sugar-loaf, drinking a cup of coffee and waiting for Bob to finish cooking a to-go order of cheese-baked eggs for Ali to take to the hospital for Leland Brooks.

"You'll take a sweet roll for him, too, won't you?" Edie asked. "Surely he'll want one of those. What about the memorial service?" she added. "It's due to start at ten. Are you going?"

Ali looked down at her jeans and sweatshirt. "I can't very well go in this," she said.

"Given what you did for Bryan Forester yesterday," Edie Larson said, "you could probably turn up stark naked, and I doubt he'd voice a word of complaint. He wouldn't let anyone else gripe about it, either."

"So Dave has let it be known that Bryan's no longer under suspicion?"

"Pretty much," Edie said.

By the time Ali got back to Yavapai Medical Center, an unmarked Sedona cop car was parked out front. When she arrived at the door to Leland's room, she found Detective Hill conducting an interview about everything that had happened the day before.

"So you didn't notice the silver Mercedes parked

at the bottom of Ms. Reynolds's driveway?" Marjorie Hill asked.

"No," Leland said. "I was looking for a truck bringing a load of tile. I wasn't looking for a Mercedes. I got out of the car, and there he was. He had the element of surprise in his favor. I tried to fend him off, but I couldn't. I seem to remember being stuck by something—something sharp. Then it was all over. The fight went out of me. I couldn't do a thing."

"He drugged you?"

"I believe so."

"What's the next thing you remember?"

"Waking up in Ms. Reynolds's bathroom. There was duct tape around my legs and around my arms and chest. He was holding my head underwater. He kept asking me about some files, and I kept telling him I didn't know anything about them. When I woke up again, I was here. That's pretty much it. I don't know anything else."

Ali heard the note of weariness in his voice and came into the room. "Breakfast is here," she announced. "The rest of the questions will have to wait until after that, Detective Hill."

"But—" began the detective.

"But nothing," Ali told her. "What Mr. Brooks needs right now is to eat and rest."

She set the food out on the rolling table next to Leland's bed and hustled the detective out the door. Once she had escorted Marjorie Hill to the lobby, Ali went in search of a nurse. "He's to have no more visitors," Ali ordered. "Got that?"

"Got it," the nurse said.

When Ali went back to Leland's room, he was sound asleep again, with his food sitting untouched on the rolling cart. She sat with him for the next hour or so while he continued to sleep. Finally, at about nine, she drove to the drugstore and put together an emergency set of makeup. At ten, having done what she could to fix her bedraggled face, she presented herself at Thomas and Sons Mortuary. She could tell from the way cars spilled down the street that the chapel was jammed to capacity. Searching for a place to park, she was surprised to see Bryan Forester standing out behind the building, smoking a cigarette.

Leaving her Cayenne idling, Ali got out and walked over to him. "Where are the girls?" she asked.

"Inside," he said, "with my folks and with all those damn hypocrites. What did they all come here hoping for? Are they thinking I'll be beside myself with grief and throw myself on her coffin, or are they hoping I'll stand up and tell them Morgan was a tramp and deserved what she got? What the hell do they expect of me?"

"They're here to pay their respects," Ali said. "And they're here to say they're sorry for your loss, even though they have no way of comprehending the real loss you've suffered."

Bryan sought Ali's eyes. "But you know, don't you," he said.

She nodded. The fact that Paul Grayson had betrayed her so thoroughly was still part of who she was, how she functioned in the world, and how she saw herself.

"But I also know that it doesn't matter," she said aloud. "What went wrong between you and Morgan doesn't matter as much as what went right—which is to say your two girls. You have to be here for them, Bryan. You have to be strong for them."

"But I don't want to be around these people," Bryan fumed. "The way they turned on me . . . When I finish your job, I'll go somewhere else. Maybe I can find work down in Phoenix. Or maybe over in Albuquerque, somewhere people won't know me and know all about what happened."

"Don't," Ali said. "Geographic cures don't work."

"You tried one," Bryan said. "You came home."

"That doesn't change the fact that my husband screwed around on me," Ali said. "Coming home didn't fix it for me, and leaving home won't fix it for you, either. And uprooting your girls from everything that's familiar is the last thing they need right now. It'll make things that much worse for them. Stay here, Bryan. Look your demons in the eye."

"Including Billy Barnes?" he asked.

"Especially Billy Barnes," Ali told him. "Especially him."

"I'll think about it," Bryan said. With that, he ground out his cigarette and strode inside.

Ali parked in a no-parking zone in front of a Dumpster. She went inside the mortuary and found a spot to sit on one of the extra folding chairs that had been set up around the perimeter of the chapel to accommodate the standing-room-only crowd. Ali could see why Bryan might have a problem with some of those folks. Cindy Martin, the manicurist who had been only too happy to blame him, was sitting there as big as life on the end of the fourth row. Ali suspected that many of the other people in attendance were ones who had been quick to think Bryan was responsible for his wife's death and to dish out rumors and innuendo.

Others, however, were clearly there in a show of support. Ali wasn't surprised to see that Mindy Farber, Lacy and Lindsey's teacher, had taken time off to be there for them.

The service, conducted by the Reverend C. W. Stowell, was a low-key affair, dignified but distant, as though the minister had been asked to officiate without knowing too many details about either the deceased or her family. From Ali's point of view, that was a good thing. It gave the two little girls sitting quietly in the front row something to remember about the loss of their mother. As Mindy Farber had told them, it was a way of saying goodbye.

Ali ducked out during the final benediction and went back to the hospital, where she found Leland, fully dressed except for shoes, waiting for her in the lobby.

"The doctor came around and told me I could go, but he said that with this arm, I'm in no condition to drive. He said I needed to have someone come pick me up. I've been trying to call you, but your cell phone isn't working."

And won't ever work again, Ali thought.

The nurse came forward to wheel Leland's chair out to the Cayenne. "Just drop me off at the house," he said once he was loaded into the passenger seat. "I'll be fine."

"No," Ali said. "We can go by your place and pick up some clothing, but for right now Sam and I are staying at the Majestic Mountain Inn, and so are you."

"That's ridiculous," Leland said. "I'm perfectly capable of staying on my own."

"You may be capable of it," Ali said, "but you're not doing it. End of discussion."

After checking Leland in to a room three doors down from hers, Ali went up to the house and collected clothing for him from his fifth wheel. At her house there was clear evidence that a search had been conducted the day before. The locked front door had been battered open and was closed now with a piece of plywood that had been screwed into the casing with wallboard screws. The padlock on Bryan's storage unit dangled unlocked on the hasp. A quick look inside told Ali all was in order, but she picked up her phone—Athena's phone—and called Dave Holman.

"It's bad enough that your guys had to break my door down," she said, "but they also left Bryan's toolshed unlocked. What if someone had come by during the funeral to steal his stuff?"

"I'll go by the hardware store and pick up a new padlock," Dave said. "Then I'll be right there."

True to his word, Dave arrived under ten minutes later.

"What were you hoping to find here?" Ali asked as Dave struggled to liberate the padlock from its child-proof plastic container.

"Syringes," he said. "But as you know, the ones we were looking for turned up somewhere else."

"And in someone else's possession," Ali added.

Dave nodded. "I'm sorry about that," he said. "Most of the time the culprit turns out to be the husband."

"Or the boyfriend," Ali said.

"You're not going to give me a break on this one, are you?"

"No," she said. "Since I was right and you were wrong, I see no reason not to rub it in."

He laughed at that. They both did.

Dave freed the padlock, threaded it through the hasp, locked it, and handed Ali the key. "We found photos," he said, turning serious and changing the subject.

"What kind of photos?"

"Souvenirs," he said. "Pictures of five dead women, one of whom happens to be Morgan Forester. We're pretty sure one of them is Rita Winter. We don't know who the others are yet, but as of now it's pretty clear that Bryan Forester wasn't involved in any of it."

"What about Singleatheart?" Ali asked.

Dave shrugged. "I asked Winter about that," he said. "He sneered at me and said, 'Figure it out.' So that's what we're doing—figuring it out. I think you and B. Simpson were on the right track. Identity theft probably played a big part in it. It made money for Winter, but I think he used Singleatheart as a way to mess around with people's lives. People signed up with them looking for romance, but he ran it with cruel—rather than romantic—intent. I've already got one suicide I can lay at Winter's door, and there may be more. I most likely can't bring him up on criminal charges for that, but the widow might be able to file a civil suit against him—assuming Winter has any actual assets."

"Won't having his files help you with all that?" Ali asked.

"That depends," Dave said.

"On what?"

"On whether or not a judge rules our having them constitutes an illegal wiretap."

{ CHAPTER 18 }

It took until Monday for things to get back to sem-inormal. Complaining about the cost, Edie and Bob Larson bailed out of the hotel first and were back home by Saturday evening. Ali convinced Leland that he needed to take it easy for a few days, but by Monday morning he insisted that he was well enough to go home to his fifth wheel. By Monday afternoon Ali and Sam were back home, too, in the house on Andante Drive in Skyview.

As soon as Ali let Sam out of her crate, the cat made a beeline for her safe-haven hidey-hole in the laundry room while Ali wandered through the house. She'd had a locksmith come through and change all the locks, for safety's sake, but knowing that the house had been invaded—that she and Leland had both been attacked there—left her feeling nervous and uncomfortable.

Chris, Athena, and some of their friends had spent the weekend cleaning up the mess left behind by the water and the investigation; they'd also reshampooed the carpets. Even though none of the damage was visible, Ali still felt Peter Winter's ominous presence in her home and in her life.

Athena's phone rang. Ali had been too busy in the intervening days to go to the store to replace the one that had died in her bathtub.

"Hello?" Ali said.

"Hello," a woman's voice returned. "Is Athena Carlson there?"

"I'm sorry," Ali said. "I'm Athena's fiancé's mother. My phone was damaged last week, and she's letting me use hers temporarily. I can give you Chris's number, if you like. You can call her on that line."

There was a momentary hesitation on the other end of the phone. "Alison?" the woman asked warily. "Is this Alison Larson, then?"

No one had called Ali Reynolds by that name in years—decades, even. "Yes," Ali said. "Who is this?"

"It's Jeanette. Jeanette Reynolds, Dean's mother. I can't believe I'm actually hearing your voice. Athena tracked Angus down over the Internet. She sent him an e-mail at work, introducing herself and asking if we'd like to be in touch. We were overjoyed to hear from her. This is the phone number she left in the e-mail in case we wanted to call. I know it's a bit awkward for us to come horning back into your lives like this after so many years, but yes, we'd be so honored to have a chance to finally meet our grandson, and we'll be thrilled to come to the wedding. He's the only grandson we have, you know. We wouldn't want to miss it."

As soon as Jeanette Reynolds hung up, Ali called Chris's number. "What wedding?" she demanded.

"Oops," Chris said. "I think you need to talk to Athena."

"What wedding?" Ali asked when her future daughter-in-law came on the phone. "Are we having a wedding?"

"Well, yes," Athena said. "We are."

"When?"

"Over Thanksgiving weekend, if that's all right with you," Athena said. "On Saturday afternoon. You said that we should do it our way, and I told Chris that if we can pull off a wedding with two weeks' notice, it'll be just about right. Not too big and not too small. The people who want to be here will be, and the people who don't won't."

"Who all knows about this?" Ali asked.

"You and Chris and me," Athena said.

"To say nothing of Angus and Jeanette Reynolds."

"Chris's grandparents?" Athena asked. "You mean they called?"

"They called," Ali returned dryly. "So tell me, where are we having this little event?"

"I'm not sure about that yet," Athena said. "Do you have any ideas?"

"Only one," Ali said. "Call Leland Brooks first, but after that, your next call had better be to my mother."

{ EPILOGUE }

On Tuesday Ali managed to purchase a replacement cell phone. As soon as she turned it on, it let her know there were messages. Several of those were from Jacky Jackson, but before she could call him back, he rang through again.

"It's over," he said dolefully.

"What's over?"

"Mid-Century-Modern Renovations," he said. "They've dropped it completely."

As far as Ali was concerned, that seemed like good news.

"That's not all," Jacky continued. "The other deal is off, too. You never should have left us standing out there on the porch like that. He's a very important man. It made me look like a complete fool, Ali. Really, it did."

Obviously, Jacky and the very important man hadn't stuck around town long enough to hear what had happened or to learn how narrowly they had escaped because Ali hadn't opened the door. She could have told him about it right then, but she didn't. Jacky was on a tear, and she let him continue.

"Having two deals blow up like that isn't a good thing," he added. "Not if you expect to be considered bankable."

"What are you saying?" Ali asked. "Are you telling me it's over?"

Jacky paused as if he'd been taken by surprise, as if he hadn't expected Ali to beat him to the punch. "I suppose so," he said. "I mean, it sounds as though you're not that interested in working, as though you're not that hungry . . ."

"Fax me the paperwork," Ali said. "We'll go our separate ways."

"No hard feelings?"

"None," Ali said.

The Saturday after Thanksgiving dawned clear and crisp. Early in the afternoon, Ali found herself standing in bright sunlight in the doorway of a flower-bedecked party tent that had been pitched in the driveway of her unfinished house on Manzanita Hills Road. Watching the arriving guests, she reflected that pulling all this off in a mere two weeks had been just about right.

And what a two weeks it had been. Edie had gone nuts over flowers and dresses and food, but she hadn't had enough advance warning to do any real damage. Athena absolutely put her foot down when Edie tried to convince her that having a storebought wedding cake or hiring caterers wouldn't do.

"You're coming to this wedding as an honored guest," Athena insisted. "You're not doing the cooking, and that's final."

Edie had been aghast at the idea that Angus and Jeanette Reynolds, the very people who had disowned their own son, Chris's father, would be coming to the event as honored guests, too. Since there wasn't a thing either Edie and Ali could do about that situation, Ali advised her mother to accept it with good grace. By the day of the wedding, however, she realized the advice was far easier to give than it was to take.

Leland Brooks's arm was still in a sling, but that hadn't kept him from organizing the wedding in jig time. He had also supervised Ali's great adventure in cooking her first ever Thanksgiving dinner, an experience enjoyed by a whole selection of guests. To everyone's amazement—a universal reaction she found quite annoying—she managed to pull off the full-meal deal: turkey and dressing, bourbon-drizzled yams, mashed potatoes, green-bean casserole, yeast rolls, and orange-cranberry relish.

Ali's folks were there, of course, as were Chris and Athena and Athena's grandmother, Betsy Peterson, who had flown in from Minnesota. Predictably, Athena's parents had decided not to come for either Thanksgiving or the wedding.

Their loss, Ali thought.

Maddy Watkins and her two golden retrievers had driven from Seattle to L.A., where they picked up Velma T in Laguna Niguel. Then the four of them had driven over to Sedona, where they had taken up residence in the pet friendly Majestic Mountain Inn. Over everyone's objections, and most especially over Edie Larson's, Maddy Watkins had insisted on baking pumpkin pies as the finishing touch for Ali's otherwise solo performance. By the time Thanksgiving dinner was over, the visitors had been invited to stay on for the wedding, which they were thrilled to do, thus adding two more geriatric attendees to the guest list.

Dave Holman and B. Simpson both showed up for the Thanksgiving Day extravaganza. They appeared upstairs only long enough to eat, however. They and most of the other menfolk, spooked by nonstop wedding planning, chose to spend their time both before and after dinner hiding out down in Chris's studio and watching football games.

With the men downstairs, Edie had recovered from being miffed about the pie situation by wowing everyone with her newly arrived replacement Taser. Ali suspected she would be carrying it at the wedding, too, "just in case." Thankfully, Chris and Athena were getting married because they wanted to be married. Edie might show up armed, but it wouldn't be either a shotgun or a Taser wedding.

Several late-breaking additions to the Thanksgiving guest list turned out to be Haley and Liam Marsh; Haley's grandmother, Nelda Harris; and Marissa Dvorak, who would be having a second Thanksgiving dinner with her own family later in the evening. When Haley had called on Monday of that week, Ali had been up to her eyeballs in wedding planning.

"Can we talk?" Haley said.

"Sure," Ali said. "What about?"

"You really don't think I'd be all that weird in college?" Haley asked. "I mean if I went. People wouldn't make fun of me or think I was odd?"

"You wouldn't be odd," Ali said. "A lot of single mothers go on to school these days."

"What if I went to the University of Arizona down in Tucson?" Haley asked. "Would I be able to find a place to live? How would I make arrangements for someone to look after Liam?"

Leland Brooks had already been on the phone looking for wheelchair-accessible accommodations for Marissa Dvorak. There were some dorm rooms available, but he had also found a terrific three-bedroom house not far from the university. He and Ali had dismissed it as being more than Marissa needed. Now, though, Ali had an inspiration.

"What are you and your grandmother doing for Thanksgiving dinner?" she asked.

"I don't know. Why?"

"There's someone I'd like you to meet."

So while Nelda Harris joined Edie's Taser admiration program, Haley Marsh and Marissa Dvorak had sat in one corner of the living room, playing with Liam and the collection of toys Haley had brought along to keep him occupied. The two girls seemed to be having fun together, but Ali spent a lot of the evening worried about whether the meeting—not exactly a blind date but close—would do its magic. When it was time for Marissa to leave, Ali was pleased as Liam clambered up into the wheelchair and gave Marissa a droolly smack of a kiss.

Nelda Harris saw the kiss, too. She caught Ali's eye and gave a slight nod.

She's thinking the same thing I am, Ali thought. *Only time will tell, but I'm betting that kiss seals the deal.*

As for Dean's parents—the other grandparents, as everyone called them—Ali was relieved when they decided not to come for Thanksgiving. Instead, they flew into Phoenix on Friday night and drove up to Sedona on Saturday morning.

You're a grown-up, Ali told herself that morning as she put the finishing touches on a face that still showed traces of bruising. *You can be civil. You don't have to be their friend.*

And those became her watchwords for the day: Be civil.

The simple outdoor ceremony went off without any complications. It was ably conducted by Judge Ruben Dreyfuss, justice of the peace, who also happened to play in the same community-league basketball team as Chris and Athena. Chris wore a tux, and Athena wore a simple winter-white silk brocade pantsuit. Athena, looking absolutely radiant, walked down the aisle on her own. She didn't need anyone to give her away.

Now, with the reception getting under way and the DJ tuning up the sound system, Ali wandered outside only to run smack into Angus Reynolds. He was standing beside the construction-crew break-room picnic table, taking in the view and smoking an enormous cigar.

"Nice place you have here," he observed. "Hope you don't mind. Jeannie won't allow me to smoke these in the house."

For good reason, Ali thought.

"Chris is a fine young man," Angus went on. "You must be very proud of him."

It was odd to be having a conversation with this stranger, a man who had once been her father-in-law but whom she hadn't actually met until only a few hours earlier. In a way, he seemed to be talking to her, but he also seemed to be talking to himself.

"Yes, I am proud," she said.

"If he had lived to see it, Dean would have been proud, too," Angus said quietly.

Ali felt her eyes filling with tears. She willed them to stop. When they didn't, she turned away and looked off in the other direction.

"Is the smoke bothering you?" Angus asked.

"No," she said. "It's fine."

"I was wrong, you know," Angus continued. "I wanted Dean to be a lawyer. I told him that if he insisted on getting a doctorate in oceanography, he'd never amount to anything and he'd never be able to do anything but teach. I didn't mean it as a compliment, either."

Ali remembered that conversation, not because she'd heard it but because Dean had told her about it in excruciating detail.

"And do you know what he told me?" Angus asked. "That no matter how little money he made, he'd rather be a dirt-poor teacher any day instead of being a rich lawyer and selling his soul to the devil."

Dean never mentioned that part, Ali thought. *He seemed to have left that out.*

Angus blew another puff of foul-smelling smoke into the air before he continued. "So I told him that if he was going to be that pigheaded, he was no son of mine, and I was writing him out of my life. If he wanted to go off and screw up his life and be poor until his dying day, he was on his own. And that's what I did, too. I wrote him out of our lives, and I wrote you and your wonderful son out of our lives, too. Pretty stupid, wouldn't you say?"

Again Ali said nothing.

"And now Chris is a teacher," Angus said thoughtfully. "Where do you suppose that shows up on the

DNA, the propensity for being a teacher instead of being a lawyer?"

"It may have more to do with being stubborn than it does with DNA," Ali said. "Chris's stepfather was adamantly opposed to his being a teacher, too."

"I see," Angus said. "But thank you for letting us come, Alison. Considering how we treated you and Chris, it's far more than we deserve, and it means more to my Jeannie than you can possibly know."

"You're welcome," Ali said. "I'm glad you're here." And when she said that, she really meant it; she wasn't just being civil.

Edie Larson stuck her head out the door to the tent. "There you are," she said. "Everybody's looking for you, Ali. They're getting ready to cut the cake."

Without a word, Angus Reynolds crushed the end of his cigar out in the ashtray on the table. Then he offered Ali his arm.

"Shall we?" he asked.

"Yes," Ali said quietly. "Let's."

TURN THE PAGE FOR AN EXCERPT FROM

THE A LIST

THE NEWEST MYSTERY FROM

J.A.
JANCE

FEATURING ALI REYNOLDS

{ PROLOGUE }

When Prisoner #74506 arrived at Folsom Prison in January of 2013, sentenced to life without parole, he came with a certain amount of celebrity. He was a highly esteemed pillar of his community as well as the scion of a wealthy founding family. His mother, a well-known area heiress with whom his relationship had been at times severely strained, would, he hoped, be able to use her considerable resources to make his time in prison less onerous.

After all, his mother's problems with him were never really with him—they were with what she called his questionable choices, first to divorce his first wife, of whom she had very much approved and loved as well, just to marry again. His mother referred to his second wife as "that bimbo," who, it turned out, managed to fleece him and then drive him into the arms of yet another piece of what his mother called "trailer trash." She considered these women beneath him intellectually, educationally, and, most important, socially and a poor reflection on herself, too. But now that neither was "in the picture," he hoped that he could become closer to his mother—and thereby closer to her seemingly unlimited funds.

Another thing on his mind, or rather in his gut, was a burning desire to avenge himself on those who'd put him away. He wanted all of them dealt with, all four of them—Leo and those three bitches as well. He wouldn't rest until they'd gotten the punishment they deserved, just as he'd been given his. Their names were etched in his brain, and he thought it would be a nice touch to etch them on his skin as well. As soon as possible, he was going to give himself a lasting and visible declaration of war—a tattoo.

Upon arrival, Prisoner #74506, a disgraced physician, soon discovered there was a thriving economy inside the prison with any number of products to buy, sell, and trade. That was especially true for inmates with salable skills, and he just happened to have some of those. By virtue of his having hired a hit man to dispose of his wife, the outside world might have stripped him of his professional credentials, but on the inside, people gave him the respect that his professional standing warranted. They also wanted to make use of his skills.

As a personal preference, the "Professor," as he came to be called, didn't smoke or do drugs, but cigarettes and drugs were highly regarded as common currency. For a package of smokes or a line of coke, he was more than happy to assist his fellow prisoners with their various health problems and issues. Thanks to his extensive knowledge, he was able to help them work their way around the system, and his ability to read people meant he could tell which guards might be bribable and which weren't, which ones might have weaknesses in the areas of gambling, drugs, alcohol, or sex that would make them suitable targets for exploitation.

Within weeks of his arrival, he was ensconced in what amounted to one of the prison's junior suites—a cell with a removable brick in the wall that allowed for keeping all kinds of contraband—hard, cold cash included.

As one of the so-called elite, he was quick to recognize others of his ilk, one of whom turned out to be a guy named Luis Ochoa, Folsom Prison's undisputed kingpin. Early on in Luis's life-without-parole sentence, he had plied his trade as a talented tattoo artist who'd transformed countless sweet-faced young kids into tough guys by covering them with walking catalogs of MS-13 tats. Over time Luis had made his way up through the ranks. His reputation as a wheeler-dealer allowed him to have a table of his own in the mess hall, where petitioners could come asking for help or favors.

When it came time for Prisoner #74506 to start on his tattoo project, he approached Luis Ochoa's table and sat down across from someone he knew to be a very dangerous man.

"What can I do for you, Prof?" Luis asked, delivering the last word in a mockingly derisive tone. Ignoring the sarcasm, Prisoner #74506 slid several packets of highly prized contraband, in this case fentanyl, across the table. He knew he was paying more than was necessary for an informal consultation, but he wanted to get Luis's attention.

"What's this?" Luis asked, while at the same time taking the packets and slipping them under his jumpsuit.

"I want some tattoos," the Professor replied. "If I'm going to do this myself, what does it take and how do I do it?"

"You're sure you don't want someone else to do the job for you?"

"Nope, I'm DIY all the way."

"All right, then," Luis told him. "You'll need india ink, needles, a candle, cotton swabs, and rubbing alcohol for sterilizing. You'll also need a guard who's willing to look the other way."

"Can you round up all of that?"

"Sure."

"How much?"

"For the supplies, three more of what you already gave me should just about cover it. To pay off the guard? That depends on the guard. Some of 'em cost more than others."

In the end the guard had cost a bundle, but he'd been happy to take his bribe in the form of a fistful of oxy. It turned out he preferred oxycodone to coke, which worked well. Pills were a hell of a lot easier to hide than cash would have been.

On the appointed night, watched over by his personally paid-for guard, the Professor did his work by candlelight, which, Luis had assured him, was unlikely to attract the attention of the cell block's security cameras. Because needles tend to grow dull with repeated use, he'd coughed up extra product for a dozen brand-new syringes, still sterile and still sealed in their original packaging. Possessing a candle or matches was also prohibited, but Luis had provided both as part of the deal.

At first the Professor thought he'd put his A List— *A* for "Annihilation"—on his upper thigh, but when it came time to actually do the deed, he had reconsidered. He wanted his declaration of war to be out there in the open, not only for him to see but for all the world to see as well. So rather than shaving his upper thigh, he shaved his left forearm. Then he penciled in five initials in all, in carefully printed capital letters.

First came a *D*, for the "bimbo." Dawn was already dead by then, but in terms of his kill list and for completion's sake, she had to be there right along with the others. He didn't know for sure that she would have testified against him, but he hadn't been willing to risk it. Then came *L*, for Leo, the punk gangbanger who'd taken his money and then thrown him under the bus by accepting a plea deal and turning up in court to testify against him. Next was a *K*, for Kaitlyn, his onetime lover, who was right there in court, spilling her guts to the prosecutor and pointing an accusing finger. Next was an *A*, for Alexandra, the ingrate woman who'd spent a decade trying to tear his life apart. It had worked, too. Here he was. The last letter was another *A*, for the news broad Ali Reynolds who'd aired the ungrateful bitch's charges far and wide, turning something that could have been handled quietly and discreetly into a cause célèbre.

Once the penciled list was complete, he sterilized the area with rubbing alcohol. Then he opened one syringe package, wrapped the needle in cotton thread, dipped it in the bottle of ink, and quietly went to work.

The first time he plunged the needle into his own

flesh, he was surprised by how much it hurt, but every poke after that was a little less painful. Each subsequent prick wasn't quite as bad as the one that preceded it, and as the inked letters came into focus, the pain turned into a perverse kind of pleasure. He was giving himself something to remember them by, and he smiled as he went along. He wasn't sure of exactly how he'd accomplish his goal, but accomplish it he would.

He'd need worker bees to do the actual wet work, but finding hired help wouldn't be that tough, not if his mother would throw a little money his way. Much to his surprise, she'd been a brick ever since his arrest, through the trial and his subsequent conviction. If he was halfway nice to her, he was pretty sure he could charm her into helping him with this, too. And why wouldn't she? After all, the woman was in her seventies and had already survived one bout with cancer. Besides, he was her only son, her "fair-haired boy," and since she was clearly living on borrowed time, she just might enjoy the challenge.

As for the Professor himself? He was doing life without parole for first-degree murder and conspiracy to commit. So what if one of his hirelings got caught or decided to rat him out to the cops? No big deal. The death penalty was still legal in California. If he was convicted in another case, a judge and jury might hand out a death sentence, but these days no one actually received the death penalty. Odds were they'd pile on a few more life sentences, just for good measure. Well, lots of luck with that, guys! Have a ball. Knock yourselves out.

The process took most of the night. Before the doors clattered open in the morning, his contraband set of tattooing equipment was safely stowed behind the removable brick in the wall under his stainless-steel sink.

In the mess hall, Edward went straight to Luis Ochoa's table to show off his handiwork.

"Good job," Luis said, examining his forearm. "So what is this?"

"I call it my A List. It's also my kill list."

"So you've got problems with these guys?"

"With these people," the Professor corrected, "one guy and four women. Make that three females still living, that is. These are the people who put me here, and I'm planning to take them down one by one."

"How do you expect to do that from in here?" Luis asked.

"I'm not sure," the Professor replied. "I'm working on it. I'll probably need some help."

According to in-house gossip, the Professor knew that running an outside murder-for-hire network was one of the many services Luis Ochoa was able to provide—for a price, that is.

"You will need help," Luis agreed, "and help costs money. You say your mother's loaded?"

"She is," the Professor said with confidence. "Even after paying off my defense team, she's still got way more money than she'll ever need."

"And she'd be willing to pay the freight for this little project of yours?"

"If I ask her, I think she will."

Luis replied with a wolfish, gold-toothed grin. "I might just be able to help you, then, my friend," he said. "If your mother's got the money, honey, I've got the time."

They shook hands on it then and there, and that was the beginning of a beautiful and very successful alliance. From that moment on, Prisoner #74506's life in Folsom Prison improved immeasurably, because everyone—guards and inmates alike—now understood that he was one of Luis's "inner circle," and they left him the hell alone.

Two weeks later, once the original tattoos were mostly healed, he gave the guard another batch of oxy in order to do an "addition and correction" to his tat.

That night, after lights-out, he retrieved his candle and his tattooing kit. He knew how to do the job now, and it didn't take long for him to ink a black *X* across the face of that letter *D* at the top of his list.

"One down," he told himself with a confident smile, studying the deadly scorecard on his forearm. "One down and four to go."